VERMILION FLAMES

VERMILION FLAMES

Midnight War: Book 1

ADAM FERNANDEZ

CLOVER HILL PRESS
New Jersey

Published in the United States by
Clover Hill Press LLC, New Jersey

Paperback ISBN 979-8-9897492-1-8
Hardback ISBN 979-8-9897492-2-5
E-book ISBN 979-8-9897492-0-1

FIRST EDITION

Book Design by Phillip Gessert

This one is for Kelly.

"Prophets will walk the land and whisper God's message to their chosen. Those with open hearts will hear God's word. Sleeping, nestled by eternal dreams, they awake invigorated, ready to mold the world."

Patriarch of Sirenum, A Reflection on the Past:
Hope in the Face of Chaos 3498 U.E.T.

TABLE OF
CONTENTS

Prologue xiii

Act 1 1

    Chapter 1 3

    Chapter 2 15

    Chapter 3 29

    Chapter 4 39

    Chapter 5 47

    Chapter 6 57

    Chapter 7 67

    Chapter 8 81

    Chapter 9 91

Act 2 99

    Chapter 10 101

    Chapter 11 111

    Chapter 12 119

    Chapter 13 127

    Chapter 14 135

    Chapter 15 147

    Chapter 16 161

    Chapter 17 173

    Chapter 18 185

    Chapter 19 197

    Chapter 20 205

    Chapter 21 217

    Chapter 22 227

    Chapter 23 239

    Chapter 24 247

Act 3 259

    Chapter 25 261

    Chapter 26 270

    Chapter 27 279

    Chapter 28 285

    Chapter 29 293

    Chapter 30 301

    Chapter 31 313

    Chapter 32 321

    Chapter 33 329

Epilogue 341

PROLOGUE

Silas
March, 4099 U.E.T. – Ymir, Saturn

For years they chased Hex beyond the asteroid belt and deep into the Far Coast. All to end up at a dusty old facility on the Saturnalian moon of Ymir, a tiny rock that was abandoned long ago when the Empire collapsed. Silas supposed it was fitting the Vermillion Coalition picked this place to make their final stand.

"We should wait for the rest of the men to catch up," Marcus said.

"We have waited long enough, and I don't want to stay in this godforsaken place any longer," he said.

"What if she isn't here?"

"That isn't an option. God wills it."

"God wills it," Marcus said, attaching explosives to the heavy iron door. "Blow it," he said.

A loud bang echoed through the empty corridor as the explosives breached the door. Their exoarmor protecting them from the shrapnel.

Silas ran into the breach first, his rifle at the ready, Marcus close behind him. The room was empty save for long rows of electronic consoles and servers that hummed softly. Red, yellow, and green lights flashed from the electronics, casting an ominous glow in the otherwise dark room.

"All units, defensive positions, secure the exits," he said, sending a message to his officers. He and Marcus had left the rest of their team behind in his impatience to reach their target.

He flashed a light from one end of the room to another, but the consoles blocked much of his view.

He was so close now. After all this time, he found her. After countless missions and countless deaths, it could finally end. There could be peace once and for all.

"Looks like no one's home," Marcus said on their private comm line.

"Take the left side. I'll check the other. She's here somewhere."

Marcus moved to the side he indicated, and Silas continued down the opposite row of consoles. He scanned for threats but found none. *She had to be here somewhere,* he thought. Jimmy's information had gotten them this far. What were the chances it would be wrong now?

He turned the corner of the last row and was disappointed to see no one there.

"All clear," he said to Marcus, but no response came.

"Marcus, where are you? Do you copy?"

He wasted no time moving back toward where they had started. As he moved the consoles began to arc with electricity, the electronics smoking and popping as they overloaded and failed under a sudden shock. He instinctively shielded his face despite his armor as the explosions intensified and fires began to break out down the rows. Whatever the Coalition had stored on this equipment, they didn't want anyone to see.

"Marcus, I repeat, where the sarding hell are you?" he shouted again, moving more quickly. The growing smoke and flames made it difficult for him to navigate.

He heard a crash a moment before Marcus's body collided violently with one of the metal racks beside him. He had his plasma blade drawn, and it snuffed out as the hilt rolled from his hand.

God's bones, he thought, drawing his own plasma blade. He kindled it just in time to deflect a savage blow that came toward his head. He prepared to defend again but a second strike didn't come.

Backing up from his friend, he scanned the room, searching for the new threat. He moved into the largest open space there was, a corridor that extended down the center of the room between the rows of consoles. He needed the extra space to maneuver.

That was when he saw her. Hex, in her green armor emerging from the smoke like some ancient deity. Tall and graceful, she held a plasma blade as she approached him. It was the first time he had seen her with his own eyes, and he could see why others would follow her in this folly.

"It's over, Hex."

"It hasn't even begun," she said. Her voice was neutral, almost to the point of seeming robotic. He assumed it probably was, but he would know soon enough who she really was behind the mask.

"The facility is surrounded. Surrender and your men will be spared. No one else needs to die," he said, holding his blade ready.

The golden hew of her visor concealed her face, but she didn't lower her blade. "Like the innocent people of Tiyas, Rihib, Dalian, New Memphis, and how many more?" she said, naming a few of the districts of Mars that burned during the Midnight Raids.

"This is different," he said, as the memories of that day came unbidden. She was trying to unsettle him, and it was working. "I am the only one here who can assure the safety of your men. Surrender and no one needs to die," he repeated, hoping she would see reason. He was tired of so much death.

"You are as much a victim as they were, Lord Beckett. If only you would open your eyes to the truth. You can still change things, but not like this," she said, and her words found purchase on his fragile psyche. The picture she painted was tantalizing and lulled him to believe things could be different, but he knew it was a lie. God had led him to this moment, and he had to trust in that divine guidance, not this siren's song.

Silas swung his plasma blade in a high arc, trying to catch Hex unaware. She twisted her wrist casually, deflecting his blow with little effort.

"Maybe one day you will see reason," she said and returned her own flurry of blows. Her form was impeccable, and it took every ounce of his skill to defend against her attacks.

She was fast and strong, impossibly strong, he thought as he fell back, losing ground. He had to do something quick, or he was going to die here.

He planted his foot and twisted, swiping his blade up into her guard while charging forward. He hoped to knock her off balance and score a hit. It was a move he had used numerous times in the dueling ring to great success, but it didn't seem to matter.

She jumped aside like a cat as her blade came down on his back. The blow knocked him to his knees, and the blade bit deeply through his armor, scorching his skin. His exoarmor worked to seal the wound, but the pain was excruciating.

"Yield!" she shouted, attempting to kick the blade from his hand. Hex was toying with him, he thought as he tried again to swipe at her. The low position gave him a small chance of hitting her in the side while her own blade was buried in his back.

The strike looked to be on target, but then the facility was rocked by massive explosions, sending them both into the air. The sudden movement separated her blade from his back, and he was able to think without pain clouding his vision.

He scrambled to his feet and swiped out again with a swift combination of strikes, but he only landed several superficial hits. He never expected she would be such a skilled duelist. There were so few outside the nobility who were.

They traded blows for what felt like an eternity as neither was able to best the other. However, he felt his strength fading while she seemed to be unbothered by the exertion. Desperation crept into his chest with each strike and deflection. Patience was the key to winning duels, but he was losing his.

Then, like a gift from God, he was granted an opening. Marcus had regained his feet and charged Hex from behind, unloading his pistol as he ran. She was forced to turn, and Silas used the opening to swing down at her body.

Hex knocked Marcus aside with her shoulder and turned back to deflect Silas's blade, but she was too late. His blade met hers, and for a moment it looked like she won, but he pushed through. His blade slid down hers and bit deeply into her leg above the knee. She collapsed to the ground, and Silas knew he had her.

He jumped back as she lunged again with her blade. She tried to get to her feet, but her ruined leg crumbled underneath her. Silas had her disabled, and now he could check on Marcus and see that she was secured and sent to his ship for questioning. His mind jumped to the future when it should have remained in the present.

Before he could process what happened next, he was slammed with tremendous force from behind and his head collided violently with the ground. He groaned as he landed, his blade knocked from his hand. Gasping, he rolled over and scrambled for it but another strike never came.

Instead, he saw Hex being scooped up by a man in jet-black armor, a plasma blade held at the ready. His helmet sported a silver visor that provided no clue to his identity. He looked back long enough for Silas to register what had happened before he ran from the room, Hex on his shoulder.

"All units, tighten the net!" he shouted through his comms.

He wanted to chase after her but then he saw Marcus's body and knew he couldn't leave him.

"Stay with me," he said, reaching his friend and was relieved to see he was still alive.

"Did we get her," Marcus said, opening his eyes.

"Not yet, but we will," he said. He knew anything less than success would only invite disaster. "We have no other choice."

ACT

1

CHAPTER

1

KAYA

AUGUST, 4101 U.E.T.—ALHAZEN, MERCURY

THEY RODE SEVERAL hours outside of the city without issue, making it all the way to the fringe of the Great Desert that covered a large swath of Mercury's equator. The area was far from the castle where city streets gave way to fields of wheat that eventually became only endless sand and desolation. It wasn't a place people chose to visit.

They had done everything right and reached the spot she had marked on the map without incident. Luckily, it was right where the engineer's report said it would be.

They stashed their borrowed bikes behind a rocky outcrop. Not far from a break in a barricade with a collection of ominous warning signs. Some of which noted the presence of landmines in the area.

Kaya knew Victoria would notice them soon, and so before she could voice a complaint Kaya took off running into the sands.

She pumped her arms in rhythm with her legs, the barren ground crunching under her footfalls. All around, heat shimmered from the surface of the windblown sands. She was breathing heavily as sweat evaporated on her brow before it could drip down her face. A light respirator over her mouth provided fresh oxygen, but her sunglasses and the thin scales of her exosuit only provided a minor barrier to the Sun's rays.

It was hot, so very hot, but it didn't matter. She wouldn't miss any opportunity to sneak away this far from the castle. The world was big, and she was tired of seeing so little of it. This wasn't the first or likely the last time she would commandeer a hoverbike for an unauthorized excursion.

Victoria had been reluctant to come along, but Kaya knew the key was not getting caught by the estate guards as they entered and left. If you

3

managed that and picked the timing window correctly, she knew no one would come looking for them. It was the perfect crime.

Victoria was happy to sneak into a mid-district club or go for a joy ride, but venturing this far outside the city on a foreign planet was far outside her comfort zone.

Kaya knew her fears weren't baseless. There were plenty of dangers outside the castle walls and especially in the Great Desert, but roving bands of criminals and crippling heat weren't at the front of Kaya's mind. Not many people lived near the Great Desert, and their exosuits did enough to guard against the heat. The real danger was the irradiated sand dunes that blanketed large areas of land in this dead region of the planet. Kaya had left out any discussion of that.

"Kaya!" called Victoria from somewhere behind her.

Kaya, momentarily startled by the sound, tripped over a rock that sent her crashing to the ground with a thud.

"Sarding hell," she moaned as she got back up to her knees, brushing the sand off her exosuit. She looked herself over but didn't notice any cuts or breaks in her suit. That was good. Getting radioactive sand on her skin wouldn't be ideal.

"I'm over here!" she shouted back. It wasn't that Victoria was slow; Kaya was just much faster and was okay with reminding her best friend of that. There was nothing wrong with some friendly competition.

As Kaya stood up, something in the sand caught her eye. From under a small rock, she could see something metallic poking out of the sand. Finding debris wasn't unusual in the Great Desert, but this seemed...different. She leaned in closer to get a better look.

It wasn't a rusted piece of scrap metal or some kind of plastic garbage. This was possibly...no, it couldn't be. Her thoughts trailed off as she was overcome with excitement and clawed at the sand. Her concern for safety was temporarily subdued by her excitement.

She may have found a relic, and not one of those fake imitations peddled by prophets and charlatans but a real-life relic. Possibly from the time of chaos or maybe even older.

It was bigger than she thought at first. She had to move several small rocks as she dug, until the full form was revealed. Although once she saw it, she still wasn't sure what it was. The material was smooth and black like obsidian but more pliable than stone or metal. It was when she turned it over and saw the emblem that she realized it was a piece of armor. Possibly a shoulder plate from an exosuit.

Not any kind of exosuit she had ever seen though, and her family owned all kinds of armor. This material was, even to her limited knowledge, of a far finer quality than anything in her family's armory. Turning it over in her hand, it wasn't the craftsmanship that held her gaze—it was the insignia.

The insignia was of a rising sun on the horizon with an inscription at the bottom. Kaya ran her fingers over the words as she read them under her breath, "Sol omnia regit," the sun rules over everything. The motto of the Solar Empire, which hadn't existed for hundreds of years. To utter those words was treason, and to have this object at all a death sentence. Her heartbeat quickened as she considered what to do.

"Kaya!" Victoria shouted again, more aggressively as she neared where Kaya was kneeling. Seeing her friend on the ground, her tone changed more to one of concern than anger at being left behind.

"Kaya! Are you okay?" Victoria said as she closed the gap between them.

Kaya's brain was still racing, but nearing footsteps forced her into action. Without thinking, she clawed at the insignia, removing it easily and concealing it in her hand.

"I...I am okay!" Kaya shouted back as she dusted off her knees. "I fell, but I'm okay."

Victoria came closer to look over her.

"I don't see any breaks in your suit, thank heaven," Victoria said. "But what is that?" She motioned to the object in the sand. "Is that a..." she said, her voice trailing off.

"Yeah, I think so," replied Kaya.

"Wow," Victoria managed as she bent down to pick it up from a corner with the tips of her fingers. She was holding it as if it were a dirty napkin.

She had found old objects out on the fringes of the Great Desert before, but nothing quite like this. Normally small rusty scraps of metal or plastic, objects that were mostly unidentifiable.

"It was lying here on the sand like this?" she said, turning to Kaya in disbelief.

"Obviously not," Kaya replied in a slightly condescending tone.

"When I fell, I noticed the edge sticking out of the sand and dug it up from over there." She pointed to a spot nearby.

Victoria turned, while Kaya slipped the insignia into her belt pouch.

"Looks like something was here," Victoria said, facing her. She was fingering the spot where the Solar Empire insignia had been attached moments before.

Kaya pretended to be curious. "Oh, yeah, I guess so. We should take it back with us. Maybe we can find out something else about it."

Victoria agreed, "Maybe one of the engineers will know."

"Maybe...but let's not show them right away."

Victoria looked at her quizzically, "Why not?"

"I want to try and identify it myself first. You know, I wanted to train to be an engineer." That was mostly true. "Put it in my backpack for now." she added, turning her back to Victoria.

Victoria seemed mollified. "Alright, but you know we are supposed to report anything we find," she said, placing the armor piece into Kaya's backpack.

"Of course, and we *will* report it, but I don't want one of the artificers to take it from me before I have a chance to study it myself," she said, lying through her teeth. She didn't want the artificers to touch this at all.

"Let me handle it, okay?" Her tone was more aggressive than she intended.

"Okay, okay. Are you feeling alright today? You are more ruffled than usual," she said. Apparently, it was Victoria's turn to be condescending. "I thought you said there was an old church out here. I don't see anything but sand and rocks. Also, when were you going to mention this was a restricted zone?" As much as they were friends, their rivalry left them prone to bickering.

"I am not *ruffled*. Ugh, come on, we are wasting time. It's out here somewhere, and if I had told you that you wouldn't have come," Kaya said. There was supposed to be an old city out here somewhere, but in truth she didn't really know where it was. "Besides, maybe we can find another relic or two."

Victoria seemed unimpressed. "My first time outside of the city on this planet, and you take me to look at rocks. Couldn't we go to the beach?" Victoria kicked at the ground.

"Let's look around a little more. If we don't find anything, we can just head back," Kaya said in the most sympathetic tone she could muster.

"Fine, but tell me everything next time, okay? I should be allowed to make my own decisions, and you don't need to keep secrets from me."

Kaya nodded before taking off in a sprint. Victoria cursed and ran after her. They traversed several more miles of desert but never came across the old city or any other relics besides the occasional bit of trash or rusty metal.

Disappointed, they returned to where they had stashed their hoverbikes on the edge of the restricted zone. Donning their helmets and connecting their comms, they rode off, sticking to the established trails that led toward the city.

They didn't see much along their route besides the detritus of time and empire. Scraps of trash and plastic blew among the rusted metal and broken concrete as they rumbled past. The population of Mercury was concentrated under the energy domes of the major cities. Just like it was on most of the settled moons and planets.

Occasionally they passed human figures walking alone to somewhere unknown or huddled in small groups. They were dirty and disheveled with their faces hidden behind large scarves and heavy robes. The clothing was their only protection from the sun and irradiated sand.

"There are so many forsaken here. We have so few of them back home," Victoria said through their helmet comms. Her tone was judgmental.

"Father says more and more are gathering along the Great Desert. Some are even seen in caravans entering the sands," Kaya replied, matter-of-fact.

She had seen the forsaken her entire life living here and venturing out of the castle. So, she felt more aware of their plight than her Venusian friend. Every planet had desperate people living on the fringe of society trying to get by, but Victoria never left her estate to see them.

"Where are they going?" Victoria asked.

Kaya kept her eyes on the path. "No one knows." Her voice grew a little more distant. "Some people say they walk into the desert to die."

Victoria paused. "How dreadful."

They rode for a while in silence.

The dunes eventually gave way to hilly plains. Nestled among the rolling hills were creeks and groves of trees surrounded by cultivated fields and pastures.

In the distance, past the pastoral landscape, the skyline of Alhazen, the largest and most important city on Mercury rose from the horizon.

The closer to the city they got, the more they had to weave around people and vehicles clogging the crumbling roads.

"Curses!" Victoria yelled as she dodged another pedestrian who attempted to cross the street amongst the traffic. "Isn't there another way we can get back?"

"Sure, if you want to get caught. They won't be looking for us here on the main roads," Kaya said, weaving around another hover truck that idled on the road. Workers were busy unloading crates of rusty parts into a vehicle repair shop as they passed. "If we go onto the upper roadways, we will be flagged down by the Mercurian Guard Dragoons. We are better off taking our chances with the local constables."

"What good is being nobility if we are only going to hang out in the slums?" retorted Victoria.

"This is a low district, but if you want to see the slums, we can do that."

"Heavens no! This is bad enough, thank you," Victoria replied. Her curiosity had much stricter limits than Kaya's.

"Then follow me. The bike drop isn't far now."

The route Kaya took skirted the outside of the city's low districts before reaching a river that separated the high districts from the low. The Alhazen Castle complex sat on a hill in the middle of the high districts overlooking the rest of Alhazen.

Before long, they arrived at the Garden District bridge. There was a short queue of vehicles waiting at the checkpoint to enter. Overhead, air traffic became more noticeable, with small transport ships, military vessels, and private yachts flying in and out of the area.

Kaya slowed to a stop a little way back and out of sight of the checkpoint. She flipped open the visor of her helmet.

"Here, take this," she said, handing an ID card to Victoria.

"What the blazes is it?" Victoria asked, looking the card over.

"Your new identity. Don't speak, just hand the constables the ID when we get to the checkpoint. Your posh accent will give you away more than your blonde Venusian curls."

"My...uhm, what? Why do we need to do all this? No one stopped us when we left," Victoria said.

"They usually only check traffic coming into the high districts, not out. Not enough manpower or something," she said, flipping her visor back down.

"Come on. It will be fine," Kaya said as she began moving her hover bike toward the checkpoint.

"Why did you have to bring my hair into this?" Victoria grumbled.

At the gate, a pair of constables wearing crisp beige uniforms and badges of the Alhazen police signaled them to stop. On the opposite side of the bridge were a small group of Planetary Guardsmen standing behind a barricade with railguns pointed out at the city. A large anti air gun pointing skyward provided them with some shade. Kaya didn't pay them much attention, but Victoria couldn't help but stare.

"Identification," the constable said, holding his hand out. The other constable approached Victoria.

Kaya wordlessly reached into the pocket of her exosuit and handed the ID to the man. Victoria did the same but fumbled with the ID, dropping it onto the ground. The female guard seemed annoyed but bent down to pick up the ID.

"You should be more careful," the woman said to Victoria, who said nothing.

"What's yer business in the district?" the other guard asked Kaya while looking over their rusty bikes and dirty exosuits.

"Couriers, pickin' up deliveries," she said, her voice muffled through the mask under her helmet. She was trying to affect the accent of someone from the low districts. Luckily, it wasn't unusual for people to keep their visors down or sunglasses on when the sun blazed high in the sky. So that alone didn't raise any suspicion.

The constable looked over her ID and then scanned it with his device. A moment went by as he stared at the screen, but when it flashed green, he eased up and handed the ID back to Kaya.

Victoria's ID likewise scanned without a problem, but as Victoria went to take it back, the constable flicked it at her.

"Oops," the woman sneered as she took a step back, forcing Victoria off her bike to pick it up.

"You cursed old bag..." Victoria began to say, but luckily the helmet muffled her words. The problem was her stiffening shoulders and clenching fists were threatening to betray her.

"Victoria..." Kaya mumbled, nodding to the constable who handed her the ID and looking back at Victoria.

Victoria huffed but climbed off the bike to get the ID, her golden hair coming out from under her collar as she bent to pick it up. *Oh no*, Kaya thought, hoping no one else would notice.

When she got back on the bike, the woman gave her a self-satisfied smile with yellow stained teeth. It was an odd change of demeanor. The two constables exchanged a look but waved them through the checkpoint without further issue.

What was that look? she wondered but dropped the thought when they crossed the threshold of the energy dome. Once they'd crossed into the high district, the air felt more substantial and was noticeably free of haze and dust, and she breathed a sigh of relief. Relief that was interrupted by Victoria's grumbling.

"By God's bones, I will see that cursed woman flogged," Victoria said as they got out of eyesight of the checkpoint.

"No, you sarding won't. She was only doing her job," Kaya responded.

"You mean treating me like a common peasant? That was completely unacceptable!" Victoria said.

"Treating you like any other citizen from the low districts you mean?" Kaya said quickly.

"Well...yes, exactly that!"

Kaya rolled her eyes. It wasn't worth arguing with Victoria about things she wasn't going to understand.

"It's not much further. We need to turn up ahead," Kaya said, signaling toward an alley.

In the historic Garden District, the streets were clean and tidy, if not a bit worn. They traveled the gently inclined road toward the hilltop where Alhazen Castle had a commanding position over the landscape below. The shining towers of the newer part of the high district gleamed beyond the castle.

The Garden District was normally the perfect place for Kaya to stash her bike. Since there was still enough low district traffic on the streets, like couriers and laborers to make blending in easier.

Except, they hadn't gone unnoticed. Twenty meters away Kaya could see a pair of Planetary Guard Dragoons riding armed hover bikes, barring their way into the alley. They had been flagged.

"Curses! Change of plans, come on," Kaya said, turning her bike sharply.

"What? Why don't we ride past?"

"That isn't a normal patrol. Now be quiet and follow me," Kaya said as she revved the engine and sped off down the closest street.

"I knew I should have stayed in and read a book today. How did I let you convince me this was a good idea?" Victoria cried out as they raced down the street, weaving around vehicles and the occasional startled pedestrian.

"That's easy. You know this is much more fun," Kaya said as she looked back to see the dragoons behind them. Their emergency lights flashed, and their sirens blared. Kaya's heart raced with excitement. "Sarding hell! They aren't far behind us," she shouted, narrowly avoiding a truck backing out of a small alleyway.

Kaya looked back to see Victoria turn sharply as sparks flew off her bike from where it grazed the truck as she passed. "Oh no!" she shouted as the dragoons thankfully got stuck behind the truck.

"Oh my God, we made it!" Victoria laughed as she sped up beside Kaya, the pair bumping their fists at high speed. Kaya couldn't help but laugh alongside her friend. "But what do we do now?"

"Let's get on the high roads. We can ditch the bikes somewhere and then sneak our way back in—oh no!" Kaya cried as she swerved seeing another pair of dragoons blocking the way onto the elevated highway. *Why were there so many of them?*

"We can still outrun them!" Kaya cried out to Victoria, who was luckily still by her side. The only response she got was a nervous scream as they sped onto the entry ramp, the dragoons close behind.

On the highway, the traffic thinned, and they were able to accelerate to the highest speeds their rusty bikes would tolerate. As they pulled away from the dragoons, she was thankful they hadn't opened fire on them.

It looked like they might get away until a startling sound roared above them, shaking them violently. They struggled to stay on their bikes as the wind from above rattled them before passing quickly. Looking up, she could see a Falcon had strafed their position before turning up ahead on the highway to face them down. Kaya's brain couldn't process why there was suddenly a fighter plane on the highway.

"No, no, no!" Victoria said, slamming the bike's thrusters in reverse to bring it to a stop. Kaya cursed but was forced to do the same. The Falcon came to hover in front of them, its engines roaring as the dragoons caught up and dismounted behind them.

"On the ground now!" they shouted as the girls dismounted, sparing nervous looks toward the Falcon. It seemed like they were as surprised as she was.

"Okay, don't hurt us!" Victoria shouted as she got off her bike and removed her helmet, throwing it aside. Kaya followed along, although more reluctantly.

"Funny joke, you got us. Can we—" Kaya was aggressively shoved to her knees.

"Hey, do you know—" She was cut off again as a hand whipped across her face.

"Shut it!" said the female dragoon, nervously holding her rail rifle up at Kaya while her partner held his at Victoria. "Lieutenant's on his way. He'll sort this out. Until then, don't move!" she looked nervously back at the Falcon and then back at her prisoners.

"If you would..."

The dragoons palm came back down on her face. "I said shut it!"

"Or what?" sneered Kaya in response. She could hear Victoria sobbing. "You dumb or just slow?" the woman said, raising the butt of her rifle in preparation to hit Kaya with it.

"That's enough, soldier!" came a commanding and familiar voice as a man dismounted from the Falcon and approached. He was several years older than Kaya, approaching his mid-twenties. He looked fit and carried himself with the air of a soldier twice his age. His long hair was tied back behind his head, and despite stepping out of a fighter aircraft he wore an impeccably pressed dress uniform. He looked as ready for a parade as for war.

The dragoons meanwhile stood dumbstruck, staring up at the man as he got close. His captain's insignia and the hilt of a plasma blade at his hip were more than enough to get them to comply.

Victoria noticeably relaxed when she saw him, and she stood up quickly, her tears subsiding. Kaya meanwhile sighed and mumbled another curse under her breath.

"Lord Vardan! What lovely timing," Victoria said as she rushed to his side.

The dragoons didn't stop her, but they did back up slowly, guns still raised as they looked to Tiberius al Vardan, her gallant brother, for direction. Their complexions becoming increasingly pale as they seemed to realize the mess they found themselves in.

"Lady Pendlebrook, always a pleasure. It's been much too long," he said, with a perfect courtly bow.

"Dear sister, I am glad you seem so happy to see me," he said, spreading his arms in greeting to Kaya.

"Hello Tiberius." She rubbed her cheek. "Nice of you to bring the cavalry," she said sarcastically. She looked at the Falcon hovering on the highway and then at the traffic beginning to build up behind the dragoons. No one seemed prepared to interrupt whatever was going on.

Tiberius laughed, making the soldiers even more tense. "When I heard you two were leading a high-speed chase, I took the first thing I saw to come and catch you both myself. What's with your face?"

"I tripped getting off my bike," she said.

Tiberius frowned and waved his hand at the dragoons. "Enough of that, you two, at ease. Surely you would have thought to take better care of my sister."

The two dragoons, as if awakening from a trance, lowered their weapons and stepped back. They looked like they wanted to say something, but no words came out. Kaya imagined they were wishing they had been assigned patrols somewhere else today.

"Well, we can address that later. Are you alright then?" he asked, and Kaya nodded. She wondered how he could be so nonchalant in a moment like this, but he did tend to be unbothered by life's pesky interruptions.

Soon after, the dragoon lieutenant arrived and looked at Tiberius with a confused expression before turning to speak with his troopers. Tiberius gave the man a friendly wave, which seemed to confuse him even more.

"You two have found yourselves in quite a mess this time," he said to the two girls, his smile returning to his face. "Father is going to love this."

"He wouldn't have to know if you hadn't gotten in our way," she said, pointing at the Falcon.

"So much gratitude!" he quipped. "You might like to know that they thought you were tech runners and were prepared to blow you to pieces." His face was horribly smug. "Yes, you are very welcome for my assistance," he said, replying to a thank you that hadn't come.

Victoria's looked on the verge of crying again, but Kaya rolled her eyes.

"Thank you, Tiberius," Victoria said with a shaky voice.

"Of course, Lady Pendlebrook, anything for you," he said with another small bow.

Kaya groaned. "Come on, Lancelot. Can you get us out of here?"
"I know neither of you are soldiers, but if you remember from your lessons, Falcons only seat one," Tiberius said. "But I expect these fine dragoons could provide an escort.
"Lieutenant, could I have a word please?" he said, waving over the young officer, who seemed to be oscillating between furious and apologetic.

"Yes, Captain, uh, Lord Vardan?" the lieutenant said, stumbling over his words.

"Captain will do, Lieutenant."

"Can you personally see that my sister, Lady Vardan, and her companion, Lady Pendlebrook, make it back to castle without further delay? I will follow close behind," he said, motioning to the Falcon.

"Yes, of course, sir. You two, clear the road," he said to the two soldiers then turned to Kaya and Victoria. "Ladies, if you will follow me this way to my vehicle?" The lieutenant motioned back to where his hovering command vehicle was parked.

The journey back wasn't long, but Victoria sat silently, making a concerted effort not to look at her. Kaya sighed as they took off, wishing the excitement had lasted a little longer before the day went sideways.

C H A P T E R

2

Kaya

August, 4101 U.E.T.—Alhazen, Mercury

Kaya sat on the edge of her bed, her mind a spinning mess of thoughts about what had happened and what would happen next. She had been in trouble before, but this... She worried this was something worse. Normally she would have been given a lecture about propriety and sent on her way, but instead her father had them locked in their rooms.

She wondered how much of that had to do with Victoria quickly ratting them out for where they had been in the first place. Although, with the high level of surveillance it was only a matter of time until authorities pieced it all together once they knew where to look.

Victoria had come to spend some time with her and her family, exploring a new place before they went on to their university pursuits. She and Victoria had worked hard to get accepted into the finest Hospitaler university on Venus, and they had been looking forward to the nearing start date.

It was the kind of school that social status alone wouldn't get you into, so the accomplishment was that much more noteworthy. Now, for the first time, she wondered if all of that could be in jeopardy and the thought filled her with dread. She hadn't considered they could get into any real trouble.

She was too distracted to worry about bathing and had carelessly tossed her backpack with the artifact and filthy exosuit into a corner but kept the insignia in her palm. She sat staring at it for a long time before walking over to one of the overstuffed bookshelves that lined the walls of her room. Her dusty hands and body left an impression behind on the bed.

She picked out a book that didn't look very different from the others.

It was entitled, *The Divine Plan: Trusting in God's Guidance in Times of Turmoil*, a thick tome written by some long-dead bishop. She opened the book, revealing a carved-out cavity. In it were several folded notes and a small pendant in the shape of a sun that her mother claimed she found digging in the garden. It had been their secret.

Before placing the insignia in the book, she rubbed at it to remove a stray bit of dirt she had missed, revealing a new detail. Inside the sun was a small symbol of three intertwined triangles. She didn't recognize the symbol. She mused it might be some kind of unit marking, although she had never heard of unit markings being combined with the Solar Empire's official insignia.

Mentioning the Solar Empire or its symbols publicly or in writing was highly illegal, but discussion of them was still quite common. Discussion of the Ageless Legion was an especially popular topic. She thought for a moment that maybe this symbol had something to do with that but dismissed it out of hand.

The Ageless Legion was an elite unit of the Solar Empire's army made up entirely of the "ageless," people who had been given some serum that greatly prolonged their lives, practically making them immortal.

Opinions on the matter varied quite a bit, and she had gotten into plenty of arguments over whether the ageless ever existed. She secretly wished it was true, but she would tell anyone else it was just a metaphor for how numerous the legion had been. It was better to deny these wild tales than be labeled an imperialist.

She placed the insignia into the book when something caught her eye. She picked up one of the folded notes and opened it. It was an old note that her mother had left for her before leaving on one of her many off-planet excursions. Except, it wasn't the words that she noticed now, which she knew well; it was the paper. There on the bottom of the stationary was the symbol. Not a similar one but the exact same conjoined triangles with the same curves and pattern.

She never thought much of it before, assuming it was the mark from some hotel. Now her mind raced with the possibilities of what it could mean.

Her daydreaming was cut short when the digiscreen clicked on. Startled by the sudden sound, she nearly dropped the book and the note. She really hated that cursed thing.

She returned the note and placed the book back in its place on the shelf as she rubbed her jaw absently. It had been hours since the escapade in the city, but her face still hurt. She moved to the mirror only absently listening to the talking heads on the digiscreen. She noticed a purple bruise beginning to paint her cheek. *Well, that's going to look bad for a while.*

She turned back to the digiscreen as it switched to a well-dressed woman on the official Republic Network, "Tonight, we discuss a growing problem. False prophets preying on the desperate with lies and fanciful tales." The screen then cut from the newsroom to images of a robed man with a hood pulled over his head. He was tall and had a neat appearance. What skin was visible was quite pale, like someone from the Far Coast.

Kaya thought there was something odd-looking about the man's face, but the scene changed too quickly for her to figure it out. Then they showed the man's back as he walked through what looked like slums. Somewhere on Mars, she thought based on the intensity of the sun and the surrounding landscape. He was carrying a plain wooden walking stick and moved unmolested through the crowds of people.

He looked completely out of place yet totally at ease, like a flower growing in a field of ash. The slums were places even armored soldiers rarely patrolled, yet this man was offering quiet words and a soft touch to the masses who reached out to him. He was either immensely brave or reckless, but she found it incredible in either case.

The screen then switched back to the newsroom where the woman stared unblinkingly into the camera. "Although con men like this one claim to speak for the divine, their false promises of salvation quickly lead to destruction," the reporter said. Her tone grew dark as the image switched again to a horrible scene of lifeless bodies in a city square.

"As you can see, where these prophets go, they leave only death and destruction in their wake." The narration matched the horrible images on the screen as the camera zoomed in on the still face of a disfigured child. There the camera hung for several long seconds before switching back to the newsroom. It was sickening. The message was clear: retribution will be swift and brutal for those who choose the wrong side.

"We remind our viewers that consorting with false prophets is a capital offense. Any sighting of these apostates should be reported immediately to your local Resident Watch office. Residents reporting such sightings will be commended for their heroism and loyalty." *And well paid,* she thought.

There was no mention of the Vermilion Coalition, but then again there never was. Kaya noticed the small strips of Vermilion cloth among the bodies. It seemed like the Frumentarii were either getting sloppy or bolder. She wasn't sure which was worse.

"We go now to the Amaranthine Palace, where High Commander Silas Beckett of the Pandora Fleet has left a meeting with his Holiness, Vox Albrecht."

The newsroom vanished and switched to an overhead shot of the sprawling Amaranthine Palace. The camera then switched to a view inside the palace. It was a familiar room adjacent to the main throne room, where senior officials would meet with the Vox and Manus.

In the center of the frame stood a man maybe a little older than her father. Silas Beckett had graying hair that was cropped short and a stern expression. His uniform was crisp and professional. He was everything someone would expect a career soldier to be. Her mother had always said he was one of the good ones, even if many others didn't feel the same.

"Citizens of the Republic, I come here today to reassure you that the Pandora Fleet, in conjunction with the Republic Army and Navy, continue to do everything possible to safeguard our Republic. Those who attempt to circumvent our laws or do harm to God's children will be hunted to the ends of the solar system, you have my word," he said, and Kaya believed him. She only wished his hunt would apply to the Frumentarii who killed nearly as many people as the Coalition did.

She tried to consider why the Vermilion Coalition continued their fight when it seemed so pointless. They accomplished nothing and often left more bodies in their wake. Then the image of the disfigured child came back to her mind, and she knew. Disgust and anger rose in her chest, but it only left her frustrated with nowhere to direct it. She had even less power than the Coalition did to create meaningful change.

Silas Beckett continued speaking as the gruesome scene flashed in a small box in the corner of the screen. The Republic was likely trying to deflect the blame for this massacre of its citizens to the Pandora Fleet by having Lord Beckett deliver this message, but his words failed to register. Her angry thoughts had full control over her now.

Even if the child's disfigurement was a product of radiation or malnutrition, she knew the Resident Watch, or more likely the Frumentarii, were ultimately to blame for the death. Her mother had always warned her quietly of the steps they would take to maintain order.

Tears began to roll down her cheek.

They didn't need Frumentarii skulking in the dark and murdering children to maintain order. If peace could be brokered with the Coalition, the resources of the Republic could be used to build anew. If there was peace, what need would there be for organizations like the Resident Watch to exist?

A knock came at the door and Kaya's mind went racing back to her own situation. She swallowed hard as a pit formed in her stomach. She hoped things would blow over like they always had.

"Lady Kaya, your father summons you," came the calm and reassuring voice of Theodore Parker, her father's Lord Steward.

"Yes, I'm coming," she shouted back while wiping tears from her eyes. She looked in the mirror and tried to remove the dust that clung to her long-sleeved white shirt and black pants. Her efforts seemed to be making it worse, so she gave up. They were clothes meant for wearing under exoarmor, but she was past the point of caring about that.

Clearing her throat with a sniffle, she opened the door.

"Mr. Parker." She nodded.

"My lady." Noticing the tear streaks on her face, he handed her a handkerchief and put a reassuring hand on her shoulder.

"Come now, it will be alright," he reassured. "I am sure your father has a plan to sort this all out."

"Thank you," she said, taking the handkerchief and dabbing at her eyes, "but it's not that.

"Have you seen the news?" she asked him as they walked. The corridor was lined with marble and tall glass windows that let in light for the plethora of plants that basked in it. It was quiet save for their footfalls and the occasional sound of songbirds in the garden.

A look of regret crossed his face. "Yes, an...unfortunate affair."

"Unfortunate..." she repeated, emphasizing the word. "What's unfortunate is that those responsible are not being hauled in by the Forge Knights or even the Void Knights for questioning!" she shouted, getting the attention of the guards stationed at the end of the hallway. They turned to look before averting their gaze once again.

Theodore pulled her into an alcove with a large window overlooking one of the courtyard gardens.

"My lady," He looked directly into her eyes. "Those who died knowingly conspired with an apostate. You understand this is a treasonous offense." He nodded slowly. "We must rejoice in knowing they will burn in the seven hells for their blasphemy," he said loudly enough for anyone nearby to hear.

Kaya was disgusted by what he said, but she got the hint.

"Yes," she drawled through clenched teeth before relaxing. "You are right. I was simply referring to the capturing of these false prophets and rabble rousers once and for all," she managed to say. Her stomach twisted with every foul word.

Theodore nodded. "Yes, I assumed that was your true sentiment," he said, looking at her with his penetrating eyes. "Come, we shouldn't keep your father waiting."

Kaya offered no protest and followed silently.

The entrance to her father's office was a large solid wooden door with the relief of a sun carved into it. It was an ancient piece transported to Mercury at great expense by the Sultans who led the way in terraforming this fiery planet. She supposed the art must have been different enough from the Solar Empire insignia to have survived the Great Purge following the end of the Time of Chaos.

The soldiers opened the door at Theodore's command. The ancient hinges always creaked awfully, even with the copious amounts of grease workers placed on them. Father liked to say it was a reminder that even the most beautiful things weren't always perfect. She hoped he would remember that when he passed his judgment for her recent transgression.

The inside of the room was as equally grand as the rest of the castle grounds. However, despite the exquisite craftsmanship, paint was fading, and plaster chipped from age. Tall bookshelves lined both sides of the room. The library was the window to one's soul, her mother would say, along with the fact that it was much harder to track a handwritten page than it was a digipad message.

At the far end of the room was a large wooden desk that was carved to match the entrance door. Her father sat rigidly in his chair, the sun illuminating him like an ancient god through the vaulted windows. The olive trees in the garden casting shadows through the room only added to the ambiance.

He wore a simple black suit with the jacket buttoned all the way down the front with a high straight collar around his neck. His vibrant auburn hair that matched her own was cut short to his scalp, the color contrasting sharply against the color of his suit. His clothing was stylish but traditional. He took pride in his appearance as a reflection of his being. Kaya looked down at her disheveled clothing and knew they would be starting off on the wrong page.

Her father, Duke Mithridates al Vardan, was only the second most powerful man on Mercury, behind the archbishop, but he still wielded enormous power as the Lord Eminent of the Assembly of Lords. He was a man who was loved as much as he was feared, a dangerous line to tiptoe within the Republic, but Kaya didn't care about any of that. This was still her father, no matter how angry he looked.

Victoria was already seated in one of the two chairs in front of his desk, and her brother stood leaning against a bookshelf, casually flipping the page of a book. She took the empty seat as Theodore closed the door and took up his own position standing next to the desk.

Kaya tried her best to look apologetic.

"Father, I—"

"Do. Not. Speak," her father said. "You three have taken great liberties with your actions, putting yourselves, this family, and this planet at great risk."

Victoria and Kaya listened quietly, but Tiberius, who had only been half listening, perked up when he noticed he had been included in their father's admonishment.

"The three of you? What the heavens did I do?" Tiberius retorted casually.

Mithridates, their father, turned to level the full weight of his gaze and displeasure on Tiberius.

"By whose orders did you commandeer a Falcon craft and involve yourself in a Planetary Guard affair?" It was clear from Tiberius's sarcastic smirk that no such order was given. How did he always get away with being so sarding smug?

"The high commander of your carrier unit has already requested you be formally court-martialed and stripped of your newly appointed rank."

Mithridates's voice remained calm, but the energy behind his words reverberated through the room. No one dared speak, but the sarcastic expression never left her brother's face. "It is by my grace alone that you remain free of chains."

"Yes...Father, it was an unwise decision," Tiberius said. He cleared his throat and stood straighter at attention, but his eyes didn't match his words.

"Unwise," his father repeated blandly. "With such wisdom, I trust your career will be as short as it has been explosive." Tiberius stifled a laugh but remained silent. Kaya wondered if his newfound power had gone to Tiberius's head. He was certainly growing bolder.

"As for the two of you..." he said, turning back to Kaya and Victoria. Kaya tried to match her father's stoic stare, while Victoria hadn't stopped crying. Pouting had always been her own strategy to get out of trouble.

"You have often pushed the boundary of what was prudent and acceptable behavior but this...this time you have both gone too far." He took a deep breath. "Not only did you both leave the castle without informing the House Guard, but you also proceeded to travel to the Great Desert, a highly restricted area, putting yourselves at risk of great bodily harm." He then quickly added, "In addition to using false identification and stolen hover bikes!"

"We paid for the bikes," Kaya mumbled.

"Excuse me?" her father replied. "I think you mean *I* paid for the bikes. Without me, you would have no money with which to fund these expeditions of yours, but that is the least of your worries. I shouldn't have to remind you both that the use of false identification and entering a restricted zone are capital offenses." As he finished speaking, Victoria began sobbing louder and more genuinely as the weight of the charges levied against them sank in.

Kaya looked down blankly at her hands, trying to think. She was so sure they would pull it off, but now here she was. No one was above the law, especially not nobility.

"I...I'm sorry. I never meant for this to go so far. I only wanted an adventure and to maybe find some relics. I knew if I asked that you would only say no," Kaya said.

"You are right, I would have. There are many reasons no one goes near the Great Desert. Aside from the high levels of radiation, it is riddled with landmines. You are both lucky to be alive," he said, shaking his head.

Victoria's head shot up at the mention of explosives, but Kaya jumped in to redirect the conversation. "What now?" she asked, reality beginning to set in.

Mithridates sighed and leaned back in his chair. "The archbishop has been quite adamant in voicing his displeasure at today's events. Normally, this type of case would be heard by the regional magistrate or perhaps even the Planetary Tribunal, but given the parties involved the archbishop was requesting the Frumentarii adjudicate the issue instead to avoid any conflict of interest."

Kaya's heart sank, and the feeling of dread returned. One moment she had been thinking about attending university, and now there was talk of Frumentarii and tribunals. She had no quips ready for that bit of news.

Her father continued speaking through her silence. "Luckily, I was able to petition him to allow the Knights of Dawn to investigate the issue and then provide their judgment, and he acquiesced."

Kaya's mind raced. It was good that the Frumentarii would have no part in this. She had some idea of what justice looked like to them.

"Wouldn't a case be brought before the Supreme Tribunal if the Planetary Tribunal is unacceptable?" Kaya asked, looking from her father to Theodore. The Supreme Tribunal was headed by the Manus, who sat above all others on the Council of Bishops and was the second most powerful person in the solar system behind the Vox himself. She was glad it wasn't being brought before the Manus, but she was still curious why.

Theodore answered. "Lady Kaya, the archbishop cannot risk a protracted legal battle that will further divide the already delicate balance between the civil and ecclesiastical administrations of Mercury. It is better a traditionally neutral body like the Knights of Dawn adjudicate the issue."

Theodore then looked to Victoria before adding, "The addition of the daughter of a powerful Venusian lord only complicates things. No, it is better for all involved that this goes away quietly."

Victoria sobbed a loud, ugly sob.

"He doesn't mean *you* would go away. Get it together," Kaya said, shaking her friend on the shoulder. "We will figure this out, like always," she whispered, trying to sound confident.

Mithridates continued, "The Knights of Dawn have already sent a seneschal, who should arrive soon. You will be asked questions about what happened. It is important that you answer very carefully. This isn't a game, and they have burned men at the stake for less than what you two have done," he said, looking at Kaya directly. She wasn't sure if he was trying to scare her. They hadn't executed a noble in at least a generation, but a shiver ran up her spine nonetheless.

"But don't the Knights only enforce judgments on behalf of the tribunals?" Kaya asked, trying not to dwell on the potential consequences.

"Officially, the seneschal is only investigating the allegations and providing recommendations. In this case, the archbishop has agreed to abide by this recommendation," her father replied.

Kaya felt apprehension.

She had listened to a lot of lectures about the knightly orders, but nothing made her think they would be any less loyal to the whims of the bishops than the Frumentarii would be.

Victoria broke the silence with a raspy and shaky voice. "Have my mother and father been told?"

"They have been informed that you are well, and I have assured them I am handling this matter on their behalf," Mithridates said. "Our families have been like one for generations. I will of course protect you the same as I would my own blood." He sounded more emotional than usual. Kaya couldn't help but feel some jealousy at the tenderness he showed her. Was it because he felt she needed it or because he didn't feel the same for his own daughter?

He cleared his throat. "I believe you all understand what is expected of you. You are to remain in your rooms until the seneschal calls for your statement. Theodore, can you see that Lady Pendlebrook makes it back safely?"

"Yes, My Grace," Theodore replied with a bow. Kaya stood to follow them.

"Kaya, you can stay," Mithridates said.

Kaya sat back down and looked nervously at her brother, looking for reassurance that never came. He had always been protective of her but never particularly tender.

"I will likewise take my leave." He bowed.

Thanks for nothing.

When the door closed, she attempted another apology, but her father waved his hand.

"I know as much as you that you aren't sorry, so let's drop the pretense," he said, his dark-brown eyes boring into her as if trying to read her very soul. "You can speak openly here. The room is shielded."

"Will this impact our admission to Hospitaller University?" she asked.

He seemed surprised as he shook his head. "You do realize how much more serious this is than that? The archbishop is talking about *executions*, Kaya. Do you understand?"

"This is all bullocks, you know," Kaya said, attempting to match her father's stare like she had seen her mother do countless times. She wasn't quite succeeding, but she was one of the only people who could or at least would try to match his stare.

"Which part exactly? The part where you forged your identification credentials or entered a highly restricted zone?"

"You know what I mean. All...this," she said, waving her hand around the room. "Our world is crumbling, and no one seems to care. The Republic hunts down so-called prophets, and Frumentarii murder children in the street while millions more die of radiation and malnutrition." She was getting fired up and her words flowed out in an unfiltered stream.

"People like you in your ivory tower," she continued, "and the brainwashed idiots in their luxurious domed districts pretend that their buildings are not as tarnished as they used to be. Vital equipment continues to fail, with no one able or allowed to create new parts to fix it. So, more people are pushed into the slums to die, and the mid and high districts become thinner and thinner. Until what? Until one day no one is left?

"Meanwhile no one acknowledges the Vermilion Coalition exists or attempts to broker a peace so we can move past this chaos. When does it end, when have we all suffered enough for the Republic and this God of theirs? They claim to deliver salvation, but instead they deliver even less than the prophets they so despise. Even if they are frauds, at least they give people hope, and hope is more than so many have right now." She was panting now, but her father remained silent.

"I want to make a difference. I want to learn how to help people. Join the Hospitallers and become a physician. Then I can cure instead of kill." Tears began to run down her cheeks and her voice grew soft and heavy.

"Mother used to tell me about the Era of Empire, when the golden spires reached the stars and human innovation was prized by all. She said there was no illness that couldn't be cured, and people lived forever in happiness and comfort. She said one day we would see it again, together as a family. She..."

Mithridates moved around to the other side of the desk to embrace his daughter. "Little sun, your mother was a beautiful dreamer. Not a day goes by that I don't open my eyes expecting to see her, only to have my heart ripped from my chest anew."

"They killed her, didn't they?"

"Who?" he asked.

"Was it the Vermilion Coalition? The Frumentarii?"

"No, little sun," he said, running his hand over her hair. "She died when her ship malfunctioned. It was a terrible accident. You already know that."

It had been nearly a year since her mother's death, but she still didn't believe what he said. He might have been satisfied with the answers they received, but she wasn't.

"That's as good as either of them doing it themselves!" she shouted into his chest. "She was a hero of the Republic, and *my mother,* but she died, and they threw her away. No one was punished for what happened. Everyone...forgot, but I didn't forget. I will *never* forget." She pulled back from her father.

"How can you sit there and say nothing?" She was angry with him for his lack of action, his commitment to his position over his family. He wouldn't be the squeaky gear, and for that they got nothing, no answers, no justice, no closure.

"The investigation was completed. There was no one to blame but metal and wires," he said, returning her angry eyes with his own calm expression like he had so many times before. "You are not the only one who misses her." His voice was colder than it had been a moment before. "Only time will heal this wound, how much time, only fate knows."

"I want answers that make sense."

"You won't find them if you die being reckless. There are consequences to actions even you and I can't escape through force of will. You need to be smart now. I am not overstating the dangers," his stern demeanor began to crack, and he looked worried. She had never seen him worried before. "None of us can help realize your mother's dreams if we are dead."

"I will do what it takes."

"You always have," he said with a weak smile. In that moment, her father looked old and tired in a way she had never noticed before. "Go now. You will need your rest," he said, his normal confidence returning.

She nodded and left the room, her head held high. Her mother had never been afraid of anything.

CHAPTER

3

AUGUST, 4101 U.E.T. – ALHAZEN, MERCURY

IT HAD BEEN several hours since she left her father's office. The gravity of his words had taken time to break through her stubbornness, but now anxiety had settled over her. It wasn't panic inducing anxiety, but it was enough to make doing anything productive difficult.

Despite that, she managed to bathe and dismissed her attendant, choosing to brush her own hair as she brooded over potential punishments. Her cheek was turning purple, but at least now her face was free of dust. Her auburn hair and emerald eyes contrasted sharply with her olive skin as the sunlight streamed in from her bedroom windows.

She stared into the mirror as she brushed, preparing herself for what came next. She would meet with the seneschal soon and would say as little as possible. They couldn't twist her words if she only answered yes or no.

"Yes or no," she repeated, taking a deep breath.

No matter how nice or kind the seneschal seemed, he wasn't her friend. He would smile and use flowery language to get her to open up and say the wrong thing, but she wouldn't listen. She wasn't going to be so gullible.

Her brooding was cut short when a knock came at the door, startling her.

"God's bones!" She sent her hairbrush crashing into the wall. She had to get it together.

She steeled herself and walked to the door. Her heart threatened to burst out of her chest. She had dressed formerly in a plain black suit like the one her father had worn. A jeweled broach on her chest was the only adornment. The broach was designed in the symbol of her house, a fox curled at the foot of a leafy tree. It was the type of outfit she would have worn at official functions when her father met with important clergy or other nobles.

The guardsman who had knocked silently guided her to the room where the seneschal would take her statement. The castle guards were normally stoic statues, but this one looked at her with a hint of concern. It didn't help lower her anxiety.

When they arrived at the questioning room, Victoria was on her way out and seemed more relaxed than she had earlier. Her eyes were dry and free of puffiness. *That was a good sign.* They exchanged slight smiles and a soft brush of their hands as encouragement. It was nice not to feel completely alone.

"Send her in," called a man from inside the room. It was the refined voice of a man who was well educated and confident in his position.

Kaya entered the room, and the guard closed the door behind her. Her heart began beating faster, and her palms became sweaty. She hated the feeling of confinement in such a small room and had to remind herself to breathe. She felt like she might be sick.

The office was commandeered from some castle administrator she assumed, based on the cabinet-lined walls and collection of hanging clipboards. Stacks of papers on the desk had been pushed aside to make room for a recording device with its yellow light glowing ominously. It felt odd they would meet here instead of in one of the larger meeting rooms.

The seneschal sat waiting behind the desk. He was around her father's age, maybe in his late fifties. He was clean shaven and wore horn-rimmed glasses, his short hair neatly quaffed. The gray suit he wore was well made but plain and unadorned. There was nothing particularly remarkable about him at all except for the golden chain and pendant that sat on his chest. The pendant was the symbol of the Knights of Dawn, a sunburst pierced by a sword pointing downward.

"Please sit," he said, motioning to the chair opposite his. His tone was detached and professional.

Kaya did, her face a blank mask. She placed her hands in her lap, back tall and straight. She held his gaze like a hunter might admire a dangerous beast from a distance, tentative but calm. *Yes and no*, she repeated to herself again. *Yes and no.*

"I am Pedram al Maziyar, a seneschal of the Knights of Dawn, here on behalf of the Archbishop of Mercury regarding incidents that occurred earlier today. Do you understand?"

"Yes," Kaya replied, her voice cold and distant.

"Do you need anything before we begin?" he asked.

Yes, to be far, far away from you and this stupid planet.

"No," she said, clenching the sides of her chair with sweaty palms hoping for some stability.

"I knew your mother, you know."

She unconsciously blew air from her nostrils and stared daggers at the man. Everyone had known her mother, but he had no business bringing her up now. She wasn't going to be his friend.

He seemed genuine, even friendly, but she assumed he would be. "You are a lot like her, I can tell, and I don't mean physically. Yes, of course you are her spitting image, but that's not what I mean," he said, beginning to ramble.

She had been prepared to answer his questions, but the mention of her mother was derailing her resolve. Her anger and anxiety were becoming tangled with confusion. She expected him to play his games and get her to open up to him, but the mention of her mother had caught her off guard.

"When we were both still young knights beginning our career, we served together. She was a model for all of us," he said, smiling broadly, and then laughed at some real or imagined memory. Kaya could only guess which. "Always the best and brightest among us, much to the consternation of some."

Kaya was apprehensive, more so because he seemed so genuine. She narrowed her eyes but managed to keep her breathing under control.

What game is he playing at?

His tone grew darker as he continued, "When the fighting began during the first Midnight Raids, well, she saved my life more than once. I owed her a heavy debt but never got the chance to repay it." He took his glasses off and rubbed his face before putting them back on. He looked...sad, but she knew that must be part of his strategy. Break her with kindness and sympathy instead of the whip. She averted her eyes and saw her hands shaking.

"We are all worse off without her. I know you have no reason to trust me, but I am not your enemy here," he said, and she felt vindicated in her suspicions.

You are right. I will never trust you.

"There was supposed to be another seneschal here who would not have been so helpful, but I arranged to make sure she never made it. By the time the mix-up is discovered, it will be far too late to change anything."

She looked at him blankly. Was this part of his ploy, a neatly laid trap for her to jump into? She looked at the seneschal and then down at the recorder on the table.

He followed her eyes and shrugged.

"You don't need to speak if you like, but the device isn't recording. Taking official statements in broom closets isn't standard procedure, but none of that matters right now. I can't keep the recorder off much longer, so I will need you to listen to me," he said, leaning across the desk.

She wasn't sure what was going on, but staying silent seemed like the best choice. She was sure he must be able to hear her heart pounding.

"You will answer my questions, being as remorseful as you can be, but don't oversell it. In the end, my recommendation will be to separate you and Lady Victoria from your families and have you sent to live as wards of the state in the capital on Mars. There you will both be enrolled in the Sanctum, the Episcopal University of New Olympia, where you will be instructed in theology and government. You will renounce your noble writs and devote your lives to the study of God and tradition as young leaders in the episcopacy."

Kaya blinked, trying to make sense of what he had just said. Her mind had raced through dozens of possibilities, but this one had never crossed her mind. On the surface, it seemed like a soft punishment, but a life under the thumb of the church... well, that wasn't a life for her at all. He may be sparing her from death, but this was a lifelong prison sentence. It didn't make any sense why any of this was happening. They had barely even done anything at all.

"No, I think you made some mistake. My father will sort all of this out," she managed to say, but her voice was shaky.

"No, I don't believe I have, and your father cannot stop any of this. He may be the most powerful man on Mercury, but the clerics wield the real authority, and they would prefer the nobility ceased to exist once and for all. You have unfortunately gained the attention of the archbishop of Mercury on one too many occasions, Milady," he spoke in a lecturing but compassionate tone. "The archbishop wished to make an example of you two, but I and many others have risked more than you could know in giving you back your life when only moments ago you were guaranteed a senseless death for little more than a child's indiscretion." His words bit into her in their admonishment, and she wondered if she was being ungrateful.

She struggled to find the right way to express what she felt "It's... This is as good as death. I will be their prisoner, even more than I am now."

"You think that now, but it's only because you lack the perspective to see the bigger picture." He looked at his watch. "Like I said, we don't have much time." He looked her squarely in the eyes. "Your mother was a dreamer, and like many others she died for that dream. The eternal dream. Even if it takes a year or a lifetime, you can carry her torch and make what she died for a reality."

She had so much she wanted to say, but he quickly cut her off.

"I'm sorry. That is all the time we have," he said and clicked on the recording device. His demeanor changed abruptly back to the cold stoic figure he had been when she entered the room.

"Lady Kaya al Vardan, do you understand why you are here today?" he said as the yellow light on the device turned green.

Her mind was thrown into chaos, spinning uncontrollably like a tornado as she tried to answer his questions. He had said "your mother was a dreamer." How did he know that? How did he know about her dream? He also mentioned an eternal dream, whatever that was supposed to mean. She wanted to ask him so much, but his questions came one after another, and before she could muster the strength to interrupt him, it was over.

She was pulled abruptly from the room by Theodore and let him take her by the arm. She was too dizzy from the experience, and her legs threatened to buckle as she walked. She thought she would be headed back to her room but was surprised to find he led her to the parlor.

Depositing her in one of the leather-bound chairs, he had a servant bring her something to drink. He likely thought it was the questioning that had wilted her constitution, but she couldn't tell him the truth. Better he thinks she was weak than reveal the traitorous conspiracy she found herself in now. Theodore then left to attend to some business.

"I'm alright," she said as the servant delivered the glass of water and offered to fetch anything else she might need. After some time to collect herself, the adrenaline subsided, and she was able to focus again.

Their family physician came next to examine her, and she repeatedly insisted she was well, but they refused to stop hovering over her. It was only once Victoria arrived in the room that they eventually departed, leaving them alone.

"Thank heaven you are here. I thought they would never leave," she said, springing up to greet her friend.

She intended to embrace her in a hug but hesitated as she noticed Victoria's less than amicable expression. There was no one she could relate with as closely as Victoria. She had spent years living with her family on Venus, and they had grown as close as sisters during those times.

They may have grown distant in recent years as they grew older, and their interests diverged, but in moments like this she still felt better to have her friend close by. She only hoped Victoria still felt the same way.

"Don't think we are okay after this," Victoria said, crossing her arms. "What do you have to say for yourself? You promised me it would be a quick trip outside of the gates," the anger obvious in her voice as she nearly snarled out each word and pointed her finger accusingly. "But then I almost died, not once but multiple times and found myself threatened with being *burned alive at the stake*!" It was then that she began swinging her arms at Kaya's body with uncoordinated strikes. "So, tell me, was it *worth it*?" She screamed as she struck again and again.

Kaya in her guilt took them without protest. She should never have dragged Victoria into this. Victoria's strikes began losing intensity, and as quickly as the storm came it passed. Victoria collapsed into Kaya's arms, and they became sisters again.

"I was so worried for you," Victoria whispered into her ear.

"I was worried for you too," Kaya said, returning her friend's embrace. "I'm so sorry. This is all my fault," she whispered into Victoria's ear through her own tears.

"You are right. It's completely your fault. It always is," Victoria said, and they shared a laugh. Even during her time on Venus, Kaya was typically the instigator.

"What do we do now?" Victoria asked, rubbing her eyes.

"I don't know yet, but..." She was looking around the room as she thought of what to say but decided it was better not to speak her true thoughts out loud. "We will do what they say and hope to stay in their good graces."

Victoria nodded.

"Have you seen Tiberius?" Kaya hadn't seen her brother since they talked in her father's office and was hoping Victoria had some idea.

"No, I was hoping you knew," Victoria said, worry creeping over her face. Kaya knew she had always admired Tiberius. "Should we try to find him?"

"No, we are supposed to wait here until someone tells us we are free to go."

"Since when are you following the rules?" Victoria said, a look of frustration on her face.

"Since I got threatened with execution," Kaya said dryly.

"I wish you would have found your sense of restraint earlier this morning," Victoria mumbled. "I guess we'll wait then." She took a seat near the large window and stared off into the garden. Kaya decided to do the same. What else was there to do but reflect even more on how things had gone so horribly wrong? In just one day, no, in a few moments, their entire lives had been changed forever.

Thankfully, they didn't have to wait long until Theodore and her father walked into the room, breaking her from her increasingly dark thoughts.

Victoria and Kaya both rose as they entered, apprehensive about what came next.

"The seneschal is gone and will deliver his recommendation later this evening to the archbishop," Mithridates said. Kaya would have sooner been able to read a boulder than her father's face at that moment.

"Where is Tiberius?" Kaya asked.

"He has returned to orbit with his borrowed craft to answer for his actions," he said, moving to where he stored some of his rarer bottles of whisky. He pulled out two glasses and began to pour out a healthy amount of the Martian bourbon into each one. "You should really be more worried about yourselves though," her father said, handing the second glass to Theodore.

"We want to know that he is going to be okay," Kaya asked again with Victoria's anxious expression adding more credibility to her statement.

Mithridates took a sip from his glass. "Yes, I imagine he will be fine." "He likely won't see a promotion for a long time but it's hardly the most reckless thing a young pilot has done," Theodore added, taking a sip from his own glass. "What a smooth vintage, Your Grace. Twenty-five-year Olympia Reserve?"

"One hundred and twenty-five-year Olympia Reserve, but close enough," Mithridates said with a chuckle.

"Hm, well, it tasted quite similar, Your Grace. I do find it harder to differentiate the years than I used to," Theodore said.

Kaya stared dumbly at the two of them and a glance at Victoria confirmed she was equally confused.

"Don't worry. You will understand one day when you get to be our age," Theodore said with a smile, likely noticing the stares.

"How can you both be so calm about this?" Kaya asked, becoming a bit angry at their nonchalant attitude.

"The worst part is done, Kaya, and it has gone better than what we could have reasonably expected," her father said, sipping from his glass. "Would you prefer being dragged to your own funeral pyre at this very moment?"

If Kaya and her father were not so similar, she would have been more upset at his choice of words. Victoria looked horrified. Kaya shook her head. "My future and everything I planned for is ruined, and you would rather drink and make jokes at my expense."

"Whose fault is any of that? Certainly not mine. So, think hard before you try to solicit pity. You are lucky to have gotten off as easily as you did. With the extra time you now get to continue breathing, you can figure out how to find purpose in your new path forward," he said, taking a seat in his favorite leather chair. His face remained its stoic mask. Gone was the fatigue and worry she had seen earlier.

Kaya fumed but couldn't think of what else to say.

"You are both free to move about the castle grounds, but do not leave the inner wall. You will be leaving in one week's time for Mars," her father said as Theodore sat in a chair opposite him.

"A week! But that's hardly enough time," Kaya protested.

"It is the time you have, so I suggest you make the most of it to arrange your belongings and prepare for your time away," Mithridates said.

Victoria meanwhile began looking increasingly panicked. "What am I to do? I only have what little I brought with me from home," she asked more meekly.

"I have already spoken with your mother and father. While you are in transit to Mars, a shuttle will leave Venus and connect with you in orbit to deliver whatever you might require. You will have time in the next few days to make your arrangements."

"Will we be allowed to stop on the planet, even for a little bit?" Victoria asked hopefully.

"No," Mithridates said firmly. "I have assured no clergy will be on board the vessel during your journey, but because of that we will not be able to make any additional stops. There is a strict deadline for your arrival in New Olympia."

"I see... okay," Victoria said. Kaya could clearly see she was battling with the fact she wouldn't see her home for several years at the earliest. Kaya's guilt returned.

"So, the bishops in New Olympia are going to hold our hands for four years? Watching our every move?" Kaya blurted out.

"What makes you think they haven't already been doing that?" her father asked. "You should assume they are and will always be watching. You already know all of this..."

"Yes, 'I must always be vigilant.' I know!" Kaya said, repeating the phrase she had heard her father say so many times. "Meanwhile, *you* can speak freely and go where you please!"

"You are right. I am the Duke of Mercury, and you are a child incapable of living by the rules we must all abide by." Her father took a deep breath to calm himself. "Do not forget that the rest of the solar system is not this castle. You breathe freely inside these walls because of my position. Outside of them, you are another one of God's flock to be tended to by the bishops. Do not underestimate their ability as shepherds. They very rarely allow one of their sheep to stray too far."

Kaya's temper flared, and it took every ounce of control she possessed not to spiral into an immature tirade. She knew that would only prove her father right. She took a deep breath. She would make her mother proud. She would endure whatever she had to if it meant making her dream a reality.

"One day, they will realize that they allowed a wolf into their pasture," she said through clenched teeth, her anger on the cusp of boiling over, "but when they do, it will be too late."

Her father stared back at her, his face a blank mask, but she thought maybe for the briefest moment there was a twitch of his lips. Maybe she hoped that was what she saw. She ached for his approval, even if it was just this once, but he only returned to his drink. Kaya took that as her queue to leave and made her way out the door, Victoria following closely behind.

CHAPTER

4

Kaya

September, 4101 U.E.T.—Alhazen, Mercury

THE WEEK PASSED quickly as Kaya continued to brood on how she had been wronged and what she would do next. Packing her belongings and organizing her affairs hadn't taken very long. She didn't care very much about possessions and had even fewer affairs. Although she still took the time to pack several of her books along with some trinkets like a vial of Mercurian sand and a piece of brick from the Alhazen Castle itself to remind her of home.

She also took several pictures of her family, the four of them posing for a portrait along with more candid photos from their vacations on the Venusian coast. There were also pictures of her and Victoria from when Kaya had spent extended vacations on Venus. She smiled looking at the family photos but realized with a pang of sadness there were no photos of the three of them without her mother. She had been the invisible glue that bound them together, Kaya supposed.

It had been nearly a year since her mother's passing and even longer since she had spent any real time on Venus with Victoria. She had spent even less time with Tiberius. He had been away in training or other military business for years now. Maybe relationships did change with time and distance.

She placed one final photo of her mother with the pile. It was her official portrait from when she was promoted to Grand Marshall of the Void Knights. Her hair tied back in a neat braid, her expression serious but her green eyes, Kaya's eyes, stared back with a depth of warmth and pride. She was Kaya's mother but also a warrior, fierce and powerful in more ways than one, and the photo encompassed all of that for Kaya. She hoped time and distance didn't weaken this connection too.

Lastly, she picked up the hollow book that held the Solar Empire insignia. She hadn't dared open the book again in the past week, and the armor scrap was still untouched in the bag in the corner. It felt like a lifetime since she went to the Great Desert, and as things unfolded it all felt more and more pointless.

However, something about the insignia and that marked note still called to her. She felt compelled to bring them, knowing full well that it was a very bad idea. If they searched her bag and found it, there would be no reversing the death sentence that followed. There were no second chances for convicted imperialists.

She gave her bags one last check and once she was satisfied left them for the servants to bring to the ship. She wanted to walk through the inner grounds of the castle one more time before she left. She thought she might miss the constant sunlight most of all, but part of her was excited to see a new planet. Mars was much bigger than Mercury and was sure to have lots of new and exciting sights to explore.

A servant found her as she walked and informed her that her father was waiting for her in the cloister. Kaya often spent time in the large open space of the cloister and under the gnarled branches of the Jiddi tree at its center. It was a quiet and beautiful place, and she found her way there quickly.

As Kaya walked to the center of the cloister from under the covered walkway, her father stood in front of the great Jiddi tree, looking up at its branches as if for the first time. Only family members were allowed inside the cloister, so she knew they were alone. Even guards were required to remain outside the doors. She approached quietly, careful not to disrupt his meditation.

"Father," she said, standing behind him, arms crossed behind her back. She had never felt completely at ease with her father, despite how similar they were. There was a gap between them that seemed to swallow any attempt at a deeper relationship.

Mithridates didn't look back as he spoke. "The Jiddi Tree, *pinus longaeva,* in the old tongue, is older than any of us. Older than the republic, even older than the Solar Empire that came before it. It was plucked from Earth and transported here, where it was forced to grow in foreign soil."

"But it still grew under a familiar Sun," Kaya said, having heard this story many times before.

He nodded but still didn't turn around. "It wasn't easy. Master gardeners worked diligently for centuries, with meticulous daily care to ensure this tree could grow into the magnificent form you see today. Even after thousands of years, through feast, famine, and war, it remains strong and sturdy. What started as a slice of Eden to remind distant travelers of the homes they left behind on Earth became a symbol of resolve and determination to see the future realized." He turned to face her, she stood almost to his height but still had to look up slightly to match his gaze. She said nothing.

"Hundreds of these cloisters exist, and hundreds of trees representing a piece of Eden remain, despite how many were destroyed through centuries of war." He took her hand and walked her over to touch the trunk of the tree, which was roughly five meters wide and stretched over twenty meters in height.

"But this tree *is* a part of Eden, of old Earth. It isn't a clone or offspring; it is the original. Through this tree, House Vardan is connected to the very beginning, to the origins of humanity," he said, becoming more enthusiastic than Kaya had ever heard him. The bark was cool and rough under her skin as she flushed with the energy of his words.

"As this tree has prevailed, so will House Vardan as its keeper, until one day the garden can be rebuilt. Even if you are far away from your home, Kaya, you will still have the familiar Sun, and you have been prepared much like this tree to survive the journey and thrive in your new home. Until we can be reunited."

Kaya couldn't help but tear up.

"I don't want to go," she said, tears running down her cheeks.

"I don't want you to go, but like this tree you have a purpose."

"What purpose? I don't want to serve the Republic. I don't want to be a stupid bishop..." she said, her anger rising. She couldn't see the big picture the seneschal had eluded to, only the cold reality of her new situation.

He looked down at her, his face softening. "Do you think this tree wanted to be moved from its quiet home on a mountain summit? From its majestic perch to this small garden? I don't think it did." He smiled a small, fragile smile. "But here it is, through the wars and the ages, waiting for the day it can return and fulfill its dream, to see the garden again."

"Restoring the garden is our dream, not the tree's," she said.

His smile grew larger. "I am glad you understand. Now you can remember that lesson when times grow dark, and you most feel like quitting. House Vardan perseveres. House Vardan remains steady. We will remain as keepers of the garden until it can be restored."

Kaya wiped her cheeks and swallowed, "I will try."

"I know," he said, and his face grew more serious again. "Follow their rules. Learn their ways. Only once you know all of that can you work to change anything."

Kaya didn't like what he said, but she didn't need to like it. She just had to survive, to live to see her mother's dream a reality. Her sadness transformed slowly into resolve.

"I didn't mean for any of this to happen." Her tears abated as she stepped back from the tree and sat down on a rock at its base. Her father took a seat on a stone beside her.

"You have always followed your own path, Kaya. I knew a day like this would come eventually." He smiled broader. "Your mother would have been proud of you. Not for so carelessly breaking the rules and going against our wishes," he corrected sternly, "but proud of you for your bravery to do these things at all. You are more and more like her each day." He looked almost through Kaya. She could tell he had gone somewhere else.

"Will you be coming with us to Mars?" she asked, which seemed to snap her father out of his reverie.

"No, with unrest on the rise and new prophets cropping up left and right, I must remain on Mercury," he said, looking back to her. "The situation isn't as dire here, but on Mars it is much worse. It is important you stay in the capital high district."

"I have seen how they handle prophets in the capital," Kaya said.

Her father nodded with a sympathetic expression. "Certain groups are given too much leeway in the capital," he said in response.

She wasn't in a mood to argue. She knew who was responsible and knew he wouldn't feel as strongly as she did about it. Although she knew her father kept the Frumentarii on the shortest leash possible while operating on Mercury, it was a tenuous thing. Without him here to maintain that leash, things might not be any better than they were on Mars.

"Theodore will be going with you and will remain on Mars to handle affairs on my behalf. You can trust him with anything," he said, and she nodded. The thought of a familiar face nearby put her at ease. "Please, just promise me you will stay in the high districts."

"I thought I was going to be under constant surveillance anyway. You won't have anything to worry about," she said, annoyance creeping into her voice.

"There are places even shadows won't go," he said before leaning in closer. "Please, promise me."

She hesitated, her face twisting in thought. It wasn't that she had any plans to leave. She had never been to Mars and had no thought as to where she would even go given the chance, but she struggled to answer.

It wouldn't cost her anything to promise, but she also felt like it was one more door to her prison cell. "I won't lie to you, but I also can't promise you I won't do anything. You will have to trust that I know what I'm doing," she said, matching his gaze.

Her father stared back at her for what felt like forever, still and unmoving. "Trust is in short supply at the moment. What would stop you from making the same mistakes again?"

"I am not the same girl I was a week ago," she said.

"In a week's time, you have learned the difference between good and bad decisions?" he asked.

"No, I already knew that. What I learned were the real costs, and next time I make a bad decision it will be for a much better reason," she said with a shrug.

Her father laughed, his stoic mask broken for a moment by her words, evidently liking the answer. "Now you really do sound like your mother, which reminds me of why I called you here in the first place," he said as he reached down and picked up a box that had been obscured by the rocks. "This is for you." He handed it to Kaya.

Kaya took the box as she wondered what it could be. Gifts were not a common occurrence from her father. As she took the box, she noticed it was light and small, about the size of a shoebox.

"What is it?"

"Open it."

She shook her head but placed the box on her lap as she unwrapped it and pulled off the top. When she did, her breath caught in her throat, and she looked down at the hilt of a plasma blade. Her mother's plasma blade, to be more precise.

The handle was shaped like the hilt of an ancient shamshir, carved with elegant floral patterns in silver and gold. Small gemstones spread through the hilt gave it a particularly pronounced sparkle in the sunlight. She didn't dare touch it.

She had been trained to use a plasma blade from a young age like any other noble and was quite proficient, but she still feared touching it. The blades were so rare and expensive that very few people even among the nobility owned one, let alone wore them regularly. This also meant they were not handed to children. Even if she was technically an adult, this wasn't something someone her age would have unless they were actively in the military at the very least.

"It's not a snake," he said, motioning to the hilt.

Kaya picked it up slowly, surprised by how light it was. The hilt seemed to mold to her hand, almost like it had been made specially for her. Taking a step back from the tree, she kindled the blade, light erupting flawlessly in the form of a curved blade. She looked at it in awe as she took a few test swings before feeling self-conscious again and turning it off.

"Surely you don't mean to give me this. Wouldn't it go to Tiberius any-way? He's the eldest after all," she said.

Her father smiled warmly, "I would have liked to wait longer, but... Well, there was no reason to wait anymore. Besides, you should know that I don't make mistakes. This one's for you. Your mother would have wanted you to have it. Tiberius already received one of the other family blades." The Vardan's were one of a small number of families that by tradition and wealth owned more than one.

"Am I allowed to have this?" she asked, turning the hilt over in her hands.

"It's not typical for students to have them, but it isn't against the rules. I would suggest not stabbing your classmates with it," he said.

"You know how I feel about promises," Kaya said, and they shared another laugh.

"I also have one more thing," he said, pulling a smaller box from his coat pocket and handing it to Kaya.

Unsure what else her father could possibly give her, she didn't waste any time in opening the second box. Inside she found a pendant made of a shiny, silvery metal that surrounded a small glass globe. The metal looked like platinum but somehow different in how it reflected the light that touched it, and the glass was perfectly crystal clear, something that wasn't very common. Suspended in the center of the coin-sized globe was a tiny and fragile seedling. She pulled it out of the box gently.

"You don't need to worry. It is suspended safely in the pendant," her father said. "Here, let me help you." He reached over to help place it around her neck.

"It's a seedling from the Jiddi tree. This way you will always have a reminder of home," he said as he finished attaching the clasp. Her heart fluttered in a mix of joy and sadness. She had longed for a moment like this with her father, and only now when she was destined to leave had she gotten it.

"It's beautiful, but...how was this made? I have never seen anything like it," Kaya replied, looking down at the pendant in her palm.

"An old antique," he said with a smile. The Jiddi tree did not produce many seeds in its older age, and even fewer would germinate successfully, making this gift exceptionally rare.

"Thank you," was all she could think to say as she began to cry again, unable to hold back that flood of emotions.

"This isn't goodbye," he comforted.

"I know. I hope I can come back soon." His gifts and words did more to fill the chasm between them in these few moments than ever before.

"Focus on getting through your studies, and the rest will follow," he said.

She nodded as she stood up. "I should go find Victoria and see if I can help with anything."

Mithridates nodded his acknowledgement, and she turned to walk away.

Kaya

September, 4101 U.E.T.—Earth Orbit

THE DEPARTURE FROM Mercury had gone off without any major issues. Kaya and Victoria boarded the vessel solemnly as an honor guard of House Vardan Marines and local dignitaries stood by. Her father had watched the entire affair from a distance with a detached expression. Right up until the last moment before she stepped onto the gangway, her heart had been near to bursting from the tension, but once she stepped onto the spacecraft, a frigate named Rubah, it somehow all washed away.

Her stress and anxiety gave way to a cool numbness. It was like the time she had climbed a sea cliff on Venus to prove to Victoria's cousins she could. She had been terrified, but once she had reached a point where she could no longer climb down, she knew the only path was up and was able to relax.

The fact her mother had died taking her own trip to Mars also weighed heavily on her mind, but a small part of her took comfort in this knowledge. If she died in the same way, would it mean she would see her mother again sooner? The clergy would say yes, and on this topic a part of her hoped they were right.

Victoria, unfortunately, took a bit longer to come around. Although she originally approached the gangway with a sense of dignity and purpose, she ended up entering the ship on the broad shoulder of a marine who had been ordered to carry her aboard.

For nearly a week after, she refused to do anything besides lie in bed, barely touching her meals. Kaya had tried to stay by her side, but it only seemed to make things worse, so she decided to give Victoria the space she wanted.

It took the arrival of the Venusian freighter to bring her back to the present. The ship arrived to deliver Victoria's belongings, and much to her surprise her mother had come to see her off. Kaya had only met with the Marchioness Pendlebrook long enough to offer a quick greeting. No one wanted to deny Victoria what little time she had in private with her family.

The rendezvous lasted less than four hours, but Victoria came out of it like a new person. Which was good considering they were only two weeks into a roughly month-long journey to Mars.

She was happy to have Theodore onboard, and his presence filled her with a sense of comfort she thought she wouldn't have had otherwise. She thought of him as her uncle, even if they weren't blood relations.

Based on tradition, each duke or duchess would appoint a lord steward to act as their voice when traveling off planet to conduct business. They would have limited authority to enter into agreements and speak on behalf of their liege. It wasn't unusual for Theodore to be traveling to Mars with them, but she also suspected he might be there to keep an eye on her.

The ship itself was a private vessel owned by her family, one of the final vestiges of the days when the nobility commanded vast fleets of starships. A ship that was small enough to nimbly travel between planets at roughly 150 meters in length and 75 meters in height and width but still large enough to accommodate a few hundred crew and passengers. The vessel also supported several Falcons for scouting patrols and deterring pirates. Traveling between planets wasn't always the safest business, so being prepared for any possibility was important.

The state room she shared with Victoria was reasonably spacious with enough room for two good-sized beds, along with built-in dressers and a writing desk for each of them. The room was worn by age but in good repair and not without its luxuries. The bed linens were made of exceptional cloth, and the carpet that covered the floor was plush. It was more like a guest room in a luxurious hotel than a spartan military vessel or simple transport ship. Theodore, as the ranking official aboard, was given the primary cabin reserved for the lord of the vessel. Meanwhile, the captain had a separate cabin.

The captain of the Rubah was an older woman, Samira al Masoumi, who had been in her father's service as long as she could remember.

Kaya and Victoria were relaxing in their quarters reading quietly when the intercom system clicked on, emitting a high-pitched whistle.

Announcements were a common occurrence throughout the day, but the addition of the loud whistle was different.

"Attention on deck. Attention on deck," came the call through the intercom system, clear and precise from Captain Masoumi.

"General quarters, all hands, man your stations. Entering Earth orbit."

"Well, that's a new one," Kaya said, looking up from her book.

"Did she say Earth orbit? Is that safe?" Victoria asked, concerned.

"Why wouldn't it be? People still live on Luna, you know. Earth has been dead for hundreds of years," Kaya said, springing up from her bed. "Let's go and see if we can get a look at it."

Kaya had traveled between Mercury and Venus plenty of times, so space travel itself wasn't impressive to her, but she had never been to Luna or glimpsed the broken Earth.

Victoria didn't move. "No, I think I will stay here."

"Come on."

"Why are you so excited? Shouldn't we stay out of the way in our room for once?" Victoria asked.

"I'm not missing a chance to see this, and you shouldn't either. It's not like you have been to Luna either or seen Earth," Kaya said, grabbing her friend's arm to lead her from the room.

Victoria put down her book with a sigh but didn't resist, "I wish for once you would ask me what I would like to do first."

"I'm sorry. I didn't think there would be anything more exciting on this trip than seeing Earth with our own eyes. Eden itself," Kaya said, pulling her out into the busy corridor where men and women walked purposefully to their required stations. None of them paid any mind as Kaya ran down the hall practically dragging Victoria by the hand.

"I have seen the pictures, and that's enough for me. I don't want to be anywhere near here. Not to mention my mother says Luna is full of pirates and other scoundrels," Victoria said, pulling her arm away from Kaya's grasp but still reluctantly following along.

"The Iron-Cage hasn't been activated for hundreds of years, and it's pointed at the surface of the Earth, not toward space," Kaya said.

"You remember what happened last time you told me not to worry," Victoria retorted. "The captain obviously worried enough to notify all the sailors."

She didn't have a good response and instead said nothing as they reached the main communal room known as the observatory.

The observatory was a large rectangular room flanked on the long sides with large, vaulted windows that curved up to the top of the craft, providing nearly full panoramic views of their surroundings. There were steel blast doors that could be deployed to guard the glass against debris or attack, but typically they were left open. The large windows had become cloudy with the passing centuries but were structurally sound.

In the room, Theodore sat at the main table near the window, looking out into space. The rest of the room was empty, with momentarily discarded drinks, books, and plates of the sailors forced to end their breaks early by the alarm. Theodore looked contemplative as they approached the table.

"See, if Theodore is here, it must be safe," Kaya said in a low voice to Victoria as they approached the table.

"Lady Kaya, Lady Victoria," he said in greeting as the pair came into the room. "Come to join me to see the view? Earth is quite a sight to behold with your own eyes." Unlike her father, he was much more personable when he wasn't serving an official function.

The two of them sat down at the crescent-shaped table, Victoria closer to Theodore and Kaya taking the seat across from the man. Their eyes were glued to the large starboard windows.

Through the window, the massive shapes of Earth and Luna came into view, their forms unmistakable as the Sun's rays cascaded over their spherical forms. The main difference was that Earth wasn't the bright blue sphere of her imagination. It was a dead sphere covered in gray clouds and coiled lightning that rippled across its surface in huge, dramatic arcs.

By contrast Luna was lit with an overabundance of light, both from the Sun and the artificial light of its cities. The lights of ships coming and going from the moon while the much larger Earth remained quiet only added to the odd image. Kaya had of course seen images of the planet plenty of times, but something about seeing it now with her own eyes made it feel so much more wrong.

"Is it safe to be this close to Earth and Luna?" Victoria asked, wringing her hand nervously.

Theodore shrugged, still smiling. "As safe as anywhere, I suppose, but if you are concerned we will be vaporized by ancient weapons, then we are quite safe."

Kaya gave her friend an "I told you so" look. "I wanted to see the Iron-Cage, but I also wanted to see if it really wasn't blue anymore. The old pictures of Earth are so beautiful," she said.

The planet had been thoroughly destroyed hundreds of years prior, but the classic image of Earth as the blue planet and Garden of Eden persisted. Its demise likewise stood as a cautionary tale, but what it cautioned exactly varied based on whom you asked.

Victoria still seemed nervous. "What about the pirates?"

"Pirates don't operate this close to the spheres. The Lunese defense fleet patrols this area," he said.

Victoria still didn't look very convinced as she lowered her voice and leaned toward Theodore. "My mother says they aren't much better than pirates."

Theodore chuckled. "Mostly old rumors and tall tales. There was a time Luna was the home of pirates and adventurers, true. That's why the capital Port Royal exists," he said, moving his hands about like a lecturer might, "but that was during the Time of Chaos, and eventually the Lunese nobility was forced to capitulate to the Republic, and they have been loyal citizens ever since."

Victoria seemed to accept that answer and sat back in her chair, as Kaya leaned forward to get a better look out of the window. She watched as the angry lightning rolled across the surface of the Earth, Eden turned to dust and ash, and for what?

Her eyes strained as she tried to make out the satellites that made up the Iron-Cage. It wasn't a literal cage, but instead a collection of weapons satellites working in unison to protect the planet from existential threats.

"There they are!" she exclaimed, as she noticed them dancing around the planet like ballerinas in an opera. "The Iron-Cage."

Theodore nodded as he looked out the window. "Yes, they are much smaller than people expect, I think," he said.

"Those little satellites turned the beautiful blue planet to ash and dust?" she said, not quite believing something like that could be possible.

Theodore's face took on a heavy and distant expression as he looked at the ruined planet, made as lifeless as the gas giants. "Yes, they may be small, but there are hundreds of them. Like a swarm of hornets, they unleashed their poisonous stingers into the Earth and poisoned it for generations to come."

"Why would people be so stupid to build weapons that could destroy themselves? I'm glad we don't have to worry about them doing the same to Venus or anywhere else," Victoria said, and Kaya agreed with her. Who would build such awful weapons and then point them at themselves. What war was worth winning that you would destroy yourself in the process?

"The weapons were meant to keep Earth safe from asteroids and anything worse that lurked in the far reaches of space. They were never meant to be pointed within," Theodore said, his tone sounded regretful.

"As we know from the Republic sources, the hearts of man were corrupted. Their precious technology rebelled against their evil hearts and brought the ruin they so desired for the universe upon themselves. The bishops say," he began, returning to lecturer mode.

"That the Solar Empire angered God by destroying the garden and opening Pandora's box. They prayed to their shrines of technology, manipulating God's perfect creation beyond recognition, and elevating themselves to the level of God's. They used their newfound power to choose who among God's creations was worthy of the gift of eternal life and in the process abandoned their immortal souls and spit in the face of their creator." He turned to them and shrugged apologetically. "Well, I am sure you have both heard this plenty of times."

Kaya had heard it many times, but it never quite sat well with her. She of course understood there was something beyond herself that existed. Some mystical force, the unseen hand that shaped the universe, but she also knew there was pain and suffering.

Much of that pain and suffering could be solved with technology. Solved with the knowledge the new prophets preach. If only humans were allowed to create, to bring to life the products of their dreams. But the bishops will point to Earth and say, "See what evil technology has created in the world," and she would have trouble proving them wrong.

"Could there still be any ageless left on Earth?" Kaya asked, wondering how it was possible that so many people could be wiped out so completely.

Theodore laughed. "You know the ageless are a myth. No, nothing is alive on the surface. Anything that wasn't turned to glass in the blasts wilted and died under the frigid cold of the nuclear winter that followed."

Kaya wasn't sure why she felt disappointed when she knew the answer before she even asked. There was something very sad about it all. She clutched at her seedling pendant absently, a new habit she had developed since leaving Mercury. The idea of rebuilding the garden seemed very silly after seeing the scale of destruction.

"Why didn't they ever try to rebuild it?" she asked.

Theodore took a moment before answering, "By the time the war ended, the people and machines capable of fixing it were dead or destroyed. Then the Republic kept the Iron-Cage in place, forever destined to guard the tomb of Adam and Eve."

"Surely the satellites must be broken by now?" Kaya said, a bit surprised.

He shrugged. "Surely some are, but hundreds of satellites remain perfectly functional. Even if their nuclear payloads are depleted, they still have their ion guns. Destroying them would be no easy proposition, without factoring in the costs. Those weapons, as old as they are, are still deadlier than anything the Navy has in its arsenal."

"So no one is willing to take the risk for a dead planet," Kaya surmised.

Theodore nodded. "Precisely. Occasionally some enterprising adventurer will descend into the swirling storms of Earth, but generally they never return. It's something of a game they play, the young, rich, and bold of Luna," he offered generously. "They take their specially made gliders or torpedo ships and see how far they can descend into the storms before they lose their nerve and turn back or die in the attempt," he said, his expression turning more dower.

She knew no one ever traveled to Earth regularly, but she had read the stories of people who claimed to have gone. Usually those adventurers were labeled frauds, or like Theodore said, never heard from again. However, she didn't know anything about this game the Lunese played.

"That sounds like a terribly stupid game," Victoria interjected.

Kaya thought she might be willing to give it a try given the opportunity. "They should dismantle the cage and rebuild, like our ancestors did before us on other worlds. Like my ancestors did on Mercury."

Theodore smiled at that. "Maybe one day you can petition for that very thing when you sit on the Council of Bishops. Maybe you will even ascend as high as the position of Vox one day."

Kaya grimaced. She knew he was only trying to be reassuring, but the thought made her ill. She wanted nothing to do with any council, not the Assembly of Lords and certainly not the Council of Bishops.

"It is hard to make changes from the shadows," he said, seeing her discomfort. "You might not see the truth of it now, but in some ways this is an opportunity very few get and even fewer make good use of."

Kaya looked over at Victoria and could see her leaning into Theodore's every word. She had no reason to think they would ever let her rise to the rank of Vox. She had spent the last week stewing on the topic, and it all felt clear to her now.

On the surface, this punishment seemed light. She would still live her life, free to rise within the episcopal polity. It seemed almost generous. In truth it was an opportunity to lock away the child of a popular noble, putting them in a cage where they could only rise as far as the Council of Bishops allowed. Meanwhile, the Republic maintained the moral high ground, having spared the life of a social apostate and showing its infinite mercy. It was all a cruel joke.

At best, she would gain a bishopric in some faraway corner of the solar system, like Pluto or, even worse, one of its moons. Her dread rose as she thought about never seeing the Sun again, and her face contorted in a worried frown.

Theodore interrupted her downward spiral. "Anyway, there's nothing to be done about it now. We all must do things we would prefer not to do in the execution of our duties." He pulled a pack of playing cards from his jacket pocket.

Kaya raised an eyebrow. "Do you have plans to spend time as a prisoner also?"

"Kaya!" Victoria yelled, smacking her friend's arm.

Theodore looked at Kaya as he began shuffling the deck of cards, returning her sarcastic expression with his own. "You aren't the only one who will be stuck on Mars for the foreseeable future. I would also remind the lady that I may serve your father, but you are not him, and I am still a baron in my own right. Others in the capital won't be as understanding as myself."

"Of course, Milord," Kaya said genuinely, feeling a little stupid. She hadn't considered that Theodore may not have chosen to be there as much as her and Victoria had. Kaya had to remind herself they were no longer on Mercury, and she held no titles of her own. Her father's name would only carry so much weight.

"Why did my father send you? To look after us?" she asked as she watched him shuffle. His hands moved gracefully in practiced motions.

"With the dukes and duchesses restricted from traveling off their respective realms, they have been ordered to send a representative to fill their seat in the Assembly of Lords," he said as he finished shuffling, placing the deck face down in the center of the table. "So here I am. Cribbage?" he asked, beginning to deal out the cards before they even answered.

Earth and Luna drifted further and further away. The lights of ships and cities faded away as they crawled ever forward toward Mars.

"All hands, stand down from general quarters," came the call from the captain.

"See, no pirates at all," Theodore said, and they settled into their card game.

CHAPTER

6

Kaya

October, 4101 U.E.T.—New Olympia, Mars

THE REMAINING WEEKS of their journey passed without incident. The biggest challenge was the crippling boredom as they passed through empty space for days on end. The brilliant views of distant stars only offered some comfort. This had been by far the longest journey her or Victoria had ever taken, and they both suffered bouts of homesickness interspersed with the longing for solid ground.

Kaya couldn't imagine how pioneers lived in these conditions for years on end, even their entire lives. The bland meals and the constant hum of machinery would be enough to drive anyone crazy, but the sailors shockingly seemed immune to it.

"All hands, general quarters, prepare for atmospheric entry," Captain Masoumi said across the comms system. "All passengers are advised to take their assigned flight seats."

The entry into the atmosphere was bumpy but uneventful. Kaya watched as the landscape came into focus from the small window beside her seat. She was excited to be on solid ground again soon. Kaya had learned she wasn't built for extended space travel.

Mars was still known as the red planet even though it had been fully terraformed for over a thousand years. From her window, she could see a mix of large mountainous outcrops, green river valleys, and large expansive grassy plains stretching to the horizon. Lush green valleys were as common as red sandy hills. Mars was large, and unlike Mercury most of the planet was hospitable to life, with larger oceans, more arable farmland, and only small, isolated deserts.

The massive Olympus Mons rose from the surface of the planet as if it was going to swallow their ship whole. The immensity of it was only truly appreciated from this altitude. On the coast of the massive Amazonian Sea, on the lower flanks of Olympus Mons, sat New Olympia, the capital of the Republic.

The city had a sub-tropical climate that lent itself to human habitation, with tall leafy plants and trees becoming increasingly visible as they descended. Mars had been the third heavenly body colonized by man after Luna, but it was the obvious home of the new Garden of Eden after the first had been destroyed. Whether that was because Mars was more resource rich, or Luna was just too full of pirates was debatable.

The Rubah banked toward a large spaceport. Kaya assumed the job of air traffic controllers must be easy since she saw very few spacecrafts coming and going from the city. As they got closer to the surface, more buildings came into view, ancient ones of metal, glass, and red sandstone extended out from a central square in the center, although the main "square" of New Olympia, Trinity Square, was in the shape of a triangle.

Surrounding this central point were the three main universities that made up the pinnacle of the Republic's education system. Her destination, The Sanctum sat on the east corner, with Olympus Mons rising ever upward behind it. The Republic Military Academy sat on the north corner and the Artificer's College of Operation and Maintenance on the west. Each university sprawled out like miniature cities behind their walls and energy domes.

Surrounding Trinity Square were various governmental buildings, including the meeting halls for the Council of Bishops and the Assembly of Lords. Most dramatic of all though was Vox's palace complex, the Amaranthine Palace, which sat high above everything else on the flanks of Olympus Mons. From his opulent palace, the Vox reigned over billions of citizens with unlimited authority.

The palace and its surrounding buildings were among the most opulent buildings she had ever seen. The clergy explained the palace and all the capitals buildings were only so grand because of the excess of the Empire that built them. So, the clergy claim practicality and enjoy their comforts while the masses suffer.

Kaya thought of her own life in the Alhazen castle, and her stomach churned at the similarity. She convinced herself there was a difference without offering any real evidence.

The ship landed in a large military spaceport within the capital district, not far from Trinity Square. There were several other ships in the space-port, including a squadron of Falcons, but none of the ships were as large as the Rubah.

Armed guards patrolled the area, and Kaya could see lookout towers and cameras liberally spread throughout the spaceport. There seemed to be at least five times as many cameras and guards as she was used to seeing on Mercury. It reminded her more of the time she had visited a military base with her father than any city she was used to.

Their presence must have been announced because waiting for them when they disembarked was a party of white-robed figures wearing red sashes. At the center of this group was one particularly ponderous-looking man who wore the same white robes but instead of a sash wore a chasuble emblazoned with the nine-pointed star and cross of the Republic.

Theodore, along with Captain Masoumi, led their small procession to meet them. Kaya feared that this man would be the one to hold the key to her jail cell and wondered if she had the strength to play along. Then she reminded herself that she couldn't realize her mother's dream if she died on a pyre. She looked over to Victoria and saw her friend looking at her nervously. Kaya reached out and took her friend's hand in what little com-fort she could offer.

"Abbot Sharpil," Theodore said as they approached, stopping to leave a gap of several feet between their party and the white robes. He offered them only a small nod and the rest of them followed his lead.

The ponderous man, who must have been Abbot Sharpil, mirrored the gesture, revealing the balding pate of his head. On closer inspection, Kaya could also see the man wore powders on his face that only accentuated his wrinkles and pockmarks.

"Lord Parker, welcome to New Olympia. Lady Vardan, Lady Pendlebrook," Abbot Sharpil said in a serpentine voice. "I am Abbot Sharpil, provost of the Episcopal University. I hope your journey was pleasant. I know you have come a long way." Each word slithered out of his mouth with a smile that never touched his eyes. It made Kaya's skin crawl.

Theodore looked the man up and down, his tall, muscular frame stand-ing nearly an entire foot above the pudgy man, though the abbot was twice as wide. The abbot pushed back his shoulders and raised his chin in what might have been a show of strength, but Kaya had to stifle a laugh.

"Thank you for your concern, Abbot. It has been a long journey, but we will adjust in time to the atmosphere," Theodore said.

"Yes, of course, Milord. You and the captain are free to proceed at your leisure. However, I was sent here on behalf of the Manus herself to see that Lady Vardan and Lady Pendlebrook were properly acquainted with their new surroundings. I must insist they come with me without delay," the abbot said, his jowls shaking as he spoke.

He seemed almost out of breath and sweat dripped from his brow. Kaya couldn't tell if he was nervous or unaccustomed to being outside the comforts of his own estate. Either way, it was clear he lacked any natural talent for diplomacy.

"An honor that the Manus has taken an interest in our arrival," Theodore replied. Unlike the abbot, his tone was practiced and conversational. Although Kaya was apprehensive that the second most powerful person in the solar system had taken a personal interest in their arrival.

"Yes, Milord, sometimes God grants us these favors," the abbot said, raising his hands and head to the sky while making the sign of the star and cross over his chest. The white-robed acolytes meanwhile moved toward Kaya and Victoria to usher them to the waiting transport vehicle. They only stopped when Theodore stepped between them.

"Allow us time to disembark and gather ourselves. I will send the ladies to you shortly," Theodore said, his face a rigid mask. Gone was the friendly man who spent hours on end playing cribbage and telling stories. This was a side of him she hadn't seen before.

The abbot seemed to hesitate before he waved off the acolytes and took a step back from the party.

"Of course, Milord. We shall wait over here," the abbot said with only the tiniest nod and turned to walk away. The acolytes dutifully followed.

"Should we be worried?" Kaya asked once the welcome party was out of ear shot.

To her surprise, Theodore said, "Yes. Now is the time to be worried. There will be no second chances. You will have to go with them now, but remember everything you have been told, both of you."

"Can't we stay with you and the captain?" Victoria asked. During the voyage she had become close with Captain Masoumi and looked from her to Theodore for some kind of lifeline.

"I will be staying here with the ship, by order of His Grace. I am not to depart Martian orbit without both of you onboard," Captain Masoumi offered, her kind hazel eyes shining brightly against her ebony skin.

Kaya had always known the captain to be a strong and capable commander, and she certainly looked the part now, but what if the Manus or Vox demanded she do otherwise? To disobey would be guaranteed death, so she knew it was a kind but empty gesture. She didn't expect any of them would willingly sacrifice their lives for hers.

"No," Theodore said, shaking his head, "staying with me or the ship is not an option. You are both wards of the Sanctum now and subject to their rules, but I will remain in the capital for the foreseeable future. If you need me, you both know how to contact me, but remember my power here is limited," Theodore stressed.

Victoria looked frightened, but Kaya was determined to be strong for them both. "We won't be needing your assistance, but we appreciate you both getting us this far. We must do our part now," she said, her voice only wavering slightly. She desperately fought to maintain her composure as her chin began to quiver.

Theodore put a hand on her shoulder. "I have no doubt you will both be fine. I will check in when I can. Take care of yourselves." And with those simple words, Kaya's mask broke, and she was reduced to quiet tears alongside Victoria.

It took all the willpower she could muster to collect her things and reassemble the pieces of her shattered mask. Victoria meanwhile didn't attempt to hide her feelings. Her grief poured out like a faucet for everyone to see. She even began looking to the abbot for comfort. From their conversations aboard the Rubah, Kaya had no doubt Victoria was convinced these people had their best interests in mind.

Kaya thought she had shed her last tears a month ago on Mercury. How naive she was turning out to be. For a moment, she had thought herself a warrior, but in mere moments she was reduced to the weak child she was. She hated herself as she stepped into the waiting transport, rubbing at her puffy eyes as the abbot and his goons leered. She hated even more giving them this victory over her.

"Here you go, child," the abbot said, holding out a handkerchief to Kaya. She stared at him defiantly, with no intention of taking anything offered by this man. The abbot retracted the handkerchief as if he had never offered it and straightened the few strands of hair that covered his mostly balding pate.

"Soon we will arrive at the university, and you will be introduced to your new homes for the next four years. You may not be happy about it now, I know," he said, adjusting his prodigious girth in the seat that struggled to contain it. "I have seen many like you come through like bleating lambs, fresh from their mother's womb, wishing they could return to where it was safe and warm. Soon you will realize that the only way forward is to accept your new condition. Graze on the gifts of God and take solace in his protection."

The abbot finished his lecture by making the sign of the star and cross over his chest while Kaya continued to glare at him. Victoria tried to put a comforting hand on Kaya's arm, but it did little to ease her anger. She wasn't privately religious, but even she felt offended that such a disgusting man would claim a close connection with the divine.

"Thank you, Abbot, this is all so new and sudden," Victoria said, and Kaya dropped her stare. She felt betrayed by Victoria's weakness.

The abbot seemed pleased with this response and said nothing else as they continued the journey. From the air, the spaceport had seemed very close to Trinity Square, but the Episcopal University could only be accessed by road through a twisting labyrinth of ancient corridors.

The clergy despised the use of technology beyond what was necessary, so they relied on the most basic tools that would get the job done. Typically, this meant ground vehicles were favored to aircraft.

This fact left her trapped with these snakes that much longer, but she needed to maintain her composure. Once she was free of this man, she could figure out what to do next.

The streets were tight and lined with buildings clad in primarily red Martian sandstone. Her first thought was that the capital resembled the Garden District in Alhazen on Mercury with its collection of historic shops, homes, and offices.

Traffic became increasingly heavy as they moved toward the center of the city and Trinity Square beyond. The abbot twitched anxiously, looking over his shoulder at the driver and out the windows as he huffed.

"Can't you go around this rabble?" the abbot said to the driver.

"Apologies, Abbot Sharpil, but there is no way around. There must be something blocking the road ahead," the driver responded in a subservient tone.

"Then go another way!" the abbot shouted.

Kaya wondered why they didn't know what was up ahead. Her only guess was that they had no means of communication, which meant the prohibition on technology must run even deeper than she realized.

The driver didn't hesitate when given the command and turned down the nearest street. Redirecting them away from the capital's center and toward the outer districts. The abbot seemed only slightly placated by the maneuver, as he still huffed audibly at the imposition.

Kaya remained quiet and stared out the window at the passing buildings and people. They were still in what must have been a high or at least a mid-district of the city. The people looked clean, mostly free of illness, and well fed. Their hair and skin seemed free of the worst ravages of solar radiation that plagued the poorer districts.

It was as they moved deeper into the city that Kaya noticed an increase in street urchins and nectar addicts stumbling through the streets in a drug-induced daze. There were many more, even here, than she would have expected to find in a similar district on Mercury. The abbot continued to squirm like the worm that he was, and she felt only a little guilty for taking solace in his discomfort.

There weren't many other vehicles on the road, but their speed slowed. Only a little bit at first until suddenly the vehicle lurched to a complete stop.

"What is the meaning of this? Keep driving!" the abbot shouted, his jowls shaking furiously.

"The road is blocked, Abbot Sharpil," the driver replied, and Kaya tried to crane her neck but couldn't see anything from her seat.

"So go around it. We have already delayed too long," the abbot said, dabbing at the sweat that dripped from his brow with the handkerchief he had offered Kaya moments earlier.

"It's... There are people, Abbot Sharpil," the driver said, hesitating slightly.

The abbot huffed louder, "I will see to this and then see to all of you when we return."

The acolytes looked more nervous as the abbot attempted to open and exit the door. The vehicle rocked from side to side, and he was struggling so mightily that Kaya got out to make room for him to pass. However, when she stepped out of the vehicle, it was into a world of chaos.

The vehicle must have been dampening much of the noise, because as she exited the vehicle the sound of voices was nearly deafening as a large crowd of people raised their fists into the air and shouted. She could see well-dressed businessmen standing beside mechanics and everything in between which was a surprising sight in a place like this.

Kaya couldn't really make out what they were shouting, but she followed their eyes to where a figure stood on a vehicle, addressing the crowd. The figure wore a large scarf that covered their head and face. She couldn't tell if it was a man or woman.

"Clear this road at once, in the name of his Holiness, Vox Ludwig, I command you," the abbot shouted, but his words had no effect on the crowd. They didn't so much as look his way. Kaya stared in stunned silence at the scene unfolding.

"God's bones! You and you, go and disperse this rabble from our path," the abbot said, commanding his acolytes. Both looked at the abbot then at each other before looking back at the crowd. It looked like they were deciding who they were more afraid of before taking tentative steps toward the crowd. As they made their approach, the masked figure managed to quiet the crowd.

"I will leave you all with one final wish. Look to each other and then look to the stars and tell me that you do not all yearn for more than this life. Why toil for an unknown reward in death when you can toil for rewards in life? Continue to dream for better and then strive to make that dream reality. The eternal dream is real, and it lives in each of you," the figure said. The accent was odd, and the voice was devoid of inflection. Kaya still wasn't sure if it was a man or woman.

What she was sure of was that they looked right at her when they spoke those last words. That might have been strange enough, but they also said eternal dream. It was the same phrase the seneschal had used. That seemed like an exceptionally odd coincidence.

Her thoughts were cut short as the acolytes reached the crowd. Instead of parting for their commands, the crowd turned to them with clenched fists.

"Kaya, get in, now!" came Victoria's voice as she felt a pair of hands pulling her back toward the open door. She only vaguely registered them as she saw the first acolyte struck with a fist as the second was hit over the head with what looked like a brick. Their blood splattered as the rabid crowd descended on the two unfortunate souls.

Kaya's brain was having trouble keeping up with what was happening. All she saw was the blood splatter as the masked figure disappeared into the crowd. On instinct, she moved to run toward the fallen men, perhaps hoping she could help them. Victoria pulled her back into the vehicle before she made it more than a few steps.

It was like everything had been in slow motion until suddenly life snapped back to full speed.

"Drive, you fool!" the abbot shouted, and the driver did as he was commanded, slamming the accelerator as they sped forward. The wounded acolytes were left to fend for themselves.

Kaya didn't have enough time to process, only realizing too late what that acceleration meant as she screamed, "No! Stop!" It was too late.

Thud. Thud. Thud. She lost count after the third one. Blood and clumps of skin or hair or...she wasn't sure what dripped on the windows as they sped forward. She wanted to scream, but all that came out was the contents of her stomach as she wretched onto the floor, Victoria following closely behind. Their bile splattered the abbot's shoes and robe. The pair continued dry heaving long after their stomachs emptied.

CHAPTER

7

Kaya

October, 4101 U.E.T.—New Olympia, Mars

Events went by in a blur, but eventually they pulled into what looked like a rear entrance to the Sanctum. When the vehicle was parked, a team came to begin washing the blood from the vehicle. No one seemed particularly surprised or concerned, which only made Kaya feel worse. Was no one at all worried about the people who were hurt? She was sure at least some of them had died.

Kaya had never seen anyone die before. She knew people who had died, of course, but she had never seen it. She never watched another person's eyes as the realization of what was happening came to them in one last brilliant flash of clarity. At least that was what she imagined they saw in those final moments.

She never considered whether what they saw was God or something else, but she couldn't get the image of that acolyte's face out of her head. The image of the brick breaking his skull and his wide-eyed terror at seeing the end. Kaya knew that moment would stay with her for a long time. Despite her own misgivings, she hoped he saw the God he believed in.

She was so engrossed in her own thoughts that she didn't consider how Victoria was holding up. She wanted to be strong for herself and her friend, but at that moment she didn't feel capable of either.

At some point, the abbot left them. She remembered another round of angry screaming but not much else. Her world had quickly become an endless loop of screams and blood. Through the noise, she didn't notice a new figure approaching them. A middle-aged woman with a stern face, who after taking in their appearance leveled a disapproving look.

"I am Head Mistress Blaiset. Collect your bags and follow me," the woman said.

67

Kaya and Victoria did as they were told and silently followed the woman into the nearest building. The building was plain and nondescript, reminding Kaya of a random clerk's office. The walls were plain and unadorned, and various people moved purposefully through the hallways.

"In here," the woman said, pointing into an open doorway. The room itself was relatively small, with a large empty table in the center. One wall was lined with shelves that contained various bins and items, and the others had doors that led into adjoining rooms.

Behind the empty table stood two white-robed acolytes who moved to take possession of their bags and placed them roughly on the table. The acolytes were unlike the ones she had seen so far. These carried polished wooden clubs at their hips and had the rough-cut faces of men who had seen a brawl or two. Their presence snapped Kaya out of her newest daze.

"What are you doing?" she asked.

"Standard onboarding procedure. All your bags will be searched for contraband, and you will be assigned your supplies for the semester," the woman said as she stood ominously beside them. She watched each item carefully as it was removed from the bags, as if her nose could sniff out contraband like a hound.

Kaya's stomach dropped. *The Solar Empire insignia*, she thought as panic and dread took over.

"Is something the matter?" the woman asked, her eyebrow twitching. Kaya knew she had to get it together quickly or something in her face was going to tip her off.

"No," she said maybe too aggressively. "No..." she tried again more softly. "I was still thinking about those people in the mid district." Kaya cast her eyes toward the ground. She didn't have to try very hard to seem upset. When the woman didn't say anything, she looked up to see the woman giving her an almost disappointed look.

"You should save your tears for real tragedies, not the elimination of malcontents. They will turn the city to ruins if left unchecked."

Kaya tried to seem disinterested as one by one her items were removed and catalogued. She hadn't caught the woman's name, but now she didn't care. She simply thought of her as the old crow now, since her expression and manner reminded her of the troublesome birds that terrorized their family garden.

The acolytes rummaged through clothing and other items until they came across her electronics and pulled them aside, causing her anger to rise again. They took away her digipad and the digislate she used to draw, locking them both away in a metal crate.

"Hey! What are you doing with those? Put them down," she asked, moving to reach for her devices. They were her only connection to the outside world, to her home. However, the old crow cut her off, putting herself between Kaya and the table.

"There will be none of that," she squawked. "You will focus your time on God and your studies. You will get these back when you have earned them."

Kaya was about to say something unwise when she noticed the acolytes beginning to remove her books one by one. They picked up the first and then the second, reading the titles and flicking through a few pages before placing them aside.

Kaya knew she had to do something. She said nothing to the old crow, and that seemed to be the answer the woman was looking for as she continued, her back turned to Kaya. "I have faith you could become a great bishop if you learn proper humility and respect before God and his chosen."

Kaya could see the book with the insignia leave the bag next, and her heart stopped. The acolyte turned it in his hand, reading the title, and then moved to open it. She knew this was her last chance to act.

She drew the hilt of her mother's plasma blade out from under her jacket. The acolyte not holding the book noticed this and shouted, causing the other acolyte to drop the book onto the table and draw the club from his waist.

The old crow turned around in a snap, snatching Kaya's wrist with a speed she didn't think the old woman capable of. The acolytes moved to her side to provide backup, but it didn't seem like she would need it.

"Did you mean to kill me with this girl?"

"No, Mistress, I wanted to make you aware I had it," she said, wincing from the pain in her wrist.

The woman snatched the hilt from her hand and admired it. "Why did you bring this here? You will have no need of weapons in the Sanctum. This isn't an academy of war."

She told the truth, "It is my right by law to carry it."

"Yes...so it is," the woman said, waving a dismissive hand to the acolytes, who holstered their clubs. Then she stared at the hilt a moment longer, and Kaya wondered what she could be thinking. "Should you draw your blade again in my presence, understand I will kill you." She squeezed Kaya's wrist tighter. It took all her strength not to cry out. *How is she so strong?* "Do you understand that is *my* right by law?"

"Yes, Mistress," she choked out, and the old crow released her and handed back the blade.

"Good, I am glad we understand each other."

When the acolyte returned to his job, he had forgotten about the book, instead choosing a new item from the bag, and Kaya relaxed. It had worked, at least for now.

Victoria's bags were likewise checked, but she put up much less fuss than Kaya had. It had been an emotional day, but Victoria looked like she had given up fighting the second they stepped into the abbot's vehicle.

Moving quickly through the rest of the process, they were given their uniforms, white robes like those worn by the acolytes, but these came with white sashes instead of red. To mark them as initiates, she assumed.

The crow made them change into their new robes immediately, which she found to be ill fitting and made of a thick and uncomfortable fabric. It was sure to be especially horrid in the subtropical climate of the city, but at least they weren't especially itchy. They were then given stacks of books and writing supplies since no digital tools were allowed.

With the distributions completed, the headmistress brought them to the room they would call home for the foreseeable future. A small, beige-colored concrete room with one small window on the far wall. It looked an awful lot like a jail cell, but without the metal bars.

By some act of divine intervention, they were kept together in the same room. A small blessing, Kaya thought as she dropped her meager belongings onto one of the beds.

They each had a desk and a small bookshelf. It was a far cry from what she was used to, but it was at least something, even if the only book on the shelf was a copy of the Holy Scripture. At least she was allowed to keep most of the ones she had brought with her. The room was plain and utilitarian, but it was clean. The one thing that would take the most getting used to were the communal bathrooms located in the hallway.

"Here are your schedules for classes, prayers, and meals. You are expected to be on time and prepared," the old crow said as she handed them the packets of paper. Her face looked like she had taken a bite of a lemon. "Any questions?"

"No, Mistress," Kaya and Victoria said in unison.

The headmistress nodded and left the room.

"That went well," Kaya said, sitting down in her desk chair, finding it horribly uncomfortable. Victoria meanwhile collapsed onto the bed, her face buried in the sorry excuse for a pillow.

"I don't want to talk," Victoria said, her voice muffled.

"We could go look around instead," Kaya offered. She was good at ignoring things she didn't like when the situation called for it. Besides, if they didn't lock her in this room, she had no intention of staying in it longer than necessary.

Victoria turned over and waved the packet of papers at her like a street salesman. "Did you even look at any of this?"

"We just got it. I was going to," Kaya said. "Eventually."

"Eventually? After everything that happened today, don't you care? And what was that back there with drawing your blade? Have you lost your mind?"

"Of course I care. No, I haven't lost my mind, but what am I supposed to do, sit here and cry? I've already given them the satisfaction one too many times," Kaya said, standing up.

Victoria shook her head. "Why do you always think they are out to get you? Maybe the bishops are right. Did you see what that crowd did to those acolytes? They killed them, Kaya. Killed them for nothing at all."

"How many did they kill when they drove through the crowd?" she asked, and Victoria didn't have an answer to that. "We are their prisoners here, you know."

"Didn't we do that to ourselves by following your stupid plan? I don't care what you do, Kaya, but I want no part of it. I will focus on my studies and wait until I can leave here," Victoria said, turning back over to face the wall. It sounded like she was crying again.

Kaya stood in the middle of the room, unsure what to do or say next.

She couldn't believe her best friend would abandon her so easily. Also, how dare she judge her? Victoria didn't know how she felt. She didn't know what she planned to do in the future. Victoria might be okay going along with this, okay with accepting that this was her fate, but Kaya didn't have to be. She wouldn't be.

"Fine then," she said and left the room.

Kaya walked through the hallway, fuming silently, searching for the way they had come in. She felt ridiculous wearing the white robes, but no one else seemed to pay her any attention as she passed. She had been angry at her situation, but now she was angry at Victoria too for giving up so easily.

Passing deeper through the building, she found other students with white robes and different colored sashes, upperclassmen, she assumed, who were studying or talking in quiet groups. No one she saw seemed particularly friendly or willing to talk, although they all appraised her as she passed.

Normally the attention wouldn't bother her, but now she felt like a fish flopping on shore. It wouldn't be long before they knew exactly who she was and why she was there. This was a school for the children of high-ranking clergy and bureaucrats, not nobility. For perhaps the first time in her life, she was the outcast.

With her devices gone, she had to search for a clock so she could make sense of her schedule. Eventually she found one in the hallway and figured she had a little over an hour until she had to be anywhere. Plenty of time to do more exploring.

Eventually she found the exit to the main square, but not before wandering into several wrong rooms where annoyed students glared at her for interrupting their activities. It all added to her feeling of isolation.

The exit she used brought her to a small courtyard that connected to the larger Trinity Square complex beyond. The square was an expansive space paved with stone and surrounded by grand and ancient structures. It was large enough for thousands of people to gather like they often did for military parades and celebration days.

On the edges of the square were several entrances to courtyards or buildings, along with the more ornate main entrances of the three universities.

Along the northwest edge of the square was a massive columned building that she knew housed the Boundless Library, the repository of all assembled knowledge in printed word. It was the one place in trinity square she knew she would be allowed to enter. The Boundless Library was supposed to be open to every citizen, but she wasn't sure how true that was in practice. Either way, it felt like a safe choice, one she had always been curious about.

She also thought it would be the best place to look for any mention of the "Eternal Dream," whatever it might be. She considered the possibility of searching for the triangle emblem from the insignia but thought that might be too much of a risk. If she mentioned it to the wrong person, they would surely turn her in to the authorities.

There was no shortage of armed guards patrolling the square, primarily members of the Republican Guard and uniformed Frumentarii. She made it a point to avoid crossing the path of either. There were also light poles with nests of cameras on top. The surveillance wasn't anything new, but there seemed to be so much more of it than on Mercury.

The library was a large building with steep steps leading to a columned entrance. Outside the building, students from the different universities, professors, and what looked like tourists all milled around in groups or alone, some resting casually on the large steps under the shade of the building. As she approached the base of the steps, three cadets, from the military academy based on their uniforms, approached her from where they had been sitting.

"Look, it's a fresh snowflake," one of them said, preening like a peacock. Kaya knew his type and attempted to walk around them. She wasn't in the mood. When they got closer, Kaya realized she knew who the two boys were and wanted even less to do with them. The girl among them she didn't know, but it hardly mattered.

"Hey, he's talking to you, snowflake," the one girl in the group said, moving quickly to block Kaya's path.

Kaya glared and without stopping drove her shoulder into her as she passed. They were about the same age and size, but clearly the girl hadn't been ready for the aggressive shove as she stumbled aside.

"You sarding bitch, get back here!" the girl yelled at her back.

Kaya could hear the rest of the group chuckling, but she didn't take the bait and kept walking. *Not today, not today*, she repeated to herself as a mantra to cool her anger.

It was then Kaya felt her legs trip beneath her. She tried to catch herself but got tangled up in the unfamiliar robes. As a result, she fell to the ground with a thud. The girl stood over her with a smug expression as she tossed her long dirty blonde hair behind her shoulder.

"That's a good snowflake," the girl said in what she could tell was a Venusian accent.

Kaya got to her feet, not bothering to brush herself off. She moved to stand before the girl, her eyes stabbing daggers into her. It looked like she might back down, at least until the peacock spoke again.

"One thousand credits on the Lady Palmona," he said in a posh Martian accent that was nearly as pretentious as his appearance. His flowery tone had a magnetic effect, and almost as quickly as he spoke a small crowd began to grow, forming a circle of bodies around the two girls.

Kaya considered pushing through them to get away, but, no, she wouldn't back down now. Not so these spoiled brats could claim some kind of petty victory. She was going to be here for a while and would need to protect her reputation.

She was properly trained for a fight, and she had no doubt she could take this girl. She felt the hilt of her mother's blade under the robe on her hip but thought better of drawing it. None of them appeared to be armed, and she surmised anyone in a group so concerned with appearances would carry one visibly as a status symbol. Besides, she didn't need to add to her list of offenses so soon.

"It's not too late to step away," Kaya said quietly to the girl. She would give her a chance to leave fairly and save some face.

"Never," the girl snarled back, "no snowflake is my better. I don't care what backwater bishopric your family comes from."

Kaya wanted to laugh, but she kept her expression neutral, "Lady Palmona, was it?" Kaya asked. She was unfamiliar with the name, so she assumed they held some small Venusian barony she had never heard of. The girl nodded, a satisfied smile on her face.

"I am Lady Kaya al Vardan, daughter to the Duke of Mercury. Perhaps your family should have taught you better and you could have avoided such an egregious mistake as to strike me. My appearance is quite distinct after all." The wind seemed to leave Lady Palmona's sails, and part of the crowd went silent as those closest to them were able to make out Kaya's words. "Your friends here could have told you," Kaya said, nodding to the two boys behind her.

The peacock who had spoken had a wry grin on his face, and the other a concerned expression. She knew they had recognized her from the beginning. Lady Palmona should really find better friends.

"Lady Vardan, I am Lord Henry Beckett, son of Viscount Simon Beckett, Lieutenant-General of the Republic Army," the one who had remained quiet up until now said.

"I know who you are," she said, not taking her eyes off Palmona. She also knew the boy with the serpentine face who slithered up beside Henry, Boniface Ajax, son of the Praefectus Frumentario, the leader of the Frumentarii and arguably the third most powerful person in the solar system.

"Kaya, how are your brother and father? It has been so long since I was last on Mercury," Boniface said, inserting himself into the conversation.

"They are well," she said flatly. It was the minimum that was expected from her to maintain social decency. She would have loved to ignore him or better yet curse him back to the hole he crawled out of, but there were some people she couldn't insult so directly.

Meanwhile, Lady Palmona looked from face to face, increasingly confused by what was happening.

It was then a man in priestly robes forced his way through the crowd flanked by Republican guardsmen clad in blue burnished exoarmor and carrying lightning pikes.

"What is the meaning of this disturbance?" the old man shouted, looking at each of them in turn. Seeing Kaya thoroughly outnumbered by the cadets, he went to stand near to her.

"Are you okay, child?" he asked Kaya in a whisper.

"Yes, it was a misunderstanding," Kaya said, looking to Palmona and the others. They all nodded their agreement.

She didn't like that she had been bailed out by the clergy, but she hadn't sought the help. It was interesting to her that she now had their blind support based on the robes she wore. A strange change of events.

"Yes, Cleric, it was simply a misunderstanding. We will clear this assembly at once," Boniface said with a sly smile. The cleric offered no protest, recognizing him.

"Very well, Master Ajax, I trust you have this in hand then," the old cleric said before taking Kaya's arm and leaning in to whisper in her ear. "Take care, child. He's not one to cross."

Kaya nodded as the old cleric left with the guards, and the crowd dispersed.

Lady Palmona took the first opportunity to extricate herself from the situation, sparing a nervous glance toward Kaya as she did. Boniface likewise left with his arm around the girl's waist, laughing as he looked back at Kaya and whispered into her ear. This was all a big game to him. Meanwhile, Henry lingered by her side.

"My apologies, Lady Vardan, if I had realized what she was going to do, I would have stopped her," he said.

"It's a shame it took violence on my person for you to feel the need to intervene. Besides, I am not sure your friend over there would have told her to stop." She motioned to Boniface as he walked away.

"He isn't a bad guy once you know him, same with Margot." It sounded like he was trying to convince himself as much as her.

Kaya knew exactly who Boniface was and what types of values his family taught, and she cared even less about Lady Palmona after her rude display. It wasn't worth it to acknowledge either of them, so she remained quiet.

Henry fidgeted nervously as the silence hung between them. She hated that it came to her mind, but there was something endearing in his awkwardness.

"Anyway...it won't happen again. Goodbye," he said, breaking the silence and leaving with an awkward bow.

She watched as he walked back to where his friends were waiting impatiently. He seemed nice enough, which left her wondering how such rotten fruit could fall from such dignified trees. All the opportunities of the solar system at their fingertips, and they sat here relishing petty competition.

When Kaya turned to continue walking to the library, a young engineer stood blocking her path. He was staring at her.

"Can I help you?" she asked, a bit annoyed to be bothered again by someone else. *Did no one have anywhere better to be?*

"Oh, um, sorry, I was on my way into the library when I saw what happened. Are you alright? I couldn't really hear, but I wanted to make sure you were alright. I got stuck in the back, you see," the boy said quickly, his hands up defensively. His accent was Martian but rougher than the cadet's had been.

Why are the engineers always so strange? she thought as she looked him up and down. He was maybe a year or two older than her, but he was shorter and thin, his body not particularly muscular. His skin was rough and pitted in the way those who had endured regular radiation might look, like those from the slums or low districts. Although his skin was healed now, the scars remained.

His eyes were a vivid gray, devoid of the yellow hew the poorer residents typically had. Although sometimes exceptional students from the lower districts did receive admittance to the three universities, it was the engineering school that typically recruited low and mid district applicants.

"Yes, I am fine. Thank you for asking," she said, trying to soften her tone. Her nerves were making her more agitated than she would like.

"Aron Trilinos," the boy said, offering his scarred hand to her.

She unconsciously hesitated a moment before taking it. "Kaya al Vardan."

"Lady Vardan, isn't it?" he asked, rubbing his hands together and trying to look anywhere but at her eyes. He looked quite uncomfortable.

"Kaya is fine," she said, feeling a little self-conscious.

He smiled, "Well, I am glad you are okay. Maybe I'll see you around in the library."

"Yeah, maybe." She returned his smile. "Goodbye, Aron."

He waved awkwardly and turned to leave, walking quickly up the steps toward the library entrance. He stopped briefly to look back at her and nearly tripped over his own feet. She couldn't help but chuckle.

What a strange day, she thought and entered the library. It was an immense and exquisitely adorned building with a series of corridors, shelves, desks, and small study alcoves stretching off in every direction. Marble columns and carved stone lined every surface and surrounded the vaulted ceilings and shimmering stained-glass windows. The worn fixtures, empty art pedestals, and dull-gold trim only lessened its grandeur slightly.

At the entrance, she passed through a series of security scanners under the watchful eye of armed Republican guardsmen. Neither guard moved nor spoke as she passed, and the librarian at the entry desk only nodded at her passing.

Entering the main space, she was overwhelmed by how many books there were. She didn't know exactly what she was looking for, but there was one thing that stood out in her mind, the "eternal dream." The phrase kept coming to the forefront of her mind, yet she had no idea what it meant, and it was incredibly frustrating. However, if there was anywhere in the solar system with answers, it would be the Boundless Library.

So, she searched aimlessly for a data terminal to aid her search but came up empty. Looking at the large clock in the main study area, she knew she didn't have time to search the stacks one by one. She found an empty table and sat down, dropping her head into her arms.

"Did you uh, need help finding something?" came the voice of Aron startling her. She hadn't noticed his approach.

"Sorry, my sister says I walk too quietly sometimes," he offered with his hands up apologetically.

"It's fine. I was putting my head down for a moment. Is there no way to search for books or topics here?" she said, lifting her head from the table.

"Yeah, there is, but it's all done manually using those cards in that case over there." He pointed to a large cabinet with dozens of small drawers. "They call it a decimal system. They should have taught you about it in one of your intro classes last week."

"I got here today."

"Oh, I see. Well, I know the library pretty well, if you want some help. I maybe spend too much time around here," he said, flushing. Kaya couldn't help finding him endearing in his own sort of way.

She hesitated before answering. She didn't know if she could trust him or anyone with knowledge of the eternal dream, whatever it turned out to be. It could be some blasphemous phrase or worse yet a weapon for all she knew, but something about Aron seemed trustworthy.

"Yes. Okay," she said, "I am trying to find any books about something called the eternal dream."

"The eternal dream..." he said, scratching at his head, "can't say I ever heard of that. What is it? Some holy scripture thing?"

"Yea, I guess so. I heard it once and was curious," she said, hoping to avoid any more questions.

He chuckled, "Got here today and already in the library doing research. I think we might see each other a lot then."

Kaya smiled awkwardly. She had no intention of spending that much time in the library.

Aron walked over to the cabinet, and Kaya watched as he flipped through the paper cards in a practiced manner. After checking several drawers, he stopped and shook his head.

"I don't see anything under that topic. Could it be called something else?"

"I'm not sure. Would these cards tell you everything that is here from each of the three universities? Is there somewhere else to check?" she asked.

"Yea, all the university collections are here together. If it's not in this library, it likely doesn't exist anywhere in the solar system."

Great, another dead end.

"Well, actually, I guess there are also the rare and historic archives on the basement floors," Aron said, motioning to a guarded staircase at the far end of the library.

"Oh, can we go take a look then?" she asked, beginning to walk toward the stairs.

His eyes went wide, and he blocked her path with outstretched arms, "No way! You need a special pass to get down there, and good luck getting one. Normally only the professors are allowed there, or the bishops and their chosen people of course. I have only ever heard of a couple students who got passes, and they were aids to someone important within the Sanctum."

She huffed. For the first time in weeks, she felt like she was going to accomplish something productive. Now, she wondered if she would ever find out what the eternal dream was and what, if anything, it had to do with her mother.

"Not used to being told no, huh," he said with a glib expression.

"Excuse me," she snapped and instantly regretted the outburst when Aron's face turned sour.

"I, uh, I didn't mean anything by it. People like me get used to being left out of places," he said with a sad expression.

"I..." She felt bad for treating him so poorly when he had tried to help, but she struggled with what to say. "I'm sure you didn't. Thank you for your help, but I need to get to prayers," she said, hurrying to move for the door, her embarrassment mounting.

"Can I walk you there?" he asked, sounding hopeful.

"No, I can find my way. Goodbye," she said more harshly than she intended and made for the door.

She realized as she walked from the library that she was acting no better than Henry and his lot. Aron had tried to help, and she slapped his hand away and failed to apologize.

If she wanted to be successful here, she couldn't go around burning every bridge in her path. This was no longer Alhazen, where everything was at her fingertips for the taking. She would have to earn her place in a way she wasn't used to, and the prospect scared her.

CHAPTER

8

Kaya

October, 4101 U.E.T.—New Olympia, Mars

Emerging into the Martian sunshine, she felt a pang of sadness at how far away and distant the sun appeared. It was a large and dominant feature in the sky back home, and she took comfort in its enveloping presence. The absence of it now was more jarring than she anticipated.

Outside, she saw Boniface and his cronies were still lingering near the base of the stairs leading to Trinity Square. Kaya found a spot near them beside several red-sashed acolytes. She raised the hood of her robe and pretended to read her schedule while she eavesdropped on their conversation. She was curious if they were waiting to harass her again.

"Why didn't you tell me who she was?" Margot said, glaring at Boniface and Henry.

"When could I have done that, Lady Palmona? You decided to knock her down before I could even process what was happening," Henry said, pointing a finger at her.

"You saw how she hit me first! Anyway, Boniface wanted to talk with her," she said, moving to put her arm around Boniface.

Henry groaned. "That was Lady Vardan, the Duke of Criophori's daughter. I shouldn't need to remind you that he is also the Lord Eminent and one of the most powerful people in the entire system."

Margot looked back to Boniface as if for support, but he was absently tapping at his digipad. "Just because your grandfather is the Duke of Mars doesn't give you any right to command me."

"This isn't your little barony on Venus. The rules on Mars aren't so easily pushed aside for your childish games. It is shocking to me you have made it this far in the Academy with such little tact." Henry said, and Kaya tensed at his sudden insults.

Margot's face turned red, and she looked ready to strike Henry when Boniface stood up from his perch. Henry seemed to stiffen as the young Ajax approached.

Kaya didn't know very much about the Becketts, Henry's family, but she knew based on his parentage he would likely never inherit the ducal crown. Boniface meanwhile was the son of the Praefectus Frumentario, Carlo Ajax, a man even dukes and duchesses didn't cross.

"Sweet Hal," Boniface cooed as he moved between the two. "We are all friends here. It was just a misunderstanding." He put his arm around Margot's waist. "Isn't that right, Margot?"

Margot stared at Henry a moment longer before turning to embrace Boniface, her expression switching to one of devotion. "Sure, of course, darling," Margot said while running her finger over Boniface's chest. "Can we go now? It's gotten quite stale out here."

The way she jumped so easily to try and please him left Kaya feeling dirty. Such a vile man didn't deserve that kind of devotion.

Henry remained silent, staring at the backs of Boniface and Margot as they left cackling like hyenas. Once they were out of sight, he kicked a step, running his hand through his hair. He was muttering something she couldn't hear.

Kaya appreciated that he seemed upset by the whole affair but couldn't say what his reasoning was. Was he angry about how they had treated her or just his position within the group? It was at least worth a conversation to find out, so she left her hiding spot and walked up behind him.

"You are right. They seem very nice," she said without announcing herself.

"God's bones!" he exclaimed with his hand on his chest as he spun around to face her. "You shouldn't sneak up on a man like that."

"You should be more aware of your surroundings. If I was an insurgent, you might already be dead," she said, appraising him. He was half a hand taller than her and muscular but with a heavier build. His wavy brown hair hung loosely to his ears, and his eyes were a similar shade of brown. His uniform was well cared for, and he looked like the young lordling that he was. He was handsome in his own boyish way.

She had never really dated back home, preferring to spend her time on other projects instead. Not that she didn't find boys appealing and had kissed one or two on occasion, but she never really made the time for anything more than that. She hated that she was becoming so easily distracted by those thoughts now.

"If there were insurgents who could make it into Trinity Square, we would likely all be dead already," he said with a smile that turned into a more sheepish expression under her heavy gaze. "Do I have something in my teeth?"

"What?"

"You are appraising me like a farmer might a goat," he said, looking uncomfortable.

"Oh, sorry." She winced, her cheeks reddening. "It's been a long day," she said and brushed imaginary hairs from her face.

She was glad when he changed the subject. "I don't know your situation, but I assume you aren't wearing those robes because you want to be." He looked sympathetic.

"No," was the only reply she could muster. That was a conversation for another day.

"Have you been to Mars before this? I had the privilege of meeting your father once, but I would have remembered meeting you." He was the one staring now.

"No, I always wanted to, but my father never thought it was a good idea. Things have been a bit unsettled the last few years," she said, hoping he would drop the subject and his staring.

"I wouldn't worry. The first time most people come to Mars is to attend one of the great universities," he said, looking earnestly at her.

"I have always heard that. It must have been nice growing up so close to the capital."

"It has some benefits, I suppose," he said with a shrug. "Maybe you can join me for something to eat? Since it's the end of the week and all..." he said with an almost pleading expression.

"Yes," she said instantly before shaking her head. "Wait, no, I can't. I still have prayers to attend." She pulled out her schedule, not entirely sure why she was so excited by the idea. She wanted a chance to release some stress of course but also wondered what alliance potential there could be with Henry. If she was honest, she wanted to sit in a restaurant with him and pretend all of this had been a nightmare.

"Oh, I understand. Maybe another time then," he said.

"Maybe I can meet you when I finish? I think I should be allowed out after that."

His eyes lit up. "Yes, that would be great. Here, take my comm number. Wait, you don't have a comm device, do you? I always forget the clergy makes you all live in the stone age. Do you know where Martyrs' Square is?" he said, motioning to a spot not far from where they were standing between the library and the Sanctum. "It is right over there. In the center is a large statue. Meet me there when you're done."

His words came out in a rush, but she found his boyish enthusiasm endearing.

"Okay, I will do that. See you soon, Henry."

"Call me Hal."

"Okay, Hal, I'll see you soon," she said, offering him a rare smile. There was a bit more spring in her step than she had felt in weeks as she made her way back to the Sanctum.

The evening prayers came and passed without any incident. Kaya had tried to pull Victoria aside to tell her about Henry and what had happened, but Victoria pulled away, choosing to focus on her prayers rather than gossip. She seemed content to commit herself to the clerics' process, even though Kaya had never known her or her family to be particularly devout.

Kaya knew the prayers of course, but outside of official government functions they weren't something she ever considered. So she spent the time going through the motions while thinking about her meeting with Hal.

It wasn't just that he was handsome, not that it hurt, but what she liked was how genuine he seemed. He had defended her when she wasn't even there and asked nothing in return. He seemed like the picture of knightly virtue.

When the final bell struck, she tried to approach Victoria a second time but found her already in conversation with a small group and decided against it. She could catch up with her friend later when she returned.

Normally she would have liked to arrange her hair or at least change her clothes, but wearing the initiates' white robes was a requirement, and she didn't feel like testing that policy, at least not this evening. So she braided her hair into one long braid that hung loosely over her shoulder and straightened her robes as best she could.

She found Martyrs' Square easily enough because it was well lit in the evening hours and there were plenty of people coming and going from the location. She assumed it was a popular meeting place within the capital.

At the center of the square stood a massive statue depicting two robed figures with their feet on top of the Sun, soldiers sprawled out behind them. One of the robed men held a sword and the other a scepter. It was a depiction of the first Vox and Manus standing over the defeated Solar Empire, God's greatest triumph over the Sun itself.

She knew the scene was a famous one depicting the formation of the Republic with its voice and hand at the forefront of the struggle. She had seen many pictures of this very statue in her schoolbooks but never considered coming to see it in person.

"I am glad you came. It's quite a piece of art, isn't it?" Henry said, coming to stand by her side. He was still in his uniform from earlier, which made her feel a little better about her own outfit.

"It is," she said, already disinterested in discussing the piece at all. "Thank you for making me feel welcome."

"Thank you for reminding me of my manners. I can promise you I will never lose track of them again."

She smiled. "I will hold you to that Lord Beckett." He blushed. "Is the restaurant far from here?"

"Ah, no, it's not far. On the other side of the square," he said, holding out his arm, which she took with only a little hesitation.

"Lead the way," she said while reaching into her pocket to make sure the hilt of her plasma blade was still easily accessible at her hip. She was willing to trust him, but she wouldn't be caught off guard again, especially outside of the square.

However, her worries turned out to be for nothing, as they arrived in front of a well-maintained building not far from Martyrs' Square. It seemed like a posh tavern that had an old-fashioned wooden sign hanging near the door that read "The Trident."

The two-story building had a facade of river stones and a neat row of large windows that revealed a bustling dining room inside. Outside the entrance was a small seating area where several diners sat enjoying meals or drinks in quiet groups. The inside was made to look like an establishment from Earth with wood-paneled walls and leather-wrapped furniture. She had been to similarly trendy places back on Mercury, and it made her feel more at home.

The clientele included other cadets as well as high district patrons in their trendy evening wear and business attire. There were even a couple of clerics off in one corner. Based on the noise level, it seemed like many of the patrons, and particularly the cadets, were well into their night of drinking to usher in tomorrow's day of rest.

Unfortunately, her classes and prayers ran every single day. She had felt self-conscious in her initiates' robes, but none of the guests seemed to find it odd. One of the clerics even gave her a nod of greeting. It felt strange that everything was so...normal.

The hostess sat them at a small table for two along one of the windows. Kaya took the seat closest to the wall where the fireplace crackled behind her. It was a genuine wood fireplace, she realized. That was quite an extravagant expense.

"Do you come here often?" she asked.

"No, not really. Boniface prefers a *livelier* establishment."

"Do you only go where Boniface wants?" she asked, taking a sip from her water glass once the waiter filled it. She found it hard to not be direct.

He shrugged. "It's not usually worth arguing with him."

"Why not go your own way?"

"His father and mine are close friends. It would only make things more difficult."

"Oh, I see," she said, disappointed. Hearing that his family and the Praefectus Frumentario were close had an immediate souring effect on the evening. Henry sensed the change of mood immediately.

"But don't worry. It's purely political. I...,"

"You what?" She raised an eyebrow.

"I don't know. We've only met, and now I'm voicing all my problems to one of my father's political rivals. As you can probably tell, I am not very good at all this, and my father would be the first to tell you that. If he had another child to send to the academy, he would have gladly done so," he said, eagerly taking the glass of wine offered by the waiter when he returned. He had turned as red as the Martian soil, and she was fairly certain he was sweating through his uniform.

"It's okay. I don't even have a comm device, remember. So how would I even tell anyone? I'm here as a friend. I don't care at all about politics. Besides, my brother is the one destined to be the next duke, not me," she said, trying to sound comforting. It was a skill she wasn't very good at, but he seemed placated.

"Thanks, you are truly a breath of fresh air when I was struggling to breathe."

"You shouldn't try so hard to flatter me. It won't do you any good," she said, looking at him over the rim of her own glass of wine as she sipped.

"I will have you know I am particularly bad in that capacity as well," he said with a laugh, and she couldn't help but join him. His laugh and smile were infectious.

"I guess we have more things in common than I realized," she said, motioning to her robes, and then raised her glass in a toast. "To the parents we continue to disappoint."

Henry continued to laugh and raised his glass to touch hers. "I can drink to that."

They exchanged more pleasantries about their families as the starter course arrived, a plate of Martian cheese and tomatoes. She told him about her brother, and he shared stories about his mother, who spent more time tending to her business than her family. She hated to see the pain in his eyes and changed the subject to asking about the beaches on Mars. He seemed grateful for the new topic.

This led to a long discussion about the differences between their two planets. He had never been to Mercury and couldn't fathom what it must be like to have daylight for months on end followed by months of darkness. Then she had to explain how the daily light cycle of Mars was already quite jarring to her after only a single day. That was followed by having to endure everyone's favorite discussion about Mercury, the heat. Any awkwardness he had shown earlier washed away as their banter strengthened under the power of wine and chemistry.

He even seemed genuinely interested as she waxed poetically about the desert canyons she loved to explore. She left out any mention of restricted areas and Empire relics, but he still hung on to her every word, which continued to flow as their entrees arrived. Fresh salmon from the Amazonian Sea for her and a plate of handmade pasta for him. Both dishes looked and smelled delish, but they barely touched them. It made her realize she might have been more starved for conversation than food.

"Did you originally plan to attend the military academy?" he asked after the waiter had brought them their second bottle of wine.

"I always wanted to be a Hospitaler," she said bluntly. "I was going to attend the military academy last year, but then..."

"It's okay. You don't have--"

"It's okay," she said, steeling herself. "After my mother died, I delayed my plans. Then I made new plans to attend the Hospitaller University on Venus and train to be a physician. I was set to attend next semester, but...now I'm here." She motioned to her white robes. "I guess neither I nor my family got what we wanted." Bitterness slipped into her voice as she raised her glass to his.

He raised his glass in silence and didn't press the subject.

"What about you? Did you always want to be a soldier?"

It was his turn to reflect bitterly on the past. "Hardly. I wanted to travel to Ganymede and study the sea life there."

The thought of him on an expedition taking pictures of fish made her smile. It was how far away from that path he was now that made her want to reach across the table and comfort him.

"Well, your father is a lieutenant general, right? That's a higher rank than most nobles, isn't it? I am sure you will be able to get whatever posting you want."

He pinched his lips. "Yeah, he's milked his relationship with the Praefectus for all its worth, I think, but I'm not really interested in staying around Mars. I would rather sail off to the Far Coast or at least some asteroid or something."

"Those are pretty unpopular assignments, aren't they? I'm sure they would give it to you if you asked."

He snorted. "My father will do anything it takes to keep me where he wants. If I could choose, I would join my uncle Silas with the Pandora Fleet. He's spent his whole life on the front-line sailing through every corner of the system. I'm sure he's even seen the whales on Ganymede." His words were beginning to slur together, and she handed him a glass of water.

"Why don't you tell me about these whales?" she said, stifling a laugh as his eyes went wide and he took a gulp of the water.

"Yes! That is a wonderful topic..." he said passionately.

They then continued to drink and eat until they were the last ones in the room, and the restaurant eventually threw them out. He was a gentleman and made sure she made it back to the Sanctum despite his inebriation.

Thankfully, she sobered up some by the time they arrived, and she made it back to her room without creating a scene. She had been excited to share the details of her evening but was disappointed to find Victoria already asleep when she arrived.

Kaya never expected this was how things would go, but she was happy for the chance to experience at least some joy despite her recent misery. She found herself excited to find out if something more would come of this, but only time would tell.

Kaya

April, 4102 U.E.T.—New Olympia, Mars

Kaya fought back the sleepiness that tried to swallow her as she listened to her professor prattle on about forgiveness and faith or some such platitudes. The first six months had gone by quickly, her time mostly filled with learning the day-to-day workings of the school, like where her assigned classrooms were and the process of daily prayers.

What spare time she had she spent exploring the capital with Hal as her guide. The boy seemed to occupy more and more of her time despite whatever emotional barriers she tried to erect. They talked constantly while cautiously dancing around their feelings. Each stolen glance, every laugh shared, carried a hint of something more profound, yet they avoided acknowledging it openly. It worried her that he was so distracting and took her away from her studies and research into the eternal dream.

Her grades were average at best, and she wasn't any further along with researching the eternal dream. She knew it must be something symbolic, but beyond that she couldn't find anyone who recognized the phrase or any mention of it in official texts.

She worried if she didn't find answers soon, she would begin to forget. Not just forget about the cryptic phrase but forget what she was trying to do, fulfill her mother's dream. She was afraid she would fall into the same happy rhythm with Hal and her life at the Sanctum, forgetting about the plight of the average citizen and the injustice they faced nearly daily. She didn't want to forget.

In her latest effort, she had begun mentioning the phrase randomly during conversations, hoping to elicit some kind of response. Besides a few odd stares, that method hadn't produced anything, but it was the best idea she had, at least until she could gain entry to the restricted area of the Boundless Library.

There were also all the mundane things she had to learn how to manage on her own, like retrieving her own meals in the communal cafeteria and laundry. These were all things she had always relied on servants for. Not to mention the lack of data devices to do anything, including staying in touch with the outside world. It was a particularly jarring experience. Even if she did speak to her father and Theodore occasionally, it wasn't nearly enough.

On the other hand, she had barely spoken to Victoria at all since the day they arrived. They spoke in passing, since it was hard to avoid completely as roommates, but it was clear that their relationship wasn't the same as it had been before. Maybe this was one mishap too many for Victoria to forgive.

Kaya had thought it would blow over, like the time she had convinced Victoria she could make them their own tandem hoverbike. Everything had gone great until they both ended up with broken legs after its maiden voyage. It had taken a couple weeks, but Victoria eventually came around.

Kaya knew Victoria's anger was fair on some level, but she had agreed to go along with her plan from the beginning, so the responsibility was as much hers after all. Why should she have to prostrate herself for forgiveness?

"Miss Vardan, are you still with us?" the professor asked, and Kaya hadn't realized she'd stopped speaking. She needed to get better at looking focused when she was busy thinking.

"Yes, Professor Moreau," she said simply. She already learned after the first couple "guided" prayer sessions that it was better to cooperate than be subjected to that experience. She would let them think they had won and broken her spirit. She wasn't proud enough to lose sight of the bigger picture. Her revenge would come one day, and she could be patient.

"As you all know, the Republic was founded when the faithful and loyal children of Eden came together to say enough was enough. The excess of the nobility, their penchant for war, and their worship of technology led to the downfall of the very fabric of society. They raised themselves to the position of God but offered the keys to heaven to only their chosen few. As a result, millions were relegated to menial and disposable lives in service to false gods, with no hope for salvation," Professor Moreau continued.

This lecture was one Kaya had heard many times in one form or another over the years. Moreau also made it a point to glare at Kaya and Victoria as she made her criticisms. They were the only members of the nobility currently in attendance at the Sanctum, and some professors were happy to use them as props for their own expositions.

"The leaders of multiple faiths came together under one banner, the Unified Church of God, the creator of all things, to show the people there was another, better way. Man is a bearer of culture but only so far as it is dictated by God. Then the church used this divine inspiration to usher in a new golden age under our glorious Republic. An age of worship and faith."

She always thought that if God was the creator of everything, wasn't he also the first artificer? The first being to create a creature capable of thought and creation in God's own image? Why would God then want to hide progress in a box like the Pandora Fleet worked so hard to do?

It never made any sense to her, and she knew there were others who felt the same, but no one was brave or stupid enough to raise these arguments publicly, except for the Vermillion Coalition anyway and the prophets that associated with them. It was one thing she agreed with them on but wished their methods didn't so often involve bombing innocents.

"We also live in an age of service," the professor went on. "We each in our own way give our lives to the Republic, and the Republic likewise provides us with everything we require. One group that exemplifies this devotion to service is the Knights Hospitaller, which operate most of the solar system medical services, particularly on the deepest frontiers. Today we have a special guest, the Grand Marshall of the Knights Hospitaller himself." She waved toward the doorway that opened at her queue.

Over the previous months, Kaya had listened to many guest speakers who all delivered the same tired messages. She didn't expect to hear anything different now, but still she was hopeful it might be something new and interesting.

She had intended to become a Hospitaller after her mother's death, and their message always resonated with her. It was one of the few truly good organizations she could think of. One of the ones that tried to make the world a better place, even if they were often limited to where and who they could help.

An elderly man with a white beard stepped through the open doorway. He wore a plain gray suit that was simply adorned with an insignia of his order, a white cross and star overlaying the caduceus staff. Despite his advanced age, he moved without a limp or need of a cane. It wasn't common to see people so healthy in their old age.

It took Kaya a few moments to realize that she knew the man and couldn't help but smile.

"Greetings, initiates. I am Grand Marshall Dario of the Knights Hospitaller. I see some familiar faces but also many new ones," he said with an easy smile as he scanned the room. When his gaze settled on Kaya, he smiled a little broader. "I am here today to talk about what we do and the opportunities available to clergy members within our order."

Kaya had known Marshall Dario for a long time, well, Grand Marshall Dario, she corrected herself. When she had seen him last, he had not reached such lofty heights, but she supposed that had been nearly three years ago.

He had come to visit her father about some new projects on Mercury, and during his visit he had taken hours to sit with her to discuss all sorts of things. She remembered him as a kind and genuine man, unlike so many of the snakes that slithered through their family estate. Her opinion was helped by the fact her mother had also liked him.

Dario went on to explain how the Hospitaller network functioned, administering state-run facilities throughout the solar system. The facilities they managed included medical facilities where medics and physicians worked to save lives, to various social programs and even a small military arm that provided security for far-off outposts where theft of valuable medical supplies was a common occurrence.

There were old stories of a time when the Hospitallers could cure nearly any disease, reattach severed limbs, or even grow new ones. Their abilities were said to be as limitless as the imagination of the practitioner. It was those legends that got Kaya interested in the profession as a young girl.

What got her to change her mind was when she got older and realized that those legends no longer held true. The Hospitallers of the present were nothing like those of legend. They were no longer allowed to perform those amazing surgeries, like attaching mechanical limbs or synthetic hearts. Now they had to make do with what limited medications they could get from the government warehouses or wealthy donors who took an interest in philanthropy. The situation got increasingly dire and bleak the further from the Sun you traveled.

Hearing him speak, she felt a pang of disappointment that she never got the chance to make a difference. Still, she appreciated the work men and women like Dario did. They were small glimmers of hope, like comets in the darkness of space.

When Dario finished his presentation, the class was dismissed, the students filing out of the room in quick succession. Only a few lingered longer to ask a question or to try and curry some kind of favor. There was no shortage of schemers among her classmates, although she couldn't blame them. It wasn't like she was doing anything different than them. Even if she knew her cause was the just one, it was still scheming.

Kaya approached Professor Moreau like she did most days, trying to develop a relationship with the woman. Professor Moreau was the only one of her professors who did not currently have an assistant, making her the perfect target. She would take the time to earn her trust, and eventually, at least she hoped, gain entry to the restricted area of the Boundless Library. Maybe then she could find some real answers.

"Ah, Miss Vardan," Professor Moreau said as she approached. Her professors never called her Lady Vardan.

"Professor, Grand Marshall," Kaya said, offering a slight bow of her head to each. "I hope you will excuse my interruption."

The professor maintained a stoney expression, but Grand Marshall Dario smiled broadly. "Lady Vardan, what a surprise to see you here today," he said, putting his hands on her shoulders and giving her a gentle shake. Kaya smiled.

"I assure you the surprise was all mine," Kaya said. "I see congratulations are in order on your elevation. I'm sorry to have missed the news."
He waved his hand dismissively. "You know that doesn't matter. Besides, it is a recent thing. My predecessor became quite ill, and it fell to me to take over her duties."

"I am sorry to hear," Kaya said.

"Grand Marshall Willan is well loved. I pray for her speedy recovery," Professor Moreau offered while making the sign of the star and cross.

Kaya had not known Dario's predecessor besides her name, but she had no reason to dislike the woman, so she nodded, offering her own well wishes.

"Yes, well, she has been in the Republic's service for nearly sixty-five years. We are blessed to have had her for so long. I only hope I can do her legacy justice," he said with a tinge of sadness in his voice.

"I have no doubt," Kaya offered with a reassuring smile. "My mother always thought you were among the finest in your order."

Dario laughed. "I find it hard to imagine she thought so, but I also know your mother wasn't one for false compliments." His face grew somber. "Her presence is sorely missed in this world. I am sorry I have not had the chance to visit and offer my condolences in person."

Kaya tried to put on a brave face, but the mention of her mother always threatened to make her spiral into hopelessness. "Thank you," she said, fighting back those negative feelings.

"I am sure the Grand Marshall has much to attend to Miss Vardan. I am sure you do as well," Professor Moreau said, breaking up the silence that had grown between them.

She considered a snarky retort but got herself under control before she could say anything unfortunate. She needed this woman and insulting her was not going to be an effective strategy.

"I always have time for Lady Kaya. There is no need to worry about my schedule," Dario said, coming to her rescue with a wink. "But perhaps we can catch up later in the evening? I plan to meet with Theodore at your father's villa. Assuming I don't sleep through my next meetings at least, it has been a long few days of travel," he said with a yawn and a laugh.

His words gave Kaya an idea, a risky idea, but thinking quickly she calculated it would be harmless enough.

Kaya feigned a laugh. "You remind me of my mother. She took any opportunity to catch a few minutes of rest. My father would say she was an eternal dreamer, with how easily she could fall asleep," she said, waiting to see if either of them reacted to her choice of words. She didn't want to draw unwanted attention, but she had to know if she was on the right track, and this was as good an opportunity as any she had so far.

Professor Moreau didn't seem to give any indication that she thought the statement was odd. If anything, she only looked mildly annoyed that

Kaya was still there talking. Dario, on the other hand... She thought for the briefest moment there was recognition in his eye.

"Yes, yes," he started to say. Kaya thought he might even be speaking a little faster than before. "That does sound an awful lot like her. She was nothing if not efficient."

Kaya was about to speak, but Professor Moreau cut her off, taking Dario by the arm.

"This is all very lovely, but I am afraid we must be on our way, as should you," she said, leveling a gaze at Kaya with scrunched eyebrows. "Oh, Miss Vardan, I could use your assistance this evening. After evening prayers, you can come and see me in my office."

Kaya took a deep breath and sighed, trying to hide her frustration. "Yes, Professor, perhaps tomorrow night, Grand Marshall?" she added hopefully.

"Oh, I am afraid I will be on my way to Deimos tomorrow morning, and I am not sure when I will return, but I will be sure to contact you when I do, Lady Kaya," he said, giving her a comforting look. Kaya thought this must be the same tone he used when he delivered bad news to patients or their families.

"I understand, Grand Marshall. Like my father always says, the business of the Republic never sleeps." She was disappointed she wouldn't be able to learn more but glad she got the chance to test her hypothesis.

She still didn't know what the eternal dream was, but the number of times she had heard it couldn't be a coincidence. She was determined to find someone who could tell her what it was and if it had anything to do with the future her mother always described to her. Her mother's dream for a better world without war and illness, where people could reach for the stars.

Her mind swam with the possibilities, but then her heart sank as she considered this wasn't very different from what the Vermillion Coalition preached. It wasn't the first time she had considered the similarity, but it seemed easy to dismiss as a coincidence. Besides it wasn't the message that was bad but the method of implementation.

Her mother would never have been involved with something like that. She was a duchess and a war hero, after all. She spent as much time fighting the Vermilion Coalition as anyone.

When she left the classroom, she was busy contemplating when an outstretched arm pulled her roughly into an alcove.

It didn't take her long to realize who had accosted her. "Grandmaster, what is..."

Grandmaster Dario spoke in a low whisper, "I cannot stay long or the professor will notice my absence. I don't know where you heard that blasted phrase, but you should forget it."

"I don't know what you are..."

"You know full well what I mean. Your mother died for that cursed dream, but it doesn't mean you have to. Now promise me you will drop this before it brings you and all of us more pain," he said, his eyes pleading.

"I...I will," she said, but the situation had caught her off guard. She hardly knew what she agreed to.

"Good. I will tell Theodore you are well. Take care, Lady Kaya," he said loudly, perhaps for the benefit of anyone listening, and as quickly as he appeared he was gone.

Although she had speculated the eternal dream might be connected to her mother's death, now she knew it was. There was more going on, and she felt like she was the last one to know. Her head swam with the implications of the new discovery.

Now she needed to know what the eternal dream was and then maybe she could make the final connections. She felt vindicated knowing there was more to this story than her father or anyone else knew, and now she would prove it, no matter how long that took.

ACT
2

Silas

January, 4103 U.E.T.—132 Aethra

S ILAS SAT IN one of a dozen occupied jump seats in the small landing craft taking them to the asteroid's surface. Asteroid 132 Aethra was an insignificant asteroid measuring only about forty kilometers in diameter with little to no minerals worth the expense of mining them. It also had a particularly eccentric and chaotic orbit, which made it especially difficult to track. In essence, it was a perfect place for a terrorist organization like the Vermilion Coalition to hide their operations.

A series of loud clanks filled the cabin, followed by the hiss of disconnecting air lines as the landing craft departed from his flagship. The Specter, as the ship was called, was the pride and joy of the Pandora Fleet and among the finest warships still in service throughout the solar system. It held a reputation as a menacing and powerful starship. Even at the age of 392, it remained in service as a symbol of the Republic's dominance. Silas only wished his own reputation had remained as positive over the years.

He had hoped to accomplish this mission with a simple orbital bombardment. Smashing the relatively small facility on the asteroid's surface to dust and then return to Mars. Quick, clean, safe. But they needed information that ash and twisted metal couldn't provide.

He was tired of the endless missions and ghosts they created. Violence had consumed most of his life, and now he wanted to enjoy a strong drink while he watched the sun set over the Amazonian Sea from his balcony. He sighed at the thought. It would be a while before he could do that if he ever could.

He had been hunting the Vermilion Coalition nearly his entire life. He first joined the Republic military when he attended the prestigious military academy in New Olympia. After completing his education, his military career skyrocketed, and he never looked back.

When he graduated, his first assignment involved eliminating insurgents who had set up shop on Elara, one of the moons of Jupiter. In the early days, the media and clergy labelled these disconnected groups of insurgents as vermin, but they would later band together and come to be known as the Vermilion Coalition.

All of this ran through his mind as he reflected on the fact that he was still here, thirty years later, hunting one of the many offshoots of those very same insurgents. Despite all their setbacks, they sprouted somewhere new, like interstellar bamboo that refused to be tamed or controlled.

He looked down at his digipad to see the asteroid's surface growing closer as his and other similar landing craft descended toward its surface, their thermal masking devices keeping their position hidden. The landing craft wouldn't be hidden to the naked eye, but the difficulty of targeting in space made fooling sensors the real priority.

He looked around the landing craft to assess the other soldiers with him. Men and women who proudly wore the symbol of the Pandora Fleet, a cube standing on one of its points, on their shoulders. The nine-pointed star and cross of the Republic was displayed prominently on the left side of their chests.

It was unusual for him to find himself with the initial landing party at this stage of his career, but their intel suggested that Hex, one of the most prominent Vermilion Coalition leaders, was behind this operation. If the intel turned out to be true, it was too big of a prize to entrust to anyone else, since taking her alive could produce intel that would save thousands, maybe even millions of lives.

That would likely only happen after the Frumentarii finished applying their barbaric methods, a detail he preferred not to consider more than necessary. His troops were among the best in the solar system, but torture and espionage were not their business. While the Frumentarii existed to gather information and identify threats, the Pandora Fleet existed to eliminate them. In this way, they were still intertwined despite his misgivings about their methods.

However, for this mission he had done his own information gathering, choosing not to rely solely on the Frumentarii's reports. He had failed to capture Hex three years ago in a similar operation and couldn't afford another failure.

That operation had left a high casualty count and little more to show for it. It would have cost him his position had it not been for the intervention of Duke Vardan, who with a tie-breaking vote as the Lord Eminent opted to keep Silas in his role. The situation had weighed heavily on Silas ever since, but more importantly it meant failure was no longer an option.

His aid-de-camp and brother-in-law, Commander Marcus Higgins, tried to assure him that they could handle the job without him taking such a personal risk, but he knew he needed to be there. His hold on command was tentative at best, and he needed to do everything possible to avoid forced retirement. He feared who would replace him and what they would do with his authority and what would become of his most loyal soldiers. He owed it to the people and his troops to maintain his position.

Despite his recent failures, his men didn't dislike him. In fact, it was quite the opposite. Many were nearly fanatical in their love for him, which became part of the problem. It was a situation the Republic leadership especially disliked and something they would gladly remedy if given a reasonable opportunity. The clergy didn't like when lay people, and especially nobility gained any high level of praise or authority.

Failing to capture Hex for a second time would give them a perfect pretense to get what they wanted. He wasn't very interested in politics, but he knew he couldn't play into the hands of the clerics back in New Olympia. They played that game far better than he ever could.

Marcus sat across from him with the helmet of his exoarmor retracted as he loudly chewed a chocolate chip cookie, crumbs spilling out over his armor. His armored fingers fished loudly in the bag for more, oblivious to Silas staring at him until he looked up.

"Where are my manners? Would you like one, High Commander?" Marcus said, extending the bag toward Silas.

He wanted to grimace but fought to maintain his placid expression. With his claustrophobia usually came a fair bit of nausea. "I still don't know how you can eat before an operation," he responded. Normally he could keep his claustrophobia under control, but the cramped quarters of the transport craft and his increased nerves made the whole experience more uncomfortable.

"Suit yourself. I don't think there is ever a time I don't want to eat. It's important for your energy and all that you know." Marcus chewed loudly.

"I would take one, Commander," replied a gruff tone from Silas's left.

With a laugh, Marcus pointed to the man with a crumb-covered finger. "Unfortunately for you, Murphy, I didn't offer you any. Now shut up and try not to shoot your own foot today. Alright?" The gruff man looked ready to offer a retort, but Marcus turned back to Silas before he could speak. "Really, where do we keep finding these buffoons?"

"Lined up outside yer mother's house," called a female voice from somewhere near the rear hatch that Silas couldn't see. The cabin erupted in laughter, and Silas allowed himself a laugh at his brother-in-law's expense.

"I know that was you, Mendoza. I hope you like filling requisition orders, because it's all you'll be doing for the rest of your career," Marcus shouted back, irritated.

"The nerve of these idiots," he said, shaking his head and leaning in as close as the safety harness would allow. "You don't really think Hex will be here, do you? I mean, we have been chasing her for what, three years since we saw her last? Every time we get a lead, she's already two-months gone. Besides, our intel isn't exactly from the most, uh, reliable source," he said, emphasizing the last part with raised eyebrows.

He knew Marcus was right. Their source was admittedly questionable, but his intel had never been wrong, merely outdated. The Frumentarii's reports tended to be both. The Vermilion Coalition was especially good at keeping their operations on the move and staying a step ahead.

"Jimmy has no reason to make any of this up. He wants the Vermilion Coalition gone as much as we do."

Marcus let out a sigh. "Great, best case we can do God's work replacing one set of criminals with another."

Silas didn't want to have this conversation here and now, so he stayed quiet. He didn't like working with criminals any more than Marcus did, but at least the Prometheus Group, among others, only wanted profits and a more comfortable life. The Vermillion Coalition meanwhile wanted to overthrow every known institution, from the church to the aristocracy and everything in between.

They would introduce anarchy and call it peace. Except the chaos they tried to sow would only breed more destruction, particularly for the desperate people who lacked the means to rebuild in a new world. Reforms were needed—they all knew that—even if they didn't say it, but Silas knew it had to be sustainable. Assassinating bishops and blowing up high district cafes was not that.

The faces outlined by the red glow of the craft's interior were largely familiar, but some were new to him. His fleet numbered over 20,000 souls spread out amongst the various ships, with the Specter alone housing nearly 10,000. Despite his best efforts, remembering everyone was an impossible task. Although he could trust all of them to be among the finest soldiers the Republic could produce. Getting assigned to the Pandora Fleet was no easy task.

Most of the troops were performing whatever pre-drop ritual they had become accustomed to. Some prayed, others chatted quietly amongst themselves, Marcus notably kept eating his cookies, but one man seated across and to the left of Marcus did nothing but stare straight at him, only breaking his gaze when it became obvious Silas noticed. *Well, that was strange.*

"What is your name, soldier?" he asked.

The man blinked with only the briefest moment of surprise. "Corporal Namtar Zambrano, Milord," he said in a steady tone.

"My father isn't here, soldier. Calling me High Commander will suffice. You are Mercurian, I take it?" Silas could tell from the accent he was likely from Mercury, but there was no harm in asking. Sometimes local dialects could sound similar in different parts of the solar system.

"Yes milor—High Commander, I arrived three months ago with several others from the Special Warfare Academy," he said before suddenly going silent, perhaps feeling like he was speaking more than expected.

"Don't worry. This isn't Mercury or even Mars for that matter. You can speak freely," Silas said with what he hoped was a reassuring smile. The man smiled back, but his eyes took on the unfocused appearance they had before.

I will have to keep an eye on him, Silas thought. New soldiers had a habit of being unpredictable when things went sideways, but he assumed Marcus chose him for a reason. So, he didn't feel the need to make it an issue now. As if reading his mind, Marcus gave him a nod of reassurance through a mouthful of crackers.

Looking at his altimeter, Silas clicked on his secure line and hailed the bridge of the Specter.

Within a split second, another voice chimed in, "Go for Fleet Command, over."

"Fleet Command, this is Firebird. Provide updates on visuals, over."

"Firebird, the building is still quiet. Minimal heat signatures and no sign of defenses or early alarm systems being activated. Landing craft shields and cloaking intact with 100% integrity. The rendezvous location is clear, and fleet defenses remain on high alert to assist if needed. Over."

"Fleet command, acknowledged. Over," he said, closing out his comms.

The landing crafts were remotely piloted to their landing spots as they descended through the ink toward the dark side of Asteroid 132 Aethra. The soft hum of the craft's engines was drowned out by the rustling of gear and bodies as the ship's warning lights switched to yellow, indicating they were approaching the landing zone.

"Ready up, everyone. Helmets on, weapons hot. Remember, our mission is information. We want prisoners," Silas said, emphasizing the last part.

He queued up his comms again, this time to speak to the other landing parties to ensure they understood their orders. They each responded in turn, and Silas took a deep breath as his helmet extended from the collar of his exoarmor and clicked audibly as the airtight seal was created. The familiar anxiety of claustrophobia washed over him, and it took well-practiced breathing techniques to calm his nerves. He knew from experience that once the shooting started, he would forget all about it.

He flexed his gloved hands and ensured his pistol and rail rifle were powered and ready. He also checked that the hilt of his plasma blade was securely on his hip. Lastly, he activated his personal energy shield that would deflect most things, at least until it began to overheat and failed. The optics inside his helmet made it possible to easily see the shields of his men being activated one by one.

Some weapons were more adept at piercing shields than others, with heavy ammunition and ceramic blades being the most effective. Luckily, the Coalition had little in the way of heavy ordinance, and ceramic blades were the weapons of the Frumentarii and Republican Guard and thus rare and illegal for anyone outside those organizations to possess.

Silas watched as Marcus unstrapped and checked the old fashioned pistol on his chest before securing it and hefting his own rifle. For some reason Marcus insisted on carrying the antique firearm.

Marcus's voice came through into Silas's helmet on their private line, a small display of his face in the corner of his vision.

"Do you remember how to use that thing, High Commander?" Marcus said, motioning to the rifle in his hands.

"I can still shoot better than you, Marcus," he replied coolly.

"Good! I was worried all that paperwork you've been doing recently might have dulled your senses. Plus, I wasn't looking forward to filling out all those incident reports if you shot your own foot like Murphy over there. Make sure you stay close anyway though, okay? Don't want any repeats of last time."

"I'm not trying to relive my youth, don't worry. I want to try and protect our careers," he said.

"Yea, well, they will be throwing you a parade in New Olympia after you march in there with Hex in chains," Marcus replied with a hint of sarcasm. "We will get her this time."

"I hope so, mate. There are one too many shadows in the dark these days," Silas said, not wanting to say anymore. His private comms were deleted from mission recordings—he made sure of that—but some risks still weren't worth taking.

Then the signal lights turned green, and a small jolt and vibration signified they had reached the landing zone. Another button was pressed by the pilot, and all their restraints were lifted, allowing them to move freely. The artificial gravity produced by the ship allowed them to stay firmly grounded.

"Lieutenant, deactivate gravity. Squad, prepare to exit," Marcus broadcast through their squad communications. "Heads up, everyone. Assume everything is an enemy until proven otherwise. God wills it!"

"God wills it!" came the resounding reply from all aboard, Silas included.

Silas took that moment to say a silent prayer and make the sign of the star and cross over his chest.

The lieutenant acknowledged the command, and they became weightless as they exited the ship's doorway, pulling on railings made for this purpose before finding themselves outside of the ship. Using the small propulsion suits attached to their exoarmor, they made their way toward the faint light of the facility in the distance.

The dim light was the only thing in the near pitch black of the asteroid's crater and made for an easy target. The lights became brighter, and a halt was called as they got to the edge of the facility's artificial gravity and energy shield dome. Their intel suggested the facility was being used for weapons and advanced tech manufacturing. So, he had some concerns there could be larger weaponry than they were used to seeing, but so far things remained quiet.

Using their propulsion systems, they hovered behind a rocky outcrop as their engineering officer went over to one of the pillars controlling the energy dome. The plan was to hack into the control console so they could pass through the energy shield. Other teams were working simultaneously at similar pillars around the perimeter. With any luck, multiple teams would make it through undetected.

Silas watched time click past on his helmet display until the officer signaled, they were clear for entry. Marcus took point and motioned to the rest of the team when it was safe to proceed. Silas meanwhile scanned the surroundings, looking for a threat behind every rocky outcrop.

It was a large, multistoried structure that covered approximately 100,000 square feet based on preliminary scans from orbit. It was constructed primarily of black metal and concrete with no windows or recognizable symbols. However, various discharging air vents confirmed the facility was operational.

The facility itself wasn't unusual for those found on asteroids and moons throughout the system. However, normally an operation this size would have considerable shipping traffic coming in and out of the docking bays. These were eerily quiet.

In their weeks of surveillance leading up to the assault, little more than a handful of vessels ever arrived, but the facility continued to manufacture...whatever it was they were making. The uncertainty of it all made him apprehensive.

They reached a blank area of the exterior wall, and two soldiers prepared plasma torches and breaching charges. They would be making a new doorway inside. The only problem was they didn't know what it would open to. Marcus took the opportunity to call in to the other teams.

"This is Alpha. Is everyone in position?" he said.

"Bravo team in position."

"Delta team in position."

The teams continued sounding off until all but one returned affirmative messages.

"Echo team, what is your status?" Marcus asked again, but still there was no reply.

Silas looked at Marcus who fidgeted with the comms device on his wrist, a concerned look on his face.

"Echo team, I repeat, what is your status?" Marcus said again, this time in a more aggressive tone.

Knowing something wasn't right, Silas motioned to the soldier with the torch to continue cutting.

"All units, continue, hold charges for the signal," Marcus said following Silas's lead and tried to reach Echo team one more time.

Another moment of silence passed before a breathless voice filled the channel. "Commander—we are...under...fire," the labored voice managed to get out. "We are making for the fallback position." The comm clicked off.

Marcus cursed and sent a communication back up to the Specter. "Specter bridge, Echo Team compromised, mobilize to provide orbital support and evac."

"We need to move now," Silas said, motioning for the explosive charges to be activated.

As Marcus issued the commands to the rest of the teams, all hell broke loose as floodlights illuminated their position. Bright flashes of weapons fire could be seen in the distance, but for the moment their own position wasn't under fire.

"Blow the charges! All units, move for central targets. I want Hex alive," Silas said as the flashes grew brighter and larger. It was getting closer.

"Fire!" he shouted, and they braced themselves for the loud boom of the breaching charges. The explosion produced a heavy whoosh of air that pulled dirt and rocks from around them into the building as the pressure equalized.

His troops moved into the building, their heads on a swivel as they searched for any immediate threats. They looked to be inside a small storage room lined with nondescript crates and drums, which they didn't take much time to inspect. Seeing no immediate threat, they moved to the only door in the room.

It was a large double door that didn't automatically open as they approached. One of the soldiers tried the switch, but it was locked. Without waiting for orders, the engineering officer set to work prying the control panel open and connecting his digipad.

The rest of the team kept an eye on the perimeter as bright flashes of light could be seen in the distance through the breech. With the element of surprise lost, there was no need to be subtle, and the fleet's canons and rail guns rained down heavy ordnance on the small facility.

After a few moments of furious typing and a small amount of cursing, the engineer gave the signal indicating the door was unlocked.

"We have control of the doors for now, but I'm not sure I can hold them off indefinitely. Their tech people are sarding good," the engineer said, shaking his head.

"All units, the gates are open. Proceed forward and remember your orders," Silas relayed to his troops.

"Stay here to maintain control as long as you can," Silas added to the engineer and motioned for a couple of soldiers to remain behind with him.

Marcus motioned, and several troopers moved into position, rifles held ready for whatever was on the other side of the door. The rest of their party took positions off to either side waiting for the all clear to enter behind them.

The switch was activated, and the door slid open with a whoosh and click, revealing an empty corridor except for a hastily erected barricade at the far end of the hall. Behind the barricade were at least a dozen insurgents with guns pointed in their direction. Silas had no time to process what he was seeing before the world disappeared in a blinding flash of white.

SILAS

JANUARY, 4104 U.E.T.—132 AETHRA

HIS EARS RUNG as he found himself on his knees. The display in his helmet gave him a series of error messages as it attempted to reboot. He tried to call out but quickly realized his comms were down, and all he could hear through his helmet were the muffled sounds of screaming and rail rifles firing. His arms and legs struggled to move as he suddenly felt like he was mired in concrete.

After what felt like an eternity, his exoarmor came back to life, overwhelming his senses with sounds and flashing meters as he regained control of his limbs.

"Commander!" came a shout through his ringing ears. Marcus was pulling him upright while firing back at the barricade. "Need to get you back in the field more. You forgot to look away, didn't you?"

Silas grumbled inwardly as his world stopped spinning and he regained his steadiness. "I swear I did. That wasn't a normal flash grenade. It cut out my electronics completely." Silas looked around and saw other soldiers similarly knocked down and slowly rising. Those who didn't were being dragged back into the room they came through.

"Glad it came back online before your air supply ran out," Marcus said, slapping him on the chest. "Now quit lying around."

The facility turned out to be a complex web of tight hallways lined with pipes, wires, and machinery. Lights flickered as the building's systems struggled to maintain power and pipes discharged water or gas where bullets had pierced them. All of this added to the chaos as they nervously passed each doorway searching for threats, occasionally finding brief resistance or more makeshift barricades.

Silas made a quick move around the next corner, firing toward insurgents who crouched behind an overturned desk before they returned his fire, and he was forced to take cover while he reloaded. Marcus switched places with him and unleashed a fresh barrage of bullets at the barricade.

"How many did you count, Marcus?" he asked as he reloaded his rail rifle. The rest of his men watched their rear, waiting for Silas or Marcus to issue new orders.

"Looks like at least four or five of them behind the barricade with some heavy rifles. If I was a smarter man, I might think they knew we were coming," Marcus said, sarcasm dripping off his words.

"I'm going to bet they are packing some bio mods and hyped up on nectar," Marcus said, breathing heavily between bursts of shooting. The disdain in his voice was obvious.

Silas didn't agree with the biological modifications many members of the Vermilion Coalition used to improve their bodies for combat either. It wasn't their place to modify God's creation with everything from mechanical bones and implanted weaponry to optic implants and neural sensors of various kinds.

Although nectar was maybe even worse than the bio mods because of the impact it had on their world, a drug that would enhance your focus and endurance while also dulling your inhibitions and emotional responses. At least for a time.

Nectar and bio mods were highly illegal, but they were a popular answer to the Vermilion Coalition's main problem of being heavily out-gunned in this conflict. They were willing to go to extreme lengths to get any kind of edge.

Silas fired another burst around the corner before ducking back as high-speed projectiles slammed into the metal and concrete around him.

"We can't stay here," he said tensely through the private comm link to Marcus.

"Yeah, I'm on it," his friend replied.

Silas could see him reaching for a pulse grenade in the compartment on his hip. It was an expensive weapon but was perfect for this type of situation.

"Everyone, take cover!" Marcus said to the squad before he slung the grenade around the corner.

The grenade exploded on impact, unleashing a blast of energy and shrapnel that shook the wall beside them.

Namtar, the new Mercurian soldier, was the first to look and step into the corridor. He deftly fired several shots before giving the all-clear signal.

The scene on the other side of the door was a grizzly mess of limbs, gore, and bent metal. Silas said a silent prayer as they passed and continued down the corridor. He didn't relish the violence.

"Entry teams, status check," Marcus called in over the comms channel.

They all reported similar resistance and heavy fire, but except for Echo Team they were all still operational. That was a good sign, Silas thought.

"Fleet Command, what's your status?" Silas asked his ship in orbit. They were too far into the building now to know for sure what was going on outside.

"Alpha Team, this is Fleet Command. Echo Team has been retrieved. We have the gun towers under bombardment. Shouldn't be long before they go quiet for good, sir."

Silas thought that was a small blessing at least. Although he didn't ask how many of Echo Team were left.

"Copy, Fleet Command, any sign of enemy vessels?" he asked instead.

"No, sir, our scanners haven't picked up any off-asteroid movement. We have Falcons deployed to intercept any escape pods or small craft attempting to flee."

"Thank you, Fleet Command, let me know right away if anything changes," Silas replied, closing the comms channel. "Alright, let's get moving. Keep a sharp eye. There's likely to be more traps or roadblocks."

He tried to keep his tone confident, but he was becoming concerned they would have a hard enough time getting out of here alive, let alone completing their mission. Despite the misgivings, he pushed on, hoping it wouldn't get everyone killed.

His soldiers nodded their understanding and took up positions in the column as they continued through the maze of rooms and corridors of the facility.

Most of the rooms were empty, living quarters, or supply rooms with food and basic equipment. Others were storage rooms stacked with hundreds of crates that on quick inspection housed various munitions destined for the Vermilion Coalition's war effort.

Even if the Republic did not consider this a war, the Coalition certainly did, and Silas was inclined to agree with them. He had been fighting the Coalition his entire life. What else could it be after so much time? The clergy back in New Olympia could call it whatever they wanted, but most of the citizens were smart enough to see what was really happening, even if they never said it out loud.

He wasn't outwardly sympathetic to the Coalitions cause, but given the Republic's moratorium on technological innovation and its death grip on what technology did exist, it was no wonder citizens were angry. The Republic may have been in power for hundreds of years, but its current state of decay was untenable.

He felt for these people and the horrors thrust upon them even in his lifetime. But the Republic's actions didn't absolve the Coalition of responsibility for their own atrocities. In the end, Silas wanted peace and to see his wife and daughter safe as he grew old and left this mortal plane.

He tried not to dwell in his thoughts as they continued down the seemingly endless corridors, encountering several patrols of Coalition fighters. They found dozens of them with bio mods or stolen Republic weapons.

Reaching another choke point where a barricade had been erected, they traded fire for several tense minutes before another pulse grenade cleared the way. Passing the wreckage, Silas saw several insurgents with scorched skin and missing limbs who hadn't been killed in the initial blast.

Their charred mouths moved to broadcast their pain, but there was only silence. It was a horrifying sight that made his prayers feel impotent and worthless. So instead, he fired a quick shot into each as he passed, stilling their writhing bodies, and ending their suffering.

The operation became a practiced rhythm, honed by a lifetime of war. Scan, swivel, shoot, take cover, scan, swivel, shoot, again and again. He didn't like it, but he fell easily into the rhythm of war. The terror replaced by painful monotony as his consciousness became separated from his body. In those moments, his mind became an absentee business owner. He was free from the menial work but still responsible for the bills in the end, and those bills were always large.

Marcus called a stop at a larger set of doors that failed to open when they hit the switch. A call to the engineering officer produced speedy results.

"Doors open, Alpha Team. They are trying to block our access, but so far we are holding." The lieutenant continued after brief pause, "They are burning data as fast as we can access it. You need to try and neutralize their access point to the system."

"Copy that, Lieutenant. We will try and shut down their tech crew if we can find them," Silas responded.

"We are working on locating them, sir. I will let you know," the lieutenant said.

Silas motioned to Marcus to open the door, as the rest of the team spread out on either side of the door ready for entry. He was breathing heavily, and his muscles ached. His exoarmor's shielding was good, but the energy of each blow still registered on his body. Much like his suit, he couldn't keep this up forever.

He was ready to immediately come under heavy fire when the door opened but instead, they were greeted with copious amounts of smoke and heat. Both disrupted their optics, making it hard to navigate, but luckily no one was firing on them.

Marcus gave the signal, and they began moving again, scanning for threats. None were found besides the dozens of burning machines spread throughout the large room, although weapons fire still rang out in the distance. They kept a tight formation in the low visibility.

Silas approached one of the burning machines to see if he could figure out what he was looking at, and then realization hit him. These were spacecrafts, something like a Falcon but bigger, and they looked well made from what he could assess from the undamaged remains. They were remarkable, he thought as he ran a hand along one of the smooth and undamaged body panels. Looking up from the twisted wreckage, he realized he had fallen behind the others and hurried to catch up.

He only made it several steps before he was hit sideways with tremendous force, his body skidding across the concrete floor like a child's toy. His slide stopped only by the smoldering remains of another nearby wreck.

"Ugh," he groaned into his helmet, the sound being transmitted to his team as the small weapons fire intensified. Through the pain he could hear Marcus calling out commands to take control of the situation.

He struggled to catch his breath as he stumbled to his feet, scanning with his rifle for whatever had hit him, but he couldn't see anything through the smoke until suddenly he got a blinking alert in his helmet display warning of an incoming threat.

He ducked a moment before a huge metal club would have surely split him open. *God's bones*, he thought. It would have been nice if the sensors picked that up the first time.

Spinning around to where the attack had come from, he could now clearly see the hulking form poised to take another swing at him. He thought of it in abstract terms because he wasn't sure if the creature even qualified as human anymore. It was a man so heavily modified he resembled a beast or machine more than a human. With so much nectar in his veins, he might even qualify as a feral animal. *Berserkers.*

As terrifying as they were violent, this berserker was even more terrifying than most. It had fully mechanical arms and legs and stood over eight feet tall and was twice as wide as Silas in his armor. Its red, bloodshot eyes showed nothing besides murderous rage as it charged.

Silas unloaded his rifle into the center of the beast, its armor seemingly absorbing the fire as he unloaded what rounds his rail rifle had left before rolling out of the freight train's path at the last possible moment.

The beast crashed into the surrounding wreckage, sparks flying from its metal limbs as it turned and lashed out again with its massive club.

Silas ducked and rolled again, narrowly escaping another crushing blow from the beast's club, but as he rolled, he drew the hilt of his plasma blade and with a practiced motion kindled it, the blade coming to life with thin plasma in the shape of a longsword. The hilt's containment field gave the blade its unique shape. Although many blades were similar, some forms were rarer than others, and those who used them tended to have their own preference.

Raising his blade above his head in a practiced fighting form, he waited for the berserker to attack again. He didn't need to wait long, as its massive club arced through the air with deadly malice, the berserker grunting with exertion.

Silas deftly stepped aside, swiping his blade toward the club burning a deep gouge into its surface that left the weapon damaged and bent. The berserker looked down at its damaged weapon and screamed as it tried to swing the awkward weapon at Silas again. This time the bent metal twisted awkwardly in its hand, and Silas was easily able to dodge.

This left the berserker momentarily confused. With so much nectar in its system, it was slow to process the situation and change tactics, its eyes having a glossy and distant appearance. Silas capitalized on the momentary pause, using it to move inside the berserker's guard and swiped left and right severing the vital connections of its mechanical legs with quick fluid movements.

The berserker crashed to the ground and flailed as it tried to get up and walk on its crippled legs. The pathetic sight made Silas sick to his stomach. He wanted to look away but instead moved closer and ended its life with a quick swipe of his blade across its throat. *Well, could he even call this life?*

He didn't know what would drive a man to turn himself into such a demon and wondered if demon was even the right word. Demons at least had hatred to fuel them. These...creatures existed in an emotionless void; they abandoned their souls in exchange for mechanical advantage. It made them even worse than robots. What greater sacrilege could there be then to spit in the face of God?

He ran to catch up with his team, all the while scanning the smokey room for anymore creatures lurking in the darkness.

Silas

January, 4103 U.E.T.—132 Aethra

Marcus ran toward him as he approached. He could hear a fire fight up ahead but couldn't see where the rest of the team was through the smoke.

"What the hell happened to you?" shouted Marcus in their private line as he got closer.

"I went sightseeing."

Marcus gave him a once over. "Inside a trash compactor? You look awful."

"There was a berserker."

"Sarding hell. Well, glad you are still with us. They are still putting up a hell of a fight. Maybe we need to rethink this," Marcus replied.

"You know this is too important. There's no turning back now," Silas said after a moment, and Marcus only nodded.

"What is the status of the other teams?" Silas asked as he assessed the rest of the team. They were constructing a makeshift barricade out of twisted metal, and he was glad to see they were in good shape. Their kept being interrupted by enemy bullets, but they still managed to make progress.

"They are converging on this hangar. It looks like we are pushing the Coalition back into the smaller bay down at the end," Marcus said, pointing. "We have Falcons covering the outside though, so I guess they are making their last stand. Valiant of them, I suppose."

Silas was only partially listening to Marcus while he scanned the room himself. It was then he noticed a cloaked figure enter a door in the distance. A lone figure looked over its shoulder and stuck to the shadows moving purposefully from cover to cover, obviously trying to hide their movements.

If there was some kind of exit, he would expect all the Coalition troops to retreat in that direction. Maybe there was something else in there they didn't want to get into the hands of the Republic. Data storage seemed the most likely answer.

"Marcus, hold here." He pointed to two soldiers closest to him, one of them being the Mercurian corporal, Namtar. "You two, come with me."

"Where the hell are you going?" Marcus sent over their private comms.

"I think I saw her. Hold this position and rally the others. Try to stop them from destroying everything if you can."

"You got it. Don't do anything else stupid please," Marcus said.

"Don't worry. I will only do things you would do," he said as he moved toward the doorway the cloaked figure had taken. He fired a few quick bursts at passing insurgents as they peeked out from behind their own barricade.

"That's exactly what I'm afraid of. My sister isn't the forgiving type, you know," Marcus said, breathing heavily as the rifle fire echoed through his comms.

Silas grimaced. "Yes, I'm aware. Focus on your part."

Once Silas got within a few meters of the door, two hulking forms he hadn't seen go in began exiting. They had to hunch dramatically to get their massive frames through the doorway.

Great, more berserkers.

These were similar to the one he had already dispatched, but instead of clubs these wielded vicious-looking steel blades. What little flesh remained on their bodies was covered in thick steel plates. They looked more like armored warhorses than men.

Before Silas could give an order, Namtar and the other soldier opened fire. Their shots bounced off the steel plates ineffectively as the beasts hardly reacted. Silas tried to fire at what little exposed skin he could see, but despite hitting their mark his shots didn't slow the berserkers' charge.

He was forced to dodge, and only narrowly missed being flattened. Namtar meanwhile dodged in a sure-footed display of athleticism. However, the other soldier wasn't so lucky and got cleaved nearly in two by the massive steel blade.

Silas got back to his feet, drawing his plasma blade and putting distance between himself and Namtar. It was better they didn't give the beasts an easy two-for-one target.

"Distract him!" Silas said to Namtar.

Namtar didn't respond, but he fired skillfully at both berserkers, coaxing them toward him. This was a dangerous game, but he knew a berserker's nectar-addled brain would succumb easily to tunnel vision. Distracting them was one of the best tactics they could use.

The distraction gave Silas enough time to get behind the two beasts and dispatch them quickly with well-placed blade strikes. He swiped at one's knees, leaving a shower of sparks and dripping oil before turning to the other and driving his blade deep into its heart and other vital organs.

He applied steady pressure as the plasma burned a hole into the beast's chest, leaving a burnt path of molten metal and charred flesh. He snuffed the blade to separate himself from the beast and moved aside as the weight of the berserker's body fell crashing to the ground.

The berserker with severed legs writhed on the ground in front of Namtar, who made no move to dispatch it. Instead, he stood like a statue staring at Silas. With a shake of his head, Silas walked up onto its back, rekindling his blade. He pressed the blade into the base of its skull, ending its movement for good. He assumed this was the first time Namtar would have ever fought a berserker, so the lack of action wasn't too surprising.

"You alright, soldier?" he said, moving toward Namtar as he kept his eyes on the door.

The man only shook his head slowly as he looked down at the bodies. Silas couldn't see his expression through his helmet.

He looked from Namtar to the mangled body of the other trooper. *Maybe Namtar knew the man*, he thought, chastising himself for not considering that.

"God wills it, soldier. We will say our farewells when this is over, right now we have a job to do," Silas said not wanting to waste more time. Although his words felt hollow. Decades of death and pain left him almost as numb as a berserker. He just lacked the capacity to absorb anymore tragedy.

Namtar looked at him seemingly confused before replying, "God wills it" he said weakly.

"Cover me," Silas said moving toward the doorway, his plasma blade in hand. He listened for a moment but heard nothing. A heat scan with his armor's sensors also came up negative. Kicking in the door, he entered, his blade at the ready.

The room contained several empty workstations with technicolor displays flashing error messages and other notifications into the dimly lit room. Silas scanned the workstations as he entered, the overhead lights flickering as the power grid continued to struggle.

He saw discarded notes, spilled mugs, and personal belongings of the people who must have worked in the facility, but there was no sign of the cloaked figure he was chasing. At the end of the long room, a hallway turned to the right, revealing a large office, nicer than the rest of the facility.

There, within the office, he saw his target, and now he knew it could only be one person, Hex. She was rummaging through paper files as she slammed a gauntleted fist into the digital displays. He would never forget her green exoarmor, suit of armor that was uniquely Hex's and frankly even nicer than his own, but it wasn't just her armor. The slender form that inhabited the armor was equally recognizable. It wouldn't be easy to find someone of a similar size and ability to fill that suit of armor.

However, something seemed off about her movement. He gained a reputation in his youth for his skill dueling. It was a skill he attributed mainly to his ability to read and remember the movement patterns of his adversaries. It was one thing he had a great memory for and didn't often forget. So he was sure her movements were off, but they were still so similar that most people would not have noticed at all.

She had been severely wounded during their last encounter. That may have been years ago, but perhaps she still suffered from poorly healed wounds. His final strike had left her with a nearly severed leg, a wound that would have been difficult for even the most accomplished Republic surgeons to repair. For the Vermilion Coalition, it would surely have been a major strain on their limited resources, if even possible at all.

"Hex," he broadcast through the speaker in his armor as Namtar took up a position behind him, raising his rifle up toward the target.

"Surrender and this all ends. The facility is surrounded, but you can still save the lives of your men."

His identity was clearly marked by the insignia on his armor, so he made no effort to mask his voice. She would know it was him anyway.

He hoped she believed him because he meant what he said. The men would be spared death if they surrendered. They would be sent to a penal colony on some far away moon or asteroid where they could labor toward absolution of their sins. The same couldn't be said for berserkers or the Coalition leaders, but it was the best he could offer.

Hex looked from the display as if startled when she heard the voice. She stared across the workstations toward the door Silas was blocking. The door appeared to be her only exit.

Silas shifted the grip on the hilt of his blade and moved into a defensive posture.

"You know there's no way out of this for you," he said while holding his position. He knew he had her dead to rights. She could try to blast through what was likely several feet of reinforced concrete, but the blast needed for that would kill her in the process. No, her only choice was to go through him.

What was odd was that she didn't move. She continued to stare at him for a long time before she moved slowly around the workstation. Her hand deftly brushed her hip where she drew her own plasma blade, kindling it in one smooth motion.

Silas tensed as the long straight blade extend from its hilt. He didn't want to fight her again. It had been a close thing last time, and he felt like he had aged quite a bit in the last three years.

Out of his periphery, he saw Namtar raising his rifle to open fire.

"Stand down!" Silas sent on their comm line. "Stay back and guard the door."

He would need space to fight if it came to that, and a single rifle wouldn't be much use against the shielding capabilities of her exoarmor.

He could hear the intensity of the battle softening and figured Marcus must be getting things under control. That was good. It meant he could focus on Hex.

They began to circle each other like apex predators. He studied her movements, looking for the familiar rhythm that he had obsessed over after he failed to capture her last time. It didn't take him long to realize she didn't appear injured at all. She was moving as gracefully as he remembered, but her movements were...different. Maybe he had misremembered.

He pushed the thought to the back of his mind; he could capture her first and then figure that out. Meanwhile, Hex continued her wordless dance, her blade held in front of herself in a form matching his own.

"It doesn't need to end this way, Hex. There is still hope for your people to make it out of this alive."

"There is no life in your prisons. Only in victory or death will my people have hope or peace. They will not yield. To yield is to forsake their souls," came a distorted voice from behind the opaque green and black helmet.

Silas sighed, tired of going down this same road time and time again. He only wished people like Hex and the Coalition would see reason and stop this pointless campaign. Spare the lives of their own and the innocent who die by the droves following their ideology.

Instead, they continued to fight and die for a reality that would never be. There was war, pain, and loss in this life and maybe a promise of something better in the next, but it was not guaranteed for everyone. That was the way of things.

"Then they will burn for their sins," Silas said, "alongside their friends. In the end, they will recognize the lies of the Coalition, but by then it will be too late. If they repent, there might still be hope of forgiveness, hope for their souls." He echoed the lines he had spoken so many times before. The doctrine of the church came so easily to his lips.

"Your words are as hollow as your soul and those of the clerics in New Olympia. The common people get sacrificed for the good of what, the few elites who benefit from their labor? No, we will not yield for their benefit. You cannot contain this storm in your box, High Commander. It is time to step aside and allow this storm to prepare the ground for new life. For a new future for all of us."

She seemed to be almost pleading.

Silas felt a slight tug in his heart but knew that the ideology of the Coalition, however flowery and however tempting, was ultimately empty. Words on a page meant to tempt those away from the proper order of the world. Like the serpent in the garden of Eden. Even if the garden had become rotten, it was still the garden he was tasked to protect. God could see him struck down now if this wasn't the path he was meant to follow.

"If you want to create a new world," Silas said, "then be a voice for peace. Stand down and implore your people to do the same. It is easier to build with a hammer than a gun." He attempted a peaceful resolution once more.

He had to try. The recording from his camera would be reviewed by the Frumentarii, and they would be sure to find any pretense to blame him for failing to capture Hex alive as instructed. Better not to give them any more reasons to have him removed from his command.

Before Hex could respond, Silas saw the familiar glow of a plasma blade reflected behind him. Marcus must have returned.

"Marcus?" he asked through his private comms channel without turning around. He couldn't risk turning his back on her.

"This peace," Hex said, "cannot be bestowed by you or the clerics. It must be earned by the people who strive for it and upon whose backs the new world will be created. The true garden of Eden." Hex took another step forward, her blade held ready and her other hand reaching for something he couldn't see. The angle of her body and the furniture in the room blocked his view. His body tensed as the world slowed down around him.

She began shaking her head when Marcus responded.

"We are a bit busy here. What do you need, Commander?" Marcus replied between labored breaths, the sound of gunfire ringing out through the audio in his helmet. Silas scrunched his brow.

His mind tried to process the new information. If it wasn't Marcus, then who? He tried to reposition so he could see behind himself without turning his back on Hex.

In the moment Silas shifted, Hex reached to her hip and threw a grenade toward him. His world was turned upside down in a blur of light and sound that overwhelmed the systems of his exoarmor for a second time.

It didn't recover like the last time and his air gauge was venting rapidly. By God's bones, a line must have been cut. He gasped as a primal fear began to take over, and he reached desperately for a lifeline that didn't exist.

Through the smoke, he briefly saw the flash of a plasma blade coming toward him before it bit into his leg, burning through armor and flesh. The wound forced him to one knee. He could smell the burnt flesh before his armor's systems were able to cycle the air and seal the wound. He attempted to swing blindly through the smoke but didn't hit anything, his heart beating faster as the oxygen gauge spiraled lower at a frightening speed.

Then he took another hard hit as something or someone collided into him from the side as he stood up, knocking his blade from his hand and sending him sprawling on the floor where he slammed his head on something hard. The helmet took most of the impact, but without functional shield systems it was little help, and his head began to cloud, and his vision blurred.

He tried to call Marcus, to warn him, but nothing seemed to work. He could vaguely see the light of plasma blades striking each until all he could hear was a muffled scream as his world went black.

"Marcus!" he cried out into his helmet, but he knew it was worthless. No sound would get through.

Was his friend already gone? He could only hear the labored sound of his breathing as his vision faded and the air left in his helmet became thick and humid. The distant sounds of battle were only a whisper as he lost consciousness.

13

Silas

January, 4103 U.E.T.—132 Aethra

"Silas…"

"Silas, can you hear me?"

Was that Marcus? Silas's thoughts were coming slowly as the fog of confusion receded. His eyelids felt heavy as he tried to open them, and the sudden light was blinding.

His helmet must have been retracted, because the air had an overwhelming smell of burnt plastic and sulfur.

Silas coughed, "Yes, I'm here." His voice was gravelly.

As his vision cleared and his coughing subsided, he took stock of the room. It looked much the same as before, but debris and dust littered the floor. He looked for Hex's body but was disappointed when all he saw was the lifeless form of Namtar being loaded onto a stretcher. *Another one dead.*

"That's it. Get it out," Marcus said, helping him sit up.

"I'm OK…" he finally said as the coughing subsided. His mind catching up to his vision. He fumbled around for the hilt of his blade but it was harder to find since the blade would have snuffed itself out when it left his hand.

"Hex! Where is she?" he shouted, attempting to stand.

"Woah, easy!" Marcus shouted back, putting his hands on his chest to restrain him. "It's over, Silas. You need to stay down. The medics are on the way."

"I don't need a medic. I need my blade!" he said, shoving Marcus away.

"Sure thing, Commander," Marcus said, moving back from Silas with a sigh.

He stood crossing his arms while Silas struggled to get to his feet. He found the hilt of his blade and reached down, but his head swam, forcing him back to the ground before vomiting, his exoarmor creaking with his movements. Without power going to the armor, it was difficult to move.

He spit the bile from his mouth and sat back down. His heart rate was steadying, and he tried to make out what was going on. Burned wreckage was all around and more soldiers could be seen searching through the rubble. He didn't hear anything more than distant and sporadic gunfire.

"Where is she?" he tried to ask, his sore throat making it sound more like a growl.

"She's gone. Looks like your armor is fried. We need to get you out of here to be safe," he said and gave Silas a hand up.

The dead armor made it feel like he was covered in cement. "You killed her then? Take me to the body."

"No, what I mean is she is *gone*, flew the coop."

Silas looked at his friend dumbfounded. "What, how?"

"Like I said, we need to get you back to the ship and then debrief. The crew can handle the cleanup here," Marcus said, putting an arm on Silas's shoulder, trying to casually guide him toward the transport that was waiting for them.

Silas stopped walking, brushing aside the arm. "What do you mean gone? We had an entire fleet in orbit outside the facility. How in the—" he started, his voice intensifying before Marcus cut him off.

"Listen, I don't have the answers, but we don't have time to discuss it now. The integrity of this hangar is questionable at best after the thousands of holes we put in it. The engineers are trying to get the shields up, but the O_2 is depleting fast. So, if you don't want to die, we need to go. *Now*," he emphasized while pulling Silas toward the waiting transport. Marcus wasn't waiting for his cooperation.

Silas conceded and leaned into Marcus, thankful for the support as his head kept spinning. Other soldiers ran over to help, but Silas waved them off. He would be fine, and it was more important they secured the rest of the facility. Hopefully they hadn't had enough time to destroy whatever secrets they kept here. He was still curious about the burnt spacecraft littering the hangar.

He replayed what happened in his mind, trying to figure out what went wrong. He had encountered Hex after dispatching her berserker bodyguards. Namtar and another soldier whose name he didn't know were with him. Both had died, but it was Hex he was most worried about now. He couldn't fathom how she could get away from him for a second time.

His heart sank as that realization set in, knowing his options for getting out of this mess were getting smaller. The Council of Bishops would only tolerate so many failures, even from a hero like him. Even the Assembly of Lords, which was predominantly on his side, couldn't defend him from this if the council decided to act.

They reached the transport, and Marcus helped Silas into a seat, his armor protesting as he tried to bend his limbs. Marcus sat in a seat next to him and signaled for the pilot to take off.

Silas let out a groan as he sat back in the seat, detaching his retracked helmet and throwing it to the side.

"Don't torture yourself. We will find her," Marcus said as they began their departure.

Silas tilted his head back staring at the ceiling. How many times were they going to say the same thing? How many times had they chased down leads just to come up short? How many more Coalition attacks will the citizens of the Republic have to endure before they finally capture their leaders and stop them for good? There were so many questions, and with every passing year he had fewer answers.

"It has been years since we were this close, and it turned into a debacle," he said, anger creeping into his voice.

He cursed as he tried to wipe the sweat from his brow. The mechanical joint of his arm refused to move, rendered lifeless by whatever unholy device the Coalition had used or just the poor state of his equipment. Even with a healthy budget, their equipment was beginning to decay like everything else.

"How can I fight when I can barely walk? Hex threw some kind of grenade, and then suddenly I was on the ground," Silas snapped, trying hard to contain his anger. The outburst was unbecoming of his position.

"We will have the engineers look over your armor and see what happened. It might have been bad luck. A faulty exosuit isn't that uncommon," Marcus suggested.

"Maybe, but my armor is not some rusty relic."

"Even new things break sometimes," Marcus offered.

Silas changed subjects.

"But what I really want to know is how she managed to escape with our entire fleet encircling her position," he said, his voice growing cold.

Raising an eyebrow, Marcus leaned in closer.

"Do you think she had help escaping?" Marcus said in a nearly silent whisper.

"What other explanation is there?"

"I'd rather think someone made a mistake instead of dealing with having a legitimate spy in one of the most elite military units in this solar system," Marcus said, and he looked unconvinced.

"I suppose...but that seems unlikely with the amount of ships and sensors they would have had to avoid. If they did have help, it was a lot of it," Silas said, finally managing to wipe the sweat from his brow. Armor got ungodly hot without its cooling systems operational. "Run through all the data when we return to the ship, but do it quietly. Handpick someone for the task and tell no one else."

"Understood," Marcus said, but he seemed distracted.

"What aren't you telling me?" asked Silas, sensing something was off, and his heartbeat quickened as he instinctively began to scan his surroundings.

"It can wait until we get back to the Specter."

"How about you tell me now," Silas pressed. He would rather get all his bad news at once.

"Well, when I got to you, I found this on the ground," Marcus said, reaching behind his back to unholster the hilt of a plasma blade. It seemed like a typical blade at first, but what stuck out immediately was how new it looked, and it was not a model that was immediately familiar to him.

All the plasma blades in existence were relics from before the Time of Chaos and the Great Solar War. There was no exception to this. There hadn't been a new blade made in hundreds of years. During those times, only the nobility and knights carried blades. After the war, what few survived began to be hoarded by the remaining aristocracy. At least those not taken as war trophies by Republic leaders.

They were complicated devices, and while their adornments often wore off or broke, the core device was very robust and extremely difficult to render inoperable. Although there were Republic artificers who could perform minor repairs on existing blades, there were none who could build a new one. There were parts they had no way to recreate. Yet this one looked like it came right off a Martian assembly line.

Silas grabbed the hilt from Marcus. He tested the hilt's heft; it felt beautifully balanced even without the blade kindled. On closer inspection, he could see what looked like an intricate series of runes carved into its silvery surface, but the symbols meant nothing to him. He kindled the blade, and it came to life casting its soft glow through the cabin.

The style of the blade was not too unlike his own, but it was thinner and shorter. However, that wasn't particularly odd. What surprised him the most was the near-perfect shape of the resulting plasma. There was hardly any distortion in the blade whatsoever. It was unlike anything Silas had ever seen.

"This is incredible," he said, staring at the blade before snuffing it out. "You said you found this in that office where I fought Hex?" Silas asked, still mesmerized by the blade's beauty. Even his old family blade, steeped in tradition, felt lacking next to this work of art.

Marcus nodded. "But there's more."

"More?" Silas asked, surprised.

"I found it with Corporal Zambrano."

Silas handed the hilt back to Marcus for safekeeping. He scrunched his brow as his brain tried to catch up with what he was talking about.

"Who?"

"Corporal Namtar Zambrano, the trooper you had with you. The Mercurian," Marcus added, surprised that Silas seemed to have already forgotten.

"Oh, yes—he was new to the fleet, seemed nervous on the shuttle," Silas said. "Seemed fine as we fought through the halls, but I'll admit I was distracted."

"This was in his hand," Marcus said, his expression serious.

"Are you sure? That can't be right..." Silas said in disbelief. "Maybe he picked it up after Hex dropped it?" No, even as he said the words, he knew they sounded wrong. He could remember seeing the glow of a plasma blade behind him before things spiraled out of control. He had assumed it was Marcus with him, but now it sounded like it was Namtar, but how could that be possible?

Marcus began to say something, but Silas waved him off.

"No, never mind, we need to find out what's going on, but this needs to stay quiet. Store that somewhere secure. Does anyone else know?" he asked.

Marcus wrapped the hilt in a small sweat towel he pulled from one of the ship's cabinets.

"No one. I was the first one in the room and spotted it right away. I knew better than to leave something like that out in the open." Marcus knew well that strange findings tended to produce worse outcomes for those involved.

"Good, let's keep it like that until we can get to the bottom of all this." His mind was racing through dozens of possibilities as to why Namtar, a young and unknown corporal, possessed such a fine blade. Even ignoring the exceptional quality of the weapon, why did he even have any plasma blade at all?

He considered the most likely answer. Namtar was a high-ranking Frumentarii in disguise sent to watch over his shoulder. It wouldn't be beyond possibility. It would explain the man's exceptional athleticism and unflinching demeanor in the face of the berserkers, although he had reacted strangely after it had been dispatched.

"Where is his body now?" Silas asked.

Marcus scrunched his eyes. "The man is still alive."

"Alive? He looked to be in bad shape when I was coming to."

Marcus shrugged. "Well, I found him lying unconscious. His armor was eviscerated, but somehow he was still breathing. Seems like he was very lucky. I had them cart him off."

Silas grimaced. "Have him put under observation, but don't make it obvious. I want to be informed as soon as he's awake."

"Of course."

"Did you find anything else interesting?" Silas asked.

"I was too busy with you to find out, but we have teams on the ground now. We should have everything swept and inventoried over the next couple of days."

"Good. Did you get a good look at those ships in the hangar bay? They looked like Falcons but larger," Silas said, his mind going back to the burning vessels.

"Not more than I could see during the fighting. It looked like they were still building them though. When we pushed into the hangar, they started torching them. I was hoping we would find one mostly intact, but it doesn't look good."

Silas nodded. "That would be ideal." He knew that was probably a long shot.

The Vermilion Coalition would sacrifice years of innovation to deny the Republic the knowledge of its existence. They had always seemed proficient at engineering solutions to their technological disadvantage, but this seemed more advanced than anything he had seen before.

He was suspicious that they had more help than usual. Someone was providing them with raw materials and high-end manufacturing equipment. A disgruntled high district magnate or disillusioned lesser noble were the prime suspects that came to his mind.

"You know we need to go pay him a visit," Marcus finally said, breaking the silence.

"Yes."

Silas knew they had to go to Tiyas to see their friend turned informant. Something they had avoided doing to protect him as much as themselves, but time was running out now, and they needed honest answers.

"Once we are done here, we will set a course back for Mars."

"Good, I look forward to it," Marcus said while stretching his arms and neck as if preparing for a brawl.

"It's not going to be that kind of meeting," Silas said, giving Marcus a look.

"I always told you that traitor was up to no good. This confirms it for me," Marcus said, scowling.

"Hex was where he said she would be. Maybe he didn't know about the rest."

Marcus grunted, "Or he set us up and they just failed to finish the job."

Silas had considered that possibility as well.

CHAPTER

14

SILAS

JANUARY, 4103 U.E.T.—SPECTER

SEVERAL HOURS HAD passed since Silas returned to the Specter. He had left his broken armor with the engineers to pick apart while he went for a medical evaluation. They performed a routine series of checks and tests before clearing him from the med bay. The wound on his leg had been deep, but it missed damaging anything vital. It would leave a nasty scar, but he would survive.

Before leaving the med bay, he stopped to speak with the soldiers who had been injured in the operation, taking a moment to laugh or joke with each of them. It was something he had always made a point of doing, and his men always seemed to appreciate it. He was surprised to see an unconscious Namtar being tended to before he departed. He said a silent prayer for the man as he left.

Lastly, he went to the morgue where the fallen were being gathered. Over a dozen bodies lined up in neat rows with flags bearing the nine-pointed star and cross of the republic pulled over their bodies. It was a sight he was much too familiar with. He made the sign of the star and cross, offering a prayer before each body. His eyes were heavy and glassy by the time he finished. With his duty executed, he finally made his way back to his quarters.

Passing through the familiar halls of the ship, he was greeted by nearly constant salutes as he passed dozens of crew members going about their assigned duties aboard the large vessel.

The Specter was a large, nearly two-kilometer-long warship and one of the largest ships still in operation among the Republic fleet, only out-classed by dreadnaughts and carrier ships. The Pandora Fleet also included several destroyers, frigates, and corvettes to round out its combat capabilities, ensuring it remained a formidable force.

For generations, the biggest naval threat had been petty pirates or the occasional obstinate lord or tyrant, so the massive warships mainly served as operating bases. There was no one alive who remembered the massive naval battles of their ancestors.

Silas had spent the early days of his career aboard other ships or stationed on distant astral outposts, but now all his time was spent stationed aboard the Specter. The unique creaking of its hull and the endless nests of pipes, wires, and metal scars that lined its pathways were as familiar as the wrinkles and scars on his face.

The truth was they both should be retired, but he feared who would replace him and what they would do with his authority. So, he fought with all his strength to stay in his position. It was for the good of his men and republic citizens.

Silas arrived at his private quarters. The large double doors slid open as the guards saluted him. As he entered the sitting room, his valet Charles stood waiting to greet him. Charles was an old man, the wrinkles on his face deep and the hair on his head stark white. His slender frame gave purchase to sinewy muscles that were easy to dismiss due to his slightly hunched posture.

"Good day, Milord," Charles said in his typical monotone voice. Charles was a serious man who was slow to trust and even slower to laugh. His world was one of strict social rules and procedures that were as sacrosanct as any the Republic could propose.

"Mr. Beach, how are you?" Silas asked. Charles insisted Silas only use his last name.

"I am well, Milord. Clean clothes are laid out, and I have requested a meal be brought up. I assumed you would prefer to eat in your quarters this evening. Do you require anything further?"

"That will do for now, thank you," he said, making his way to the next set of doors leading to his office. Charles was right that he had no desire to dine formally with the senior officers. It was then he looked at his watch to check the time.

Time in space was relative after all, but aboard any naval vessel day and night cycles were simulated to match Unified Earth Time, which was used throughout the solar system. He was surprised to confirm it was already dinner time.

"Very well, sir," Charles said with a short bow before returning to other business in his adjoining room.

Silas thanked him again with a nod and passed into his office. In the middle of the office sat a large wooden desk flanked by a small sofa and a pair of chairs that created a small sitting area. The walls were lined with ornate wooden bookshelves that felt out of place aboard the otherwise metal-clad and largely utilitarian vessel. The shelves were lined with books, picture frames and various medals and war trophies Silas had collected over his career.

After passing through a small dining area and day room, he arrived in his bedroom. In the bathroom, he ran a shower and walked back to his bedroom while he waited for the steam to accumulate.

He sat down at the foot of his bed with a sigh and rubbed his face. The pressures of the day beginning to catch up with him all at once. He knew that tough times were approaching, and there would only be so much he could do to navigate them. The clerics and his rivals would be coming for him soon.

His eye caught the framed photos on the dresser across the room, and he got up to examine them. It was a photo of his wife Diana and daughter Catherine, who was young in the photo, maybe about ten or eleven, he thought. It was from a family vacation to a beautiful resort on Venus. One of the rare vacations they ever took since Silas rarely ever had the time.

They had taken a couple of trips after that one, but by the time Catherine was a teenager they had effectively stopped completely. It was around that time that she stopped looking at him with that unconditional love and respect a child has for their parents, but he knew that was the way of things.

Their relationship became increasingly strained as his duties grew, and he was off planet more and more, which was one of his greatest regrets in life. He didn't blame her for resenting him, but his position was what offered his family the best opportunities for success. He only hoped she would realize as she got older and had children of her own why he did what he did to keep her safe.

His wife Diana always argued he could do better if he wanted to, and maybe she was right. He did put his work first in a sense, but it was only because he saw the success of his career being hand in hand with the success of his family. Maybe she was right though, and all that was an excuse to justify his own selfishness.

There was a time he enjoyed the fame that came with being a hero of the Republic, but now he could only shake his head at the memory. He had been so naïve in many ways. Now in these moments he missed his family and wanted nothing more than their loving and supporting presence. Maybe that was even more selfish of him.

Reaching for his digipad, he selected his wife's contact and hit connect. In the familiar silence as the delayed transmission went through, he waited for a connection to be established. He realized then that he hadn't considered the time difference or even what he would say. All he knew was he wanted to speak to his family.

As the silence dragged on, he knew it was because she hadn't yet accepted his comms request. He was too close to Mars for the delay to be that bad. Finally though, there was a familiar click as the connection was established. A moment after that, a soft but firm and slightly annoyed voice responded.

"How bad are you hurt this time?" Then there was a pause. People used to off-planet communications were practiced in allowing time for delays until you became accustomed to what the conversation speed would be.

"I... I'm not hurt. I wanted to speak to you." He wasn't sure what else to say.

Diana sighed, maybe from relief, but he wasn't sure.

"I am sure it will be okay," she said next. She knew the conversation was at best being recorded and at worst actively surveilled. So she was careful not to say much.

"Maybe. Is Cat with you?" Silas didn't have a reputation for exaggerating anything, so she would know that maybe was likely serious.

"No, she's gone off world." There was an uncharacteristic pause. "To the Far Coast, she left slightly after you did for your last tour."

Silas let that hang in the chasm of space between them. His daughter had left for the Far Coast months prior, and no one thought to even mention it to him. Surely if his family hadn't told him his own intelligence officers would have known and thought to mention it. His emotions danced now between concern and anger as he considered all the possibilities.

"The few times I could call, you told me she was indisposed. Then when I finally spoke to her, she was already gone?" he said in disbelief, thinking back to the last time he spoke to her what had to be several weeks earlier.

It was a quick call, and their connection had been poor, so they barely shared more than a few words. Their relationship had been strained for a long time, so he just assumed he would try again to reach her in a few weeks' time and hope she was more open to speaking.

"She didn't want you to worry," Diana said to fill the silence. He knew what that meant. She didn't want him to know because she didn't want him to stop her.

"Where did she go?" He finally managed to get out, his voice holding back on the precipice of rage.

"She accepted a job as a physician at the hospital of St. John...on Oberon," she added the last part after another delay.

Silas cursed audibly as his head swirled with anger and confusion.

The Knights Hospitaler administered hospitals all over the solar system. Their headquarters were even close to home on Phobos, but she picked an outpost on the Far Coast, a place filled with pirates and other miscreants, as far from the watchful eyes of the Republic as possible.

It was a place where lesser nobles went to earn fame and fortune or lose both in dramatic fashion. A desperate place for desperate people. A place littered with the lifeless husks of the solar system attempting to cling to whatever semblance of life they had left. Some might say it was a place where the help of the Hospitallers was most needed, but all he knew was that it was no place for his daughter.

"You...allowed this?" he drawled out through clenched teeth.

Diana let out a short and sarcastic laugh. "She is an adult, unless you have forgotten, and even worse, a Beckett. There is no controlling either of you. I'm sure she was going to tell you soon," she said, at least throwing out one sorry attempt at sympathy.

Silas unclenched his jaw and took control of his anger. This wasn't the time or place.

"I'll be back on the surface soon. We can talk then," he said, his voice returning to its typical neutral tone. He had made the switch back to the void as Diana put it. Turned off from the world.

"OK." The line clicked dead. She had given up on humoring him years ago when he got this way.

He stared at his digipad, keying in the numbers to Catherine's device but unable to press connect. He was angry but also didn't know what he would say even if he reached her, so he cursed again, throwing his digipad aside and went to take the shower he originally intended.

The water had turned off automatically due to water control measures aboard the ship, but luckily the faucet in his quarters could be easily turned back on. One of the best perks of his position, he thought.

Although their water supply was effectively infinite, they rationed water to lower the strain on the aging infrastructure. Despite these kinds of measures, it seemed to Silas like repairs became more costly and challenging with each passing year.

The water was hot and refreshing as it fell over his head. He lingered there in the heat until the water automatically shut off again but didn't turn it back on. He still had a lot to do, so he made his way back to his room and dried off before dressing in the clean black fatigues Charles had laid out on his bed.

He wanted nothing more than to slip into the bed, but he resisted the urge and walked back to the small dining room in his quarters. He was momentarily startled to see Marcus sitting at the table, quietly scrolling on his digipad.

"You know you have your own quarters, Marcus," he said, walking toward his usual seat at the head of the table. "You are lucky Charles lets you in."

Marcus scoffed, "That shriveled mummy doesn't even know I'm here."

As if on cue, Charles's voice could be heard from the other room. "Will you be staying for dinner, Sir Marcus?" Charles said, using Marcus's knightly rank like he usually did.

Charles was a believer in following the ancient social etiquette of the Solar Empire, which made him a bit eccentric, but he was far from the only person who held onto nostalgia for a different time. Luckily Charles knew how to walk the fine line of avoiding treasonous behavior, and lucky for Marcus he was Silas's brother-in-law and as family got more of a pass to break with proper etiquette around Silas.

Marcus cleared his throat. "No, Mr. Beach," he said, trying to find his previous confidence. Silas only chuckled as he sat down.

Marcus's expression suddenly grew serious. "Don't get comfortable. The Vice Admiral called a meeting," Marcus said, standing up.

Silas cursed silently, rubbing his palms into his face.

"Couldn't he wait until tomorrow," Silas said, rhetorically. Vice Admiral Zhou served as the Republic Navy liaison, and although he wasn't in control of the Pandora Fleet, he outranked anyone else aboard and could call such a meeting whenever he wished.

The Pandora Fleet operated largely independent of the greater Republic Navy and Army, but it was still privy to its chain of command. In this case, since the company was not operating on land, the Navy took precedence.

Marcus shook his head. "I tried to tell him you were stuck in the medbay, but he had his lackeys check the records. Damn bureaucrats track everything. They might be worse than the Frumentarii," he said sarcastically.

Silas grimaced at that, but there wasn't much else to do but get the conversation over with. "Mr. Beach, we will be back for dinner."

"Of course, Milord. I will have it prepared for your return," Charles said, having arrived in the room beside Marcus, seemingly out of nowhere.

"Curses, man!" Marcus exclaimed, momentarily startled.

Silas laughed as he slapped Marcus on the shoulder and walked for the door. "Come on. You can ask Mr. Beach for stealth lessons later."

"You know it's unnatural," Marcus said as they walked out into the corridor. "What are you going to tell the esteemed vice admiral?" he said, becoming serious.

Silas only offered a small shrug as they walked, the crew of the ship buzzing past them going about their assigned duties like bees in a hive.

"What more can I say but the truth? If he hasn't already watched the recordings, he will soon," he said quietly while returning a salute with a fist to his heart to a passing officer. Despite the recent failures, there were many among the crew who remained immensely loyal to him. He was thankful to have the support but wary of abusing the faith and trust they put in him.

The meeting room was not far from his quarters, so they arrived there quickly. The door was flanked by a pair of guards in crisp uniforms, their rifles slung over their shoulders at the ready. They saluted with fists to chests as Silas and Marcus entered. The room held a large meeting table in the center with comfortable chairs. Empty glasses and pitchers of water and wine sat on a small banquet flanked by a ready servant in a steward's uniform.

Only a few of the seats had been filled with the most senior leadership available aboard the Specter. Vice Admiral Fu Zhou occupied one end of the table with a young captain who served as his aide-de-camp, and Colonel Taylor, the Republic Army liaison, who was a no-nonsense type of officer.

Captain Lancaster of the Pandora Fleet, a grizzled veteran who served as Silas's second in command and captain of the Specter anchored the other end of the table where an empty seat waited for Silas.

A few other lower-ranked officers were present, but the captains and commanders of the other vessels within the Pandora Fleet had not been called to attend, so many of the seats remained empty. Silas had no doubt this was on purpose to limit the number of friendly voices he had in the room.

Silas offered a salute to Vice Admiral Zhou before taking his seat at the opposite end of the long table while Marcus took a seat across from Captain Lancaster.

The vice admiral was a slim man of average height in his late fifties that, unlike Silas, looked every year his age. Despite his aged appearance, his hair was perfectly coiffed and his uniform impeccably tidy. He looked more like an old courtier than a senior military commander.

"Thank you for joining us, High Commander," Zhou said, making it a point not to call him Lord Beckett. His speech was a well-practiced Martian lilt common amongst the highest social rung in the capital. His words were full of venom but masked behind a veil of propriety. Zhou might be the ranking military commander, but he was no aristocrat, despite his obvious aspirations.

Zhou enjoyed reminding Silas that he could tighten his collar if he chose to, but he was at least smart enough to know that power could only be used once, and even then, it would be a dangerous proposition.

"Vice Admiral," he responded curtly, "I expected to have this debriefing tomorrow with the entire fleet high command present." He motioned to all the empty seats in the room.

"Unfortunately, High Commander, time has grown tight on dealing with these matters. The Council of Bishops is expecting my report promptly," Zhou said in a mock apology.

Silas was too practiced at this game to let Zhou get any kind of rise out of him.

"I am sure you are anxious to provide your report, but the facility has not yet been cleared and inventoried."

Zhou waved his hand dismissively. "I am sure your techs and engineers will have that busy work completed soon. The important point is that I understand the Vermilion Coalition leader—Hex, I believe—has escaped you once again," he said with a smile on his face.

Silas knew Zhou was enjoying this little show, but he wouldn't give him the satisfaction of playing into it.

"We are combing the area, but she escaped the facility. With the rushed nature of this meeting, I have not had an opportunity to gain more details. As you likely already know, I was in battle with several berserkers before being incapacitated." He knew this wouldn't sound much better, but it was the truth, and there was no point trying to cover up his own failure with flowery words or vague statements. That was a tactic of cowards and politicians, and he was neither.

Zhou's smile never left his face as Silas spoke. "Yes, how unfortunate," he said before continuing in an even more pretentious tone than before.

"As undoubtedly you are aware, the Vermilion Coalition presence has been escalating unabated for the past two years," Zhou began as he summarized a common list of events and failures in a tired speech Silas had heard too many times. "Meanwhile the Prometheus Group has gained a stronger foothold than ever before among the seedier aspects of our republic and seem to have ceased hostilities with the Vermilion Coalition."

At that last statement, Silas's ears perked up. Now that was something he hadn't heard. The last intel report he had received suggested the Vermilion Coalition and Prometheus were still thoroughly at each other's throats, a state of affairs that the Republic was happy to allow so long as it weakened both treasonous groups and limited the use of Republic resources. Although both groups sought reform, their methods and end goals kept them at odds.

"To make matters worse, prophets seem to be proliferating at an unprecedented pace. One in particular seems to be amassing a large following. Some have even taken to calling him 'Aelius the Divine' because of his ability to heal any sickness with a single touch," Zhou said this with complete incredulity.

Silas was becoming exasperated with these proceedings. "Thank you for this update, Vice Admiral, but let me remind you that I receive the same security briefings as you and fail to see your current point."

Zhou's lips tightened, and his cheeks reddened. "The point..." he emphasized slowly, "is that your failures are beginning to mount, and excuses are ceasing to be sufficient."

"Don't you mean our failures, Vice Admiral? Or am I to be blamed for the failings of every aspect of the Republic's Strategic Command? If that is the case, let me know and I will bare my neck now and warm the block for you," Silas responded coldly. Although the Pandora Fleet played a significant role in providing security to the Republic, it was also only one part of the overall security and military infrastructure.

Zhou blanched slightly, losing his previous fervor. He knew as well as Silas that this could easily become a very slippery slope.

"Yes, well," Zhou cleared his throat, "some of us play more prominent roles than others in these failures."

Silas wanted to roll his eyes.

"Hex was found where we expected her to be. She may have gotten away for now, but we have still disrupted one of their largest manufacturing locations we have uncovered in years." He kept his voice steady as he spoke, careful to keep his irritation in check.

"We have also destroyed dozens of ships, new ships by the looks of them, that were surely destined for piracy." He would have also mentioned the minimal losses suffered by his own forces, but that was a statistic that mattered very little to a man like Zhou.

"So, you see, Vice Admiral, to call this operation a failure would be a gross misrepresentation of the facts," Silas finished, letting the silence hang in the air.

As the exchange became increasingly tense, the others in the room looked from the face of Silas to that of Zhou, attempting to gauge how far this would go. Each camp formed at the table as subordinates whispered amongst themselves.

A long, tense moment passed before Zhou finally spoke. "I am here as a friend to help you, High Commander. We are of course on the same team.

I will send my report to the council tomorrow. I trust by then your full report should be prepared."

The others relaxed when it became clear that violence wasn't imminent, even if no one believed that the matter had been settled. Silas, however, remained tense as he stared down Zhou.

"I will meet with my team and provide you with the necessary information," Silas replied curtly.

"Then I will leave you. I believe I have done enough to stress the importance of the situation to you," Zhou said as he stood up abruptly. The others at the table stood up in response to offer salutes as he left the room, while his lackeys followed him out.

Silas, stayed seated and merely offered him a nod, finally relaxing as the man left the room. Silas then dismissed his own officers, except for Captain Lancaster and Marcus, with instructions to provide their compiled reports before morning.

"Sanctimonious prick," Captain Lancaster said as soon as the room had cleared.

"I reckon if we release him out of an airlock no one would miss him," Marcus added.

Silas shook his head. "I hate that man more than most, but he is right that this looks bad. Hex has escaped twice now on our watch. Did you also hear what he said about the Vermilion Coalition and Prometheus Group coming to some kind of...arrangement?"

"Yeah, and I have been telling you for years that Jimmy was a rat. Looks like I finally have proof," Marcus said enthusiastically.

"We don't know he had anything to do with Hex getting away. I mean he gave us her location in the first place. Besides, we did take the facility. You saw how much equipment they had in there."

"Yeah...but maybe that was before he made a deal with the devil and decided to sell us out," Marcus replied, crossing his arms, a sour expression on his face. Captain Lancaster nodded along with Marcus. "It seemed pretty obvious to me that they had at least some warning that we were coming."

Before Silas could respond, a young officer, serving as one of his administrative aids, came in and saluted smartly.

"Lord Beckett, I was told to inform you that the High Engineer is ready to present his report."

"Thank you, Lieutenant, and once again it's just High Commander," Silas said, dismissing the young lieutenant.

There would be plenty of time to discuss the involvement of the Prometheus group and the day's events. For now, however, they had to understand what this facility was used for and learn as much as they could about the devices discovered inside.

"Let's focus on digesting this report for now. We will meet with Jimmy as soon as we return to Mars and get to the bottom of all this," Silas said.

Both Marcus and Lancaster grumbled under their breaths but made no attempt to argue. He wasn't sure if they were more annoyed by the situation with their informant or the fact neither of them enjoyed engineering meetings.

Silas activated his comms and spoke to his aid, "Lieutenant, please send in the high engineer and his team."

They were all in for a long night of discussions.

CHAPTER

15

Nearly two years had passed since Kaya arrived on Mars. In that time, she had eventually conformed to what was expected of her. On the surface, she showed proper deference and obedience to the Republic and its clergy. Despite trying to resist it in the early days, she knew now that cooperation would be the only way to get by with some semblance of freedom and any hope of a life after she was done.

Although she remained roommates with Victoria, their relationship had only continued to sour as they grew more distant. When before they would at least converse in passing, now it was hardly at all unless necessary. They went from best friends to strangers who passed each other tentatively, unsure if the other meant them harm.

From Kaya's perspective, it seemed like Victoria had fallen happily into her new life, embracing the process of study and prayer with a zealous fervor Kaya would have never expected. Well, good for her, she supposed. If that was what Victoria thought she wanted, then who was Kaya to try and stop her?

Things with Hal had also flourished in the absence of any other distractions. She was glad she had given him the chance and convinced herself that it wouldn't get in the way of her actual goals.

Either way, she was glad when she finally received instructions from Professor Moreau to retrieve a text for her from the archives in the Boundless Library. She was so excited after the messenger delivered the message that she had nearly embraced the man. He of course didn't know what the message said, but rarely was anyone so excited to receive instructions from their employer.

Only months prior, the professor had finally seen fit to take on Kaya as her assistant. In no small part, Kaya assumed, because of her constant pestering. At first the work had been boring tasks, like transcribing seemingly endless hours of lectures into handwritten documents or even menial tasks like managing the professor's laundry. All tasks she would never have done had she remained on Mercury. It was maybe exactly for that reason that the woman saw fit to give her those jobs.

What she might not have known about Kaya was that she had been raised by a mother who preached the importance of remaining humble in service to others. Because of that upbringing, Kaya believed there was no job beneath her dignity.

However, this wasn't a point of view shared by many others of the ruling elite, especially the likes of Ajax and his cronies. Luckily for her, they had kept their distance after that first day in the square. Whether that was because of her own intervention or the fact she had continued seeing Hal so often she didn't know. Ultimately, she was glad Hal had been smart enough to separate himself from them. She knew he was better than all of that.

The day was cool and crisp as she strode through the square toward the library's entrance. Her white robes ruffled in the breeze, and she adjusted her sash, the white one having been replaced with green. It was a crisp and sunny day, but smoke hung in the air, and she looked around for the source. She saw a crowd growing in the distance but couldn't see where the smoke was coming from.

Unrest in the capital, well, most of the cities of the solar system really, had continued to grow in intensity and frequency. With that unrest came fires that sometimes burned for days, because no one except the military would go into the slums to extinguish them.

There were near-daily incidents, mainly clashes between citizens and the local guardsmen or even Frumentarii if the rumors were to be believed. She always assumed the Frumentarii were behind the bulk of the violence committed under the guise of keeping order. So, she had no reason to doubt the rumors.

The whole situation only left her increasingly numb to the horrible scenes of death and violence. After that first day and the incident with the protest, she had run out of tears to shed. She told herself it was a simple matter of survival. Being labeled as a sympathizer could see her hauled in front of the Frumentarii for questioning or worse.

As she got closer to the library, the crowd grew, but she couldn't make out the focus of their attention. Whatever it was, she figured it must be some kind of official Republic business, since only lawful assemblies were allowed in Trinity Square.

Making her way up the stairs of the library, she turned to get a better look at what was happening.

"What is everyone gathered for? Do you know?" she asked a young girl who was staring out over the square, her jaw clenched.

"Heretics," the girl said simply. She sounded ashamed to even utter the word. "At least we will be free of them soon."

Kaya wasn't sure what the girl meant until she noticed the pyres set in the middle of the crowd. There were two pyres, one burned and charred and another fresh and ready. *Good God, executions.*

"Are they..." Kaya asked, struggling to speak.

"They already burned one of them, Sol worshipers I think or maybe just Coalition members. I'm not really sure. You should have heard the screams, what awful sounds. Well, serves the devil right, don't you think?" the girl said as if she were describing the weather.

Even if she wasn't surprised by the girl's callousness, she still found it unsettling. It was the symptom of the disease the Republic suffered from. The disease she hoped to cure one day, like her mother dreamed of.

"Yes, of course," Kaya said, her stomach turning in knots. "When did they start doing this?"

"I heard the Vox issued a new decree yesterday. They began carrying out execution's planet wide. These are the first here in the capital though. Did you not see the notices? They posted them all over."

Was this why the professor sent her to the library today? To make sure she saw this spectacle with her own eyes?

"No, I must have missed them. I have been so busy with my studies," Kaya said. It was then that she saw them dragging a limp figure to the fresh pyre.

She couldn't tell who the person was from this distance, but she could see that they were bloody and disheveled. As they tied them up, she could see that it was a man who stared up defiantly, spitting into the face of one of his captors before breaking into laughter. She turned away, unable to look, but his laughter was haunting.

She vowed in that moment to find a way to put an end to these barbaric rituals.

"Well, it looks like you made it in time for the next one," the girl said, but Kaya had already begun to move away. "He seems to be a lively one. You would think he would take this time to repent."

"He will meet God soon enough. He must plan to repent in person, but unfortunately I don't have time for distractions, especially heretics," Kaya said, and the girl only shrugged as she went back to watching her show.

The crowd began to cheer louder as they listed off the man's crimes, real or imagined, she couldn't say, but his laughing continued. She turned back one last time and saw a smile on his face. She knew death smiled at us all, but she didn't think she would have the strength to smile back like he did.

She resolved to have the strength to at least watch that man's final moments and give his death meaning by being there to witness it. What good were finding answers to her own questions if she wasn't going to follow through on her promises to create change?

When it was over, she bowed her head in a silent prayer. She hoped he found his way to whatever afterlife he believed in with the same joy he showed at the end of his first life. The excitement she had earlier was gone as she continued her walk to the library.

Once inside, she passed by the guards, waving casually to the entry clerk, who waved back. She had become well acquainted with the staff from spending much of her free time within the library. Despite thinking she never would when she first arrived. There wasn't much else they were allowed to do as students besides pray and study, and she found studying to be much more fulfilling.

Unlike most days, she made her way down the stairs to where the entrance of the archives was located on the below-grade levels. Presumably this was where the texts could best be kept safe in the event of a calamity. There on the basement level, a pair of guards blocked the main entrance to the archives, along with a body scanner and clerk who was there to check credentials.

The guards watched her with suspicious gazes as she approached, adjusting their rifles ever so slightly. This wasn't a job they took lightly. On the first day she came to the library, the security hadn't been quite so intense, but over the last year security concerns had only grown, and that was reflected everywhere now.

She handed the clerk her credentials and was admitted after she was given a long list of rules and procedures that she must adhere to. In particular, she was only allowed to leave with the specific text from her clearance document, a treatise on the rise and fall of the ancient American Empire.

Kaya had no interest in tales of ancient civilizations. Several others had risen and fallen in the wake of the American's, so why the professor found this one interesting was unknown to her. Either way, she had her own purpose. The other primary rule was that you couldn't take any notes or otherwise document anything within the archives. That rule would be easy to follow since she hadn't brought any writing supplies and carried no recording devices. What they didn't consider was that she had a very prodigious memory.

Kaya nodded to the clerk and made her way through the large bronze doors that were intricately carved with a motif of God descending from the heavens to bestow his blessing.

Once through the doors, she was temporarily stunned as she realized the sheer immensity of the space. Seemingly endless rows of shelves, books, and cabinets lined the perimeter of the room while in the center a railing guarded against a precipitous drop down many levels below. Feeling a sudden sense of vertigo, she stepped back from the edge and continued walking amongst the shelves.

She passed only a handful of people who mostly avoided interacting with her as they went about their own business. It was emptier than she expected, and she wondered if that had anything to do with the executions in the square. The faint hum of cheers from outside seemed to confirm her suspicion.

It made her sick to think how many people were taking pleasure in the torture and death of another man, one who had likely not done anything to any of them. However, she assumed most of these people were also ignorant of history. There had been more than one revolution that began in earnest with the death of a martyr.

Finding the location of the decimal cards, she began searching first for what the professor had requested. After a year working with this system, she had become proficient with its use, finding the location of the text easily enough. She then went on to search under eternal dream, looking for any possible reference.

Over the last two years, she had reminded herself this would always be a long shot, but she still hoped to find something. Any kind of reference that would shed light on what she already knew from Grandmaster Dario.

Except when she got to where the index card would be, she found nothing. She searched again, looking at cards before and after where it would have been, hoping, even praying, that it might be out of order. It didn't help because it wasn't there. She had put years of hard work into gaining Professor Moreau's trust, and all the emotional energy that entailed, to get to this point. Now she found out it was all for nothing. She had failed.

She watched the last whisper of her mother's dream die before her in real time. She wanted to rage and scream, to knock the case over and burn the cursed library to the ground. They would kill her for that, like the laughing man but she hardly cared.

Then she considered her father and what he would think when he heard the news of his only daughter's death, and she quenched her murderous rage. He didn't deserve that. He had always tried to do his best for her.

She rubbed her face, the anger coalescing to stone in the cold reality of the moment. If this had been two years earlier, she knew she would have collapsed and cried, but she was stronger now. She had been so sure that it would be here, but this wasn't the end. She wouldn't let it be the end.

Her mind had become used to tedious labor over the last two years of service to the clergy. Maybe that was why now, in her moment of greatest stress, it searched for some basic tasks to complete. Some tiny shrivel of success to cling to in a job well done. So, she turned to search for Professor Moreau's book, finding it easily several isles over from the decimal card cabinet. Grabbing the book, she tucked it under her arm and continued.

The task wasn't nearly enough to help her forget the pain of her recent loss. So, she walked silently like a ghost, descending the stairs of the library for no other reason than to see how far this new hell would go.

However, as she descended several sets of stairs, she realized that each floor had its own collection of decimal cards. In the main section of the library every floor held the same cards, but she thought maybe that wasn't the case here, however illogical that seemed. Maybe the librarians had some organizational reason to separate the cards that she couldn't devise in that moment. The universe had sent her this tiny lifeline, and even if it only lasted for a moment, she was determined to cling to it.

She checked the first cabinet then the second and found no reference to the eternal dream in either, but she kept descending. At least she was able to confirm the listings were in fact unique to each floor. However, after the third and fourth cabinets, she began to lose her grasp on the tiny lifeline.

Her heart sank, and her legs became shaky, but she tried to will her desires into reality. Reaching the fifth cabinet, she slammed her balled fist down on top of it and searched yet again for the eternal dream, her mother's dream. They were becoming one and the same in her mind.

Then there it was, one single card, worn and yellow, directing her to another section of the archives, where one book resided. The book was titled, *A Reflection on the Past: Hope in the Face of Chaos*. It was written by one of the Patriarchs of Mars roughly five hundred years prior.

The tears she swore she no longer had began to swell in her eyes, and she dropped her head onto the cabinet. "I finally found you," she said under her breath. Lifting her head, she studied the card, committing its contents to memory before closing the cabinet.

Her feet carried her swiftly toward the designated shelf, and she felt lighter than she had in years. *It was worth it.* All the pain, the hard work, the loneliness, all of it. She had done it. She *wasn't* a failure.

However, as she got closer to the designated shelf, she heard the shuffling of feet and the movement of books on and off shelves. It had been a while since she had seen anyone, and the archives had been eerily quiet.

She of course had permission to be here, but it still made her uneasy that anyone might see where she was and what exactly she was looking for. She may have permission to be in the archives, but she already had the book she had come for, and this area was nowhere near the exit. She didn't need to be arrested now for collecting more than what her permit allowed, especially after all this time.

Then she heard what she could have sworn was a familiar voice say, "Eureka, I found it!"

Kaya peeked around the end of each shelf looking for the source of the voice. When she came to the third row, the one she needed to enter, she found it.

A man stood looking down at a book, he wore the robes of a cleric, but something seemed wrong. It only took her a minute to realize that the style of the robe was incorrect. It was similar, and most people may not have been able to tell the difference, but she could.

This man's robes were made of the wrong material, and the stitching of the hems was all wrong. As he turned absently toward Kaya, still engrossed in the book, she saw his face and had to suppress a gasp.

Standing there was the engineer, Aron, who she had met on that first day in the square. The same pitted face and mop of hair. She could easily recognize him through what she was sure was a disguise. He wasn't a cleric, and she had experience pretending to be people she wasn't. She would have said she was good at it too if not for her current situation.

She quickly considered what to do from her hiding spot. She wouldn't have much time before he walked past, but she didn't know what to do. She could ignore him and wait until he left, but how long might that be? And why was he even here?

She did know he was pretending to be someone he wasn't, and if she got caught with him, doing whatever it was he was doing, she would surely face the same punishment. She wanted to ignore him and leave, but he was in the row where she needed to be. It was too strange of a coincidence to walk away.

She had to move quietly as Aron began walking toward her, the book he had been reading under his arm. She shuffled down to the other end, looping back behind where Aron had walked. At first it seemed like he heard her, because he stopped to look around but satisfied that he was alone went back to walking down the main corridor between the stacks.

Kaya cursed to herself. That had been close, but now she was where she needed to be, and scanned the shelves looking for the book. *A Reflection of the Past* but immediately realized it was not where it was supposed to be. Instead, she found a gap. An obvious gap free of any dust from where a book had only recently been removed.

"God's Bones!" she said out loud. What could an engineer possibly want with that book of all things? How did he even know to look for it? Then she remembered asking him about the eternal dream all those years ago. Had he remembered after all this time, and how did he even get in here, on the same day as her? These questions and so many others raced through Kaya's mind as she stalked out into the corridor looking for that good-for-nothing engineer.

Seeing the back of his head as he walked between the shelves of books, she followed him. It didn't seem like he noticed her. As she turned the corner, she saw him and with a quick series of steps closed the gap.

Raising Professor Moreau's book like a cudgel, she slammed it down on the back of his head while simultaneously kicking the back of his knee. Years of frustration directed toward disabling her latest roadblock. She didn't want to hurt him, but she had to stop him, and he needed to know she meant business.

Aron collapsed in a heap under the sudden assault with a shocked groan and rolled onto his back, trying to make sense of the situation. Luckily for Kaya his first reaction wasn't to scream, and before he could work up the sense to do so she covered his mouth with her palm and jabbed the hard spine of the book into his side as if it were a knife.

"Not. One. Word," she snarled. He nodded weakly with wide eyes. She used her free hand to take control of the book he carried. Glancing at the title, she confirmed it was the one she had been looking for.

"I'm going to guess since we aren't already both in chains the guards didn't see any of this on the cameras, at least not yet. I am going to take my hand off your mouth, and we are going to stand up. You aren't going to say a word unless it's to answer my questions. Do you understand?" she asked as she pushed her knee into his abdomen a little harder. Aron nodded with a groan of pain. She felt a little bad for what she was doing, but only a little. As they stood up, she put both books under her arm, and Aron rubbed at the back of his head.

"Why are you here?" she asked. He remained silent for a moment, glaring at her. "You can speak now."

"The same reason as you apparently," he said. Kaya could tell he looked concerned, but then he narrowed his gaze at her, as if he thought of something. "Who sent you for that book?" He motioned to the dusty tome under her arm.

"I'm the one asking the questions," she said, hoping they weren't attracting any attention. "What do you want with it?"

Aron bit his lip, like he was deciding how much he should say.

Kaya glared at him and tilted her ear up toward the ceiling. "Do you hear that? They are burning a man alive. That is what they do to traitors now. You better tell me what you are doing here if you want any chance of avoiding the pyre." She felt disgusted with herself, but she had to know, and she would do what she had to do, even if it meant continuing to act the part.

He narrowed his eyes at her, his indecision turning to anger. "All of you are the same. Frumentarii in training, are you? You can sard off with your threats. I won't say a thing. I'm dead already anyway." He looked at her, defiant. "So turn me in then. Let's be on with it while the fires are still hot."

Those words stung worse than almost anything he could have said to her. Her threats backfired so fully in her face, and now what? She would have to either follow through or, or what? Let him go? So he can tell his conspirators and murder her in her sleep? She had to think fast.

She sighed. He had called her bluff and won. "We don't have much time. Someone will notice our odd behavior and come to investigate. How did you get in here and what is with the costume?"

"Why would I tell you? So you can tell your friends and earn a promotion while I burn and you all cheer about what paragons of justice you are? Sard off," Aron said, crossing his arms. "You go your way, and I will go mine. Keep the book. I don't know what's so important about it anyway."

"You don't even know what it is?" she asked.

He put his arms out in a shrug. "I was asked to come and get it, same as you, I assume. I even got to it first, but I bumbled it," he said and sighed. "Pretty typical honestly, I wish they had never sent me in the first place. I'm no spy. My first and last mission right to the gallows."

"No one sent me. Well, not for this book anyway. I was looking for it on my own," she confided in him, deciding to be honest. How useful could that tidbit be anyway?

He shook his head. "So all that time ago when you asked me to help you search for the eternal dream, it was a random guess? I mentioned it to my, um, associate. He seemed to know what it meant right away, but he wouldn't say anything more. I figured I was the last to know. What is it then?"

"I don't know," she said with a shrug as she looked over her shoulder, "but we can't talk about this now. We need to get out of here." Then she considered how she would leave with the book in hand. She had assumed she would have time to read some of it and memorize it over several visits, but now she was worried it wouldn't be there when she returned. Glancing at the pages, she realized it wasn't even written in a language she understood. *Sarding perfect.*

"Do you have a way for us to get out of here? We need to take these with us," she said, holding up the books she was holding. She knew they probably couldn't walk out the way they'd come, not now, and she hoped he had a plan for how he was going to do that in the first place.

"Did you not think about how you would get out of here with the book?" he asked.

"I wasn't going to take it at all, but now I'm worried if I don't that you will," she countered.

"You're right. It's worth more to me than your little research project."

"Why would you care so much about some dusty book?" she asked.

"I need it to pay a debt," he said, sounding ashamed.

"There are easier ways to make money."

"It isn't the kind of debt money can pay, not that I have any anyway," he said, and she wondered what he was hiding.

"Do you have a way out of here or not?"

"Now you need me to figure it out? After you tried to bash my skull in?"

"I only hit you with a book. You will be fine."

"'Fine,' she says. Some of us can't afford proper medical care, you know," he said, shaking his head at her.

Kaya grumbled, "You know what I mean. So do you have a plan or not?" she said, glaring at him again. He could insult her after they were out of here and somewhere more private.

"I do, but you might not like it."

"It's not the sewers, is it?" Kaya asked, suddenly feeling concerned.

"The...what? No, of course not. You've watched too many movies," he motioned for her to follow him as he made his way down several more sets of stairs and past seemingly endless stacks of books.

"Where are we going? Shouldn't we be going up?" she asked.

"Trust me," he said in a hushed tone.

"You already told me you are a terrible spy. Why should I trust you?"

"Because I might be a terrible spy, but I'm a pretty good engineer. I know the ins and outs of these buildings better than anyone has any business knowing them," he said only a little sheepishly, looking around nervously for any signs of other people as he walked.

Eventually they reached a dead end where a desk was pushed up against a wall, nestled between the stacks of books. Kaya thought the workspace looked claustrophobic, but she assumed some studious bookworm probably loved the space.

She looked around for signs of cameras or other surveillance but didn't find any. However, she also didn't find a way out.

"Where are we supposed to go now?" she asked.

"Down here," he said, dropping down onto his hands and knees and disappearing under the desk. Kaya wondered what in the worlds he was doing until his voice called out from somewhere further away. "Are you coming or not?"

She grumbled but followed suit, readjusting her robes, and once she got under the desk she saw where he had gone and laughed. It was an uncovered air vent large enough for an adult to pass through.

Noticing her surprise, he smiled back. "Wouldn't expect someone like you to notice a mechanical hatch. Close the vent behind you, and let's go. There's a vehicle waiting." He turned on a small handheld light and led the way through the darkness of the vent.

She did as she was told, and shuffled behind him through the dusty and dirty air vent. The dust kicked up as they moved, and she was forced to cover her mouth to suppress a series of coughs. Aron let out an admonishing sound. Unlike her, he seemed unbothered by the dust and stale air.

"I'm sorry the air quality isn't up to the lady's standards," Aron said. She assumed he had a glib expression on his face even though she couldn't see it.

"It's fine," she said while stifling another coughing fit. Her lungs felt especially sensitive as she breathed in the stale air and dust. "Shouldn't there be air flowing through here?"

"Typically, there would be, but this isn't a real air vent. It was added in secret by one of the old bishops who managed the library decades ago. He used it to leave the capital in secret to visit his courtesans, but don't worry, he's been dead for a decade now."

"Then how did you find out about it? I'm guessing it's not on any building plans," she asked.

"No, it was very secret, but someone still had to build it. Lords, bishops, the rich, they all forget real people still need to do the work. Those people have memories and often use them to their own benefit," he laughed. "My father was the one who led the project, and he kept very thorough notes."

"I guess that's why whoever hired you picked you for this job," she said.

"Maybe, but like I said, this was my first and last job," he said, looking back at her.

"Whatever you say. I don't care what you do," she said truthfully.

She didn't care beyond finding out what he knew about this book and why he was here in the first place. She figured she had to go to whoever was actually in charge and ask some questions. For now she was content to follow Aron as he led them through a labyrinth of tunnels from memory, a feat that impressed Kaya a little bit more than she would have liked to admit.

Kaya

February, 4103 U.E.T.—Tiyas, Mars

AFTER WHAT FELT like an hour of crawling and coughing, they finally reached the end of the fake ventilation system. They exited into a large room with what looked like bins of dirty linens, disorganized shelves, and no windows.

Kaya coughed and spit out a mouthful of dust as she tried to clean herself off. It looked to her like some kind of laundry room. They must still be inside the university grounds, but it didn't look familiar, so she knew it wasn't part of the Sanctum. Given her present company, she assumed it might be the engineering school.

"Here, change into these," Aron said as he rifled through a pile of clothes on the other side of the room, tossing her what looked like a mechanic's jumpsuit.

He pulled off his white robe and began changing into a similar jumpsuit. Unlike her, he was still wearing normal clothes under his robe. She had done that for a while, but at this point she had become used to the garment and opted for a more...streamlined approach.

Kaya looked at the outfit as she caught it and grimaced. The clothes smelled of stale sweat and were covered in stains. She had worn plenty of disguises before, but they had all been her own clothing, not some stranger's beat-up old rags, but she knew wearing her white robe was probably a bad idea, so she started taking them off. As she started removing the robes, she saw Aron awkwardly turning around to avoid looking at her.

"This is a strange way to try and get my clothes off," she said, trying to break the tension or, better yet, make him more uncomfortable. It turned out to be the latter as he turned around red faced. She laughed to herself. Her underwear wasn't much different from a swimsuit, so it didn't really bother her. She kept the belt holding her plasma blade strapped around her waist.

She took off the robe and donned the dirty jumpsuit. Then she folded the robe and placed it into an empty bag she found nearby along with the stolen books. She tore a hole in the pocket of the jumpsuit so the hilt of her blade would be easy to access.

"You can turn around now," she said.

"We can't do anything about hiding your eyes, but can you at least do something to hide your hair?" he said. She wanted to be angry at him, but she knew that was a good point. She would be easy to recognize if her description was shared with the local constables.

Kaya walked over to the shelf where Aron found the jumpsuit to look for herself. There she found a large plain blue cloth she could wrap around her head as a scarf. Since New Olympia was such a cosmopolitan center, she hoped the very Mercurian style wouldn't appear too out of place.

"That should work," Aron said, so she thought her assumption was probably correct.

"Where are we going now? You said there would be a vehicle."

"There is. Get in," he said, motioning to the laundry basket full of dirty linens before diving in headfirst.

"Really? Like this?"

"Do you want to get out of here or not? Get in the basket," he said forcefully. She wasn't used to dealing with someone with such little deference. She wondered what had happened to his previously pleasant demeanor.

"Fine, move over," she said as she likewise jumped into the bin that smelled like stale sweat and other things she didn't want to think too much about. The oily rag wrapped around her face and head turned out to be a godsend for masking the odors.

They both buried themselves into the linens, jostling with each other for a comfortable position within the large, wheeled basket. She slapped at him as his leg or arm jabbed into her side, and he struck back out at her in turn.

"Will you cut it out?" she said.

"I will when you do, you entitled little..." Aron began to say, until they heard the sound of a door opening. Kaya took that opportunity to give him one final punch to what she hoped was a sensitive part of his body. The quiet groan made her think she had hit her target.

"Remember who's in charge right now," she whispered.

"Yes, me, because I'm the one getting you out of here."

Okay, he had her there, but she was still in charge.

The cart began moving soon after. It rumbled loudly as the wheels clattered on the floor and shook them violently. If it wasn't for the bed of smelly laundry they were nestled in, the ride would have probably been quite painful.

The cart got particularly hot as they were wheeled out into the sunlight. She could feel Aron squirming beside her, but she had no problem remaining still. The heat here was unlikely to ever compare to what she was used to back home.

It felt like they were wheeled up an incline, maybe into the back of a truck, she thought. An idea that was confirmed as a heavy door shut and they began an even bumpier ride to somewhere she could only guess.

The ride began to take so long she couldn't help but start to doze off, despite her best efforts to fight the feeling. Until she was awakened by Aron's pained groans.

"I think I'm going to be sick." She could barely hear him over the sound of the road and vehicle.

"Get it together. This is barely even bumpy. Haven't you ever broken the atmosphere before? This is nothing compared to that," she said.

"No," he responded angrily, "not all of us are so lucky." She felt instant regret for her assumption. Not everyone lived the life she had, and she needed to remind herself of that. She was also quickly proving all his preconceived notions about her correct, but she still didn't trust him, so she didn't intend to apologize for anything.

They were quiet for the rest of the ride, which seemed like hours, but she couldn't be completely sure. She spent the whole time wondering if people were already searching for them. She would have been expected at prayers by now, and absences weren't handled lightly.

Except, more importantly, she worried about where they were being taken and who would be there when they arrived. Aron for his part seemed relaxed, so she hoped it would be reasonably safe.

Luckily Aron did manage to hold the contents of his stomach long enough for them to get dumped unceremoniously out of the basket. He then proceeded to empty said contents on the floor in front of several large men holding rail rifles. Looking up at the men, she considered Aron had been lying to her the entire time.

Her eyes took a moment to adjust to the light as she took stock of the room. It was a lot like where they had come from but much more rundown. The walls were broken, and rusty pipes and machines lined the walls of the building. It was a wonder the building stayed standing at all, she thought. She attempted to stand up to face the two big men when a rough hand pushed her back down onto her knees.

"Stay right there. What's this about? The boss said there would only be one boy. Why's there two?" a gravelly voice said to who she could only assume was one of the two big men.

"I'm surprised yous can count that high," the one ogre said.

All she heard was a snarl behind her as the figure kicked Aron. It was then she got a better look at him.

He was a local constable by the looks of his uniform. Although it was thoroughly tattered and stained. He looked more like a goblin than a man. Her stomach dropped as she put the pieces together, realizing the slums were the only place she could be right now. *Oh no*, she thought and scrambled for something, anything she could do to get herself out of there.

"And yous, why you dirtying my floor? Whose yer friend?" the goblin said.

"Why does everyone keep hitting me?" Aron groaned as he got up. "And your floor is already filthy, Maengar. Listen, get out of our way. We need to be moving."

Maengar kicked at Kaya next. He hit her in the stomach, and she doubled over like Aron trying to catch her breath. "I asked who's this," he repeated.

"None of your business, now get out of our way or the boss is going to find out about this," he said in a dangerous tone that seemed out of character.

Maengar laughed. "Yous don't call the shots here, kid. Yous see this badge?" he said, jabbing a dirty and deformed finger at the faded insignia on his shirt. "Yous are just a wee pup. I need what you went to get, not yous."

He then snapped a finger toward one of his goons, who proceeded to wrap his muscle-bound arm around Aron's neck. He struggled and gasped for air, but it was a battle he wasn't going to win against the significantly larger man.

Kaya wouldn't have expected to find these kinds of toughs here, although she also knew the use of nectar and steroids were very common, especially in the slums.

"Ha, ready to tell me now?" the goblin cackled again as he then snapped his finger at his other goon. "Remove his hood. Let's see our new friend."

Before the ogre could get close enough to her, she drew her plasma blade, kindling it in one practiced motion. The sudden heat and glow stopped the goon in his tracks, and Maengar stopped laughing.

"You heard him. Step aside, cretin, and let us pass", she said, motioning to the goon who held Aron. He didn't even look at Maengar before dropping his grip and stepping away. She gave her sword an unnecessary twirl as she walked toward Aron to help him up.

"We's didn't mean anything by it," Maengar began to say, putting his hands up apologetically until Kaya was on him in a blink of the eye, her blade pressed toward his face, the heat of it singed what scraggly beard hairs he had.

"We will make the delivery ourselves. Understood?" she said.

"Yeah, course," he said, shrinking away from the blade.

Kaya grabbed Aron and led him out of the curtain that served as a door on the dilapidated building. In the next room, a row of workers fed fabric into massive washers and steaming vats, pausing only momentarily at the sight of them before returning to their work. They didn't seem to want anything to do with whatever was happening.

Once they reached the exit to the street, she snuffed the blade and holstered the hilt once again.

"Okay, quick, where are we going," she said, shoving him out of the door ahead of her.

"I didn't think that was real," he said, stunned.

"My father is the duke of Mercury. Of course it's real," she said, annoyed. "Do you know where we are going or not?"

"Oh uh," he hesitated, looking around. The street was quiet except for the occasional passing truck or pushcart. The locals didn't seem to pay any mind in their disguises though.

"You don't, do you?" she asked, feeling a bit scared now.

"We can't be far."

"We can't be far? We were in that cursed bin for hours!" she said, slapping his arm. Was he dense? "You said you had a way out of there!"

"I did!" he said, shirking away from her blows. "They tried to kill me. Obviously their plan was different than mine. They should have been taking us back to the mid districts."

"You are welcome, by the way," she said before walking randomly down the direction she saw the most people going.

"Wait, why that way? Where are you going?" he said, chasing after her.

"We need to go somewhere, and this way is better than no way." she said, wanting to take action.

He pulled out his comm device next to her and began to type into it before she slapped it out of his hand and stomped on it.

"What the sarding hell are you doing?" he said with a look of shock on his face.

"Are you an idiot? That is the first thing they will think to track."

"How would they even know where to look? They have no idea who I am!"

A fair point, she thought. *Oh well, what's done is done.* "Well, better safe than sorry," she offered.

Aron only let out an exasperated sigh. "We need to find a way out of here, and you broke our best tool to do that."

"We will find another way," she said, almost believing her own bravado and continued walking again. Aron reluctantly followed behind.

The ramshackle buildings shot up into the sky supported by concrete and steel that was so rusted and pitted that she worried one of them could come down at any moment.

As they walked down the street, they began seeing more and more people. Most looked dirty, ill and much too thin. Like old rotten mummies, too tired and broken to even hunt its tormentors. Their sunken faces cast down to the ground as they marched slowly toward their own deaths. Unconsciously, Kaya moved closer to Aron as they walked down the street and tried to avert her eyes from the horrid sight.

"You should look at them. See what the real world is like outside your shiny palace," he said in a low whisper.

"We must be in the slums?" she asked, already knowing the answer.

Where else could it be? Even with his admonishment, she had trouble looking. They weren't nearly this bad on Mercury. At least not that she ever saw, but maybe she never wanted to see it.

He nodded. "I'm not sure which one, but maybe one of the worst, Tiyas, Ziyun, New Memphis maybe. I'm not sure. I don't come here often."

"Aren't you from the slums?"

He laughed. "You would think so, wouldn't you? No, a lower mid district, but I have had to come into the slums once or twice. I didn't expect to be here now, but I guess it makes sense."

"How does it make sense?" she asked.

"If they planned on killing me, what better place to do it? No one is coming looking for me, well us, here," he said with a grimace.

"I think you need to find new friends," she said, still staying close to him as they walked, her hand clutching at the hilt of her plasma blade under the jumpsuit. "But you didn't tell me why you agreed to this in the first place."

He hesitated. "I took the job for my sister. I need to get her out of a bad situation."

"Couldn't you go to the authorities for that?"

"Maybe in your world, but not in mine."

"Right, working with criminals makes more sense."

"This wasn't the original plan, at least I don't think it was. I think Maengar back there decided to make a move for himself," he said, and he seemed genuinely upset.

"Not surprising that criminals would only look out for themselves."

"That's easy to say from a position of privilege. Why do any of these people even need to live this way in the first place?" Kaya was taken aback and prepared for a further barrage, but he only sighed. "But you are right. He wasn't my choice of partners. Some people are formed by their circumstances. Others find a natural home for their pain and malice in them."

"Which type of person are you?" she asked. His face became tight and rigid, but he didn't answer.

Continuing in silence they came to a square that was crowded with people going about their business or loitering in the street, high on narcotics or slumped from malnutrition. Kaya found it hard to tell the difference. Many buildings were burned, rusted, or damaged beyond repair, but they remained occupied.

Vendors guarded their rusty old carts with watchful eyes. She knew there was no justice or security here in the slums beyond what you could provide for yourself. There were gangs who offered protection for a fee of course, but they were as likely to be the ones robbing you. It was a vicious cycle of loss and predation.

It was one thing for her to understand these facts on an intellectual level but quite another to see them with her own eyes. The heavy weight of the truth was crushing.

The foul odors and dirty streets felt like penance for her ignorance, but they hardly amounted to understanding the real pain of these people's lives. Aron was right to criticize her.

"Over there," she said, nodding to a small cart where a sickly-looking boy was selling some kind of food product. "He looks harmless enough. Let's find out where we are."

Aron grabbed her arm, stopping her before she could move. "Remember where you are. Everyone could be dangerous."

She pulled her arm away. "Weren't you the one who told me to acknowledge these people? That is what I am trying to do, and that starts with trust," she said, hoping her optimism wasn't going to get them killed. Better to die for a good deed than a bad one, she supposed.

"That's true, but a lot of people here are so hungry and sick they would sooner slit their mother's throat than pass up an opportunity to improve their situation. That is a level of desperation neither of us truly understands," he said before following her over to the boy's cart.

The food smelled rotten, but she feigned interest in it. The boy was gangly, and his skin looked like old leather, covered with sores and open wounds. It was a pitiful sight, and she wondered how he managed to stay upright through what must have been excruciating pain.

"We will take two," she said, pointing to the rotten meat on a stick and then motioned to Aron. "Sorry, I left everything in my robe."

He gave her a disgruntled look but pulled s larger denomination credit chip out of his pocket and handed it over. It was far more than this meal could have possibly cost.

"You owe me," he said in a low voice.

"Keep the change," she said to the boy as he snatched up the credit chip. "What's your name?"

"Brandon," the boy said through a raspy voice. Although it seemed like he had just noticed Kaya for the first time, and he began to stare. "Yer eyes, I ain't seen anything like them," he said, almost as if in a trance, his own yellow and sickly eyes digging into hers.

Aron grabbed her arm again and whispered into her ear, "This is a bad idea. We need to get out of here. People are beginning to notice." He began to look around nervously, which she thought would only attract more attention. She ignored him.

"Thank you, tell me, where are we right now?"

The boy blinked at her. "Uh, Tiyas. Where else?"

"I think the lady is lost, Brandon," came a gruff voice from behind the cart. Kaya looked to see where it came from and saw a large man rise from where he had been sitting out of view. "I can help you find yer way back for some of them credits," he said, looking greedily from Kaya to Aron as he cracked his knuckles.

"Leave them alone, Gram. They ain't causing trouble," Brandon said in their defense.

"Why don't ya take off that scarf and show us yer pretty face?" the man named Gram said as he got closer to Kaya.

In the moment, she didn't really know what to do, but she began to reach inside her pocket for the hilt of her plasma blade. "Stay back. We don't mean you any harm."

The man laughed at her. "I know that, and don't go reaching for any of yer fancy toys," he said as he pulled a wicked-looking device of rusted steel that crackled with energy. Some kind of makeshift stun rod. "Keep yer hands out of yer pockets."

Kaya did as he said, beginning to be frightened. Aron tried to put himself between her and the brute, but it was too little too late, and the man effortlessly swung out with his homemade weapon, striking Aron in the gut. The strike left Aron doubled over and Gram easily closed the gap before Kaya could reach for her blade.

The man laughed. "They make yous so weak. Why do they call us vermin? Now let's see here," he said and yanked the scarf from her head, revealing her long auburn braid and unblemished skin. It was obvious she didn't belong there. The commotion drew a small crowd that upon seeing the reveal gasped and began rushing toward her.

"Hands off, she's mine," he screamed as he grabbed her with one arm and swung out with the stun rod in the other.

Gram was forced to hit several men who tried to touch her hair and face. Kaya screamed, hoping to push and kick them away, but the press of bodies became overwhelming. She tried desperately to reach for her blade, but between the mass of people and Gram's grip she couldn't get her hand on it.

She screamed and kicked until she felt her voice going raw. She kicked one man in the face who made it through Gram's defensive swings, leaving him pawing at his bloody face on the ground. Aron was still doubled over on the ground, where he became tangled up in the crowd. The madness likely only lasted a minute, but it felt like it went on for hours.

The loud sound of gunshots rang out, forcing the crowd to run away or dive for cover, but Gram didn't let go. His body was hot, sweaty, and reeked of rotten eggs and the putrid smell of puss.

"What do we have here?" came a confident female voice. "Drop her, Gram, or I'll drop you."

Gram hesitated but then eventually dropped her on the ground. She was panting heavily, and the tears blocking her vision made it difficult to make out what was going on, but she scrambled on hands and knees toward the voice.

"Please get us out of here," she shouted, unable to get a hold of herself.

"There, there, girl. Stand up," the new woman said as she holstered one of her pistols on her hip. Kaya could tell now she was heavily armed with pistols on either hip and a rifle strapped over her back.

Her hair was black and long, except where it was shaved on one side. She had several tattoos on what skin Kaya could see, but what caught her eye was the crossed torches on one forearm and a more faded tattoo on the other forearm of a cube standing on one of its points. The sight of that tattoo brought her back to reality as she brushed hair from her cheeks and stood up.

"Pandora?" Kaya asked desperately, hoping this was the salvation they needed. Even if getting caught would only lead to her eventual death. At that moment, she only wanted to get away from all this.

"How observant," the woman drawled, "but, no, not anymore." Her voice was cool, calm, and almost sultry. It was completely at odds with the current setting, as was her attractive form. She was as foreign to the slums as Kaya was.

"So, who's going to tell me what's going on?" the stranger asked.

"Gram tried to attack her. I tried to help, but yous know I can't," Brandon said, offering an explanation first and motioning to his sickly body. He seemed happy to throw Gram under the bus.

"Is that right, Gram? Did you attack this girl?"

"She's some high district bitch. What does it matter?" the brute said, spitting on the ground.

"Tisk, tisk, tisk. You really should know better, Gram. Remember what I told you last time you attacked a girl? Well, it looks like you can't learn after all," she said as Gram began to speak, but before he could utter a word, the woman drew her pistol and fired a single shot in the blink of an eye before holstering the weapon.

Gram stood there stunned for a moment. Everything, including time, stood still as that one shot rang out, and its echo reverberated through the square. Then his body fell in a heap with a single line of blood dripping from the wound between his eyes. "Oh God, protect me," Kaya muttered.

"Come on, princess. You are coming with me," the woman said, motioning to two exosuit-armored figures who had been standing behind her. The two helmeted figures grabbed her by the arms and began leading her away.

"You can't take her!" Aron screamed as he finally got to his feet approaching the woman.

"Is that so? And who might you be?" she folded her arms with an amused expression.

"I am a lieutenant of the Children of Men. The Father is expecting her. He will be very displeased if he finds out you harmed his property," Aron muttered, and Kaya looked on stunned. *The who of what?* she thought as her head spun. His property? What was he saying?

The woman laughed. "Kid, I'm much more afraid of my boss than yours. I like your spirit though, so you can come too," she said with a cat-like smile and nodded at one of the troopers. The trooper released Kaya and swiftly dropped Aron with a blow to the back of the head before throwing him over his shoulder effortlessly.

Kaya screamed, "Please don't kill me. I will cooperate!"

The woman turned her feline smile to Kaya next. "I am sure you will, but I can't have you seeing where we are going. Nighty night, princess." They pulled a heavy hood over her head and the world went dark.

CHAPTER
17

Kaya could feel before she could see. Rough hands half carried and half dragged her across the floor before leaving her to fall on her side. Her hands were bound behind her back, so she gasped as she hit the ground unexpectedly.

"By God's bones, what is this?" said an unfamiliar male voice.

"I found some lost birdies," came the voice of the woman from before. How much time had gone by? Where was she?

"Take the hoods off. Let's see what we have."

The hood came off with a yank, and Kaya tried to stumble to her knees, shaking the strands of hair from her face. One of the armored figures who she assumed dragged her here helped her get into the new position.

Aron was next to her, but he still seemed to be unconscious. She didn't know what game he was playing, but he had tried to help her. So for that at least she hoped he was okay, even if it was only so she could be the one to beat him.

The room went silent when her hood came off, and she took stock of the room. It was nondescript with no windows and unadorned walls save for the large banner with two crossed torches on it. A large table that could have belonged in a meeting room dominated the center surrounded by several chairs.

There were a few people in the room, but her eyes were drawn in front of her, where a man stood leaning casually on a table, arms crossed on his chest. When he looked down at Kaya, his eyes went wide.

She tried to steady her breathing. She had to be strong, now most of all. Not for her or Aron but for the dreams she had worked so hard for that were so close to being realized. She couldn't let these...criminals or anyone take that away from her. At least not without a fight.

"A lost birdie? You brought us a royal pheasant," he said, walking forward. He dropped to one knee in front of her, so their eyes were on the same level. "Amazing, such a rich emerald," he said as he looked into her eyes, "I didn't believe them when they said the color was unlike anything you had ever seen before, but I bet you have heard that once or twice, eh?"

Kaya stared at him. "Who are you and where am I? I demand answers," she said, her tears from earlier forgotten as she fought to regain control despite the bindings on her wrists.

The man smiled at her, a toothy boyish smile. His teeth were straight and clean, along with his skin that only showed minor blemishes of age. She guessed he was in his middle years based on the amount of gray hair on his head and beard.

He wore a simple and clean uniform like cadets wore at the Academy, except his was solid black. He wore a gun at his hip but otherwise appeared unarmed.

What her eyes were drawn to most however was his forearms, where he had his shirt sleeves rolled up. There was the same Pandora Fleet insignia on one arm and the crossed torches on the other, like the woman had.

He looked deeply into her eyes and then suddenly stood up and returned to lean on the table, facing her. "You have certainly put me in quite a position."

"Let me and my friend go, and I promise you won't be harmed. I could perhaps even see to a reward for you and your men," she said, straightening her back. She thought they seemed like the kinds of people she could negotiate with, unlike the brute from before. She had never encountered such animalistic behavior up close. The memory made her shiver.

The woman from earlier laughed and moved to stand beside the man. "Where was all this fight before, princess? First you ask for my help, and now you are making demands of your host. Not very ladylike," the catlike woman said in her sultry drawl.

"I'm no princess. Stop calling me that," Kaya said.

"Yes, of course, Your Highness."

"That's enough, Kwon," the man said. "If I have my men untie you, will you behave yourself?"

Kaya nodded, and he motioned to one of the armored men to cut her bindings. With the plastic restraints off her wrist, she took a moment to survey the room before reaching into her pocket, but her heart sank as she felt nothing there.

"Looking for this?" Kwon said, holding up the hilt of her blade, waving it teasingly back and forth.

Kaya tried to get up and lunge for it, but Kwon was quick. Before she even took a full step, she had one of her pistols drawn and pointed at Kaya. "Now, now, you promised, remember?"

Kaya seethed but took a step back, and Kwon holstered her weapon. "Maybe the first smart thing you have done all day," she said mockingly and tossed the hilt to the man who attached it to his belt.

"I will hold on to this for now. If you behave yourself, maybe you will get it back," he said.

Kaya brushed her hair from her face and took a moment to see if the Jiddi tree necklace was still around her neck, and her heart sank a second time as she realized it was missing.

"Where is my necklace?" she said. "It's not a weapon. Give it back." Her voice rose with panic. She was quickly losing everything that connected her to her home.

Kwon rustled through a pocket before producing the necklace and likewise tossing it to the man who gave her a questioning expression.

"I wasn't going to keep it," she said.

The man fingered the surface of the necklace and sighed, looking from the necklace to her and back. "If you answer my questions honestly, I will let you have this back. Deal?"

"And let me and my friend go?"

"I can't promise you that." He rubbed at his beard with his free hand. "I can promise neither of you will be harmed if you cooperate."

Kaya looked around at the unsympathetic faces staring back at her and the armored soldiers guarding the doors and decided she wasn't going to get a better deal. She nodded.

"So, what now, who are you guys, Pandora Fleet?" she asked. Meanwhile, Aron began to stir next to her. That was good at least.

"Name's Jimmy. You already met Reina Kwon there," he said, motioning to the female gunslinger. If Kaya wasn't terrified of the older woman, she would have found her fascinating.

"And everyone knows who you are, princess. If they don't already, they will soon. Alerts have already gone out to look for you, and you aren't difficult to spot," Reina said.

"What do you mean?" Kaya asked.

Jimmy was the first to respond. "Well, the reports are only through official channels for now, but there's been a theft at the Boundless Library, and a high-value asset was missing. Namely a certain duke's daughter."

"What's that have to do with me?" she asked, trying to bluff poorly.

"Lady Kaya al Vardan," Jimmy said slowly, "I never had the pleasure of meeting you, dear, but I have met your mother, and you are her spitting image."

"Besides, who else would be dumb enough to wander through the slums looking like you two with a bag of contraband and flashing credit chips," Reina said, motioning to one of the soldiers, who took their bag and tossed it onto the table, the pilfered books and white robe spilling out. "The robe only made it easier to put it together."

"Where am I?" Aron moaned as he rubbed his head. He had gotten hit in the head perhaps one too many times today. However, Kaya's sympathy only went so far with him. She still wanted to find out what he knew and what she had to do with it.

"Safe," Jimmy said, "for now anyway. So think carefully before you tell me any lies. Who are you?"

Aron looked from face to face, taking in the room, "Aron Trilinos, lieutenant of the Children of Men. The Father is expecting me back soon."

"That sorry lot of zealots? Maybe not the best bargaining chip to use with me, kid. Did you kidnap Lady Vardan here?" Jimmy asked.

"What? No! If anything, she kidnapped me," he said truthfully, but Jimmy and Reina looked skeptical.

"Now there's a twist," Reina said.

"But you know who she is?" Jimmy asked rhetorically. "What were you doing in the library?"

"I was looking for a book, what else?" Aron said, and one of the soldiers promptly smacked him in the back of the head.

"Next time it won't be so gentle. Want to try again?" Jimmy asked.

With a sigh, Aron continued, "The Father sent me to collect a book while everyone was distracted with the executions. She got to me first and asked me to get her out of there with one of those books," he said, motioning to the bag. "I don't know what's in either of them or why it's important. I'm just an engineer."

Jimmy thrummed his fingers against his biceps, presumably gauging if he believed Aron or not.

"Did you expect the girl to be there?" he asked. Aron hesitated, and Kaya stared at him. How could he have known Professor Moreau would send her on that specific day?

"It was mentioned as a possibility, but I didn't expect her to *actually* be there. I was supposed to bring her back if I found her, and—"

Jimmy cut Aron off, "And what? Watch her be killed or sold for ransom by that lunatic you call the Father? Well, that won't be happening today." He motioned to one of the soldiers. "Grab him and take him to a cell. I will figure out what to do with him later. As for you," he said, turning to Kaya, "there's no shortage of reasons someone would want to kidnap you. The question is which one is the real reason."

"I need to get back to my sister," Aron pleaded. "Please, let me go. She has no one besides me!"

"You should have thought of that before you got mixed up with the Children," Jimmy said, and there was no sympathy in his voice.

"Wait, leave him. I think he's telling the truth," Kaya blurted out before they could drag Aron away. Jimmy stopped to consider her words. "He could have killed me many times over, but he didn't. His own men even tried to kill him. He's as much a victim as me."

Jimmy raised an eyebrow at that. "Is that true, kid?" Aron nodded in response. He looked like he was afraid to speak lest Jimmy change his mind.

Jimmy let out another sigh. "Fine, leave him, but if he so much as looks at the girl crossways, kill him."

"Why do you care so much about what happens to me?" she asked.

"There are plenty of people who would love to see you dead, but there are plenty of others who would rather you stay breathing. I work for that second type," Jimmy said.

"So you're a soldier of fortune," she concluded.

Jimmy shrugged. "There's some people who would say that about me." He pointed at the crossed torches on his forearm. "Do you know what this is? It is the symbol of the Prometheus Group, our little organization here."

Kaya could tell he took pride in that, but she had no idea what this Prometheus Group was or what they did. There was no shortage of mercenary groups, gangs, pirates, and other would-be insurgents within the Republic.

"What is Prometheus?" Aron asked.

"He was an ancient god of fire," Kaya said.

Jimmy nodded. "Prometheus stole fire from the gods on Mount Olympus and gave it to humanity in the form of knowledge and technology." Aron seemed to consider the story, but Kaya had heard it before from her father.

"Seems at odds with your other tattoo," Kaya said, eyeing the Pandora Fleet insignia.

Jimmy seemed thoughtful as he fingered the outline of the tattoo. "There is truth to that, but I keep it as a reminder."

"A reminder of what?" Kaya asked curiously.

Jimmy ignored her question and went on, "The Republic of course believes all the world's evils, like technology and knowledge, those gifts of Prometheus from the gods must be locked away in Pandora's box. Never to be opened again lest evil overwhelm us. The legend says that within Pandora's box of evil is also hope, preserved for mankind, but to me it is withheld from mankind."

His voice began to rise as a fire burned in his eyes. "Not only is hope withheld, but also the tools needed to make life better. I plan to break open that box and return the torch to mankind as it was originally intended."

"What's to stop evil from taking over? Order is what keeps us safe," she said.

Jimmy shook his head. "Good men with the tools to do great things are what will keep you safe, princess. Everything else you have now is an illusion, made possible by willful ignorance. The regular people, the ones from the slums and low districts see it every day. They see the truth when no one else is willing to."

"That sounds like a recruitment pitch," Kaya said, and Jimmy laughed.

She didn't know what she thought about his little speech. It was certainly interesting, and he even said things she agreed with, but she wasn't sure what the point of all this was. To be petty terrorists? That wasn't something she wanted to be a part of. If that was even what he was getting at.

"I said you wouldn't be harmed, not that you can join us, princess. I am going to return you to your father at the first available opportunity."

"She would be a good addition to your team," came a new voice from the side of the room. Kaya had not even noticed someone was quietly sitting there. The man wore a heavy scarf and spoke with a strange accent, not Martian or Mercurian, yet it sounded familiar.

Then her heart skipped a beat. She remembered. It was on her very first day in the capital when the abbot's car had driven through the crowd, a crowd that stopped to hear this man, the prophet. She was sure it was him. Jimmy seemed to consider the man's words. Was he really the one in charge? The boss he mentioned maybe.

"Did you see it in the orientation of the stars and moon, old man?" Jimmy said, and Kaya felt that her assumption was probably not correct.

Before either of them said another word a soldier opened the door. "Boss, she's here and in the main hall waiting for you."

"I will be right there," Jimmy said scratching his beard.

"Reina, don't leave the princess's side. She can stay here in my office with the old man until I get back."

Reina nodded.

"What about me?" Aron asked.

Jimmy seemed to consider for a moment. "Show him to a room and keep him there until I figure out what to do with him. Make sure he has what he needs," he said to one of the soldiers, who then moved to lead him off. Aron seemed relieved and didn't offer any complaint.

"I would take anything he says with a grain of salt. I'll be back soon," Jimmy said, tossing the sapling necklace to Kaya. He then left the room followed by his soldiers. That left only her, Reina, and the prophet together. Kaya took that moment to finally stand up and stretch. Reina meanwhile took a seat and picked at her nails.

"You are Aelius the Divine, aren't you? The one all over the news reports. The one everyone is looking for," Kaya said.

"You hear that, Aelius? I told you that you were famous."

The man Reina called Aelius removed the scarf that covered his head, revealing clear alabaster skin and a completely smooth and bald head. Kaya was taken aback by his appearance. It wasn't that it was inherently strange; it just hadn't been what she was expecting. Although, she found it amusing they called him an old man. If it wasn't for the bald head, he would have looked younger than Jimmy.

"You can call me Aelius," the man said in his hard-to-place accent. Kaya prided herself on being able to place people's origins, but this one had her stumped.

"My name's Kaya."

"I know." Of course he did, thought Kaya. Everyone seemed to know everything but her.

"Why are you here? Are you part of the Prometheus group?" Kaya asked.

Reina chuckled but didn't say anything.

"No, but I think I am here for the same reasons you are."

She narrowed her eyes on the man. She was tired of everyone assuming they knew what she wanted.

"It doesn't matter," he said, walking closer to her, "I knew your mother and your father once, long ago."

"Everyone tells me that."

"I know, but it doesn't make it less true. I am here to complete a mission, like you."

"You don't know anything about why I am here."

His mannerisms didn't change. He remained rigid and calm, almost unnaturally so.

"Careful, princess, this is where he will start giving you a long speech on the existential threats to mankind and how only you can stop them," Reina said, giving Aelius a sideways glance.

"We can save those for another day, but there are threats that need to be stopped. There is also knowledge to be gained. I know you want answers," he said, looking at her, his face unmoving.

"I know you have quite a following, but I'm not so easily convinced, Prophet," Kaya said. "I'm not interested in the Prometheus Group, or you, or even the Vermilion Coalition. I have my own plans."

"It seems you haven't considered that all of those groups have the same interconnected plans."

"I'm not interested in riddles right now. Especially from frauds like you," Kaya said, taking a seat next to Reina, who seemed to enjoy her berating the man.

"What if I told you everything you have heard from the Era of Empires was true? All of the stories, and their implications, that have been withheld from you based on lies? Countless innocents dead when they could have lived."

"We have heard your speeches before, old man. They are just words. Besides, ancient legends aren't what we need to win this fight. We need soldiers and guns," Reina said.

Aelius didn't smile, smirk, or make any outward emotion at all. He simply held out his hand to Kaya. "Let me see that pendant."

Kaya hesitated, not wanting to let it go again. "Why?"

"I promise no harm will come to it," he said, and Reina looked to Kaya. "If he breaks it, I'll shoot him," and Kaya believed her. So, she handed over the necklace.

Aelius handled it deftly. "Do you know how you would remove the sapling?"

Kaya shrugged. "I would break the glass and plant it. What else would you do? There's no way to open it." She knew that because she had tried countless times when she sat alone, missing home.

Aelius moved the pendant through his fingers in circular patterns. At first it seemed random, but then Kaya picked up on a pattern to where he was pressing and swiping on the surface.

It was some kind of lock, she thought, but how did he know how to open it? Then suddenly he held his palm out, and in the center the pendant whirled before opening like a lotus blossom in his hand, revealing a thriving sapling that rustled briefly in the air of the room. Kaya reached out to touch it gently.

"How did you know how to do that?" she asked, stunned. Even Reina looked impressed.

"Were you sure there was no way to open that, princess?"
Kaya shook her head. "Even my father didn't know how besides breaking it. I have never seen anything like this. Look how perfectly it all worked. What's even powering it?" She had so many questions.

Aelius pressed the pendant again, and it reverted to its egg-like shape with a resounding click, and he handed it back.

Kaya held the pendant and desperately pawed its surface looking for some kind of seam or mechanism, but its surface was perfectly smooth.

Reina also snatched it from her hand to do her own assessment and looked equally surprised when she couldn't find anything.

"Well, that's a neat trick, old man. I'll give you that," Reina said.

"How did you know how to do that?" Kaya asked.

"There are many things that have been kept from you, all of you," he said, looking at Reina before turning back to Kaya. "I can help show you the way, make the eternal dream a reality, but first I have a plan that I think you can help with, if you are willing to listen," he said.

Kaya moved to rummage through the bag with the books that had been discarded on the table and pulled out the book about the eternal dream, slamming it on the table in front of Aelius.

"Everyone keeps talking about an eternal dream, but what is it? Why is there only one book in the entire Boundless Library that talks about it?"

Reina picked up the book and flipped through several pages, squinting. "What language is this even written in? I don't recognize it."

Aelius didn't look at the book. "It is a very old form of Imperial English, far removed from the current Standard Tongue by some five hundred years."

"How do you even know that much? You didn't even look at the book," Kaya said, beginning to get angry.

"There was a time, before the Time of Chaos, during the Era of Empire, when the phrase was popular. The idea was that humankind's innovation and expansion would be as limitless and unending as their collective dreams," he said.

"I have never heard it before," Reina said.

"Most haven't. It has only survived in small circles. The Republic did a good job erasing mention of it during the Great Purge."

"Why would they leave this book around, least of all where it could be found in the Boundless Library?" Kaya asked. This all seemed like too much of a coincidence.

Aelius remained eerily passive in his demeanor, which was off-putting to Kaya. "The author, the Patriarch of Sirenum, was a clever man. He wrote the book with quite a bit of allegory and religious undertones, so it managed to evade censure. It also helped that very few people could read the language then or now."

"So the book is important?" Kaya asked.

"The message in it is important, but that message exists in more than this one book."

"I think my mother believed in the eternal dream."

Aelius nodded. "She did and so do many others."

"This is an interesting history lesson, old man, but what does it mean now? Dreams are great, but the reality right now is a nightmare," Reina said, fully engaged in the conversation. Meanwhile, Kaya was struggling to process what was going on. Who was this man who claimed to know so much about her mother and the world she dreamed of? A world no one had seen for nearly a thousand years.

"The dream will be a reality again soon. Pandora's box will be opened, and mankind will have the tools it needs to endeavor once again to reach for the stars and beyond, painting the cosmos in its image," Aelius said. He delivered it with the same steady tone he said everything, but it still resonated within Kaya.

"I'm only one person, little better than a prisoner right now," she said.

His smooth white face broke from its passive mask, and the corners of his mouth turned into something resembling a smile, or at least that was what Kaya thought it looked like.

"You are more than that, so much more. You are your mother's daughter, and there is an important part for you to play in all of this," he said.

"I want to know everything you know about my mother."

"In time. For now, there is other work to do, if you are ready to listen."

"Someone told me my mother died for this dream. What do you know about that?" she pushed.

Aelius nodded. "She devoted her life to the eternal dream and the cause it represented. Are you ready to follow in her footsteps?"

Kaya knew what she wanted to say but didn't know this man or any of these people. Everything was moving so fast. Things had finally settled down into some semblance of normal in the past year with school, prayers, and especially Hal, but now that had all been turned upside down in an instant.

She looked desperately to Reina for some kind of guidance, even if the woman wasn't her friend. Reina shrugged. "I have no idea what he's on about, princess, but he usually talks like he's in charge. Even if he isn't," she said, glaring at Aelius. Her gaze softened. "But I would hear what he has to say. Even Jimmy listens to him."

After a quiet moment, Kaya finally nodded. "I have never wanted any-thing else more." Her father had always told her life was a series of hard choices, and you couldn't shy away from making them. So she took this leap, whatever it would mean for her now.

Aelius's strange smile returned. "How much do you know about the current state of the Republic?" he began, and Kaya knew she would be in for a long night.

Silas

March, 4103 U.E.T.—Tiyas, Mars

SILAS KNEELED ON the cold, hard stones of the small church. His head bowed low, gloved hands pressed to the floor in front of him.

Candlelight flickered in the dark and cramped space as the cleric gave his benediction, the junior officers of his command kneeling next to him on either side. The occasional rustle of armor and weapons were the only sounds interrupting the cleric's prayer and the metal creaking of his censer as it swung over their heads.

He didn't appreciate having to play the social games of clergy and politicians, but the commitment to his family, faith, and mission kept him moving forward.

He would sacrifice what he had to if it meant keeping his family safe. He preferred to pray in private, not in a spectacle made for prying eyes to film and judge.

He knew even now a clergyman would be delivering a message to the local bishop of his presence here. However, if he had to be seen in a church in the capital, he would choose one that served the poorer districts, like the one he found himself in now.

The church sat along the banks of the Agyre Basin in a town called Tiyas and was humble compared to the large cathedrals nearer the capital.

He felt the cold touch of holy water hit his head before dripping to the stone floor between his hands as the ritual neared its end. He focused on communicating with God and not the machinations of the clergy, but the ghosts that haunted him made him question if he deserved God's blessing at all.

"Go with the light of God and fulfill your duty," the cleric concluded with a tinge of superiority in his voice.

To that the assembled knights replied, "God wills it!"

"God wills it," Silas replied with the others. Rising to his feet, he cursed in silence, his knees aching from the effort. He was beginning to feel his age.

Stepping into the sunlight, he took in his surroundings. Tiyas was known more for its slums and troubled history than anything else, but despite its problems it was a place where he could reliably interact with the Republic's common citizens.

In Tiyas, the citizens didn't deal constantly in secrets and schemes, at least not ones that involved him, he thought dryly. His journeys to the capital were typically fraught with political danger he strived to avoid.

Marcus opened a pack of cookies as he walked up beside Silas offering him one.

"No, thanks," he said. "Do you really need to eat right now?"

"I would have eaten inside, but I figured you wouldn't approve."

Silas gave him a disapproving look anyway.

Religion was one area he and Marcus didn't see eye to eye on, even though Marcus had been destined for the clergy once long ago.

"You know, it is never too late to take up that career with the clergy," Silas said.

"And finally make the ghosts of my parents happy after all these years? Absolutely not. Besides, I'm still holding out for your job," he replied as he bit into another cookie.

"You better get in line," Silas replied, shaking his head.

He turned to the armored escort as they approached their transport craft. "You, you, and you," he said, pointing to three of the soldiers. "Come with us. The rest of you return to the ship. I will call when we are ready for transport."

The three soldiers, one an old and stocky first sergeant named Gwen Lin and two young and physically imposing soldiers, moved to join himself and Marcus. The lieutenant in charge of the transport, who Silas didn't recognize, spoke up.

"High Commander, I cannot leave you without a craft on the ground and a satisfactory escort," the young lieutenant said with a tone indicative of his noble upbringing. He looked like he had barely left the academy. Gwen stepped up next to him, and Silas knew he wouldn't have to say another word.

"Don't worry, Lieutenant. We have the commander here well taken care of. We promise to have him back before dark," she said in her rough Martian accent with a deadpan expression.

"I don't…" the lieutenant began to say in protest, looking back and forth between Gwen and Silas. He had been in his position before and didn't envy the boy. The lieutenant might outrank Gwen, but she had enough authority to make his life a nightmare for the foreseeable future. He knew this and decided this fight wasn't worth the extra paperwork, so he saluted and made his way onto the transport as ordered.

"You always know how to make friends with the new ones, don't you, Gwen?" Marcus said to her through a mouth full of crumbs.

"I'm tired of these academy drones. One more year and I can finally retire," she said, sounding wistful.

"Hey, hey, easy on the insults. We were academy graduates once too," Marcus said, feigning a wounded heart. Silas smiled. He had a soft spot for Gwen and found her banter with Marcus amusing. She was one of the few people who could always put him in his place.

"Yea, well, that's why I've run out of patience for the bullshit and can't wait to retire next year," she said gruffly, adjusting the rifle strap on her shoulder.

Silas let out a chuckle and Marcus an exasperated sigh, but before they could respond she asked, "Where are we going anyway? This place is a dump."

"We have to go see someone discreetly," Silas said, emphasizing the last word. Marcus seemed more interested in his snack, but the two young soldiers next to Gwen looked nervous. Luckily, they were well trained enough to stay quiet.

Gwen looked them all over. "We aren't exactly inconspicuous, you know."

"If it's the few of us, we shouldn't create too much panic. We aren't looking for a fight," Silas said.

"Not to question you, sir, but is that smart right now with how volatile the situation is around here?" Gwen asked.

"We will be fine if we stick to the main roads. Hands off triggers. We don't want anyone killing someone because they got jumpy," Silas said, eyeing the young soldiers especially.

"What are you worried about, Gwen? Aren't you from around here anyway?" Marcus chimed in.

"If by around here you mean the slums, then yea, but not this one," she said, glaring at Marcus. "I left for a reason. Anywhere else is better than the slums."

Silas knew a lot of the Republic's military was recruited from the slums. It was one of the very few opportunities for regular meals and any kind of future.

Gwen turned back to Silas, speaking in a low voice. "I'm all for non-violence, sir, but don't you think we should have more fire power with us than this to go in there?"

"We aren't trying to start a war, just quietly and discreetly get some information. This isn't the midnight raids. If we bring more people, they will assume the worst, and it won't lead to anything good."

Gwen nodded, understanding the assignment. He normally wouldn't let a soldier question him so much, but Gwen had earned that right a long time ago.

Silas addressed the other two soldiers who were too far away to hear what they were talking about, "If everyone does what I say and keeps calm, we will be in and out in no time. This is still Republic territory."

"Yes, sir," they said in unison.

"Alright, well, let's get to it then. I don't want to navigate this hell hole in the dark. You two," Gwen said to the soldiers by her side, "take point. Don't shoot anyone unless they try to shoot you." Then she stopped as if she had a thought. "You know what, switch to stun rounds just to be safe. I will watch the rear."

Silas gave the signal, and they moved out. Stepping through the gate was like passing into another world. The cathedral offered one of the only green spaces for miles in any direction and stood in stark contrast to the dilapidated city around it.

However, the church grounds were only open to those lucky enough to obtain a permit, which was why he knew they would be nearly empty when they came through on this mission. Only the upper crust of Tiyas would earn a permit to enter this oasis, and that group was shrinking every day.

Once they moved a couple blocks past the ancient stone and metal gates of the church grounds, they were overwhelmed by sights, sounds, and especially smells.

Tiyas sat at a low elevation on the flanks of Olympus Mons, giving it a warm and slightly humid climate that only seemed to make the aromas particularly unbearable for those unaccustomed to it.

Silas scanned the buildings as they passed, most of them so deteriorated he was amazed they were standing at all. Without proper maintenance, the solar radiation took its toll, along with water damage, vandalism, and exploding gas lines.

As he walked, he was careful to keep his hands away from his weapons, lest anyone get the wrong idea. Although he had been to the Tiyas church numerous times recently, he hadn't ventured into the slums themselves in years. There was a part of him that dreaded the experience, and the memories it dredged up, but this meeting was something he couldn't trust to anyone else, not even Marcus.

His eyes moved from one burned-out building to the next. Through broken or missing windows, he saw families of equally bedraggled humans existing in some kind of semi-conscious state crammed together into whatever area was not already occupied by trash or machinery for the units above them.

Those on the higher levels of the buildings lived in relative luxury compared to the abject poverty of the ground dwellers as they were called. However even the upper crust was crammed into tiny units with far too many people in what most from any other neighborhood would consider squalor.

He couldn't help but feel pity for these people as they drifted from one hell to the next trying to eke out some existence from the detritus of the past and the meager resources of the present. Each burned-out building and shattered family only reminded him of what used to be and the part he played in creating this reality.

It was undeniable that the Midnight Raids had changed these places forever, and despite constant promises from the government the light never returned to them. There was a time he believed he was doing something good to improve the lives of normal citizens, but year after year the false promises mounted, and it became harder to accept that narrative.

The thought always took Silas to a dark place. The guilt and hopelessness were nearly overwhelming, but he would keep trying to atone. Until one day, God decided he had suffered enough and relieved him of his burden.

Marcus's voice broke him free of his stupor.

"I never understood why he chose to set up shop here of all places," Marcus said while scanning the assembled crowds around them.

The people of Tiyas were shuffling along with a look of weariness he couldn't imagine. Seeing it made him feel guilty about his own lamentations. He knew any of these people would gladly switch places with him given the chance.

The deeper they traveled into the slums, more and more of the disheveled masses took notice of their presence and cried out for alms or other aid. His team ignored them as they passed. There was nothing the few of them could do or offer to fix their situation.

"You know, he thinks he can help these people, so he sits here in plain sight, doing that in defiance of the Republic's decrees," Silas replied in a low voice.

"Only an idiot would think they could change anything here. Look at them. What a sorry lot," Marcus said, his face a mix of contempt and empathy.

"Maybe one day there will be a way to really help them." Silas knew there wasn't any easy solution to this problem, but it pained him to admit it out loud. Marcus was too pragmatic to agree with him.

The road became more congested the deeper they got into the district. Food vendors with dirty, rusty carts sold steaming strips of questionable meat, along with ration or vitamin packs that were likely well past their expiration dates. Other vendors hawked various sundries or nearly destroyed pieces of old tech.

Silas found the resolve these people showed to toil through this type of misery and eke out an honest living incredibly admirable. They showed a level of resourcefulness and inventiveness he rarely saw. However, he wasn't delusional and knew for every honest citizen there were at least two others preying on the most vulnerable.

In the deeper shadows, vile figures lurked selling nectar or other narcotics surrounded by the withered husks of their worshipers. Unfortunately, that scene was far too common.

As they walked, they came across a pocket of people crowded around a man in heavy robes pontificating on a box next to some assembled items. Silas hated these grifters most of all.

They were the ones who sold ancient pills guaranteed to bless you with agelessness or some other mythical gift. There were plenty of desperate people happy to believe their lies for a chance at that promised future.

As the group approached the false prophet, the whispers from those nearby started to grow and carry down the crowded street. Word would spread quickly that soldiers were here, and that couldn't mean anything good for them.

"Should we handle this?" asked Marcus, nodding in the direction of the robed man.

"He's too far away. By the time we get close, he will be long gone anyway. Let's carry on," Silas replied.

It was then one of the young soldiers hefted his rifle, perhaps looking to make a name for himself and sighted the man through his rifle. "I have a clear shot," he said confidently, his finger inching toward the trigger of his rifle.

Thankfully Gwen was there in a flash jerking the rifle down and pulling him in close. "Are you a sarding moron, Corporal?" she growled into his ear.

"I thought..." he began to protest, his voice a mix of confusion and anger, but Gwen cut him off.

"You aren't here to think, Corporal. You are here to keep your eyes sharp and avoid doing anything stupid. Look around you," she growled in a low whisper. "What do you think will stop them from tearing you apart once you fire that shot? Tearing us all apart?"

She shoved him away as the corporal stuttered, struggling to come up with any reasonable answer. He eventually nodded and put his gun aside.

Silas knew that could have gone poorly, but he was happy with how Gwen handled it.

"Stay sharp. We still have a little further to our destination," Silas said, motioning them forward through the crowd.

However, as they got closer to the robed peddler, someone in the crowd shouted, "Soldiers! It's a raid!" It was then that madness took over.

"By God's bones! Tighten up! Stay close, fingers off triggers," Silas shouted as they kept on their course, trying to part the turbulent sea of bodies.

The crowd surged around them, as people tried to flee in every possible direction. They knocked each other over and toppled carts to get away, creating even more chaos as people swarmed the fallen scraps of food and sundries, trying to scoop up what they could in the confusion.

"Everyone, calm down. There is no raid!" Silas shouted over the crowd in a worthless attempt to establish some order. His unaided voice wasn't loud enough to get through the noise. It was then that Marcus drew his antique pistol and fired several shots into the air.

"Hey, listen up. Clear out peacefully!" He began motioning the people away in the opposite direction to where they were heading, the sudden gunfire making them a bit more agreeable. "Yes, that's right, slow and steady," he said, giving a good shove to another bedraggled man who bumped into them in his haste to get away with arms full of pilfered goods.

Well after the crowd began to thin out, three constables could be seen running over to their position. The three men were out of shape, disheveled, and as sickly looking as most of the slum's residents. However, they had stun batons held at the ready.

Once they got close enough to see who the party was, they nearly fell over each other in their haste to salute.

"We uh...came running when we heard a gunshot," the senior of the three said. He was a short man with a hefty gut and pockmarked face, his uniform faded and straining to stay together at the seams.

"Yes, thank you, good sirs. I feel instantly safer," Marcus said in a dry tone. "I think we have it under control."

"We, uh, didn't know yous would be here," the constable said.

"You and me both," Marcus responded under his breath before waving the three on. "Why don't you go back to...maintaining safety and order in these parts. Here, you three find the nearest thing that passes for a pub here and see that there aren't any more dissidents." He reached into his pocket and came out with a credit chip for each man.

"Uh, yes, yes, sir! We sure will," the senior constable said as he greedily took all three. Silas assumed the man would be keeping them and deciding what the other two might receive. The three men then tripped over each other in their haste to leave, maybe thinking Marcus would change his mind and take the chips back.

"Well, that should keep them from reporting seeing us," Marcus said. "At least for now."

"Let's hope so. We are almost there. Hopefully we can get there without any more—" Before he finished, a loud groan filled the air. He'd spoken too soon.

Hearing the groan from under a toppled old cart, Gwen motioned for the corporal to investigate the source of the noise while she and Marcus kept an eye on the windows and rooftops with their rifles ready.

The rickety old cart had toppled over, dumping old military-issue ration packs among other odds and ends. The soldiers moved the debris and pulled back the tattered old sun cloth, revealing the crumbled form of a young boy whose legs were trapped under the weight of the cart. Gwen motioned for them to lift the cart, but as one of the soldiers moved to comply the corporal hesitated, causing his partner to pause.

"What are we doing this for, Sarge? He's another slum rat. Let's leave him for his friends and keep moving," the corporal said, looking from the boy to Gwen.

Moving closer, Silas could clearly see that the boy's body was deformed and covered in sores, a sign of the radiation sickness that was rampant in the slums where they couldn't afford regular anti-radiation meds or rad scrubbers to filter the tainted air and water. The situation here, and everywhere, was getting worse and worse, he thought.

Gwen looked at the corporal with a steely gaze. Silas could have sworn she was taunting him to challenge her command, but she never said a word and didn't have to. After a moment, the corporal thought better of complaining and motioned for his partner to help him lift the dirty cart off the boy, making his disgust with the task well known.

The soldiers righted the cart with relative ease, the flimsy metal not offering much challenge for the two men. With the cart righted, the boy's legs were free, but he still groaned in obvious pain.

Silas approached the boy with Marcus by his side. Once he got a better look, he could clearly see that the boy's legs were even more deformed than he had realized. If he had been able to walk at all, even before this accident, it could have only been with exceptional pain. Then he noticed the trail of blood coming from the back of the boy's head.

"Boy, can you hear me?" Silas said, waving his hand in front of the his cloudy eyes.

"It hurts so much," the boy stammered through groans and whimpers. The sight broke Silas's heart, even if he wouldn't let anyone else see it.

Tears wouldn't do the boy any good, so he snapped his hand out to the corporal. "Give me a morphine shot."

"High Commander, what for? Look at'em. He will be dead by tomorrow," the corporal said, disbelief evident on his face.

"Corporal, now," he replied sternly, not pulling back his hand. He wasn't in the mood to play these games. Not today.

He would thank Zhou later for these new recruits who made it obvious they would prefer someone else to lead the Pandora Fleet, although that was a problem for another day.

With a sigh, the corporal opened his med pouch and handed over a morphine shot. Silas took it and hesitated for only a moment before jabbing it into what passed for the meatiest part of the boy's leg. It was a dose strong enough for a soldier more than four times his size.

Silas knew what it would do in such a frail boy, but the corporal was right that he wouldn't survive through the night, and he hated that reality. There was nothing more he could do but try and make the boy comfortable.

The drugs began to work, and the boy's eyes opened slightly as the pain eased. "Th...thank you," he groaned hoarsely as he looked deeply into Silas's eyes.

"What's your name, boy?" Silas said, steeling himself against his own emotions.

"B...Brandon, sir," he stuttered out.

"Brandon, I am Lord Beckett, High Commander, of the Pandora Fleet. It is an honor to meet you," he said, grabbing the boy's forearm lightly. It was so small and frail he worried he would break it. It all seemed so pointless.

The boy's eyes widened as much as they could in his state, "M...milord," he said, averting his eyes.

"None of that, lad," Silas said, taking his other hand and placing it on the boy's cheek. "Today you look at me as a knight of the Pandora Fleet." The others looked from Silas to each other, but none of them said a word.

He knew there was no saving his body now, a body that had been crippled long ago by a harsh world that offered no comfort for people like him. All he could do now was try to offer some comfort for the boy's soul.

"Do you swear to uphold the laws of man and God, face the darkness without fear, and stay steadfast in your duty to safeguard the realms of man from the horrors kept locked away, for as long as you draw breath?" he said, reciting the Pandora Fleets oath of service.

The boy's eyes lit up in a way unimaginable a moment prior. Silas could only guess what fantasies raced through the boy's mind. Dreams of commanding starships and leading soldiers across battlefields or visiting distant moons. Those were the kinds of dreams he had as a child.

It was the dream of being someone who commanded the respect of their peers and left a lasting mark on the world, the dream of being someone whose life mattered. In that moment, Silas wanted the boy to know that he also mattered.

"Yes, I swear it," he said, confident and proud. A tear rolled down his face as his eyes became cloudy again and his eyelids heavier. Silas could tell he was struggling to stay awake, but he never looked away, never wavered. He had the heart of a lion.

"Malum contineri debet," Silas said, still cupping the boy's cheek with as warm of a smile as he could muster. The motto of the Pandora Fleet, "evil must be contained."

"Rest now, soldier. Tomorrow, we sail for distant worlds, and your strength will be required."

The boy's smile radiated as his eyes began to close. Silas motioned to Marcus with a nod. He didn't want to let go of the boy.

Marcus leaned over and grabbed another morphine shot from the corporal and unceremoniously jabbed it into the boy's leg. It took only a few more moments before his body became lifeless in Silas's arms. Marcus shook Silas's shoulder, and he reluctantly let go. Silas would have shed a tear then if he had any tears left, but this was another terrible ghost to add to his already crowded mausoleum.

"To God we belong, and to him we shall return," Silas muttered, making the sign of the star and cross, and the others followed suit as he stood up.

Marcus shoved the empty morphine cartridges into the chest of the corporal as he walked past, and they continued on their path.

CHAPTER

19

It wasn't much longer until they arrived at the location they were looking for. It was a large skyscraper by the standards of the slums. The building was clad in glass that was still mostly intact or repaired with whatever patchwork the workers could find.

It was a building that was the legacy of a more prosperous time in this district of the city, before the Midnight Raids changed things, before he changed things. He had been to this building once before, during those times. Begging the magnate who owned it and controlled this part of the city to acquiesce to their demands, but he had refused. The memories of that day came unbidden to Silas at that moment.

"You okay?" Marcus asked, stopping beside him. Then he seemed to have his own realization. "Is this–"

"Yes, Orzone Industries."

"I hardly recognized it," Marcus said, still looking up at the building, but then he noticed two figures by the formerly grand entranceway eying them with guns held tight. "Looks like the goon squad is watching. Are you sure this is a good idea? We could still send a message."

Silas shook his head. "No, we need to do this in person. As it is, we might not even get another chance when I meet with the Vox. I need something to tell him, and I need it now."

Marcus nodded and took a deep breath. "Well, then let's get this over with, shall we?"

As they approached the door, the two guards made no move to stop them, but they also didn't seem scared or concerned by the presence of armed soldiers at their doorstep. On closer inspection, Silas could tell they were professionally trained soldiers, not local toughs.

When they made it to the doors, the guards stepped into their path.

"You two only," one of the guards said, motioning to Silas and Marcus.

Gwen looked like she wanted to protest, but Silas waved her down. "It's okay. You three stay out here. If you don't hear from me in fifteen minutes, kill everyone," he said. She nodded, eyeballing the two guards, and searching for other threats, like snipers in nearby buildings.

Silas knew that if Jimmy wanted them dead, they probably already would be. He just hoped the risk he was taking was worth it.

"You boys are looking good. Glad to see Jimmy is feeding you well," Marcus said, slapping one of the guards on the shoulder. He didn't seem amused.

"No weapons," the guard said, not stepping aside to let them pass.

"Well that isn't happening, mate, so better to move aside and let us through," Marcus continued, creating a standoff with the guards. Silas remained silent, but he had no intention of giving up his weapons either.

"It's fine. Let them in," a woman's voice said from the doorway, causing the men to break their staring contest.

"Hello, Captain Kwon," Silas said, looking at the woman.

"Hello, High Commander, and is it Commander now, Marcus?" she asked as the guards relaxed and let them pass.

Marcus pointed to the oak leaf on his lapel. "Yeah, that's right. I finally outrank you."

"Congratulations, darling. It's nice to see you both again. It's been a long time."

"That makes one of us," Marcus said, and Silas cast him a look.

"Good to see you too, Reina," Silas said more amicably.

"As pleasant as ever, Marcus, but we can catch up later. Jimmy is expecting you."

"I guess word got here fast," Silas said.

Reina shook her head. "Why is it everyone thinks they can stroll in here like we wouldn't know? We have had you tailed since before you left the church grounds."

"I'm glad to know you were so concerned for our safety," Marcus said sarcastically.

"If we wanted you dead, you know you would be already. You could have made a quieter entrance though."

"Unfortunately, the situation escalated, and asking for an escort wasn't exactly an option," Silas offered, and Reina grunted.

"That seems to happen a lot lately, doesn't it?"

"Taking the moral high ground, eh? That's rich coming from you," Marcus said.

Reina didn't take the bait. "I do what I must, like you. I just happened to pick the right side."

They rode the elevator in silence until they reached one of the higher floors, well above the smells and sounds of the slums below.

Reina led them to a large pair of doors flanked by more armed guards. Inside the room was a large conference table surrounded by a dozen chairs, but only one person sat at the table waiting for them. He rose as they entered and waved them in.

"High Commander, Commander, please come and sit," Jimmy said affably.

"Commander Torress, you are doing well for yourself, I see," Silas said, using his former rank. He had retired in good standing, so he wouldn't take that from the man. Even if he didn't agree with what Jimmy chose to do in his retirement.

Also, he did look good. His skin was pale, but it had always been pale, a legacy of his heritage beyond the belt. "How long has it been now, five years?"

"More like ten," Jimmy said, taking his seat. "Please, sit."

"I'd rather stand," Marcus said in a cold tone, placing his hand on the pistol at his chest. "You remember what I told you last time I saw you? Screw me again and it would be the last time."

Reina instinctively moved her hands over the guns on her hips. "Really, Marcus? Do you think you can outdraw me now?" she said confidently.

"I don't need to be faster than you, just fast enough," Marcus said, never taking his eyes off Jimmy.

"It's alright, Reina," Jimmy said, waving at her to relax. "Shoot me if you think it will help, Marcus. Whatever you think I did, I can assure you I didn't. I don't know how many more times I can tell you that," Jimmy said.

"No one needs to shoot anyone," Silas said, trying to de-escalate things. "We didn't come here for this, Marcus."

He was afraid this might happen, but it had been worth the risk. At the end of the day, Marcus was the only one he trusted to be in this room at this moment, despite the personal issues Marcus had with Jimmy.

Marcus paused, considering something and then took his hand away from his gun. "You better have something good to say, or I swear before God—"

Silas raised his hand taking his seat, and Marcus let his words stop there. Marcus decided to stand beside Reina where he could watch them both.

"So you are working with the Coalition now, Jimmy?" Silas asked.

He shrugged. "Working is a strong word. You know the Coalition has dozens of players. Everyone is trying to accomplish different goals, and most of them don't even play nice together."

"You didn't answer my question."

"I do what I have to survive here in my little slice of Eden, while also collecting the information my clients need," Jimmy said, leaning back in his chair. "How are things going for you these days? Prophets on the rise, riots, even the missing daughter of the Lord Eminent. Must be tough."

"What do you know about any of that?" Silas asked.

"Not much, everyone wants to find Lady Vardan, but I am sure she will turn up sooner or later in some private estate partying like other lost socialites in the past. She's only been gone a few weeks," Jimmy said.

Silas nodded. "The Frumentarii are working to find her. My concern is the prophets and putting an end to their cabals. Particularly the one they are calling Aelius the Divine or Najm Alarshad, the guiding star."

"It's a catchy name. He has really gained quite the following, but I don't know any more than you," Jimmy said. "But I wish I did so I could thank them for the comfort they have given to the people. Not to mention the miracles, diseases healed, and wounds fixed. It is quite impressive."

"Don't tell me you are falling for these charlatans now too, mate. It must be the radiation getting to you," Marcus said.

"You can joke if you like, but I have seen it with my own eyes, he is—different," Reina said, and Silas could tell she was very serious. Marcus only scoffed. He had always been a skeptic.

"Let me know if you find out anything more," Silas said, and Jimmy nodded, "Another thing I need to know now, the information you gave us on Hex and the Hermes Conglomerate at 132 Aethera? Did that information come from your new—not partners, as you say—acquaintances?"

"No, that information was old, and I told you as much when I gave it to you," Jimmy said, leaning over the table. "If she wasn't there, that's not my fault."

"They were waiting for us, you pasty white bastard," Marcus said, "and I think that's because you tipped them off."

Jimmy scoffed. "As if I had those capabilities. If I did, do you think I would be here in this lovely palace?" he said, motioning to the deteriorating building around him. "No, if they knew you were coming, it was because they saw you from miles away. Hermes has more resources than I have seen from anyone short of the Republic military. I wouldn't underestimate them."

Silas stayed quiet, thinking. He was right that Hex and her Hermes Conglomerate had shown a level of organization and resources unrivaled by nearly anyone.

Maybe it was less that they were waiting for them and more that they were organized and prepared in a way he didn't anticipate. If they had time to mobilize the fleet of aircraft they had burning in their hangars, maybe things would have ended differently.

"They might be organized, but they are still a small rebel group. They will all fall eventually," Silas said.

Jimmy smiled. "I know you still think that, but you really should open your eyes."

"I thought you were on our side, mate," Marcus said.

"Can't a friend be honest? Besides, I don't need to like what the Republic stands for. I am a businessman now. I will keep taking your blood money and using it to help these people. It's the best I can do for now while the clergy continue to run things."

"You are many things, but my friend will never be one of them again, Jimmy," Marcus said.

Jimmy turned back to Silas. "Look, High Commander, you know times are changing. The cities are crumbling. People are sick and dying. It gets worse everyday. None of this is sustainable."

"So bombing peaceful districts and murdering innocents is the way to fix it?" Marcus asked.

Jimmy looked angry. "You know I have nothing to do with any of that."

"Marcus, why don't you wait outside?" Silas said.

"I'm not leaving you–"

"I will be fine," Silas said, cutting him off. "Just right outside the door." He then looked at Jimmy.

"Why don't you join him, Reina?" She looked at Jimmy and likewise hesitated, but the two of them eventually left the room, watching each other like two hungry dogs fighting over a bone.

"You know we have nothing to do with the recent attacks," he said once they had all left the room.

"I believe you, but he doesn't. Along with many others. You have flown under the radar for now, but the news of your association with the Vermilion Coalition isn't good. I can't protect you forever," Silas said, leaning back in his chair. "It's becoming hard enough to protect myself. I really need your help here."

Jimmy nodded. "I appreciate everything you have done, and despite what Marcus might think we have made some real progress here."

"And set yourself up as a rich little warlord."

He shrugged. "Positive side effect, I guess. Either way, it puts me in a position to influence others. Groups like the Children of Man who prefer a more violent approach."

Silas stared at him. He hoped that was the real reason and not some petty turf war.

"It has been in the works a long time, but now that Prometheus is finally recognized as part of the Apex Group, we can start making more changes. It also means," he said, pulling out a data chip and sliding it across the table to Silas, "that I am privy to more and better information."

Silas didn't reach for it. "What's the Apex Group?"

"Think of it as the Assembly of Lords but for the Vermilion Coalition. The strongest groups that keep the others in line."

"So it's a crime syndicate?" Silas said, snatching up the data chip. "And what's this supposed to be?"

Jimmy laughed, "Some might think so, but at best it's a loose organization to avoid stepping on toes and trying to reach a consensus on big-picture strategy. So far it's been more productive than our naval command meetings used to be."

Silas was forced to laugh. "That is a pretty low bar."

"Isn't that true? And that in your hand there is my gift to you.

Information on where Hex is, and it's recent, including specifications of their hideout and all."

Silas looked at him suspiciously. "Why would they give you this?"

He smiled. "What makes you think they did? I stole it, of course, during a meeting. Despite their sophistication, we have a strong espionage team here."

Silas knew that was true. There was no shortage of former military members among the Prometheus Group. Even some former Frumentarii if the stories were true.

He slipped the chip into his pocket. "Where is the base? Somewhere near Pluto?" he asked in a sarcastic tone.

"No, nowhere so nice. Deimos," Jimmy said in a mock apology.

Silas looked surprised. "Deimos, how sure are you?" It wasn't impossible, he knew, but it seemed exceptionally odd the most wanted individual in the solar system would choose to hide so close.

"Very sure, it seems like they have run out of distant hiding spots. Good job on that by the way," Jimmy said, raising his eyebrows. "Anyway, it was information pieced together by my team from their internal reports. It would have been difficult for them to fake our conclusions. Anyway, it's not far. If they aren't there, what's the harm?"

Silas looked at him for a long moment. He knew Jimmy could and did lie, but what he was saying made sense. Unless it was a trap, but everything could always be a trap. They could mitigate those risks. He didn't exactly trust Jimmy, but he had always dealt with them honestly.

"Thank you, Jimmy, your fee will be transferred," he said, and Jimmy nodded.

"Always a pleasure doing business with you. On a personal note, how is your father holding up?"

Silas stood up to leave. He didn't plan to linger here longer than he had to. Especially the direction this conversation was going.

"He is a fighter. I am sure he will be with us for years to come," he said but knew Jimmy wouldn't believe him. It was common knowledge the Duke of Mars was aging and ill. It was only a matter of time now, and then Silas would be duke.

Jimmy nodded. "He was always a good man. Good luck, High Commander."

Silas returned the gesture. "You too, Jimmy." He made to leave the room but then stopped at the door without looking back.

"Why did you pick this building to set up shop?" he asked, and there was a long pause.

"I think it was for a chance to change things. To make the right choice, even after all these years," Jimmy said, and in the silence that followed they shared a common memory. Although there wasn't anything more that could be said and Silas continued out the door.

Kaya

March, 4103 U.E.T.—Tiyas, Mars

THE DOOR CLOSED, and Kaya peeked out from behind the secret alcove in the meeting room. Her heart had threatened to beat out of her chest, and she wondered how no one had noticed it making so much noise. If the high commander had seen her, things would have gotten ugly.

She had been missing for nearly a month and knew there was no shortage of people looking for her. Lord Beckett would have taken her back and arrested everyone in the building, or at least tried to anyway. In any case, she was confident it would have led to bloodshed if they had tried.

"Why did you let me see that?"

"If we are asking you to help us, to risk everything, you need to understand the stakes involved. This is too important now for doubts or indecision," Jimmy said, looking at her.

Aelius made it easy for her to decide to stay, at least in the beginning. Then it turned out he had very little to say about her mother specifically.

He was more interested in explaining the intricacies of the conflict they found themselves in and how people like her mother had supported change. She was thankful for the information but what she really wanted to know was more about her mother.

Kaya wanted to help people of course, but she knew in her heart that wasn't the main reason she stayed. The problem was that before she got the chance to press Aelius further he had disappeared to some parts unknown.

That left her spending more time with Jimmy, and in that time she had grown to like him. He had been true to his word and treated her and Aron with kindness despite their circumstances.

Kaya pushed for Jimmy to allow Aron to contact his sister, despite her misgivings about what had happened between them. Even if it was as much to find out if she was real as it was to help him. It turned out she was, and Kaya was glad she pushed for it. It was clear from the relief on Aron's face that it meant a lot to him too.

She knew Jimmy was also taking a big risk keeping her there, but she was worried about what her father and brother must think. She wanted Jimmy to allow her to contact them, which he assured her she would soon. She could win a victory for Aron, but it seemed much harder to win one for herself.

"Have you ever met the high commander before?" Jimmy asked.

"No, I have only seen him from a distance, when he came to visit my father once, but I'm sure he would recognize me anyway, even with these contacts and dyed hair," she said.

"Maybe, he's a smart man and a keen observer, but he also isn't expecting to see you here or looking like that," he said, motioning to her appearance.

They had given her contacts that made her eyes a plain brown, and her auburn hair was cut to her shoulders and dyed dark brown to match. She wore black trousers and a simple blue blouse and could pass for any of the thousands of young mid-district office workers who populated the city's larger businesses.

"People like to make sense of what they see in the world, so they won't usually question things below the surface. That is one of the problems with the world today."

"Do you really think what all of you are doing here will make a difference?"

"I wouldn't be here if I didn't," Jimmy said.

Kaya thought for a moment, something the commander had asked sticking with her. "Why did he ask about this building? Why would he care about this random place?"

Jimmy gritted his teeth, and she narrowed her eyes. *What was he hiding?*

"They are gone, boss," called Reina from near the door, Aelius following in behind her. With how focused Kaya had been on Jimmy, she hadn't even heard them come in. She was glad to see Aelius had returned but the newest interruption amplified her frustration.

"Have a team shadow them back to the church grounds," he said.

"Already done," Reina said, but Kaya was busy glaring at the three of them. "What? Is there something in my teeth?" she said, running her tongue under her lips.

Kaya wanted to scream. She hated feeling invisible and hated even more not knowing what the sarding hell was going on.

"I have been here for weeks, but I feel like none of you have actually told me what's going on," she said angrily. "You all talk in circles and vagaries until I lose all sense of which way is up. Do you even want my help? What am I even doing here? Why won't any of you give me a straight answer?"

Jimmy looked sympathetic as he walked over, putting a hand on her shoulder.

"There is a lot of history here, most of it occurring well before you were born. Someday I can tell you about it, but right now it isn't important."

"So, what is important? Sitting here doing nothing, working with the Pandora Fleet to hunt your allies? Letting innocent people be killed by extremists? Whose side are you even on?"

"I am on the side of the people. Maybe the only one who is," he said harshly. "There are a lot of things to balance, and battles need to be prioritized. Right now, the Children and their campaign of fire and blood are not my priority."

"So, you will let them continue to escalate violence, killing thousands while you sit here and play politics?" she said.

"There is a bigger plan, bigger than anything the Children could hope to accomplish with their simple-minded vision. In time we will deal with them, but for now they have their own part to play, and we need them."

Kaya was seething but didn't really know what to say to counter his arguments. It was difficult to argue without any information.

"You still haven't told me what the plan is or what my part is in it. You have kept me here locked away while everyone searches for me. Am I a prisoner then, a pawn you can use as a bargaining chip when it becomes convenient?"

"It is time you tell her," Aelius said, looking at Jimmy. "The moons are in motion now. There is no breaking them from their orbit."

Jimmy rubbed his beard. "You have never been a prisoner. If you want to leave, I will see you taken safely back to your room in the university." Kaya was about to respond, but he cut her off.

"But if you choose to stay, you will be committed to this path. There will be no turning back. Death will be your only escape. Think carefully before you speak."

Kaya didn't need to think. She was a person of action, and something about all of this felt important to her. Since that day she found the insignia in the desert, life had been different. A whirlwind of change that had shown her so many new and wondrous things, but also terrible things. A world decaying below the surface of marble and gold.

One thing she did agree with Jimmy on was that the world she was born into wasn't sustainable. If there was any chance at creating a new one, at making her mother's dream a reality, she had to take it.

"I am committed," she said boldly. "What is the plan? Leverage our numbers to demand better rations? Maybe demand infrastructure repairs in the slums?" She looked in turn to each of them. "Why are you all looking at me like that?"

Reina smiled, a wicked, mischievous smile, "You are thinking too small, princess. We are starting a revolution! We have a Republic to destroy."

Kaya was thoroughly stunned.

Had all these people lost their minds? As if something like that was even possible. The Republic had ruled the nine worlds for centuries, which wasn't by accident.

"You have all gone mad, haven't you?" she said finally.

"Although many people think so, no," Jimmy said calmly. "The plan is more refined, but Reina summed it up."

"I need to sit down," she said and flopped into one of the chairs, the worn springs creaked and sank under her weight.

The leather of the chair was worn and cracked like the rest of the room around her, but she sank into it anyway. Dust clung to every crevasse of the chair like it clung to the tall glass windows that once looked out over the towers of industry and progress that filled this city. It reminded her of the remnants of that golden age her mother used to talk about.

The others took their own seats.

"So what are we doing, storming the Amaranthine Palace or something? This is crazy. They will murder everyone. They have murdered thousands for less!" She couldn't believe what she was hearing. It was total madness. She should never have agreed to stay here. This wasn't a plan. This wasn't going to lead to her dream. It was suicide, plain and simple.

"All you need to know is that there is a plan," Jimmy said.

"So you want me to hold a rifle and storm a castle?" she said, still in disbelief.

"No, we have soldiers for that. What we need from you is to help us get the lord high commander, Silas Beckett, on our side," Jimmy said with a serious expression, and Kaya wasn't sure if it was a joke. It must be.

"Why didn't you ask him yourself? He was just here."

"He wouldn't listen to me if I had."

"But he's going to listen to me? He doesn't even know who I am," she protested.

"Everyone knows who you are, and your presence adds credibility to the story. Your mother was well loved, and your father is well respected. Without the nobility, this plan is destined to fail," Jimmy said. "Well, all of that plus some information that will be of personal interest to the high commander."

"What information is that?" she asked.

"I am sure you are aware that the duke, his father, has been ill for quite some time. However, it turns out his illness is not entirely natural."

"You poisoned the duke?" she said angrily. "How is that supposed to get him on your side?"

Jimmy sighed. "No, we didn't do anything to the duke. It was his own progeny that did that. Viscount Simon Beckett, now a general of the Martian Planetary guard. More importantly, a close friend of the Praefectus Frumentario."

Kaya stared at him, and Reina spoke as if reading her mind. "Yes, princess, your boyfriend's dad is a murderer. Well, not yet, but he's trying to be."

"Why would he want to kill his own father? He isn't even in line to inherit. Silas is," she said. Except, she believed it, even without any evidence. The stories Hal had told her during quiet moments were enough for her to read between the lines. She had no doubt his father was capable of this kind of cruelty.

Jimmy shrugged. "Maybe he hates a father who never loved him, maybe he plans to kill his brother as well, or perhaps it's something else entirely. Nobles have done worse for less. Either way, we still need as many of them as possible on our side."

"Why?"

"The nobility are the ones trained in military strategy. They command starships and lead armies. They–" Jimmy began to say, but she cut him off.

"Why me?" she asked again, more sternly this time. "Do you think I will convince my father next to support your little rebellion?"

Jimmy stared at her, obviously trying to formulate an answer.

"It was meant to be your mother," Aelius said, and Jimmy and Reina both looked at him angrily. "They didn't want me to tell you that, but it's better that you know. She was originally supposed to be in the position you are now."

Kaya didn't think her head could spin any faster, but then it did. Her mother was directly involved in this somehow, or were they lying? Was this why Aelius spoke in so many vagaries, to hide the truth until it was too late for her to leave?

She couldn't think of any other reason why, but it made more sense that who they really wanted was her mother and not her. She took a deep breath. "My mother was a part of Prometheus? Did my father know?"

"I was in communication with your mother for a long time, but she was never a part of Prometheus. As for your father, I can't say what he knows. This was your mother's story to tell," Aelius said in his typical monotone way. Although she had gotten used to it in the last few weeks, she still found it off putting.

"Why didn't you tell me until now? Were you ever going to tell me?" she asked, looking at Aelius.

"I told him not to," Jimmy said before Aelius could reply.

"Why?" she asked, trying to keep from crying. Not because these people had lied to her. No, she didn't expect anything else from them. They didn't owe her anything, at least until now.

She wanted to cry because she missed her mother and wished she was here to explain all of this and tell her what she was supposed to do.

"I thought you needed to be here because *you* wanted to be, not out of some sense of duty or family honor. Besides, would you have even believed me if I told you that in the beginning?" Jimmy said.

He wasn't wrong in thinking that she thought. If he had told her that in the beginning, she may have thought he was a liar, but she may have also agreed on the slight chance she could learn more about her mother and what had happened to her. It was what Aelius had done to get her this far anyway. That still might be the only reason she stayed. Family honor never mattered to her as much as it did her father or brother.

She wanted to know the truth and make those responsible pay. She always thought it wasn't an accident, and now she had all but confirmed it. Now it was about finding out who was responsible. She took a deep breath and, at least for the moment, was filled with new resolve.

"Do you know how my mother died?"

"I only know about the explosion of her ship, but everyone knows that," Jimmy said.

"Do you know if it was an accident?" she asked, hoping he knew more.

He shook his head. "I can't say, but I can promise you this. I will help you find out if I can."

She nodded. She hadn't expected him to know, but she needed to ask, and his promise to help seemed genuine enough. He had kept his word so far, even if he did keep information from her.

"Okay, I will help you, but I have some conditions," she said confidently. If she was going to follow her mother's legacy, she was determined to make her memory proud.

Jimmy looked at her seriously. "What are they?"

"I want my plasma blade back. I want to inform my father I am alive, and I want to retrieve things from my room in the university."

"The first is no problem, but it is too dangerous to send you back to the Sanctum ground. Speaking to your father, at least right now, is also not a good idea," Jimmy said.

"It is nonnegotiable. I can take word to his lord steward that I am alive. That is all they need to know."

Jimmy stared at her, pausing for a long moment. "We can send word on your behalf. It's too much to risk otherwise. We can't have them following you back to us. They might not agree we had your best interests in mind this entire time. Also, Reina will continue to accompany you until I decide otherwise."

"Fine." That would have to do, she thought. Besides, she felt confident she could lose the older woman if she had to.

"Anything else?" Jimmy asked.

"I want you to release Aron so he can get his sister. I also want to try and go to Hal," she said before correcting herself. "I mean Henry Beckett. You know who he is. If it's the high commander we want, he could help us." She hoped they would go along with the idea.

"You do realize, darling, this isn't some party to invite all your boyfriends to?" Reina said, shaking her head.

"The boy, Aron, is an officer with the Children of Men, the same zealots you asked me why we weren't fighting, and now you want me to let him go?" Jimmy said.

"You said they were a part of this too right? What would be the harm. Besides, he has a lot of useful skills."

"He tried to kill you, didn't he?" Reina said in disbelief.

"I don't really know that," she said hesitantly. "Jimmy won't let me talk to him. Besides you will be my shadow, right? You can always take care of him if you need to," she said, looking at Reina and making a stabbing motion with her hand. Reina rolled her eyes in exasperation.

"Are you both sure about this? I think the girl's lost it," Reina said.

"I will let you speak to Aron. Based on what he says, I will consider it. As for the young Beckett, we can talk about it. There might be something helpful he can do, but we need to be careful of what is said for obvious reasons," Jimmy said, standing up from the table. "Now, I have other business to attend to, as I am sure you all do as well." He reached to his belt and pulled off the hilt of Kaya's blade, placing it on the table. "Don't let me regret this, kid."

She reached for the hilt, happy to have it back in her hand, the familiar shape molding to her palm. It was the strongest connection she had to home, and most of all, her mother.

"I won't," she said as he left the room.

"May I see that?" Aelius asked.

"My blade?" She hesitated, having just gotten it back and was remiss to let it go again so soon. Then she considered what he did with the pendant and figured there was no real harm, so she handed it to him. "Sure, be careful not to press—"

He stood up and activated the blade, moving it deftly in his hand, almost studying it like a sculptor admiring his work.

"How did you know how to do that? Are you actually a noble on the run?" Kaya asked, and even Reina seemed surprised. She had assumed he was a commoner from some distant moon in the Far Coast based on his alabaster complexion.

"No."

"Artificer than?" she asked.

"No," he said again, deactivating the blade and studying the hilt before handing it back to her. "This one is quite old."

"It was my mother's. All the plasma blades are old. There hasn't been a new one made since before the Time of Chaos," she said.

"They were always rare, even during that time. Only the greatest knights carried them, even among the Ageless Legion. The grand artificers who made them were the finest craftsmen this system has ever known. Responsible for some of the greatest artifacts of their age. If you look at the hilt, above the pommel is a small tree, the mark of Widukind, the best of them all," he said.

"A great story, old man, but how would you know all of that?" Reina said.

"History is trapped in everything and everyone. You just need to take the time to look and understand," he said in his typically cryptic style, then he got up and began walking towards the door.

Aelius was a difficult person to have a conversation with because he always seemed to be living in his own world. Yet somehow he purported to know so much about so many things, and much to everyone's surprise they typically turned out to be true.

"So all of the stories, the ageless, the grand artificers, their amazing creations, you are saying they are all real?" Kaya asked.

"I have been saying that since you arrived and before," he said, pausing at the door.

"Wait, come back a minute," she said and jumped from her seat.

She rushed to the nearby table, grabbed a pen and paper, and sketched a design. It was a design that had become completely etched in her mind. The three conjoined triangles from the insignia she found in the desert and on her mother's note.

"Do you know what this is?" she asked, pushing the paper toward him. Reina came over to look as well, but her face showed no signs of recognition.

"Aelius didn't hesitate in responding. "It is the mark of the Ageless Legion, but now I really must go," he said and left the room.

She considered going after him but was too stunned to move.

Reina laughed, "It's a nice doodle, but I wouldn't listen to him. You asked him about those old legends, and then suddenly he tells you some lie to back up his claim. Those charlatans are quick like that. I think he has started believing in his own delusions, but he has connections to the people and other operatives that we can't do all of this without. I would say his storytelling was harmless if it wasn't for the poor souls that believed it."

Kaya regained her composure and considered what Reina said could be right. Kaya did set him up to say what she wanted to hear. "What if he is telling the truth? What if he's even one of the ageless?" Kaya said, raising her eyebrow.

Reina rolled her eyes. "Don't you start falling for his delusions too, princess. Come on, let's go talk to your boyfriend."

"Stop calling me, princess, and he's not my boyfriend," she said forcefully.

"Sure, whatever you say, Your Highness," Reina responded and led the way out of the room toward where Aron was being kept in an old office.

His room had a large window that allowed somewhat of a view, as well as a bed and small writing desk. As far as prison cells went, it looked comfortable, Kaya thought. Aron looked up from a book he had been reading when they came in. The title read, *Astronomical Spectroscopy*. Kaya could only fathom a guess what it was about. He had a surprised expression.

"You look so different. I hardly recognized you," he said.

"Contacts and hair dye. How are you holding up?" she asked as she sat down next to him on the bed. Meanwhile, Reina took up a bored stance in the corner, one foot flat against the wall. She tapped quietly at her digipad.

"I didn't think I'd see you again," he said in a low whisper. "But Jimmy said I have you to thank for finally speaking to my sister. Thanks for that."

She was glad she was able to help, but it didn't make her any less angry about what had happened in the first place.

"I wasn't sure I ever wanted to see you again."

"I owe you an apology, Kaya."

"You owe me much more than that. You were going to hand me over to a psychopath who wants nothing more than to see every noble in the system dead!"

"I...I didn't know that would happen," he said weakly. "I thought it was going to be for some ransom or something but...but I didn't have a choice."

"Didn't have a choice? Of course you had a choice. You always have a choice!"

"They have my sister! What was I supposed to do?" he shouted back at her.

"It's time for you to explain," she said. "The entire story."

He sighed. "Fine. When I learned I got into the Engineering University, I was the only one in my district since my dad did went. Well, when he died, I was the only one left with my sister," he said, his eyes distant.

"What happened to your parents?" she asked.

"Radiation, well, they got sick, but I know it was the rad poisoning. Even in our district, we couldn't afford to repair the rad scrubbers. It was only a matter of time." Kaya could see he was trying not to cry. "Anyway, it left me in charge of my little sister, who's thirteen now. I did what I could to make money, repairs around the neighborhood, that kind of thing, but it wasn't nearly enough. I wanted to keep us out of the slums." Reina had stopped tapping at her device and was listening intently now also.

"So I knew this opportunity was the best one I was going to get. I had to try and make a living for us, to keep us safe, but I needed the money to attend. The Children offered to loan me the money, more specifically the Father did. That's what they call their leader," he said.

"You didn't think that would come with strings?" Reina asked. "And here I almost thought you were one of the smart ones."

"What was I supposed to do? What would you have done?" he shouted at her, and for once she didn't have a snide answer.

"So you took the money and then what?" Reina asked.

"Nothing at first. I did some work for them, repairing machines and stuff like that. They considered that payment for my debt, but then they started asking for more."

"Like what?"

"Information first, like about the security in Trinity Square and around the capital. Then more detail about building layouts, systems. I mean, all sorts of stuff. It didn't always make sense what they were asking for, but I did it. Then one day they told me it wasn't enough anymore and that Clara would have to start working for them too," he said.

"Doing what?" Kaya asked, concerned.

"Nothing specific. They basically made her a servant, like those refugees that go to the far coast who collect debts they could never repay. It isn't much better than slavery," he said, and the thought made Kaya's stomach churn.

"They said if I did this next job for them they would let her go. That's how I ended up here, with you," he said as tears ran down his cheeks.

"But then they tried to kill you anyway," Reina said.

"Yeah," he whimpered, "and I left her all alone with them. This is all my fault. That's why I need to get back to her. I need to get out of here and get her out. Before they blame her for my mistake."

Kaya's heart broke at the useless tragedy of it. She couldn't even blame the Republic for this. There was nothing to do now but try and set things right.

"Your sister, is she with the Children now?" Kaya asked.

"Yeah, kind of, she's still at our home, but they decided to use it as a new base of operations in our district," he said looking increasingly despondent.

"That's good," she said, rubbing her temples as she thought.

"How is that good?" he sneered.

"It means we know where she is and can still get to her. Reina, can Prometheus send a team to get her out?"

Reina considered the question, then shook her head. "Getting the girl would be easy, but Jimmy isn't going to risk a fight with the Children, not now," she said, giving Kaya a look.

"Sarding hell," she mumbled, "I have one more idea. Aron, I need to know, are you with us or not? You need to decide now."

He looked up at her, his eyes red and puffy, cheeks streaked with tears. "They took my sister. She's all I have left. I would have killed them all myself already if I could." He looked ashamed. "But if you can help me get her back, keep her safe, I will follow you to my last breath." The fire in his eyes told Kaya everything she needed to know about his sincerity.

"Good, then tell me everything you know, and we will get her back," Kaya said, and Reina looked at her with a curious expression.

CHAPTER

21

Silas

April, 4103 U.E.T.—Amaranthine Palace, Mars

Silas arrived at the Amaranthine Palace promptly after he received the summons from the office of the Manus. He was to meet with the Vox and other senior officials to discuss the deteriorating security situation within the capital and beyond.

It had been some time since he walked through the halls of the palace, since he spent most of his time aboard the Specter. His orders would typically travel through liaisons and other high-ranking naval officials. That he was being summoned personally was not a good sign.

Marcus as his aide-de-camp walked by his side. They both wore their formal uniforms, as was customary within the Amaranthine Palace. They had left the rest of their escort behind at the palace barracks.

The palace was the one place almost unblemished from the Age of Empire, except for the missing or altered artwork on display. The nods to antiquity were replaced with modern depictions of God's majesty, although the memory of what came before was almost completely faded from discourse except among the most dedicated scholars and history-minded nobles.

The palace itself was immense and sat perched high above Trinity Square on the tiered slopes of Olympus Mons. The views from almost every window of the capital and the ocean beyond were truly magnificent. The added backdrop of the impenetrable snowy landscape above only added to its allure.

The palace was by any account a small city, complete with extensive defenses. It would take nothing short of a full-scale siege to take it. Something that had only ever happened once before.

Even though he had been here several times before, he couldn't help but marvel at its craftsmanship. Vaulted ceilings stretching up to the sky, clad in marble, glass, and polished metal. Different materials melded into a beautiful symphony of colors and textures surprised the eye at every angle. Even staring at one spot, you would be amazed at new details your eye had originally missed. It was truly a marvel of a different age.

"It's a good thing very few people ever actually see this place up close. The riots would never end," Marcus said in a hushed whisper, shaking his head. "Imagine what we could accomplish today if we had the means to build things like this."

"They say a man named Widukind was responsible for all of this. I can't imagine anything short of God's hand creating such beauty," Silas said as they walked.

"Divine inspiration or not, it's still the work of man," Marcus said as they came to the antechamber of the designated meeting room.

The door to the room was clad in intricately carved wood, and it seemed as if there were no seams at all until one of the guards pressed an invisible button and the wood slid aside, allowing them to enter.

Through the doorway was a smaller antechamber with several comfortable seating areas where invited guests could wait for their assigned meetings to begin. Several others were already in the room when they arrived.

Silas scanned the faces to take stock of the attendees, when he locked eyes with someone he had not seen in quite some time, Carlo Ajax, the Praefectus Frumentario. Beside him stood his brother Simon speaking animatedly about something.

Ajax was roughly the size and age of Silas, carrying himself with a rigid, military demeanor. He wore his formal uniform, and his ceramic blade hung from his hip. The blade was the practical and ideological counter to his own plasma blade.

Simon meanwhile was heavier set than Silas and lacked the rigid features he inherited from their father. His brother appeared soft in a way he did not, and perhaps that was one of the things Simon disliked him for.

"Brother," Silas said coolly, looking to Simon, as he approached the two men. "Praefectus," he added, nodding respectfully to Ajax, even if he despised the man. There was no benefit to insulting one of the most powerful men in the system. Even if he would have liked to.

Marcus followed suit and took several steps back behind Silas. Close enough to be useful but far enough to maintain propriety. Silas had worried many years ago that he would be unable to fill this role, but much to his surprise he realized Marcus could play the proper aid when required.

"Silas, brother, how good to see you," Simon responded in his posh accent. Silas found it thoroughly grating. "I thought I would have seen you back at the estate to visit Father. Unfortunately, he is too ill to attend today."

"Yes, I read the reports daily. Of course, duty has required my presence here first," Silas replied.

"Yes, duty, as you and Father have always reminded me. Oh, how your family has suffered for your duty," Simon said, and he clenched his jaw. He wouldn't let the weasel bait him, not here.

"I was just informing General Beckett of your continued bad luck with capturing the dissident known as Hex," Ajax said, laughing as if making a joke, but the venom in his words was clear. "Had I not known of your...commitment to duty, as the general tells me, I might think you were working with the Coalition yourself." His brother joined in the Frumentario's mirthless laughter.

It was then that Silas realized the star on his brother's shoulders. A promotion for a noble to such a high rank was unheard of in recent times. It made him instantly suspicious of what his brother had promised the clergy in exchange for such a gift.

"Congratulations on your promotion, brother," he said, through their jibes. "I am sure our father would be proud if he was able to see it." They both knew their father would not be. He never thought very highly of Simon and even less of his choice to serve within the Planetary Guard.

Simon stared daggers at him, but the Praefectus seemed unconcerned. "Come, General Beckett, I have others for you to speak with. We will speak again soon, High Commander," Ajax said, pulling his brother toward another group of waiting individuals.

He recognized the others as generals and admirals from the Republic army and navy. There was even a representative from the Knights of the Forge, more Frumentarii, and the Republican Guard represented.

Silas watched them go and saw how they whispered and plotted with the others. It sickened him what this Republic had become. No longer a haven of God but a den of fiends.

"Lord Beckett," a man said, clearing his voice to get his attention. He wondered how long he had been standing there.

"Yes, sorry, I..." he paused, realizing who it was, "Lord Parker, it is good to see you."

"Please, just Theodore," he said, holding out his forearm in greeting. Silas took it gladly.

"Of course, Theodore, it has been a long time. You are here in place of the lord eminent then?"

Theodore nodded. "Yes, sadly given the state of affairs, traveling off planet remains unwise."

"That is true, but I assure you we are working to resolve those issues with great haste. In fact, I have news to share today that should go a long way to improving conditions," Silas said, speaking so only Theodore could hear. The room was likely being recorded of course, but with so many voices it would still be hard to hear every word.

"Yes, I am sure you will continue to do all you can, but that wasn't what I wished to speak about," he said, his expression turning more serious.

"The Lady Kaya then?" he said, assuming the only other topic that could be important to this man from Mercury.

"It has been over a month now, and we have yet to hear anything promising. Last I heard, she was seen leaving the Boundless Library through some service tunnel with an unknown cleric."

"I have not been actively involved in the search, but that is the information I have heard as well."

Theodore let out a breath. "I am sure you can imagine how anxious the Lord Eminent is to hear that his daughter is well. Especially after the unfortunate loss of his beloved wife," Theodore said as he stared into Silas's eyes.

"The situation is unfortunate, but I assure you we are doing everything—"

"Let me speak more plainly, High Commander. You will make this a priority of yours. I don't think I need to remind you that His Grace was one of your biggest supporters over these recent, trying times. Even after the unfortunate incident involving his wife."

Silas returned the man's stare and nodded. "I will do everything within my power, Lord Parker. You have my word under the eyes of God," he said, looking up to the sky.

"Thank you, Milord. You will continue to have my support for now. I am sorry to hear of your father's illness. I understand he has been in a coma for some time now."

"Yes, he has fought for a long time, but the physicians have run out of tools to aid his condition. It is in God's hands."

"I will offer my prayers then," Theodore said before taking his leave. He wasn't surprised by the request given their history, and at least he could appreciate the directness of the request.

When Silas was alone again, Marcus returned to his side. "What did the Mercurian want?" he asked.

"He came to demand his pound of flesh like the others. Soon there will be nothing left but bones to claim, and even then I wager the dogs will come to fight over them," he said dramatically.

"They will have to wait in line. You still owe me for joining you in this man-made hell," Marcus said.

"Have I told you I always appreciated your support?" Silas said, eliciting a laugh.

Soon after, acolytes opened the doors to the main meeting room, and the assembled dignitaries filed inside. The room was open in the style of ancient courts with a wide space for petitioners to stand except for a few small, cushioned stools for those unable to.

The room was dominated by two thrones at the far end, surrounded by fine tapestries and carved stone reliefs. One of the thrones was larger and intended for the Vox, and a slightly smaller one was placed to its side for the Manus. The voice and hand of God in this world. The room was magnificent to behold, and it wasn't even the primary throne room of the palace.

In ancient times this would have been where the emperor and empress met with their councilors on day to day matters or with high-ranking officials who came to bring news or air grievances. Now the room served largely the same purpose all these years later.

Once everyone had entered the room, the Camerlengo, resplendent in fine embroidered robes, tapped his ceremonial staff on the stone covered floor and the room instantly fell silent. "Her Holiness the Manus Gremory," he announced, and everyone immediately dropped to one knee and bowed their heads. Even the Praefectus Frumentario fell to the floor in deference.

Silas raised his eyes slightly to see a tall, lithe woman with long black hair and smooth ivory skin enter the room. Her robes were white and embroidered with intricate patterns of gold, silver, and lace. The fabric flowed off her body gracefully as she strode into the room and took her seat. Silas thought her form exuded beauty and strength in equal measure.

"His Holiness the Vox Albrecht," came the Camerlengo's voice again as the Vox entered.

In contrast to the Manus, he was a short and stout man possessing little hair and sagging skin. He also always appeared to be displeased. He had begun to look quite elderly since Silas had seen him last, and he thought about how much time he may have left. Not much, he surmised sadly.

Albrecht's support had been one of the few things keeping him in his position in recent years, so losing him would be quite dangerous. Although many believed Manus Gremory might be the type of force needed to really turn things around, and her ascension would certainly be popular.

"Stand," the Manus said in a commanding voice once her and the Vox were fully seated. The assembled dignitaries rose from their kneeling positions, and the acolytes closed the doors behind them. The room felt crowded, and Silas felt his claustrophobia beginning to creep to the surface.

The Republican Guardsmen lining the walls, their weapons at the ready, only added to his unease. Silas disliked having to leave his plasma blade behind, but the inner palace was the only place no one besides the Republican Guard and Frumentarii were allowed to carry weapons.

"You have all been summoned to this conclave to discuss the need for action, given the increasing violence in our Republic," the Manus began in her steady but oddly melodic voice. "There is not a single moon or planet that has not dealt with some level of dissidence. We even received word today that Triton is in open rebellion." A gasp went up as the Manus continued.

That news hadn't yet traveled very widely, Silas knew, but he had seen the reports already. The situation was certainly becoming more dire by the day. He worried for his daughter on Oberon, but there was little he could do from so far away. He just hoped the issues wouldn't spread to neighboring worlds.

"These events, should they become public, will certainly embolden others to follow the example of their brethren."

A clergyman, one of the Martian Patriarchs, stepped forward and bowed his head in deference, "Your Holiness, if I may, is it the Coalition who is leading this rebellion or the Duchess of Triton?"

"Our understanding is that the duchess still holds some ground against the Coalition rebels," the Manus replied. The Vox followed the conversation with his old glassy eyes. Silas began to wonder if he chose not to speak or was simply unable.

One of the admirals moved forward to address the patriarch, "We have dispatched aid from nearby outposts and expect the situation to be rectified soon," he said confidently.

The Vox took this opportunity to speak, his jowls shaking as he slammed his fists on the arms of his throne. "If you had the situation under control in the first place, none of this would be happening. You have all allowed the heathens to continue their apostasy unabated!" he shouted, and everyone was forced to avert their eyes.

"Your Holiness, I have news that should aid us in this fight against the heathens," Silas said confidently. It was better to get his news out early on before the others had a chance to disparage him or his efforts. The Vox was prone to sudden outbursts, but there was not much else to do but try and make his case.

The Vox waved his hand with a scowl, indicating he could proceed. Meanwhile, the manus watched him closely. He found her stare to be very unsettling.

"We have located the last hiding place of Hex and the Hermes Conglomerate. With your authority, we will move at once to eliminate their operation once and for all," he said, keeping his head bowed and eyes averted.

"You have had many chances, yet you continue to fail in capturing this fugitive High Commander. I do not believe you are the one to manage this effort, if the information even proves to be accurate," the Manus said. "The Republic continues to bleed, and you have not staunched the wounds."

"Your Holiness, the information is reliable. There is no other possibility save for success in this now," he said.

"Incorrect, High Commander. There is in fact a high probability of failure," she said in her cold tone. "Your mounting failures border on dereliction of duty and perhaps even treason."

The Vox looked to Manus Gremory, but it was difficult to judge his reaction.

"I live to serve, Your Holiness. I have no greater calling from God," he said, speaking honestly.

"That may be so, High Commander. Your service in aggregate has been exemplary, but in recent years it has fallen to an unacceptable level. I am afraid we must consider alternate options. This menace, the Vermilion Coalition, must be contained before it spreads through the rest of the system like a cancerous sore," the Vox said.

"I must concur with your most divinely guided assessment, Your Holiness," added Ajax from his place in front of the assembly. Condescension oozed off his every word. "I believe another would be more suitable to finish this once and for all. Perhaps General Beckett could replace his brother in this effort." There was a slight murmur as he said this, and the group split into different camps.

"The Assembly of Lords has not lost faith in High Commander Beckett and believe he should maintain his role until his mission is completed," Theodore said, shouting over the growing sound of voices.

Looking to his left and right, Silas could see that although he had some support in the room he did not have nearly as much as he needed. Others began murmurs of "imperialist" and "sympathizer," which began to devolve into a series of insults being traded among the crowd's different representatives.

"Silence!" the Camerlengo shouted, tapping his staff on the stone floor again, and order was quickly restored. The Manus stared at Silas without sympathy. His brother and the Praefectus looked at him with obvious contempt.

God's bones, he had a fear something like this would happen, and so he did the only thing he could think to do.

He prostrated himself on the ground. His hands flat on the ground and forehead pressed to the cold stone floor. His action did more to silence the room than the Camerlengo's staff.

"Your Holiness, I throw myself at your mercy. Should you find me wanting in my duty, take my life now as you please. Everything I do is for the glory of God and Republic. Allow me this last chance to prove my ability."

He spared only a momentary thought for what his death would mean. It would thrust his daughter Catherine into this den of fiends as duchess when his father eventually died. He only hoped she was prepared to navigate it.

"You have had enough chances already," the Manus replied, and his heart sank further. So, this was how it would end, shamed, and discarded like so many before him. He kept his head on the ground as he absorbed the news of his certain death. He couldn't imagine a scenario where they simply let him go.

"Then I–" he began to say but was cut off by Vox Albrecht's gravelly voice.

"You have humbled yourself before God and his chosen voice and hand. This does you great honor and is an example others in this room could heed," he began.

"Your Holiness, perhaps we should confer in private before casting judgment," Manus Gremory said, but he waved her away.

"No, I have heard the voice of God within my mind and have the information needed to make this decision."

Silas kept his head to the ground so he could not see the expression of Ajax or his brother, but he assumed neither was pleased.

"It seems God has seen fit to allow you this additional opportunity, although success and failure will be decided by your actions alone. Should you fail, it will be clear that you are no longer favored, and that kind of rot must be removed before it spreads," the Vox intoned. "Rise, High Commander, rise and fulfill your oath."

He stood as he was commanded, and he was right that his brother looked furious, but the Praefectus Frumentario simply stared, his face unmoving as he spoke.

"Your Holiness, in the interest of prudence, should we not send additional reinforcements, perhaps a retinue of Frumentarii knights and perhaps soldiers of the Republican Guard?"

The Manus this time answered first, "Yes, Praefectus Ajax, that would greatly improve the probability of success. See that it is arranged," she said.

"Yes, I concur. It is always best to be prudent, as we are not privy to all the plans of our almighty God," the Vox said, casting a narrow expression at the Manus. Silas found it odd they confronted each other so openly, and the sight was unsettling. He was sure the exchange was not lost on the others as well.

"God wills it," he said, slamming his fist to his chest in salute. "Hex will be captured, and we will mark the end of the Vermilion Coalition, marking a new era of prosperity," he said to a cry of support from his allies. The others remained silent.

"Go by the grace of God, High Commander, we all pray for your success. Now, let us move on to the next topic," the Vox said, and they all settled in for the discussions. Silas thought the most volatile part of the meeting was likely done, but now he had to wait to find out if the information Jimmy gave him was reliable. That left him with much more hesitation.

CHAPTER

22

Silas

April, 4103 U.E.T.—Viragos High District, Mars

Silas walked along the street, taking in how much it had changed in the last year. Marcus walked by his side as he normally did. He had the transport drop them off several blocks away so he had time to think about what he would say to her when he arrived.

They wore no uniforms, and their escort followed discreetly, so they were able to walk unmolested through the tree lined avenues. In any event, it was not unusual for wealthy businesspeople in the High Districts to walk the streets with added protection.

Despite the beautiful architecture, verdant gardens, and dazzling skyscrapers, it was impossible to ignore the impact the recent string of attacks by the Coalition had on daily life. Even here, near the capital, he passed the boarded-up windows of a cafe that was recently bombed. The attack had left six dead and a dozen more injured; it was a horrible thing.

He couldn't help but feel some responsibility for the continued violence. He had been fighting the Vermilion Coalition most of his life, but the situation had only deteriorated to the point that a moon was in open rebellion and high districts within the capital city were no longer safe. It was a sorry situation. God willing, he would set things right soon.

His destination was a tall glass building with silvery spires that rose into the sky like ancient gothic fingers, clawing for heaven.

Security was tight here too with private security officers in tactical gear manning the entrance. Silas flashed them his identification, and they made no moves to stop him.

"I can't deny my sister's good taste," Marcus said, admiring the ornate lobby of the luxury tower. "I know you didn't pick this place."

Silas grunted, "I was always partial to the coastal estate, but she likes it here closer to her work."

Marcus took a seat in one of the lobby chairs and pulled out his digi-pad.

"Aren't you coming?"

"I figured you two have some catching up to do. I'd rather not be there for that," Marcus said, not looking up from his device. Then he waved at the few guards who had trailed in after them. "There's a cafe across the street. Why don't you lot keep yourselves busy for a little while?"

The guards hesitated, looking from Marcus to Silas, who nodded, and they reluctantly left the building.

"Don't need those seagulls looming over my shoulder all evening," Marcus said. "Call if you need anything, but if I hear any screaming, I will ignore it."

"Your kindness, as always, overwhelms me," Silas said on his way into the elevator, taking it to the top floor.

The elevator opened to a large vestibule and a pair of copper clad doors. He knocked and waited for a response. Given the late hour of day, he was hopeful she would be home.

The door opened slowly, and a slender man in servant livery opened the door. "Milord," he said, directing Silas inside with a bow.

He walked into the main room, a simple but elegant seating area where his wife sat with a book. As he entered, she placed it down, removing the clear-framed glasses from her face.

"You could have called first," she said.

He took in the sight of her. It had been nearly a year since the last time he saw her in person, and every ounce of his being ached for her. Her shoulder-length brown hair was clipped behind her head, and her slender form was covered by her simple physician's uniform.

Age had done nothing to stunt her beauty, the wrinkles and freckles only added to her allure. He admired the way her uniform clung to her curves, and in that moment he wanted nothing more than to embrace her, but he knew that was the one thing he couldn't do. Not yet.

"I was afraid you would tell me not to come," he said, moving toward her. She stood to meet him and looked up into his eyes, her arms folded across her chest.

"You're right. I would have," she said.

"Diana–"

"I'm not interested in your excuses, Silas. They are as tired and old as we are."

He sighed. "Have you heard from Catherine?" he asked to change the subject to their daughter.

"Not recently," she said, but her expression was one of concern.

God, please let her be alright, he thought.

"Why would you let her take that post? It's on the other side of the far coast," he said, shaking his head.

"Do you realize she is a grown woman now? She isn't the little girl you left at home for years at a time while you went on campaigns. If you did, you would know we don't have control over what position she chooses to take," she said, glaring up at him.

"She took a position with the Hospitallers. You could have talked to the Grand Marshall. You could have–"

"I could have what, tried to control her life like you and the Republic have controlled ours?"

"Everything I have done, I did for you, for her, for us. We have been called by God to serve and–"

"God didn't make you leave. God didn't make you miss birthdays and graduations. That was your choice," she said, digging her finger into his chest. "Yours and the Republic that has done so little for us."

"You need to stop now," he said in a low warning tone.

"I don't care if they hear me. Our hospital is packed beyond capacity with the sick and wounded. I save one life to watch four more extinguish, all because we lack the resources to do anything more," she said, beginning to cry as she slammed her fists into his chest.

All he could think of doing was pull her in close as his own heart began to break. His facade was crumbling.

"I'm sorry, Diana. I wish I would have said it more often. Told you both that I loved you and explained why I did what I did," he said as he began to tear up.

Tears in solidarity with her pain and tears for the joy he felt at holding her again. Hopefully tears of shared joy would come in time.

"You have always kept your feelings behind vague decrees of duty and honor. How would she know that it had anything to do with love? How would I?"

"It feels like a lifetime ago that God came to me and delivered me from hell and then blessed me with you and then again with Catherine. Blessings I never deserved and have been thankful for every day, and since then my duty has been to protect you both. To protect God's blessing with all my strength," he whispered into her head, and she clutched at him tighter.

"Step outside with me," he said, and she nodded, following him out to the large balcony while wiping tears from her eyes.

"Things are deteriorating rapidly. Triton is in open rebellion," he said in a low voice, hoping the wind would make it hard for any listening devices to pick up his words.

"Oh my God," she said, holding her hand over her mouth. "We need to tell Catherine. We need to–"

"There is nothing we can do. Triton is a long way from Oberon, and the duchess is still resisting, at least for now. You need to keep this knowledge to yourself," he said, emphasizing the last part.

"Are you going to the Far Coast then?" she asked, turning away to look out over the city.

"No, there is something more pressing here. Diana, I need you to listen to me."

She turned back to look at him, concern written on her face. "What is it? You are scaring me, Silas."

"I can't say too much, but–" he hesitated.

"What is it?" she pressed.

He let out a breath. "I had to prostrate myself before the Vox and Manus. If things go poorly, well, this will likely be my last chance." His words left a long silence as they hung in the air, the unspoken realities of what they meant materializing in their imaginations.

"I am sure you will come out of this. You always have before," she said reassuringly.

He shook his head. "This time is different. I'm forced to make a bad decision on bad information and hope it all works out," he sighed. "But it's not me I'm worried about. I'm prepared to meet my fate."
"Then what is it?" she asked.

"If I am gone, Catherine would be in line to become duchess, but I worry they may come for her, for you, to avoid that happening. Prune the entire rotten branch," he said, the words tasting like bile in his mouth. "I also worry about the machinations of my brother. He continues to rise higher, and I wonder what it is he's promised them in return."

Her expression turned sour at the mention of Simon.

"Do you think they are trying to trap you?" she whispered.

"I don't know. I don't think so, but either way they backed me into a corner, and with my father ill my support is drifting away."

She pulled him in close. "I missed you," she whispered.

He stroked her hair, not wanting to let go. "I have missed you every day. I'm sorry things went so wrong with us, with me."

"I always knew what I was getting, even back then," she said, looking up at him. "But I realized later I can't be the one to fix you."

"I have fallen so far down this hole. I'm not sure I will ever get out of the darkness."

She put her hand on his cheek and leaned in, kissing him tenderly.

"You will see the sun again, even if you need to stumble around in the dark for a while," she said. "Stay with me a little longer?"

"There is nothing else I would rather do," he whispered back, and she smiled. A playful, girlish smile he hadn't seen in years. It was infectious. She grabbed his hand and pulled him back inside toward the bedroom.

"Good, you can start your stumbling here then," she said, and they both laughed. The tension of before was forgotten in their embrace, but his joy was short lived when the servant interrupted their path.

"Apologies, Milady, but there is an urgent communication," he said in a neutral voice.

"Who is it?" she asked.

"The hospital, Milady."

"I will call them back," she said, still smiling.

"Apologies, Milady, they said it was quite urgent," he said with a bowed head. Diana's joy disappeared as the weight of her responsibilities fell back on her shoulders.

"Tell them I will be there soon," she said, her face growing serious. She sighed and looked at Silas longingly.

"It's my turn to leave for duty, it seems."

He grabbed her hand in his and kissed it. "The world is better for it," he said, meaning every word. She blushed. "My people can take you there."

"Oh no, I wouldn't want to impose. I can make it there alright," she said.

"Really, I insist."

She nodded and moved inside to grab her things while Silas admired the penthouse apartment his wife had been calling home in his absence. He didn't blame her for wanting to live away from their large estate and its empty rooms.

Looking at the shelves of photos, he smiled to see photos of their youth, photos of their wedding, and of course photos of Catherine as a baby. However, one picture in particular caught his eye, and he picked it up.

It was a photo of the three of them smiling on a quiet beach with rocky cliffs in the background and a bright blue sky. It was like the one he kept on his dresser aboard the Specter, but this one was from the last trip they took together as a family. Catherine was a teenager, and he and Diana still looked like little more than children to his old eyes. He sported a particularly bad sunburn, and he couldn't help but laugh.

Diana came up behind him laughing when she realized what he was looking at. "That has always been one of my favorites. The one impromptu vacation we ever took as a family."

"Yes, I don't remember looking that red though," he lied. He would never forget that painful sunburn.

"I don't expect you would. It only got worse from there. It was your first time on Mercury in years, and you insisted on not wearing any special protection. Your space-locked skin wasn't ready for being so close to the Sun," she said with a giggle.

"I paid for my hubris."

"Yes, the great Silas Beckett, laid to waste by a beach vacation."

"The troops didn't let me live it down for months," he admitted painfully.

She smiled, wrapping her arms around his. "Why don't you take the photo with you?"

"Thank you. I think I will."

"Good, now let's get going. If they called me in, it's because the knight commander I left in charge is losing control."

He leaned in and kissed her deeply one more time. "Thank you, Diana, for everything."

She kissed him back and whispered into his ear, "Come back to us and make it all worth it."

They made their way down to the lobby, arm in arm. Silas was reluctant to let her go until the last possible moment.

"Glad to see you two getting on again. I can't take anymore awkward holidays," Marcus said as he saw the two come out of the elevator.

"They have been substantially less awkward without you, Marcus," Diana said, glaring at him.

"Marcus, get the men to bring the transport for Diana. They will take her to the hospital," Silas said, breaking up the sibling quarrel.

"Are we going with her?" he asked.

"No, they can come back for us. There is a tavern down the street, and we don't need to be back right away," Silas said with a grin.

"I like that plan," Marcus replied then he radioed the escort and gave them their new instructions. Despite Marcus's assurances, two of them insisted on staying behind.

"Buzzkills," he said in annoyance.

The group stood out on the street. With the string of recent attacks, the streets were quieter than normal, and only limited traffic passed them by. He could see only a few vehicles flying overhead through the navigation corridors.

Their transport vehicle touched down gently in front of the building, and the soldiers took their position around the craft. They saluted Silas and Diana out of respect for her rank within the Knights Hospitaller.

"How much longer will you be on Mars?" she asked before getting into the vehicle.

"I'm not sure, but at least a few days," he said, brushing a stray hair from her cheek.

She smiled. "Good, hopefully–" she began to say when suddenly a blast rang out down the street, followed by screaming as people ran every direction away from the blast.

"Get in!" Silas shouted, pushing Diana into the craft. "Get her out of here, go!" The soldiers' training kicked in, and they took off in a blur, two remaining behind with their rifles at the ready, searching for threats.

A slender form came out from the alley where the smoke was billowing and shouted, "Please, someone help! Hurry up!"

Silas turned to direct the armed building security but saw they were already locking themselves down inside the building. "Cowards," said Marcus, spitting in their direction.

"Our orders are to protect this building, sirs," the man said and then locked down the door.

"You two, call in backup and secure another transport. Marcus, let's go see what's going on," Silas said, turning to leave. "That's an order!" he shouted at the lingering soldiers who saluted and jumped into action. Silas and Marcus meanwhile ran the short distance down to the alley.

By the time they reached the alley, the crowds in the street had dispersed, but something felt...wrong. He looked at the ground and didn't see any debris or shrapnel. Marcus must have noticed the same thing, because he stepped defensively in front of Silas and said, "Should we wait for backup?"

"No," he said and drew the hilt of his blade from his belt, kindling it. He held the searing plasma out in front of himself as he crept cautiously into the smoke, Marcus following close behind with his own blade kindled.

Through the smoke they came to a small open door leading into some kind of service building. They wouldn't have noticed it at all if it wasn't for the faint glow that came from inside.

"Let me go first," Marcus said and stepped inside, his blade at the ready. His response came swiftly. "Uh, High Commander, you might want to get in here."

Silas, confused, came into the room, ready to face berserkers or whatever other trap waited for him, but he wasn't prepared for what he saw instead.

There standing alone in the middle of the empty storage space was a girl, her hair spilling out from under the hood of a heavy cloak. The strangest part was she stood casually holding her own plasma blade.

She gave the blade a few flourishes and then snuffed it, clipping it to her belt. "It took you both long enough to come. I assume we don't have much time until your men return," the girl said in a heavy Mercurian accent.

"Who in the nine hells are you?" asked Marcus, channeling what Silas had been thinking. Neither of them snuffed their blades.

She pulled the hood off her head, revealing a dark olive complexion and emerald-green eyes that seemed to glow in the dim light of the room. "Lady Kaya al Vardan, daughter to the Lord Eminent, and I have a message for you, Lord Beckett."

His head swam as he tried to process what was happening, which meant it went to the most logical explanation first.

"Lady Vardan, there's no time. We need to get you out of here. Then we can talk–"

"I won't be going anywhere, Milord. There is no threat. You can put away your blades, unless you plan to skewer me here and now. The smoke will dissipate soon, and I'll be gone."

"I don't understand," Silas said, snuffing his blade but keeping the hilt in his hand. Marcus followed suit but then moved his hand to his pistol as he looked cautiously around the room.

"I wasn't kidnapped like they are saying. I left, and I don't intend to come back."

"Listen, we don't have time for this. Apologies, Milady, but you are coming with us," Marcus began to say as he walked up to grab her. He was stopped in his tracks when she deftly rekindled her blade.

"No, I'm not," she said, holding the blade out defensively. "I will make this quick. I know you both went to meet with the Vermilion Coalition, but I don't intend to tell anyone. Unless I need to anyway."

"You are working with the Coalition?" Silas said. None of this made sense. "What do you want if it's not to expose our meeting?" Marcus took a step back, but she kept her blade ready.

"You could say I'm recently affiliated, but that's not why I'm here. I came to tell you something else. Since we are short on time, I will spit it out. Your father isn't ill. He has been poisoned," Kaya said, her voice unwavering. If she was a liar, she was a very good one.

"How do you know that? Was it the Coalition then?" Silas asked rapidly. "This better not be some game, girl. Tell me what you know."

"I don't play games because I'm not a girl. My sources are my own, but the information is accurate. It wasn't your favorite demon, the Vermilion Coalition," she said, never looking away from Silas. "As for what I know, you aren't going to like it."

"Tell me," he growled. Something in her tone or maybe the series of events, created a deep sense of dread in him at what she was about to say.

"Well, Lord Beckett, it was your brother Simon who did it," she said.

"Lies," he said instinctively, "they have run every possible test and found nothing. Why are you coming to me with this?"

"Because it is true. Here," she said, tossing him a data chip. "Your reports have been altered. The originals are on that chip."

"Yours are likely the fakes."

She shrugged. "Inspect them yourself. Better yet, perform your own tests personally. I assume you haven't already done that."

He said nothing. Partly because he was ashamed to admit he hadn't. He had been relying on his father's physician, but now that this seed of doubt was planted was it really the right choice? Could he be certain that the man hadn't doctored the records? He had no reason to doubt them before now.

"Why would you tell me any of this? What does someone like you have to gain from any of this?" Silas said.

Kaya paused before answering. "The truth," she said simply. "It might not mean much to you, but for me it's everything. The tides are changing, Lord Beckett. Pandora's box will open soon, and everything that has been kept from man will be returned, and a new age will be born."

"That sounds like something Jimmy would say," Marcus said, glaring at the girl.

"You have a chance to be on the right side of history. You both do."

"God and the Republic will lead us on the right path and deliver us all," he said, doubling down on the party line.

Kaya frowned. "The only place the Republic will lead us now is ruin, but if God exists, maybe they finally decided to intervene. So here I am, your intervention."

"I always thought Mercurians lost their minds after baking under the sun for a long time, but it seems like you lot are just born nutty," Marcus said.

Silas meanwhile didn't know what to say. The girl obviously knew something, and that was dangerous, but if they took her in and she talked...that might be even worse for him. He considered for a moment a third option but abruptly dismissed it. He wasn't a criminal. Theodore had asked him to find her, and in a way he had done that now. It would have to be enough.

Shouting could be heard in the alley, and he knew his men were coming. They would have sent an assault team to investigate and extract them from the situation.

"It looks like my time is up. Remember what I said. Help us. Be a part of the future. Investigate my claims yourself and see the truth. You have been lied to as much as any of us," she said before dropping a smoke bomb and disappearing into the building.

He and Marcus tried to chase after her but quickly realized it was a waste of time. She had been prepared to meet them and had a well-planned exit strategy. They were chasing a ghost.

"Sarding hell," Marcus said, "she's definitely connected to Jimmy somehow. That trick with the smoke, something Reina would have done."

Silas shook his head. "I have no idea."

The extraction team arrived, and he ordered them to search the surrounding buildings while he and Marcus made their way to the transport, but he was sure they wouldn't find anything.

"Do you think it was really even her? What would she be doing with that lot anyway?" Marcus said.

"I have no idea of that either, but it was her alright. I knew her mother. She looked nearly identical. It's why I still don't understand, but I am going to find out," he said.

He didn't want to believe her, but at the same time had he ever actually questioned the data he was being given? Would his family's physician really hide records from him? He didn't like to think his brother would stoop so low, even though he knew in his heart he was capable of this and worse.

He had so many questions and so few answers. That was becoming a common problem, he thought, as he got onto the transport and immediately contacted Diana to make sure she was alright. Things seemed to be spiraling out of his control, and he was desperately grasping at any semblance of normal.

CHAPTER

23

Silas

Silas

May, 4103 U.E.T.—Thessalonica, Mars

THE WEEKS HAD gone by in a blur. April turned to May, and Silas continued the relentless march to his destiny, or was it going to be his doom? He tried not to dwell on the thought, but it always came unbidden in quiet moments when he wished things could be different. Times when he wished he had never met that girl, Lady Kaya, in that empty warehouse.

Not that things were simple before that meeting, but at least they made sense. He thought he had become immune to secret plots and intrigue at this point in his life. Maybe this was God's way of punishing him for his hubris.

At the same time, God gifted him with the magnificent view from his family's estate in New Thessalonica. The tiered gardens and buildings built to complement the sloping landscape of the Olympian Escarpment.

To the north he could see the Iasus River and to the south the Pelasgus as they spilled icy cold water into the Amazonian Sea from the dizzying heights of Olympus Mons. Down the escarpment and all the way to the sea, a chaotic network of streets and buildings filled every inch of land leading to the piers that shot out into the sea itself. The city of New Thessalonica was one of the largest and oldest on Mars, and it was his home.

He was sipping a cup of coffee that steamed in the cool crisp air, seagulls crying out overhead, when he heard footsteps behind him. He spoke without turning to look at who it was.

"What dark tidings do you bring me now?" he said.

"Maybe it's good news for once," Marcus said as he came up beside him. The sound of a snack bag crinkling in his pocket gave him away.

"Is it?" he asked with a raised eyebrow.

"Not really, but it could have been," Marcus said with a grin. "Preparations are nearly complete for the mission to Deimos. We should be ready to leave in the next couple of days."

Silas nodded. "Good, but what's the bad news?"

"A detachment of Frumentariis and Republican Guard have begun their transfer to the Specter for the mission. The rest of their forces started dispersing on Deimos in place of regular security details so they will be in place ahead of time," Marcus said.

"I don't like it, but we knew that was coming. I also plan to be part of the landing party again," he said, turning around. Marcus had an annoyed look on his face.

"What else is it?"

"They plan to send your nephew Henry and Boniface, the Praefectus Frumentario's boy with us. They both graduated from the academy, and this is going to be their first major assignment."

"Absolutely not," Silas said. "This mission is no place for fresh graduates. Too much is at stake for this type of political stunt." He couldn't imagine why else they would suggest something so nonsensical.

"I tried to tell them all of that, but it turns out they have been assigned to a special detail with Vice Admiral Zhou," Marcus said with a scowl.

"Fine, they will be relegated to the ship then, and I will hear no more of it."

"The vice admiral thought you might feel that way, so he made it a point to join us as well, along with his new proteges," Marcus said.

Silas sighed. Things only continued to get worse. "I continue to be challenged at every turn. I can only imagine what fresh hell awaits us next on Deimos."

"None that we can't handle. God wouldn't deliver the challenge if we couldn't meet it head on," Marcus offered, slapping him on the shoulder. He knew Marcus didn't believe any of it but he appreciated the attempt at comfort.

Silas tried to force a confident grin, but he wished it could look more genuine.

"Did you bring Diana with you?" he asked, changing the subject.

"Yeah, she's waiting with him now. We can start whenever you are ready."

"Good, let's get on with it then," he said and moved to go back inside toward his father's bedroom. Along the way servants scurried past him about their regular business, most attempting to keep their heads down or appear especially busy. They all felt it, knew it like he did. His father was not long for this world, and his death would mean change, and this was a job none of them wished to lose.

He knew at some point he would have to consider all this business, as he would become duke, but for now he had ignored it completely. He wished instead to pretend none of it was happening, a survival mechanism that had served him well all these years. At least so he thought.

Silas moved purposefully to his father's chamber, ignoring the sights and sounds that assaulted anyone who walked through the lavish halls of the Beckett Estate. He had been raised in these halls, so for him they offered a different message, one of comfort and majesty but also crippling expectations.

The ornate columned walkways that had been designed and built by his ancient ancestors in the grand style of the time served now to remind him of how little he had accomplished. A constant reminder that what he had done wasn't enough. He would have to work much harder if he ever wanted to match the achievements of the past.

The room was situated in one of the oldest wings of the complex, and its vaulted ceiling and large windows offered a clear view of the sea as it stretched to the horizon. On the walls hung tapestries and other art, objects that had always brought his father joy.

There was also a place for pictures of family, him, his brother, their father, and their now long-deceased mother. She had been a kind woman, maybe too kind for the world she found herself in. A sadness for another time, he thought as his eyes grazed those photos. He turned to see his father lying near lifeless in the four-post bed, the machines that surrounded him like somber sentries beeping and flashing as they kept death at bay.

Such a strong and vibrant man laid to waste by the insidious march of illness, or at least so he had been made to believe. Waiting in the room was his wife Diana, who sat in a chair beside the bed holding his father's hand. She had developed a close relationship with him over the years and had spent more time with his father in recent years than he had. He could see by the expression on her face that she was experiencing this pain as acutely as he was.

"Were you able to get the necessary equipment?" he asked moving to stand beside her. He put his hand on Diana's shoulder and looked down at his father's sunken face. He looked so very frail, but even now, with the light of the Celestial City so close, he held on. Unwilling to give in.

"Yes, it wasn't easy to get the testing equipment out of the hospital unnoticed, but I have it," she said, motioning to the equipment that had been arranged on a nearby table.

Marcus came in, shutting the door behind him. "The estate is secure, and the servants have been told not to disturb us. We should have some time before they get suspicious."

Diana nodded. "This shouldn't take very long."

"How sure can we be of the results?" Silas asked.

"Unless whoever did this used something unknown since the Age of Empire, one hundred percent," she said with a serious expression on her face.

"Are you already convinced there is someone to blame?" he asked.

She shook her head. "I have seen the old reports, and I never had any reason to doubt them, but it was shocking how sick he got in such a short time. He was as healthy as anyone I have seen and then suddenly was on death's door. It does happen, but it just always felt...off to me," she said with a sad but thoughtful expression.

"Of course, this explanation," she said, motioning to the test equipment, "would mean there were several people actively doctoring and hiding information within this household and at the Republic level. I would normally think this would be too complicated to pull off, but with how things have been going recently I'm not sure it's an impossible scenario."

"Well, let's get on with it then. I don't think I can wait much longer," Silas said, taking a seat opposite the bed by the window, leaving Diana to her work. Marcus meanwhile posted himself by the door and opened a bag of dried apricots. Silas glared at him.
"What? Isn't this going to take a while?"

Diana finished drawing a blood sample, her movements with the needle quick and practiced. "That part is quick, but the analysis will take a bit longer," she said as she placed the sample into the machine and began typing on the digiscreen.

Seeing that there would be no quick results, Silas thought his time would be better spent elsewhere, not looking over Diana's shoulder. "Can I trust you two to get along if I step out for a moment?" he asked jokingly.

"If I'm forced to silence him, I will. It won't be the first time," Diana said with a smile.

"That's not how I remember it," Marcus said, turning to Silas mid chew. "Sure you don't want me with you?"

"No, I'm not going far, just to speak with the Lord Steward." Silas trusted them more than anyone and knew they could handle this part.

Marcus nodded. "Alright then, I think I saw him nearby somewhere on our way in."

"Thank you, Marcus. That is very helpful, as per usual."

"Anytime, mate," he said through a mouth full of apricot, and Silas sighed, pushing his friend out of the way of the door.

Silas found the old man close by in one of the sitting rooms. He was speaking quietly to a pair of young staffers, who he dismissed when he eyed Silas approaching. Lord Hill had served his father as Lord Steward since Silas was a child. So, if anyone knew the happenings of this estate, it would be him.

"Lord Beckett," the man said, bowing his head.

"Lord Hill, if I may have a moment of your time."

"Yes, of course, My Lord, how can I be of service?" the man said, looking more annoyed than helpful.

"Perhaps you can walk with me. I haven't seen the water garden in quite some time."

"It was always your favorite, My Lord," he said, seeming to force a smile, and moved to walk beside Silas. He was breathing heavily, which Silas was quick to notice.

"Are you unwell, Lord Hill?"

"Oh, old age, I'm afraid," he said with a bitter laugh. "What was it you wanted to talk to me about, My Lord?"

Lord Hill was a vibrant and joyful man once. At least that was how Silas remembered him as a child. However, at some point he turned into something of a shrew.

This was most exemplified in the incident where Lord Hill had taken liberties to cut salaries and reduce incentives for the estate's employees. It had taken his father well over a year to regain the trust of his people, and

Silas believed their personal relationship never truly recovered. Although for some reason his father kept Lord Hill in his position as steward, perhaps out of some sense of duty or out of respect for their past friendship. He couldn't be completely sure.

Silas didn't answer right away, and the man's breathing became heavier as they made it into the water garden. Their footsteps were overpowered by the sound of water cascading from ornate, tiered fountains in amazing designs. It was an exquisite work of art depicting the many stages of the history of man. He stopped next to one statue.

"What do you see when you look at all these sculptures, Lord Hill?" he asked while admiring one of his personal favorites, a scene depicting Saint George slaying a dragon.

For too long, Silas had allowed others to manipulate the world around him, and he made his sacrifices hoping to appease the great serpent. However, this was now the result. His father dying, his own house in disorder, his career in shambles, and the list went on. It was time for him to remember he was a knight, and the serpent was his to destroy, not appease.

"I, well," Lord Hill stuttered, seeming confused by the question. "They are statues of stone and metal, My Lord. I don't think of them much at all beyond their surface beauty."

"That is a pity. Personally, I have spent countless hours here studying these works, as you know," he said, running his hand along the stone of the sculpture's base. "The entire history of man summarized into a few dozen sculptures of stone, metal and glass. How do you think the artists managed to do that?"

"I don't know. They were students of history, I suppose. I'm not sure I understand the purpose of your question, My Lord."

Silas continued talking as he walked to the next statue, "Oh, they were certainly students of history. As students of history, they were able to distill the vastness of human history into these few vignettes. It took me a while to discern how this was possible, until I realized these stories had the same few things in common."

He turned to face the old man and could see that he was sweating now. *Good*, Silas thought. He had spent a lifetime hunting charlatans and terrorists, but he blinded himself to the possibility he had serpents within his own home.

The girl had opened his eyes to the truth he always knew but preferred to ignore. It was better to live in his happy lie than face the reality of his crumbling life. Now was his opportunity to take it back. To rebuild something new and better.

Silas didn't need to see the test results to know something more was going on here. The test would only confirm what he only briefly considered before. Now it was about finding out how deep this betrayal ran.

"Have you studied this one in particular?" he said, motioning to the scene carved into the fountain in front of him. "It's a lesser-known story from ancient Earth. It shows the Roman Emperor Caracalla at the height of his power. After killing his ailing father, he murdered his brother in their mother's arms, all to claim his father's power for himself." The Lord Steward looked like he was hoping to be anywhere but in that garden.

"Do you know what happened then?"

The Lord Steward didn't speak, only watched Silas nervously.

"Well," Silas said, pausing dramatically, "he was emperor for a time, until he was murdered while taking a piss by an angry soldier," Silas said, while staring deeply into the man's eyes, and his face betrayed his guilt.

"The greed of man is a constant companion, no matter what planet we find ourselves on. Then, like now, it rarely ends well for those who seek their fortunes through dishonorable means."

"My Lord is right," the old man stuttered, "it is truly a cautionary tale."

He had no proof the man had been involved, but Silas could feel the guilt radiating from him like a child who had been caught where they knew they didn't belong.

"Tell me, was it your idea or my brother's?"

"I...I don't know what you mean, My Lord. I only aim to serve your house to the best of my ability," the man said, and Silas felt that was as much of a confession as he could hope to get. He knew his brother was a coward and would have someone else see to the dirty work, and Lord Hill had the access required for the job.

Marcus arrived unexpectedly in the garden and called for Silas.

"High Commander," he said with a serious expression and a nod indicating the results were in. Silas didn't need to be told what those results were. The look on Marcus's face said it all.

"I will be right there," he said, giving the Lord Steward one last appraising look. The man looked paler than he had moments earlier.

When he had gotten out of earshot of the man, he turned to Marcus. "See that an honor guard is placed in my father's quarters. Also, instruct them that Lord Hill is not to leave the premises under any circumstances."

Marcus nodded.

Silas didn't spare another look for the Lord Steward and made his way back to his father's chamber. He would need to figure out what to do next with this information. It was clear to him Simon was responsible, but his connection to the Frumentarii made it difficult for him to discern a clear path to justice.

CHAPTER

24

Kaya

May, 4103 U.E.T.—New Olympia, Mars

THE BUILDINGS SPED past as their service van made its way down the bumpy mid-district road toward the capital. Reina sat up front with their driver, another Prometheus Group member, leaving Kaya in the back of the van with Aron. It was the first time he had been out of the Prometheus Group headquarters since his capture nearly two months prior.

He seemed happy for the first time since Kaya had known him. His cheeks had filled out, and his features seemed more vibrant. She hadn't noticed until it was gone how the constant stress of his situation had been weighing on him, and with it gone he was a new person.

"Thank you," he said for what must have been the hundredth time.

"I told you to stop doing that."

"You did more for me in one meeting than I could in years. She's safe with Prometheus now, and that's thanks to you. I don't think I can ever pay you back for that."

"I told you before that I don't want anything from you," she said more forcefully.

It had been an easy thing arranging for the return of Aron's sister. Jimmy made it clear he needed the boy and the girl to secure important allies, and in exchange they could keep the house they had already stolen anyway.

Well, that, and the message was delivered by some of Jimmy's soldiers, and the Children became amenable. She felt like she had done very little to make this a reality.

"It's Jimmy you should be thanking."

"Jimmy only cared because you did. That's why I'm thanking you." He seemed genuine as he smiled at her. The attention was making her uncomfortable.

"He's right about that," Reina said from the front seat. "We are almost there though. You love birds can finish your flirting later. Remember to stick to the story and don't say anything more than you must. Your credentials are pretty good, but they won't hold up under scrutiny." It almost made her laugh to think how far she had come from the days of cobbling together her own fake identities to sneak around Alhazen. She would have reminisced more if not for Reina's commentary.

Kaya had stopped taking the bait from the older woman, but she still hated how easily Reina got a rise out of her. So she glared ineffectively at the back of her head. Aron didn't seem at all bothered by Reina's frequent quips, which only made her more annoyed. They weren't a couple, and she had no intention of making them one. They were friends and nothing more.

Now she was only concerned with completing their mission. Well, a mission and fulfilling her request. She missed Hal and was looking forward to finally seeing him again. Luckily everyone agreed having another high-placed ally could only help their cause.

Jimmy had suggested sending a team to retrieve Hal but worried a second high-profile kidnapping would only attract more attention. Kaya convinced Jimmy it would be a good idea to try and reach out to him directly. He had been reluctant but eventually agreed after Aelius seemed to speak in her favor.

The plan they devised was simple. They would go to Trinity Square posing as cleaners and they would investigate Henry's typical haunts. He lived in an apartment near the square, and she knew where he hung out most. Aron meanwhile knew the corridors well enough to move them around relatively unseen. Reina and the other soldier were there in case of an emergency.

What Kaya didn't mention was that she also planned to make a stop at her room in the Sanctum, despite Jimmy's refusal to allow it. She wanted to retrieve the insignia she left behind along with photos and her mother's note. That note was the one thing beside her blade that connected her to her mother, and she didn't want to leave it behind.

Kaya had originally wanted to go to Theodore and then back to Trinity Square to find Hal, but Jimmy had continued to refuse so she was forced to pen a simple note that Jimmy's men delivered to Theodore. She hoped it reached him and gave her father and brother some peace.

Kaya didn't know what Hal would say, but she wondered if he missed her too. She didn't know if he had been working toward finding her this whole time and how worried he must have been. She also knew he wasn't happy with his life here, and now she could offer him a better option or at least a more fulfilling one.

"We will drop you both off near the main service entrance. If you keep a low profile, no one should even notice you–" Reina began to say, but Kaya cut her off.

"I was thinking it's better if I go alone. I don't want anyone else to risk anything for me," she said as the truck lurched to a stop.

"It's too late for that, princess. The plan is the plan, and we never deviate from it. That is when things go wrong and people die," Reina said, sounding like Professor Moreau. "Aron will stay with you, and I will be nearby keeping an eye on things. You have a couple hours max. If lover boy doesn't show up, I'm sorry, but it will still be time to go. When I call you, it's time to come back to the truck, and I don't want to hear another word about it."

Kaya thought better of pushing it. It would make her seem suspicious. What she didn't want was Aron hanging over her shoulder, but she could manage him better than Reina. The woman was as observant as a Falcon and twice as mean.

It would be more suspicious if a work crew arrived and left without performing any work so she knew there would be some time to kill before they tracked down Hal. It was during that time she planned to sneak into her room. No one had to know, and no one would get hurt. She only hoped Victoria wouldn't be there, but she rarely spent much time in the room, so she figured it was unlikely.

"Alright," Kaya finally said.

"Do you both understand the plan then?" Reina asked, and they both nodded.

"Good, don't get yourselves killed," she said, waving them off dismissively with her hand. Kaya almost thought she heard a tinge of concern in the woman's voice.

"I won't let you off that easily," Kaya joked as they stepped outside and grabbed their mops and cleaning supplies from the truck, and Reina smirked. It was as close to a genuine smile as she could have hoped to get. Despite their differences, Kaya found the older woman had grown on her.

Aron led the way confidently through the service entry into Trinity Square. Their passes worked flawlessly as they scanned their way into the walled compound, the security personnel doing little more than looking at the contents of their basket of cleaning supplies before waving them through the scanner. From there they didn't expect to run into much more scrutiny, at least if they kept a low profile. Kaya's hair dye and contacts hid her most identifying features, and Aron blended in fairly naturally.

"Now remember to look the part. Don't do or say anything out of the ordinary," she whispered to Aron.

He laughed, "You do realize I have worked a normal job before. When was the last time you even picked up a mop, let alone used one?"

"Not *that* long ago," she said defensively. "There was one day last year that they made us clean as a sign of penance."

"What about back home on Mercury?" he retorted.

"Let's focus on what we are doing here," she said, and he laughed harder, gaining the unwanted attention of other nearby workers.

Kaya gave him a dirty look, and he composed himself, but he didn't look very apologetic. She found him considerably irritating with his constant "observations," as he liked to put it, about her life. She hated them more because they were usually accurate.

"I need to make a detour," she said suddenly as they neared the side entrance to the Sanctum's compound.

"That isn't part of the plan."

"Now you sound like Reina. I don't need you to come. Stay here and look busy."

"I'm not going to let you run off on your own," he said raising his voice slightly.

"Can you keep it down?" she said angrily. "Fine, but you need to keep this to yourself, okay?"

"Alright," he said hesitating, "but where are we going?"

"I need to get something from my old room. It's important."

"Can we go in like this?" he asked, motioning to their disguises.

"Yes, it's all the same cleaning crews, but you are going to have to wait outside the building anyway."

"Why don't I go along with you?" Aron asked.

"Because you are a man, and men aren't allowed on that side of the building," she said simply.

"Fine, I will wait for you near the common area then. Meet me there when you are finished." There was concern in his voice. She appreciated that he cared but didn't need him to protect her.

She nodded and made her way alone down an adjacent corridor toward her old room. Her plan was to collect a few things, the insignia and her mother's note, and get out before anyone noticed her. The quicker she finished, the sooner she could find Hal.

She made it to the room without drawing any unwanted attention, going slowly as if she was one of the staff. She remembered from her own time in the Sanctum how the cleaning staff tended to come and go, invisible to the students and faculty. Even when she tried to get to know them, she was frustrated to find they rotated regularly. This was why she had suggested this disguise to Jimmy and Reina in the first place.

One day she had even commented to Professor Moreau about how odd it was that she never saw the same faces. The older woman stared at her and said, "Of course, dear, you wouldn't want possible spies and dissidents wandering these halls, learning our patterns, day in and day out. What easier way would there be to ambush us?"

At the time, Kaya thought that explanation made sense. Although now she wondered if it wouldn't have been better to properly vet trustworthy staff. She supposed that must be hard when the clergy tended to distrust everyone who wasn't one of their own.

She wasn't sure what she would say if she saw Victoria and hoped she didn't need to figure it out. It was the one wrinkle in her plan, but she felt like it was worth the risk, even if others wouldn't think so. She stood in front of the door and took a deep breath to steady her nerves before turning the handle and walking inside.

The room was much like she had left it, her belongings still neatly arrayed where she had left them. She was surprised no one had taken the time to inspect them, but she supposed they may have and did a good job of hiding their passing.

Most of all she was happy to see that Victoria wasn't in the room. Although there was a part of her that missed her friend, she didn't trust her. She couldn't afford to get caught, not now when all their work was finally coming together, and she felt like she was making a difference for once.

Kaya moved to her desk, pulling open the drawer where she kept her old family photos. She flipped through them, smiles coming to her face before she held them briefly to her chest and then slipped them into a pouch she had hidden inside her worker's jumpsuit.

She looked around her desk for anything else that might be useful but didn't come up with anything before turning to the small shelf of books next to the desk. There she had kept all the new books she had acquired in her time at the Sanctum, along with the ones she had brought from Mercury. She found the specific book she was looking for and opened it to reveal the Solar Empire insignia and her mother's note. She was excited to see they were still there.

She was drawn to both objects and their seeming connection. She didn't know if Aelius had told her the truth and they were somehow linked to the Ageless Legion, but part of her hoped they were.

Either way, they reminded her of home and the possibility of something better. One last link to her mother's dream. She picked up both items and slipped them into her pouch with the photos.

It was then that she heard the door open and shut behind her, followed by a high-pitched scream.

"God's bones! What are you doing in here? Get out this instant! I will see that the head mistress is notified immediately..." Victoria shouted, her face full of anger as she waved her arms.

Kaya turned quickly at the sudden shouting and threw her arms up innocently.

"Victoria, please be quiet," she whispered, her own panic setting in at Victoria's sudden appearance. Maybe Kaya should have kept Aron around to keep an eye on the hallway after all.

"How do you know my name? Get out of here, you..." she was shouting nearly hysterically until suddenly she stopped and stared quizzically. "Kaya?" she asked, looking her up and down with a scrunched brow. "Is that you? Where have you been, and why are you dressed like that?" Victoria's words came out in a rush, but she maintained a cautious distance, as if Kaya's disguise came with some kind of disease she would rather not catch. Kaya moved closer anyway.

"It's a long story," she said, trying to figure out how she would extricate herself from the situation, while simultaneously cursing herself for not thinking through this part of her plan more carefully. "I can tell you all of it, but you would have to come with me now," she said, reaching out to grab Victoria's hand. "You can pack a few things, but we don't have time to discuss it. You would have to trust me," she said knowing that was likely impossible after all this time.

Kaya wasn't surprised when Victoria pulled her hand away, but her heart still twisted from the pain of being rejected again by her oldest friend.

"I don't know what's going on with you, Kaya, and what is going on with this new disguise of yours," she said waving her arm, "but I want no part of it."

Victoria walked towards the door, but Kaya moved to block her way with an outstretched arm. Kaya might not have been surprised by Victoria's rejection, but her leaving now and telling someone would be disastrous.

Was this why Reina always harped on sticking to the plan? She had to think fast, but what could she do? Was she prepared to tie up her friend? To kill her?

"Wait, don't go. I can explain everything," she pleaded as she watched her plans unraveling in real time.

Victoria laughed. It was a cruel laugh, one Victoria never had before they arrived in this place but now seemed almost natural.

"I haven't trusted you since the moment we stepped foot off Mercury, Kaya al Vardan. My life has been nothing but chaos with you in it, and you know what?" she said, and her laugh gave way to an even crueler smile. "I have quite liked not having you around these last weeks. I only wish they could have separated us sooner."

Kaya's eyes became cloudy, and tears threatened to pour from her eyes. Kaya knew what she said was true, and she didn't even say anything that Kaya hadn't thought about Victoria. None of that was why it all hit her so hard.

She wanted to cry, because she knew the friendship they had as girls was gone, and it was never coming back. What thin thread of hope she had in her subconscious that it could be repaired was gone in that instant. Kaya noticed Victoria's eyes begin to water too as she turned to look away.

"I should turn you in. Everyone is looking for you, you know. Not that you care, I'm sure," Victoria said, wiping the tears from her cheeks. A part of Kaya wanted to reach out and embrace her friend, and another put up a cold steel wall to guard against the pain that threatened to consume her.

"Please don't, I–" she said pleadingly. "I am so close."

"So close to what?" Victoria said, quizzically. Sadness replaced by the anger and distrust that had been there moments earlier.

"The truth."

Victoria stared for what seemed like an eternity before she folded her arms across her chest and shook her head. "I don't know what you got yourself involved in this time, but I want no part of it. You are going to leave now, and I won't say anything, but I better not see you here again. This will be the last favor I ever do for you. Do you understand?" Victoria said, practically snarling out the last words.

Her mind raced with every possibility. Victoria seemed genuine, but it might also be a trap. Either way, it was the only lifeline in front of her, and she had to take it.

"Thank you," she finally managed, staring at her former friend one last time.

"I said to go. You have done enough damage already, and I am not interested in picking up the pieces," she said, turning her back to Kaya.

Kaya didn't know what else to say, so she walked quietly to the door, wiping her face with her sleeve. At the door she paused to look back one last time, and they locked eyes. Kaya saw nothing but contempt as she took the final step out the door, closing it behind her.

By the time she found Aron again, her tears had dried and her stoney expression had returned.

"Come on, let's go," she said more harshly than she had intended.

"Alright, but what's going on?" he asked startled by her tone.

"Nothing, I got what I needed. Now we can finish what we came here to do."

"Do you want to talk about it?" he whispered as they made their way back to the square.

"No."

"Alright, follow me. I know a better way to go. You said we should check Martyrs' Square first, right?"

"Yeah, that's where he's most likely to be. He likes to sit and watch the birds at this time of day. Should be just him and the elderly clerics," she said, and the thought of Hal softened her mood.

"Alright," he said hesitantly, "bird watching then. You sure you're alright?"

"I'll be fine," she said and followed him as he led the way through the labyrinth of service corridors that connected Trinity Square to the three universities that surrounded it, until they were forced to exit onto Trinity Square proper to cover the final distance.

Once out on the square, they were stopped at several checkpoints and asked to provide their badges. At the first one, Kaya had almost given them away in her anxiety, thinking Victoria had already given her up, but it turned out to be regular security protocols.

"Do you think they added all of this extra security for me?" she asked when they had some privacy.

"You sure do think highly of yourself," he said with a smirk, "but I don't know, maybe. Bombings have been on the rise for years. Maybe they finally couldn't ignore it anymore, even here in the heart of the capital. I already graduated, so they definitely aren't looking for me."

Kaya contemplated that as she looked up at the Amaranthine Palace, which loomed above them. She wondered if there had ever been a time that the palace brought a sense of security and hope instead of fear and pain.

"It's only going to get worse, isn't it?" she said.

"If it's anything like what happened in my district, I expect it will. Maybe not now, but eventually it's bound to." His words darkened her mood even more.

When they got near Martyrs' Square, the security increased, and it began to settle on her that this was a terrible idea. In that moment, she also took the time to realize Aron's obvious unease. She had taken him right from the fire and back into the frying pan.

For the first time she felt guilty for dragging him into all of this. He had gotten his sister back, and she was threatening to ruin everything. He trusted her, and that only made her feel worse for betraying it.

"Why don't you go back? I can do this alone," she said pulling him to the side discretely.

He seemed taken aback but shook his head with a reassuring smile. "I won't do that. We are a team, right?"

He was so much sweeter to her than she deserved. "Thank you, Aron," she said, and they continued deeper into the square.

When they arrived at Martyrs' Square, she was disappointed to see Hal wasn't there. They waited for a little while making the rounds of the square, cleaning benches, and picking up nonexistent pieces of rubbish.

During that time, Reina reached out to them via their comms, but she reassured her that everything was fine, and they would be done soon. Kaya knew they were running out of time though.

She led Aron to the other most likely locations where he could be. The Trident Tavern or outside his apartment. She even went to the dreary pub where he used to hang out with Boniface and Lady Palmona, but he was nowhere to be found.

She wanted so badly to talk to him, to tell him everything that had happened and hold him tightly. Now it seemed like she might never get that chance, and her heart ached. She wanted him to come with her, and she would help him see the whales of Ganymede he loved so much, and they could live out their lives on their own terms.

Aron looked at his comm device and said, "We are out of time. I'm sorry."

Kaya knew he was right, but she didn't want to hear him. She kept staring at every doorway, willing Hal to walk out of one of them, but all her staring was useless. At least he hadn't rejected her, she thought.

She let out a deep sigh. "Alright, let's get back," she said. Her voice was low and far away. Aron briefly put a comforting arm on her shoulder before quickly removing it again. "Sorry, I–" he began to say, but she cut him off.

"You don't need to apologize, thank you," she said, offering him a genuine smile. She appreciated his kindness and hadn't thought any more of it.

They began their walk back to the pickup location, the mood lightening as they got closer. That was until she saw them.

There, meters ahead of them, Hal walked by, and her heart rose near to bursting. She almost ran to him, but he wasn't alone, so she hesitated. Then almost as fast as it rose, her heart sank when she saw Victoria's blonde curls and her arm draped over his.

They passed by oblivious to her presence, but she was stopped in her tracks. Aron pulled at her arm. "Kaya, what is it? We need to get out of here."

Absently she could feel her comms device buzzing as Reina no doubt called for them.

"I...I need to go back," she said, starting to move back in the direction Hal and Victoria had gone. Aron blocked her with his body.

"I don't know what's going on, but it's time to go," he said again more forcefully.

"I need to talk to him. If I do, he will understand," she said, trying to work her way past him. She had forgotten everything else in that moment of panic. She had lost so much already and now this, but Aron held her close and tried to calm her down.

She considered knocking him over and going past, but instead she slammed her fists angrily into his chest, oblivious to the world.

"Shh," he whispered forcefully, "you need to get it together! You are creating a scene."

She noticed him looking over her shoulder at something, so she turned to do the same. She saw what he did, several patrolmen taking notice of them and heading their direction. Her fear began to break through the fog of anger and sadness.

She rubbed her eyes, trying to compose herself before she unraveled. *So much for never crying again*, she thought dryly, as self-loathing momentarily replaced anger.

"Everything alright here?" one of the patrolmen said as he approached, eyeing the pair up and down. Kaya averted her eyes, bowing her head deferentially.

"Yes, sir, I received some bad news and lost my composure," she said, opting for the truth.

"Credentials," he said with one hand on his rifle and the other on his badge scanner. They displayed their IDs. He scanned them and, seemingly satisfied, waved them along. "If you can't compose yourself, vacate the square."

Kaya and Aron breathed a sigh of relief once the patrolman walked away. These close calls were becoming much too common, and worse yet this one had been completely avoidable.

She looked back at the way Hal and Victoria had gone, but they were out of sight.

"You are going to need to tell me what that was about," Aron said as they continued walking. "I haven't seen you get so upset before."

She felt embarrassed. Normally she was good at holding it together, but this time she couldn't. Luckily Aron had been there. She shuddered to think what could have happened if he wasn't.

"It doesn't matter. It's just more reason to focus on our work. Jimmy should have more for us to do now that things are in motion. As much as I enjoy writing pamphlets, I would like to be doing something more practical," she said changing the subject. She spoke softly so only Aron could hear.

"He has kept me busy repairing equipment. I can't say I mind it," he said. "It's better than what the Children had me making." Kaya could hear the shame in his voice.

"That part of your life is over now. It doesn't need to come back," she offered in an attempt at comfort.

He nodded. "You should consider your own advice. You talked to me about creating a new world. Why not start now?" he said looking at her with a knowing expression.

She didn't know how much he knew, but it felt like enough. He was smart, maybe too smart, and she ignored the possibility that he had already put everything together. That realization must have been written on her face because he continued.

"I told you I will support you for what you did for me. Even if I think it's a bad idea, which this trip absolutely was." he emphasized, "but my support won't always come with my silence."

"I'm sorry," she said, considering her own mistakes that once again led them to this situation. This time it had worked out, but it could have so easily gone badly.

She would consider his words for the rest of the journey back to Tiyas. She may have lost two friends that day, but maybe she also gained a new one. More importantly, she would need to learn to be a better friend herself.

ACT
3

Silas

June, 4103 U.E.T.—Metus Low District, Deimos

Silas sat in a troop transport, geared and mission ready for what felt like the hundredth time this year. Marcus sat across from him, snacking on a bag of pretzels. His appetite was truly prodigious. Silas assumed it was part of his process, like a nervous tick, but he had never asked. Silas would pray, and Marcus would eat. It was a combination that just seemed to work and who was he to question the way of the universe.

Unlike the last mission to 132 Aethra, this troop transport wasn't only loaded with his own loyal troops, like Gwen who sat beside Marcus.

To Silas's left sat a group of Frumentarii Knights, their exoarmor was gleaming white with ornate gold trim. They held rail rifles and their golden hilted ceramic blades rested easily at their hips.

Past the Frumentarii were a group of elite Republican Guardsmen with their blue-tinged armor. They carried an array of firearms and lightning pikes, a long spear with a sharp blade that could also emit a short arc of electricity to debilitate an enemy. It was quite an unusual conglomerate, and they sat separated like warring clans within the transport.

To Silas's right in the remaining seats sat Vice Admiral Zhou with a couple of his own marines. Plus, the addition of his nephew Henry Beckett and Boniface Ajax, the Praefectus Frumentario's son.

Silas tried to argue that it would be unsafe and unhelpful for two recent recruits to be a part of such an important mission, but his opinion was ultimately ignored. Vice Admiral Zhou outranked him, and if he wanted them there, it was his prerogative. Silas had no doubt Zhou received a strongly worded recommendation from his brother and the Praefectus.

Silas tried to have Henry stay close to him, but Zhou managed to keep the two of them from speaking more than a few words to each other. He was never close to the boy, primarily due to his brother's wishes and the lack of an opportunity to get to know him well. His brother had always gone to great lengths to separate himself from the rest of the family.

Silas had always feared that would lead to Henry becoming a copy of his less scrupulous brother, but by all accounts Henry was a good kid and a better soldier. His reputation preceded him in all the right ways, and it seemed like he was generally well liked by those around him.

"T-minus five minutes to the landing zone," came the calm voice of the pilot into their helmets. No one spoke, and the banter normally present among his own men was gone.

Everyone was tense, and he worried the wrong move could trigger an uncontrollable reaction amongst all the parties involved. There was a reason inter-organizational missions were rare within the Republic.

The transport vibrated as they entered the thin atmosphere of Deimos. Their destination was a small landing zone the troops on the ground had already marked. The troops they had been moving into position quietly for weeks had been fully mobilized an hour earlier.

They had moved fast and aggressively into the Metus low district and, like a tsunami, crushed what resistance they encountered. Then surrounded the compound and secured the landing zone pending further orders.

Now Silas and the others would arrive to be a part of the final breach teams, to ensure nothing went wrong and for the vice admiral to garner most of the credit, he thought dryly. Meanwhile, the Pandora Fleet patrolled the atmosphere with their Falcons, ensuring there would be no repeat of the last mission with a craft that got away. They were leaving nothing to chance.

The party disembarked about a dozen of them in total as they fanned out from the transport. The guardsmen and Frumentarii knights knew their business well as they efficiently took up defensive positions around Silas and the other officers with their rifles and pikes at the ready.

"Vice Admiral, as discussed, I advise you and your retainers to remain in the rear," he said through their comm line.

"Thank you for your opinion, High Commander, but we will be fine on our own," Zhou replied in a condescending tone and waved his group, which included his nephew and Boniface, forward ahead of the others.

The boys hesitated slightly, perhaps surprised to find themselves among the vanguard, but they eventually followed as Zhou raised his rifle and shouted, "Forward unto glory!" The rest of his troops echoed the call and moved into the facility. Their exosuits provided them with an added element of speed.

"God's bones," he cursed on a private line to Marcus, "he is going to get those boys killed. Henry is the one hope my brother's bloodline doesn't end in ruin. Come on, let's follow them." He left his lack of care for Ajax unsaid, but he would do what he could to keep his nephew safe. Even if they were estranged, family was family.

"With me!" he shouted to the Frumentarii and guardsmen, and they fell in line without argument. They had been ordered to stay with Silas, so that was what they did.

The compound was a large warehouse facility, like what they encountered in 132 Aethera. However, instead of large open hangars, this place was a maze of underground tunnels and rooms. It had once been an early settlement structure when life on the surface was too difficult to maintain so people lived a dark and gloomy life underground.

By the time they had reached the opening that the vanguard had breached, Zhou and his group had already proceeded inside. The blasted entrance led into a narrow hallway full of pipes and wires that only allowed for two men to walk side by side. Rifle fire could be heard echoing through the halls and smoke, and sparks billowed out from broken equipment and burnt-out rooms, but they didn't immediately encounter any resistance.

"Vanguard Alpha, status check," Silas sent to the advance entry teams.

"Slow progress, heavy resistance deep, route sent," came a disjointed message between heavy breaths. The sound of rifle fire was loud and violent in the background.

"I think I see an alternate route. We can maybe cut them off," Marcus said as he assessed the three-dimensional map in his visor.

"Let's do it then," Silas responded without hesitation, and the party redirected down a different corridor.

It didn't take long before they began to encounter resistance. The first corner they came around, a small squad of Coalition members opened fire on them, but in these close quarters the superior exosuits of their elite force, with their personal energy shields, made for easy work.

The two guardsmen who had taken point rushed forward, their shields absorbing the enemy fire until they were in range to stab out with their lightning pikes, crackling energy arcing out from the tips as they pierced the enemy troops.

It was a brutal display that left burned and twitching corpses. These were weapons designed to kill heavily armored knights, not the lightly armed masses that made up most of the regular troops on both sides of this fight.

They crossed paths with two other similar patrols, and each time they were dispatched with the same ruthless efficiency. During the last encounter, the Coalition soldier knew they were outmatched and detonated a bandolier of grenades in close quarters. The resulting blast took out the two forward guardsmen along with one of his own from the Pandora Fleet and one of the Frumentarii. In their rush to get to the front, they had neglected their defenses. It was a careless move on his part.

"Zhou, report, what is your status?" he said as the men regrouped from the blast and began pulling the dead and injured back to waiting troops who would bear them up to the surface. However, no response came.

"Zhou, repeat, what is your status?" All he got back over the comm line was a crackle of static and strained groaning.

"Shit," he said out loud. "Come on, on me," he shouted, rallying Gwen and Marcus along with the remaining guardsmen and Frumentarii.

He turned the next corridor to find a flight of stairs leading downward, and Marcus after a brief pause motioned them down, Gwen taking point. At the base of the stairs, she fired a quick burst from her rifle into a surprised young girl who looked much too young to be holding a weapon.

Anger rushed into him at the thought of the Coalition using these poor children as their pawns. Then he wondered how much different it was that Zhou paraded Ajax and Henry into this mess. Not to mention the Republic military's countless young recruits, although at least they were trained soldiers.

Then they approached what would have been the old communal meeting hall for this one-time settler's colony. He knew the governor's office would be beyond that. These early homesteads, as they were called, were all built in largely the same layout. A useful tool to train future settlers on the same equipment no matter what planet or moon they would eventually be sent to. Now it made them a familiar battleground. It was odd the Coalition would pick somewhere so obvious. Perhaps, they were more desperate than he realized.

One of the Frumentarii moved to check around another blind corner, and heavy machine gun fire instantly overloaded his shield and the structural integrity of his armor. In an instant, his head was torn from his body in a spray of blood and viscera. It was likely ammunition meant to take out aircraft, but it proved equally useful at destroying bodies.

"God's bones," Marcus shouted, "stay back. I got this." He moved forward, taking a grenade from the bandolier on his chest and throwing it into the hallway. It expertly bounced off the wall before detonating farther down the hallway.

They could hear shouting from the enemy, and the remaining Frumentarii and guardsman rushed into the breach, dispatching the remaining resistance as Silas turned the corner.

They breached the large doors and walked into a scene of chaos. The space was a large, vaulted room with doors accessing it from multiple directions. Inside the room, different groups were locked in brutal firefights as each side vied for position in the large space. Having blasted their way through what must have been one of the main checkpoints, they didn't immediately encounter resistance on the other side.

Silas looked around the room, hoping to see a sign of Zhou and the two boys. When he passed through the smoke and fire, he saw them moving into what he expected to be the section of offices at the rear of the complex. He had raided many of these old colonial offices. Those rooms would be the most secure in the compound and the most likely place for Hex to be hiding.

However, before he could motion to the others to follow, a piercing scream rang out as a berserker bared down on them. Gwen and Marcus opened fire, and the remaining Frumentarii knight drew her ceramic blade to combat the beast that stood over a foot taller than the woman and roughly three times her width. This one seemed even larger than the berserkers he had faced on the asteroid.

The berserker swung down with a brutal-looking iron sword, and the knight was forced on the defensive. She moved gracefully and managed to land several slashing strikes on the body of the beast, but it was far too little. The ceramic blade might be best for defeating knights in exoarmor, but it was largely ineffective against the steel-clad berserkers. The special ceramic of the blade could do little against the thick metal, despite its incredible sharpness.

The Frumentarii swung out several more times, but it was obvious the woman was becoming fatigued as Silas approached with his plasma blade kindled. He was wary of getting in her way since they were not accustomed to fighting together, but he managed to swing out with a few well-timed blows burning into the beast's armor and skin.

Although his blade did not instantly cut through the iron, with enough force and precision it was possible to deliver piercing or slashing wounds through the heavy iron plates.

The berserker reeled back in pain as the knight moved in hoping for a killing blow, but it proved to be a fatally mistimed maneuver. The berserker recovered and swung down with a massive two-handed strike, overpowering her shield and nearly cleaving her in two. Despite the gruesome sight, Silas took the opportunity to get behind the beast and jab his blade between two armor plates, burning deep into its body until it collapsed.

Panting, he saw Marcus and Gwen providing covering fire to their rear. It looked like the Coalition had rebounded and was engaging in an effective counterattack. The three of them moved to a more defensible position deeper in the room behind one of the now abandoned barriers and reloaded.

"I need to get to the offices. You two, link up with Alpha Team and follow as soon as you can," he said to Gwen and Marcus, who were too busy to argue with his command. He ran off on his own, shooting quick controlled bursts from his rifle to take out another insurgent that crossed his path.

He cursed as he made it into the open doorway, several rail rounds slamming into his shield causing it to flicker. He continued to be careless, but he knew he had to reach Zhou and the boys before they ran into other berserkers or Hex. He knew that would be a death sentence for any of the three and by extension himself if he ever made it out alive.

He passed several adjoining rooms that were littered with bodies, many of them still writhing in pain or shouting for aid. He checked quickly to see if any of them were who he was looking for, but seeing that they weren't he moved on. He didn't even spare the time to end their suffering. Others would have to care for them now.

Silas heard shots ring out at the end of a long hall and began a mad dash for the source but was momentarily stifled as one of the writhing bodies swiped his leg with a knife. His armor's shield flickered one last time as it failed against the strike, which bit into his armor and left a bloody gash several inches long on his calf.

Cursing, he turned to the man on the ground who was pulling back for another swipe, a crazed expression in his eyes. Silas kicked the knife from his hand and drawing his pistol put two shots into his body. The man clutched at his chest and despite the life slipping from him continued to snarl with disgust, and in that moment Silas felt a pang of guilt.

He didn't enjoy this part, but it was the job. It was what kept his family safe. It was what kept the Republic safe. So he pushed those thoughts aside and continued toward his destination, the old colony governor's office at the end of the hall.

At the door, he had to vault over the body of a dead berserker. Since its flesh and metallic corpse blocked a large portion of the doorway. It looked like it had suffered numerous small wounds, but its iron blade was equally bloody, causing his heart rate to increase.

Inside the room, he was greeted with a nightmare situation.

In the center of the room stood Hex, her green armor vibrant and bearing only minor damage. At her feet was the lifeless body of Zhou, his detached arm lying off to his side, his snuffed plasma blade still clutched by the hand of the severed arm.

Hex held her own blade at the ready as she circled with Boniface, who had his ceramic blade drawn. Silas cursed, knowing that he was likely no match for her ability, even if he was a gifted swordsman.

Finally, his eyes darted around the room looking for Henry, who he found semiconscious near the door with a large bleeding gash across his chest. It looked like he had taken a heavy hit from the berserker in the hall. Sarding hell.

His breathing quickened, and he wanted to rush to Henry's side, but his eyes locked back on Hex and Boniface. He only prayed the boy was still alive.

"Marcus! Hurry to the governor's office. Bring backup and medics. Henry's down," he sent on their private line before turning to his nemesis.

"Hex! It's over. End this and no one else needs to die," he shouted for what he hoped was the last time. The circling pair stopped, but neither turned their heads to see the source of the sounds lest they be taken by their enemy. Silas moved closer, his own blade drawn defensively.

When he came into view, Boniface spoke, "With all due respect, High Commander, step aside. I will end this now." He spoke with all the bravado only youth can provide.

"She will kill you. Step aside, Lieutenant Ajax. That is an order," he said more forcefully.

"The son of the Praefectus Frumentario, how fortuitous. I would listen to the commander, boy, or you can end up like your heroic leader here," came a modulated voice from Hex as she motioned to Zhou's body.

"Don't speak to me of heroism, vermin. You wear a mask to hide your villainy, and where Zhou was weak, I am strong. God will show you the right of it through my blade," Boniface shouted, and Silas tensed even more. The boy was brave but a fool.

"Surrender, Hex. It's over. No one else needs to die," Silas repeated.

"No," came the modulated voice again, "but since this seems to be a bit of an ending, perhaps the boy is right and there's no more need to hide."

Boniface smiled broadly as Hex retracted her helmet revealing an unblemished face with light-brown eyes. Her brown hair braided tightly on her head, and a regal expression on her face. She carried herself with the confidant demeanor of a woman in her thirties.

It took Silas time to process what he was seeing, but when his brain finally caught up with his eyes, his heart completely stopped. Time went into slow motion as Boniface lashed out with his blade as soon as the helmet retracted.

Hex easily deflected the blow and countered with her own riposte that left Boniface with even deeper wounds through his armor. They traded several blows in quick succession before Silas could get his body to function.

He didn't think, only acted out of pure instinct as he moved his own blade in a practiced motion, dashing forward to jab it deep into the side of Boniface. Hex backed off, and Boniface glared back at Silas in complete surprise as he dropped his sword. His body fell to the floor, the surprised expression glued to his face. Silas likewise fell to his knees from the shock of it all. Hex meanwhile snuffed her blade and stepped forward.

Silas rose slowly on shaky legs as he stood to meet her, looking down into her eyes. He retracted his own helmet; he was having trouble breathing. He reached out with a shaky hand to cup her face.

"Catherine," he whispered, "I...I don't understand."

"Hi, Dad," she replied, putting her own armored hand onto his cheek.

Meanwhile a groan came from the corner of the room where Henry had remained injured and semi-conscious throughout the ordeal.

Silas

June, 4103 U.E.T.—Amaranthine Palace, Mars

Silas stared blankly at his daughter as she sat in the transport heavily shackled. Guardsmen and Frumentarii alike stood poised with their weapons drawn and pointed at her. Time had been a blur since the events of the old governor's office. Hex—Catherine, he reminded himself—went along easily after the death of Boniface. Neither of them spoke and instead stared at each other until Marcus entered the room.

Silas was glad it was Marcus, because he was able to take control of the situation until Silas could regain his composure. He had sent Silas to tend to Henry. The boy was unconscious but alive, although to Silas's shame, in that moment he was more concerned with what the boy might have seen than his well-being.

He tried to think of a way he could get his daughter out of there, save her from whatever madness this was that she had gotten herself involved in, but there hadn't been enough time. The room was full of others in short order, and the task was largely taken from his hands as Frumentarii arrived and threw Catherine into chains, but not before beating her ruthlessly.

His words of protest did nothing but intensify their actions. Gwen and Marcus did their best to pull him away and shut him up. There would be a time and place for his outrage, but that moment wasn't it. Luckily, they knew it better than he did.

However, none of that stopped him from seething now as he looked at her bruised face and battered body. They had hurt the one person he loved more than anything in this life, but there was nothing he could do. He was impotent in the face of this outrage, like he was when he kneeled before the Vox and Manus and begged for another chance. He had begged for that chance so he could protect his family.

Instead, he was here, his daughter beaten and in chains. The anguish and guilt threatened to overwhelm him. God had obviously abandoned him now, and he was sure he knew why. He was finally being punished for the sins of his past, and it disgusted him that Catherine would be the one to suffer for it. Maybe because God knew this was the only way to make him truly suffer. He would find a way to make it right, whatever it took.

Except he knew it wasn't that simple. It was more than Hex being his daughter that he would answer for. Zhou was dead, and he would answer for that too, not that he felt particularly sad about the loss.

Then there was Boniface Ajax, the Praefectus Frumentario's favorite son. He knew the news had already reached the man, and the response had been as bad as he imagined. With so many Frumentarii around, it had been impossible to slow down the transmission of information.

He still asked Marcus to erase his camera footage. That it was missing would raise questions, but having it present would only seal his death, which wasn't likely to be quick.

Then there was his own nephew, not dead but nearly so. Silas knew he had no business being there and had said as much, but no one would remember that now. They would only see his failure to protect them.

Catherine was the only one he actually cared to save, and he stared at her now as if he could will her somewhere else with just his mind. She offered him a small smile, and his heart skipped. He didn't deserve that smile, but it was all he wanted. He had let her down, not only now but for years, and he would need to answer for that too.

The transport was made worse by the ruckus celebrations of the troopers. They had finally captured the most wanted person in the Republic. They didn't shy away from their glee, even when he scowled. Although, he would have been happy too if it hadn't been his daughter inside that green armor. It was what he had been working towards all these years. Now that he had it, he wished he could give it back.

They landed in the main landing pad of the Amaranthine Palace, where a large column of Frumentarii and Republican Guardsmen stood poised in their gleaming armor to take Catherine into custody. They also came to carry the bodies of Zhou and Ajax, along with the other slain officers to the Basilica of the Divine Hand where they will begin their journey to the Celestial City.

News of the capture had not spread to the populace yet, but he was sure they would be filming the proceedings for use in official reports as soon as possible. None of this would happen quietly, which only made his job harder.

When they disembarked, Silas, as the most senior officer remaining, was forced to present his prisoner to her holiness, the Manus Gremory, who met them at the end of the promenade. It was a ritual he had taken part in numerous times, but only now in these circumstances did he realize how ludicrous the affair was.

He bowed deeply before her, raising his arms in the traditional ritual. "I bring before your blessed hands the rotten fruit of the orchard so that it may be pruned and discarded, lest it infect us all."

There was no emotion in Gremory's face, not even pleasure in seeing the most sought outlaw finally brought before her. No sign that it mattered at all in her eyes. This only made Silas angrier. Catherine's sacrifice and pain meant so little as to not even register a reaction.

"Go with the blessing of God, child, and tend to the unripe crop so it may grow and nourish future generations," she replied mechanically. He knew she had never behaved any differently, but where it was unsettling before, now it was painful.

He handed Catherine off to the Frumentarii, and they roughly took her away. Likely to the palace's prison cells, which were reserved for the most politically sensitive prisoners.

He noticed that Praefectus Ajax and Simon had been missing from the welcome party. He assumed they must be tending to their own grief. He selfishly hoped they felt at least as bad as he did in that moment.

"Lord Beckett, come with me," the Manus said, turning to leave toward the main Palace building. The guards who attended her were more aggressive than normal in ushering him to follow. Whatever happened next would be away from the prying eyes of cameras and witnesses. He took a deep breath to steel himself against the coming tide.

To his surprise, they'd led Catherine into the Vox's audience chamber, not straight to a prison cell. When he arrived, she was lying prostrated on the floor, her hands and feet bound with her head pressed into the cold stones. The Vox sat on his throne with a bemused expression.

His brother and the Praefectus Frumentario stood to the side in front of a larger group of military officers. A group of clergymen stood opposite them. He supposed Ajax and Simon preferred to relish in his pain than dwell in their own.

When Silas reached the dais that held the thrones, the guards stopped and went to their stations flanking the doors. The Manus walked to her throne and gracefully took a seat.

This left all eyes in the room focused on Catherine and Silas at the center. The room was silent and the tension threatened to strangle everyone. Ajax seethed openly like a tea kettle that had already boiled over, but Simon was only slightly more composed. Likely only because his boy still lived.

"High Commander, how grand it is to see you succeed again after so long," the Vox said through the quiet murmurs. "I wonder why it took you so long to capture this miscreant when she was under your own roof the entire time. Were you perhaps never really looking? Catherine Beckett," he said, shaking his head. "Not who I would have guessed."

"I claim no kinship to this vermin," Simon shouted before spitting at the ground. Others on both sides of the room followed suit, and it took every ounce of his self-control to not draw his blade and lash out at each one.

Silas had been about to speak in his daughter's defense, but her muffled voice filled the room first as she fell to her side, attempting to sit up despite the restraints.

"All the better, Uncle. I would prefer no association with a coward like you," she said despite the swelling in her face, and even then Silas felt a tinge of pride at her display of strength. He leaned down to help her to her knees, and the guards moved to stop him, but the Vox waved them off.

"Let him aid her. I would prefer to see the face of this traitor. Hex," the Vox said, leaning forward in his throne, "your list of crimes is long and well documented, and today you have only added more. Do you have anything to say for yourself? Perhaps you care to repent."

Silas got her to her knees and held her briefly before he was forced to step back. Her body was cold and damp, and he worried for her condition.

"Never," she said flatly. "I have killed your commanders and your future," she said, staring directly at Ajax as she did. "And I would gladly do it again."

"You lack the strength to kill my son," Ajax snarled, and his supporters joined him, shouting their own expletives as they shook their fists and spit in her direction.

"Your son was raised on the rotten foundation of this so-called Republic, and he fell easily, like a weed beneath my boot. Your precious Republic is next, because it can't stand the weight of what's coming," she said with a crazed and bloody smile. It was then she began to cackle, and Silas was taken aback. This wasn't the daughter he remembered. This was someone else entirely.

However, her words didn't have the intended effect, and instead the men and women before her scoffed and fell into their own terse laughter. Not all of them, but enough that even the Vox joined in with their mocking merriment.

She only laughed harder. "Kill me then and begin your demise. I'm becoming impatient," she said through gritted teeth, her laughs subsiding. Silas batted at her arm to silence her, but it was ineffective. What she was saying was suicide.

"No, no, no, little mouse. That is what I will call you, little mouse," the Vox said, and the others laughed their cruel laughs. Whatever love the Vox may have had for Silas was surely gone, or at the very least it didn't extend to his family.

"As you know, our Republic has laws, and you will stand trial for your crimes. If..." he said with a sarcastic smirk, "you are found guilty, then and only then will you burn." His expression cold.

Catherine shook her head. "Then let us get this farce over with, so I can meet our real maker and free myself of your pretension," she said before spitting her own bloody phlegm onto the floor toward the Vox, who looked incensed as he made the sign of the star and cross on his chest along with the other clerics.

The Manus meanwhile stared at her unmoving. To Catherine's credit, she was able to return that stare, a feat not many could manage.

"Your blasphemy will not go unpunished. You will repent, if not now then when your skin begins to melt from your bones," he said and waved his hand dismissively. Silas wondered if they had gotten their fill of this spectacle.

As if to answer his question, the guards moved swiftly to lift her off the ground and carry her away. Silas tried to reach out for her, but he was too slow, his mind too sluggish to make contact. He was having trouble processing the situation and even more trouble formulating a solution.

"Your Holiness!" he shouted through the growing conversation and murmurs as they carried Catherine toward the door. They paused when Silas cried out, and he then dropped to his knees before the Vox for the second time. This time the disgust of it threatened to overwhelm him, but he would do anything to protect her.

"High Commander, we will discuss your failures soon enough when the trial is concluded and the apostate is dead," the Vox said simply.

"I beg of you, Your Holiness, show her leniency. Allow her another chance to repent and rejoin the flock," he said as tears began to fall from his cheeks, and spittle shot from his lips as they quivered. He was surely a pathetic sight to see. A legendary commander reduced to a whimpering dog.

"You are lucky you are not joining her," Ajax said, rushing forward as if to strike at Silas. However, several of his fellows held him back. Silas considered telling the truth, telling Ajax it was he who killed his son, but if he did there would be no opportunity left to save Catherine.

"I only beg for her life, Your Holiness," he repeated, ignoring Ajax. "Imprison her for life, allow her a lifetime of contrition. I will gladly sit beside her if it would bring you to amnesty." At those words, the crowd gasped, and the Vox looked curiously at Silas.

"You would relinquish your titles, your lands, everything... to sit in a prison cell beside your traitorous daughter for the rest of your life? Is that correct, High Commander?" the Vox said.

He further prostrated himself, his head to the floor. "Yes, Your Holiness, I would offer everything I am and everything I could ever be before God and beg eternal forgiveness." He would gladly bow before God in his heart. That thought kept him from deviating from this path. God's eternal light would be his salvation, even if this life were lost.

There was a long silence, and all he could hear was his own breathing as he waited for judgment. "I will take it into consideration. You are all dismissed," the Vox said finally, and Silas lifted his head to see the guards exit the room with Catherine in tow.

"Your Holiness, this is an outrage!" Ajax shouted as he stepped forward toward the throne. "Hex is responsible for the death of thousands—no, millions—of soldiers and citizenry alike. She must pay for these crimes and more. This shell of a man can burn with his evil spawn if he likes, but no amount of contrition will absolve him and her of their wrongdoing–"

"Enough," the Vox said loudly, cutting off his tirade. "I said I will take it into consideration, and I will remind you, Praefectus Frumentario, I am the voice of God in this solar system. Not you," he said with a menacing glare and stood up to leave. The Manus followed closely behind and whispered into his ear. They were too far away, the words too soft for Silas to hear.

Hearing the others begin to chatter and disperse, Silas stood up. He wiped at his face, and the tears dried on his cheeks. The guards remained close at hand, but it appeared he remained free, at least for now.

He looked for support in the room but even his most loyal supporters seemed hesitant to get near him. However, Ajax had no such reservations and got directly into his face. The guards tensed and moved closer to the pair but did not intervene.

"I don't know what happened, but I will find out. My son is dead, Zhou is dead, and how many more. I hold you personally responsible for every one of them, and you will pay for it alongside your bitch of a daughter. You will finally burn after all these years of failure."

He leaned in even closer, whispering into Silas's ear. "Like those poor souls in the slums all those years ago. Poetic, isn't it?" he said and leaned back, a satisfied smile on his face before he walked away, Simon following him close behind.

Silas, through all of it, remained silent, even as others jeered at him. There was very little he could think of saying at that moment and even less he wanted to. Ajax was right. He would answer for his sins, he knew that, but he would answer to God and God alone.

Kaya

June, 4103 U.E.T.—Amaranthine Palace, Mars

KAYA FOLLOWED SILENTLY behind Aelius, the hood of her white robe pulled down to her eyes, concealing her face from all but the most curious observer. She kept her eyes down and didn't speak. It was expected that acolytes would be like ghosts unless called upon for something. They certainly wouldn't speak unless spoken to.

She was apprehensive, but the presence of Aelius gave her confidence as they passed each subsequent guard station. He had a quiet confidence about him that put her at ease even here, deep inside the bowels of the Amaranthine Palace. Their cover story was simple. They were there to try and coax a confession from a prisoner, an action that would not draw excessive attention. Kaya prided herself on being able to blend into different roles and environments, but Aelius made it look natural.

He spoke intimately with the guards at the next checkpoint, offering them perfunctory blessings, which they accepted gladly. Kaya kept her head down and followed him through the checkpoint in a show of well-practiced subservience. The guards never paid her any mind at all.

The ease with which Aelius conducted himself made Kaya wonder, not for the first time, about his real origins. In her short time with the Coalition, the man had been nothing but helpful, but there was something strange about him.

He was always aloof, keeping himself separate from the others. That wasn't particularly strange for a group of saboteurs and revolutionaries, but it was one aspect of many. He also seemed to know entirely too much when others around him knew next to nothing. He even knew about things she had never heard her noble parents speak of. Subjects and ideas that weren't found in the books of her family's secret library. When taken in aggregate, it made her wonder who he really was. More importantly, it made her wonder what he really wanted.

Most called him a prophet, especially among the populace, but she refused to do so. Others might believe he was blessed by God with secret knowledge, but she certainly didn't. Others within the Coalition leadership didn't seem to care one way or another. Kaya figured they were just happy to have someone so well connected and competent among their resources.

Leading a revolution wasn't a cheap or easy proposition. Finding people who were willing to help with connections, power and money was a difficult, if not impossible task.

Aelius seemed to check all those boxes, but no one she asked, even Jimmy, could tell her for sure where he came from. He was like a specter that appeared one day, and no one questioned the haunting.

The latest guard checked their credentials. She was a Republican Guardsman, standing tall with her blue armor gleaming and lightning pike held at the ready in her left hand. She had a serious expression, like a bird of prey. These weren't the type of people Kaya was used to fooling. The guards back on Mercury had been little more than impoverished security guards. These people in their blue armor and flowing capes were real knights.

Soldiers that had been combat tested suppressing revolts in the Far Coast or hunting pirates through the belt before being chosen for the Guard. It was a position of honor given only to the most loyal soldiers. Their business was death, and they knew it well.

The guard handed back their identification and waved them forward. The same woman led them through the well-lit corridor. They were deep within the bowels of the palace now, where no one ever went and even fewer even knew existed.

Kaya remained quiet, but internally she was a ball of panic and apprehension. This could all go awry at any moment, and if it did there would be no escaping this time. There were far too many guards and nearly three times as many cameras, but somehow Aelius remained calm and collected.

Kaya didn't want to trust him, but he hadn't asked her to come. She decided that herself after she found out where he was going. She knew coming to the palace would get her closer to Theodore, and then all she had to do was figure out a way to separate herself from Aelius. It wasn't much, but it was the best chance she had to finally go see him. With things escalating, she wanted her family to know she was safe, and she wanted to do it in person.

That wasn't her only reasoning. Kaya had always heard whispered tales of Hex, the champion of the Coalition. Discussion of her or the Coalition was of course not allowed, but it was impossible to stop every strand of information and legend that leaked out onto the web. There was always enough that got out for people to create their own legends in the absence of facts.

She wanted to see for herself who this woman was and understand what Aelius had planned for her. Not the beaten and drugged version that they paraded on digiscreens throughout the Republic. The real Hex, the real Catherine Beckett. Hal had mentioned her before and how she trained to be a Hospitaller like her mother. He described his cousin as a confident woman with a kind heart, an image directly at odds with the picture painted by the Republic's media.

Her trial had already begun in earnest with the Republic wasting no time turning it into a circus. The Vox presided over her trial like God himself upon his golden throne while the Council of Bishops and Seneschals from the Void Knights asked probing questions and leveled an endless stream of accusations for crimes real and invented. Being with Prometheus made it easy enough to know the difference. It had become a spectacle unlike anything she had ever seen.

They were led past endless rows of nondescript doors until finally they came to one at the far end guarded by another guardsman. The woman leading them whispered a few words into the man's ear, and he saluted before going back down the hall.

She tapped at the lock controls inputting a code before scanning her palm. The door whirled to life in a series of distinct clicks and clanks as metal rods slid open on the heavy door. Kaya felt confident this cell could withstand any conventional attempt at breaching it. Even an atomic blast would likely have no effect after seeing the thickness of the door.

"You have five minutes. I can't promise you more," the woman said, and Aelius nodded as she walked a few paces down the hall, leaving the door propped open. So this was another one of his contacts, Kaya thought. The surprises never seemed to end with him.

"Are we breaking her out?" Kaya asked hopefully.

"No, that isn't possible now," he said simply, stepping into the room. Kaya followed, wrinkling her nose at the sickly smell that hung in the air. Hex was on the bare floor, curled into the fetal position, her arms wrapped around her knees. She didn't move when they entered the tiny room. Save for a waste port in the opposite corner, there were no other features in the room.

The plastic walls were marred with scuffs and carvings, likely made by the nails of prisoners long since gone from this world. Uplighting near the ceiling provided only an eerie reflective glow that made the space even more uncomfortable. Kaya felt claustrophobic as her shoulders brushed into Aelius as they moved into the small room.

Aelius seemed unbothered by the smells or even the state of the woman lying on the floor in rags. "Can you help her?" Kaya asked, unsure of what to do. She came here wanting answers, but it was clear now that Hex wasn't in a condition to give her any. She wasn't going to see the real Hex after all.

Aelius handed her a mini lantern that illuminated the room and she knelt beside him casting the light where he directed.

The light only made the ragged woman look worse. Her rough-spun slip was filthy, and her skin had grown taught from a lack of food. Where her skin wasn't covered, Kaya could see a myriad of bruises and cuts that had been left untreated, several of which had begun to fester in the squalid conditions. It was a horrible sight.

Aelius pulled a device from under his robe. It looked like a typical metal syringe but much larger. It also glowed faintly, so she assumed it was some kind of powered device, but it wasn't something she recognized. He cleared a spot on her thigh and pressed the end of the needle into her skin. The device hissed to life with a sound like air being released from a balloon.

"Was that morphine?" she asked.

"No, something better."

Kaya was still taken aback by how calm he was, even now. Deep within the enemy's stronghold, he spoke like he had taken a stroll through the quiet boulevards of the high districts.

"Here, hold this," he said, taking her free hand and wrapping it around the device that protruded from the frail woman's leg. Meanwhile he fished another bundle from under his robe.

He unscrewed the cap of a small pouch, some kind of nutrition packet she thought based on the look of it. Squeezing the contents into Hex's mouth with one hand, he opened a second pouch containing water. Trading one for the other, he slowly administered the water in the same way. It took a moment, but Hex eventually began to swallow. Slowly at first and then hungrily like a starved animal, her eyes suddenly opening with a wild expression. Her body didn't move save for small twitches of weak muscles.

"Good, very good, relax," he whispered in his monotone voice.

It took a moment, but her eyes calmed, and she focused on Aelius. Her body still appeared rigid and unmoving, but her eyes were focused now. No longer lost in the mist. Aelius fished another small bundle out from under his robe and placed it in the crook of her arm.

"Consume this as soon as you are able. Your condition will continue to improve as long as you do. Remember the plan and have faith it will work," he said before placing a hand on her cheek. "Good luck, Catherine. You are doing us all a great service." She didn't speak, but her eyes locked onto his before they closed in assumed recognition.

Kaya didn't work up the strength to ask Hex anything, but even if she had it was unlikely she would have gotten an answer. She was in a bad way, and whatever drugs Aelius had given her seemed to help, but who knew for how long? She wondered if it was even worth it.

Everyone knew how the trial would end. There was only death for traitors to the Republic, and recently those deaths had been exceptionally gruesome. So wouldn't it better to be unconscious and dreaming of better days? Dreaming of a better time before the pain, before the suffering? Kaya would have thought so. This could so easily have been her had things gone differently two years ago. It could still be her in the future.

Her and Aelius didn't speak further until they had returned to their vehicle outside the palace grounds. Their exit had been stressful, at least for her but thankfully uneventful.

"I need to go see Theodore," she blurted out as they loaded into the vehicle.

"There isn't any time."

"You know that there is, please. This might be my last chance to do it."

"Do you intend on going somewhere?" he asked, turning to look at her.

"Well, no, but...with the trial and our plans. I mean, who knows what will happen next?"

He seemed to be weighing her words with a blank expression like someone trying to solve a mathematical equation in their head.

"What will happen is what is meant to happen," he said in his prophetic manner, and Kaya resented him for it. She was tired of being patronized.

"Don't give me your prophecy mumbo jumbo, Aelius. I don't subscribe to it, and it lessens both our intellects to engage in tiresome rituals. We both know we might all soon be dead if this fails. We might die even if everything goes well. I would prefer to settle my affairs now." *And make alternate arrangements for my escape*, she thought.

"Very well," he said after a long pause. "It might have been a mistake keeping you with Reina for so long." The monotone nature of his voice and his expressionless face made it difficult for Kaya to tell if he wasn't being serious. She found him to be a frustratingly difficult man to understand.

Kaya

June, 4103 U.E.T.—New Olympia, Mars

THEY ARRIVED AT her family's villa in the capital a little past dark on the same day. It sat on a hillside below the palace, not far from Trinity square. The area was surrounded by similar homes for off-planet lords and ladies when they visited the capital.

Her family's estate was constructed in a Mercurian style with rough-hewn sandstone blocks and large arched windows. There was also a series of connected buildings, rather than one large one that included living quarters, a small barracks, workshops, and official offices for conducting business and accepting guests.

Her mother had always talked about how she loved the large gardens, fountains, and especially the small orchard of fig trees. Kaya hoped she would get a chance to see them.

Aelius stopped the vehicle near the front gate.

"I won't be long," she said, stepping out of the vehicle.

Aelius followed her. "I will go with you."

"I will be fine."

"Yes, but I will still go, just in case."

Kaya wanted to argue, but she knew there wasn't much point, and if things went south he might be useful. He always seemed to have a solution.

In this case, she knew sneaking in wouldn't be the best strategy. So she led them openly to the gate where two guards kept watch. Predictably they were stopped, not harshly but sternly. The guards were well-trained veterans, chosen from among the most loyal Vardan house guards for positions like this.

She didn't know if they recognized her, but she wordlessly gave them the passcode Theodore had provided. The guards didn't seem surprised, and one of them moved into the guardhouse, presumably to verify the code against their logs. The other kept a watchful eye with his rifle at the ready.

Aelius meanwhile maintained an easy stance. She supposed it wasn't strange for a bishop and his aid to be visiting the estate.

They didn't say anything else, but the gates were opened, and she began to walk inside when the guard spoke.

"Only the girl," he said, raising a hand to stop Aelius.

"He's with me," she offered.

"The code is for you."

"I can wait here. It will be alright," Aelius said, his calm demeanor putting her at ease. Maybe yet again he knew more than he was letting on.

Kaya nodded and followed the guard inside. They hadn't searched or restrained her, and she thought that was a good sign. They brought her to a small waiting room attached to the office complex and asked to wait while another guard watched over her.

She hadn't told them who she was, and they hadn't asked. She assumed they either already knew or were well trained enough to follow whatever protocol that code she gave them prescribed.

It wasn't long until Theodore himself came in, flanked by several well-armed guards. His face was tense, and his body rigid as he entered the room, but it quickly changed when he saw her sitting there.

"My God," he said, "I couldn't be sure it was you. Come with me." She followed his lead deeper into the building, passing several offices with workers going about their business.

"Seems like it's busy around here," she said, trying to affect a more Martian accent for the benefit of eavesdroppers.

"Yes, that is an understatement," Theodore said until they made it into a large private office, she assumed was his. The guards remained outside.

"Everyone has been hard at work," he said as he closed the door. "Looking for you, Kaya. I received your note, but I wasn't sure if I could believe it. We weren't going to stop looking for you that easily."

"I'm glad you didn't change the code."

"What good would it be if we had? I am glad you are back safely, but more importantly what the devil is going on? Where have you been?" he said, his expression weary. "Your father is beside himself, and your brother has even come to aid in the search personally."

"Tiberius is here?"

"In orbit, but he just arrived yesterday with a small detachment of the Mercurian fleet. Do you need some water?" he asked, moving to a small bar in the corner of the room.

"The fleet? What for?" she asked, confused. She didn't know what the need was for warships between Mercury and Mars.

"Pirates continue to be a problem, and it's escalating. With the spectacle of the trial and the unrest it's creating, the authorities are having a hard time putting out all the fires," he said with a neutral expression.

"They are strained to the breaking point, which is why your brother came with more support to help find you. We couldn't trust the Frumentarii or the Martians to handle it themselves," he said with no small amount of disdain.

He filled a glass from a condensation-covered silver pitcher. "Now tell me what is going on? Are you well? Where have you been all this time?" he said, handing her a glass of water.

She took the glass and drank deeply from it, not because she was particularly thirsty but because she needed a chance to organize her thoughts.

She was glad to hear her brother was here but disappointed she wouldn't be able to see him. She knew things were becoming more unsettled in the Republic, but official news from the capital was becoming more difficult for the Coalition to get. Many of their agents had gone dark. They were either already discovered or hiding out from the increased Frumentarii presence. News from farther away was even slower in reaching them.

"I have been safe. I wasn't kidnapped like they said. I left the Sanctum of my own choice," she said, vaguely.

It wasn't that she didn't trust Theodore; she trusted him almost completely. He had been there her entire life, but he was also her father's most trusted advisor. She didn't want to give him any more reason to keep her there for her own well-being or some other such reason.

"That's it? You walked out and left and went where?" he asked, raising an eyebrow.

"Well, something like that," she said, suddenly realizing how ridiculous she sounded. "I have friends. I am safe," she added quickly, trying to salvage the moment.

He looked at her dubiously but didn't push the subject. "I'm glad you made it here safely. Your father will be even more glad when he hears. We can transfer you to your brother's ship immediately."

"No!" she said more harshly than she intended, "I... I don't plan to leave. I only came here to let you know I was well and to warn you."

His brow scrunched, "Warn me? Of what?"

"There is trouble coming."

He laughed, "Trouble coming? I think anyone could have told you that, Kaya."

"No, I mean something big. Something that will change everything, maybe forever," she said with a deathly serious expression.

He studied her face and his laughter eased. "You know something, don't you? Have you been with the Coalition? You have been. It all makes more sense now," he said running a hand over his face. "Your father thought you might be lying low somewhere, maybe with some other Sanctum runaways, but I thought there must be more. Your note only amplified my feelings."

"That part doesn't matter. I—" she hesitated, not knowing how much to really say, "I want you all to be okay. Things are happening none of us can control. It's going to get dangerous."

His face grew more somber as he leaned in to speak with her, "Kaya, there is much more going on than *you* know. This isn't something you want to be involved in. Please, come with me. I don't want to have to force you, but I will if I must." His expression was more serious than Kaya had ever seen it.

"No," she said, sure of herself. She was tired of being questioned and shielded from responsibility or danger. She would finish what her mother wasn't able to. She would see her dream become a reality. "If my mother believed in this, then so do I. I can finish what she started," she said confidently and stood to leave, but Theodore reached out to stop her.

"It was Prometheus then," he said almost to himself before looking at her earnestly. "Kaya, whatever they have told you is likely not the truth, not the complete truth anyway."

Her mind jumped to his mention of Prometheus but then landed on his final words. None of what he said was news to her. They had lied to her once about her mother's involvement and probably other things. She didn't trust them, but they had done what they said they would, which was more than she could say about others.

"I know enough. I can help where others can't. Even if it's not for them, it's for me, my mother, and the regular people who can benefit from a changed world. I might not be able to convince my father to help, but there are other Lords and Ladies who can be convinced. Lord Beckett—"

Theodore cut her off abruptly, a scowl creasing his face, "Lord Beckett is the reason your mother is dead, Kaya. Why would he ever help the Coalition?" Kaya could barely process what he said as he continued speaking. "I don't know how his daughter Catherine got mixed up in this now, and I am sorry to see it, but maybe it's finally his punishment for the blood on his hands."

Her mind swam. How did Lord Beckett kill her mother? Her mother died in the ship explosion. Did he plan it? *No, that doesn't seem very likely. That isn't what the Pandora Fleet does. It's true they never found any evidence after the explosion and, oh no,* she thought. *It was supposed to be your mother. That's what Aelius had said.*

"Kaya..." Theodore said, "are you okay?"

"My mother didn't die when her ship exploded, did she? She was never on any ship at all," she said, tears forming. "She was Hex, wasn't she?"

When he hesitated to answer, she knew immediately she was right. How long had he known? Did her father know? How long did they plan on keeping this from her. Probably forever.

It had been her mother all along. That was why she had been absent so often and why the investigation into her death was dropped so quickly. A fact that had always bothered her, but now she was even more furious.

If her mother was Hex and the Pandora Fleet was her primary enemy, than it made sense that Silas Beckett was the one who killed her, but in that moment that revelation wasn't what she was most angry about.

"You all lied to me, all this time. My mother sacrificed her life for people who couldn't fight for themselves, and then her memory was brushed aside and shoved into a closet like an old pair of shoes!" she shouted angrily, pulling away from his grasp. "I *will* finish what she started." She stormed out of the room. The guards grabbed her as she attempted to pass and held her firmly in place. She attempted to break free, but she didn't think she could without hurting them.

"You have no right to detain me," she shouted.

Theodore caught up to where she writhed, trying to remove herself from the guard's grip to no avail.

"I have every right, but I am not your enemy." He let out a deep sigh. "I am only here to keep you safe."

"Then help me," she said, staring into his eyes, "Help me finish what she started. You have told me before you loved my mother, so prove it now." His face twisted, and she knew he was at least considering it.

"There is much more at play than you could ever imagine. This is hardly the beginning or the end," he said.

"It is at least *a* beginning, and that is enough."

He waved to the guards to let her go, and she didn't try to run.

"The conclusion of the trial is only days away. There is no telling what might happen next," he said, a look of concern etched on his face. "I assume you will be there to witness it."

"I will be there to stop it," she said confidently.

"There is no stopping fate," he said shaking his head.

"Then I will change it and create a new path."

He sighed and nodded gravelly. "Then I will help you." He looked defeated.

"You are going to let me go?" she asked, surprised.

"Your father will kill me, but I have seen that fire in your eyes before. Your mother had the same fire, and like her I expect you aren't going to listen to a word I say."

"You could force me to go with you, lock me away, and ship me back to my father." She didn't want him to do that, but she wanted to understand why he would let her go. Why would he risk so much?

"I don't have the heart for that. The future is as much yours as it is mine. Besides, you aren't a child. You understand the costs," he said solemnly, and he was right. She hadn't been a child since that day her mother died, and now that was even truer.

"Where will you be?" she asked.

"I will remain near the Rubah. We need to be ready to leave. Look for me there, and I will get you off this planet when the time comes."

Then it dawned on her, that was why her brother brought war ships with him. It wasn't for her, not only for her anyway. It was to make sure they could get off the planet, no matter what happened, and she considered how much more he knew. She would have to warn Jimmy and the others.

"I will," she said and wondered if she would ever actually see him again.

"Be careful, Kaya, and I will see you again soon. Remember why you are doing what you are doing, and don't succumb to weak emotions. Arrogance and anger have no place in this."

She only vaguely understood what he was talking about, but she nodded anyway. She had to get going and didn't want to give him time to change his mind.

"Thank you, Uncle Teddy," she said.

He smiled, and she could have sworn she saw moisture forming in the corner of his eyes as he pulled her into an embrace. "Go make her proud," he whispered and let her go.

She was happy for his support, but it didn't change that he had lied to her. That was something he would still need to answer for, along with her father if it turned out he also knew.

She didn't look back as she went to Aelius and the vehicle. She found him there sitting quietly and staring off into the distance like he had a habit of doing. She began to seethe again when she saw him, but her words remained calm and icy as they came out.

"Did you know Lord Beckett killed my mother?" she said.

"It was always a possibility that he could have killed her," he said without hesitation.

"My mother was supposed to be the one on trial. I thought she was helping to recruit Lord Beckett, but she was going to be the one to sacrifice herself for the cause, wasn't she? You lied to me."

"No. I told you it was supposed to be your mother. You chose not to understand what that meant," he said, and she hated him for it. Like some ancient genie, he twisted her words to fit his own narrative, and she understood now why the others disliked him.

"Now an innocent woman will burn at the stake, put there by her own father. For what, revenge? As a sacrificial lamb? What lies did you tell her?" she asked, her voice rising as she berated him with questions.

"She is no more innocent than any of us and even more a part of this cause. She knew your mother and loved her. Is she not allowed to take up the mantle of Hex and finish what your mother so bravely started? I have never told her anything but the truth," he said in his typical dry fashion.

"It should be me in that cell, not her." It was her mother's legacy, and so she should be the one to bear that burden if someone had to.

"One day there may be a need for you to wear your mother's mantle or maybe your own, but right now it is Catherine's duty. Now you can help me make sure she survives the ordeal. Like you, she will be needed for what comes next," he said cryptically, and she scrunched her brow.

"You plan to get her out?" she said, suddenly excited.

"Her life will not end in martyrdom," he said without expanding further, and she was left to ponder what he could possibly have planned.

CHAPTER

29

Despite his constant pleas and requests, Silas was declined access to his daughter during her trial. He was left to look at her from a distance in the viewing area with the rest of the lords and ladies that had assembled in New Olympia.

They had all watched the trial with varying levels of interest and concern, but most avoided looking at Silas directly throughout the ordeal. He wondered if they avoided him out of pity or out of fear that they might become guilty by association.

His brother Simon, however, watched almost gleefully alongside Ajax as each accusation and condemnation was lobbed at Catherine. The sight of it nearly drove him into a manic rage, but luckily Marcus was there to stop him from signing his own death warrant.

Now that the verdict was nearing, and nothing was left to influence, his old allies came to his aid and arranged for him to see Catherine at long last. They didn't say it, but it seemed clear that this might be the last favor he ever received from any of them.

The bridges were burning, and it wouldn't be long before he was left nearly alone on his island of despair. Marcus and his wife Diana, the only ones left beside him. Through his pain, he made a mental note of who lit their torches first.

He had questioned Diana to no end about what she knew regarding their daughter and her involvement with the Coalition. She swore she had no idea and Catherine had left her in the dark as much as him. He had no reason to doubt her, and so they suffered together. Except while he spiraled deeper into depression, she buried herself in her work at the hospital. He knew it was her way of finding comfort and meaning in the face of senseless tragedy.

Marcus would offer to stay with them to the end, but he would order him to leave before he wasted his life as well. He cared about the man too much to see him fall as far as he had in such a short time. With any luck, they might still consider him for a high position in time. Maybe not within the Pandora Fleet but somewhere. Soldiers of his experience and skill were always in high demand.

He didn't want it to come to any of that and held out hope that the Vox and Manus would decide to spare Catherine's life, despite their refusal to meet with him. He continued to pray for guidance, but God remained silent, which wasn't unusual for him in recent years, but it only amplified his unease. Diana at least maintained her faith in his ability to get them out of this. He didn't want to fail her too, not more than he already had.

Silas was only given limited time to see his daughter, and even then, it was from the other side of the glass and steel of her prison cell. This was the one condition they wouldn't budge on in exchange for the privacy he now had with her. She had been sitting on the floor, with her knees drawn into her chest.

Now that he was up close, he realized that the room had no furniture or amenities besides the waste hole in the corner. It made him want to smash the glass with his bare hands and pull his daughter to safety. Yet he stood there weak and impotent, merely knocking for her attention.

"I told you that I won't confess. Leave me alone," Catherine said without looking up. Her voice was stronger than it had been through much of the trial, which he found amazing. She was stronger than he could have ever imagined. She endured so much and somehow maintained her health and composure.

"Catherine, it's me, your father," he said weakly. He was ashamed to even call himself that, but her head sprang up in recognition.

"Dad," she said, more confident and excited than he would have dreamed possible as she sprang to her feet and came to the glass.

He was struck immediately by how tired her eyes looked, even if her body seemed energetic. He had seen eyes like that far too many times. They weren't the eyes of defeat, more like eyes that acknowledged the inevitable and resigned themselves to what came next. It was what the loss of hope looked like.

"How...are they treating you? Are you doing okay? Last I saw you, it seemed like you could barely stand, but now..." He appraised her more closely. "...you almost look like nothing has happened."

She shrugged. "I don't know, maybe some kind of illness. I'm terribly hungry, but otherwise I feel much better. The accommodations could use improvement," she added with a sarcastic smirk. "The room service is even worse."

He laughed, a shallow, pitiful sound, but the tension still decreased noticeably.

"It isn't your fault," Catherine offered generously.

He didn't want to spend what little time he had with her talking about his own blame. There would be a time for his penance.

He reached into his pocket, his hand shaking slightly. "I didn't bring any food, but I thought maybe you might want this," he said, passing the photo through the slot in the glass.

She didn't move right away, her eyes scrunching together appraising him. He wasn't sure if her situation had made her so suspicious or if he was only noticing now how she viewed him, but the moment passed quickly as she took the photo.

His doubts washed away as she smiled at it and laughed. Her laugh, more of a chortle, was uniquely hers. It was so unique that when she made it as a child, he often worried she was choking. Diana had hated it for the primal fear it instilled in her, but he always found it endearing, even now in this place.

"I still remember how you limped around for days, unable to sit or move because of your blistered skin."

He let out his own stifled laugh in solidarity with her. His skin still chafed at the uncomfortable memory.

"I want to have more memories like that, Cat. You, me, and your mother and maybe even grandkids one day. Tell them what they want to hear, and they will let you live." Then he hesitated. He knew what he wanted to say, but he still hesitated as he choked out a simple, "I love you."

Her lips pursed as she offered an understanding nod. She opened her mouth to speak several times before responding, as if she was trying to find the right words.

"You may have forgotten how to love, yourself most of all," she finally said.

He shook his head, looking into her eyes fervently. His words caught in his throat, but he knew they had to be said. "Love is all I have. Love for you, your mother, and God. It is what I have sworn to protect and the well from which I draw my strength. To protect those things, I would give up everything and anything. I have already offered them everything I have to spare you. My title, lands, wealth, everything," he said, pressing his palm up against the glass.

In response, Catherine slammed her fist into the glass. If it wasn't for his battle-hardened nerves, he would have jumped back at the unexpected outburst.

"Yes, I remember. I fought against my chains while you offered them our necks. You are too smart to be so foolish," she snarled. Whatever love she had shown him vanished in an instant.

"I..." he hesitated now in the changing winds. She put him off balance in a way only someone so close to his heart could. "Whatever I give up now is nothing compared to your life, nothing compared to the glory we will receive in the future when this life ends," he said, his voice choked with emotion.

Her face wrinkled as her gaze dropped to the ground. "You are a fool. You don't need to make yourself a martyr to balance the scales. The Republic tramples over your body, and yet you plead for more. You yearn for the yolk that binds you to their wagon. You cower and concede when you should stand your ground. You say you fight for me, but that is a lie. You are only fighting for the bishops and their rotten system that has doomed us." She looked up, pointing a finger at him. "Not only you and me but all of humanity. It is an unprecedented darkness that you personally help maintain." Her judgment was swift and condemning.

He didn't have the will to fight her. A part of him knew she was right. Even now he cowered under the weight of her accusations, unable to produce any coherent retort.

Yet his love remained unbroken. He knew the meaning of sacrifice, the ghosts that clouded his memories and the scars on his body were testament to that. Now before God he would sacrifice even more if it meant the return of his daughter to him.

"I don't want to live long enough to see your final resting place," he said.

"Then fight with me, fight with the millions of others who are willing to give up everything to protect not only themselves or their families but all of the others who can't protect themselves from the corruption of the Republic."

He shook his head. "The only way is to cooperate. The Coalition can't win this war."

"The Coalition is already winning. The Far Coast is in open rebellion, and more will follow. With your help, with the Pandora Fleet, we can take the fight to them. Our world is stale and dying, and I have no interest in standing idly by in my villa while it continues to crumble around me."

"What you are suggesting is suicide. There is no other possible outcome," he said, attempting to speak low, although he knew it would all be picked up on the security audio anyway.

"What difference does it make if I am already destined to die?" She turned away from him, stepping deeper into the cell before pausing and looking back. "You say you don't want to know my final resting place? Then fight with me, and they can bury our bones together."

He stood stunned for what felt like eternity, but before he could say another word the guards returned and forced him from the hallway, Catherine's pleading eyes etched into his memory.

Silas arrived back aboard the Specter hours later. He had found out en route that his wife was already there waiting for him to return.

Marcus had insisted she remain close to them instead of on the surface as a precaution, and Silas was glad that he did. They had no shortage of enemies now.

"Welcome back," Marcus said as he entered the airlock into the main corridor. "Come on, you are needed in the war room."

"I didn't call any meetings. Can this wait until tomorrow? I would prefer to go to my quarters," he said, exhaling deeply.

"No, this is important," Marcus replied, leading him toward the designated room.

"The trial is ending tomorrow. I don't know what could possibly be more urgent."

"This is about that," Marcus said, opening the door to the war room.

Inside were all the senior officers of the Pandora Fleet, save only a few.

A quick look at the faces confirmed these were the most loyal among them. Veterans of dozens of campaigns who for one reason or another gave him their unquestioning loyalty. Strangely, Colonel Taylor was also in the room. He was surprised to see the Republic army liaison among them but said nothing.

"Is this some kind of intervention then?" he said, tentatively taking his seat.

"Something like that, Milord," Captain Lancaster said in his gruff voice. "This situation is near to boiling over, and we are ready to stoke the fire."

"I'm not sure what you are suggesting, Captain," he said, his eyes narrowing.

"What the captain is saying is that we are all with you on this," Marcus said, and the room filled with ayes and nods. Some even beat their fists onto the table.

Silas raised his hands to quiet them.

"I appreciate your support, but there is no fire to stoke. We will wait for the verdict and abide by it. I only pray they choose the righteous path." He found their support flattering and great comfort, but this wasn't the way.

"Sard that!" Lancaster shouted. "Those pricks wouldn't know the righteous path if a holy book bit them in the ass. The writing is on the wall, High Commander, even if you don't want to see it." The cries of agreement and fist pounding came back in earnest.

Silas pinched the bridge of his nose, sighing loudly until they quieted enough for him to speak, "What you are suggesting is treason. If you don't think of yourselves, at least think of your families. You would throw all of that away for what? A self-admitted criminal of the state?" It was ridiculous what they were suggesting. The laws were in place for a reason, no one, not even his daughter, should be above them.

His own men seemed undeterred in their fervor, but it was Colonel Taylor who spoke up. He had sat quietly up until now, but his voice commanded the room with ease. Silas always knew the man to be a straightforward operator. A military commander who appreciated the rules and did his duty honorably. In his time as the Republic Army liaison to the Pandora Fleet, he had always been stern but fair in his dealings with Silas.

"This republic is ill beyond saving, High Commander. It continues to crumble around us, and only the poor and helpless have had the courage to rise to the challenge. To use what ability and resources they can muster to build a new world. Meanwhile those of us here continue to fight them, for what?" he asked, looking around the room to each of their faces. "To protect our own wealth? Our own families? Our own lives? Are we all so petty and selfish to cast aside our fellows thus? I am not a religious man, but I do know the scripture doesn't condone such action."

"We protect the will of God through his voice and hand in this world." Silas said, quoting scripture instinctively, but even to his ears it felt hollow now.

"They are men and women just like us, not gods. What divine will could order the deaths of so many? Not just directly by their hands but also by their policies that keep the masses poor and hungry. I for one am sick of it," Taylor continued slamming his fist on the table, his brow furrowed in anger as his eyes dug into Silas.

It was as if he was measuring him for the first time, deciding if this was the man who would lead them into the future. Silas wasn't sure he was prepared to be that person. He still hoped the system he devoted his life to would at least this one time bring him salvation.

"There is another way—" Silas began to say but was cut off.

"There is no other way but by the sword. There was a time in my life I bought the lies they told me. I believed my actions would make the world a better place." Taylor's eyes became glassy and distant. "Then I heard the screams of Tiyas and Ziyun. The screams of the children as they burned. Not a night goes by that I don't face their judgment. They pry into my very soul and reveal the weakness that has hidden there all these years. They are right to find me wanting, but now is a chance to do what is right." A few of the older soldiers seemed to nod knowingly, and Silas was forced to push aside his own ghosts. He couldn't succumb to their pressure now. "I don't expect it to bring me peace," Taylor said, shaking his head, a sorrowful expression on his face, "but I hope that the lives we save can find peace and happiness in their own ways. I think that is enough." The room hung silent for a long moment as many were lost in their own thoughts or watched Taylor and Silas, waiting for an answer.

Silas was prepared to give another canned response, but his mouth failed to open as if held closed by those same spirits that haunted Colonel Taylor.

He knew they were the same spirits, even if he often denied it. The screams were distant though, like a strange noise masked by thick windows. He had heard them secondhand through recordings and the radio transmissions of his men. If he hadn't tried to find another way, if he had been with his men instead of that office tower... He sighed as his thoughts wandered down a well-trodden path. He rubbed at his eyes to try and refocus.

"Emotions have been running high this past week. Everyone, get some rest, and we can reconvene tomorrow," he said, and the men and women in the room nodded, some with grins, others with more serious expressions. By God's bones, what had he done? He didn't say no, and that was treason. Did it even matter anymore? Deep down he knew how this all would end.

As the officers filed out of the room, some offered words of encouragement or support, while others maintained a stony silence. Marcus waited until they were the last ones in the room before approaching him.

"I know you are hurting, but don't forget Cat is my niece too. You aren't in this alone," Marcus said, putting a hand on his shoulder, "but this goes beyond any one of us now. The Far Coast will require attention, and you know how hard it is to operate a campaign that far from the Sun. There will be no better opportunity than this.

Marcus continued, "You tried to do the right thing once. What happened wasn't your fault. All those men and women in this room know that too. This is your chance to try again, be that man you aspired to be, the man God called you to be," Marcus said, tapping his chest forcefully. Suddenly everyone had the measure of him but himself.

"Like I said, I will give my answer tomorrow," Silas said, keeping his tone firm. He didn't have the energy to argue point by point.

"Remember, this isn't only your choice anymore. It's mine, Diana's, Catherine's, and every other soldier in this fleet. We all have our own part to play in this," Marcus said, stepping back. "These men are loyal to you, but if you choose the wrong path, I can't guarantee it will stay that way. You have assembled a group of people who strive to be better with their every action. You have bred that mantra into the culture of this fleet. You can't expect them forget that now when it matters most." Marcus clasped his arm pulling him in close and said, "Never forget." Then he left the room.

CHAPTER

30

Sleep never came, and Silas tossed in bed for hours until eventually deciding to give up the futile exercise. Diana managed to have slightly better luck, so he left her to rest as much as she was able. They had spoken for a long time into the night. She supported her brother's plan and was ready to fight for it, but she ultimately deferred to him to make his own decision. The question had left him wide awake and no closer to an answer.

He had been haunted as much by ghosts of the past as by the hungry eyes of the present. Everyone wanted something from him, which wasn't new. He had always been surrounded by pestering summer flies, but now they were becoming the insatiable demons of nightmares.

He spent hours staring out at the seemingly endless void of space and its distant stars that offered the illusion of a better world.

As a boy, he had looked up at the sky from Mars and dreamed of a better future. Reading adventure books about his heroes, like the great ancient American explorer Milton Krane from the early Imperial era, who was one of his very favorites. Even now, in the age of the Republic he is credited in large part for the successful colonization of the Far Coast.

Then there were the tales of Marchioness Julia Rothbard, who served as High Admiral of the Fleet. She had fought with distinction throughout the war between the Solar Empire and the fledgling Republic, accounting for a large portion of the Empire's early victories.

However, she later changed sides, joining the Republic after the destruction of Earth. Despite her early service to the Empire, stories of her ability and battles were still taught today within the naval academies of the Republic.

Silas had originally told his father he wished to be an explorer like Milton Krane, but that idea was squashed early when he was told in no uncertain terms that his place was at the helm of a warship in defense of God and the Republic, so it was in the steps of Julia Rothbard he walked instead. Although in times like this he wondered how different his life could have been if he had left for the Far Coast or maybe even beyond.

There were always those farfetched tales of the Sanctuary, a mythical ark akin to the one constructed by Noah during the great flood on Earth. Except instead of a simple wooden ship, the Sanctuary was said to be the largest starship ever made.

Legend has it the Sanctuary was commissioned by the last emperor of the Solar Empire before the end of the war as a last-ditch escape plan. Other historians argued that construction on the ship began well before the war ever did and that it was meant to facilitate human exploration to the distant solar system of Alpha Centauri.

It was a story that had captivated millions over the years, including Silas, but there was no evidence the ship ever existed, and even less that humans ever reached Alpha Centauri. Even the most generous historians agreed there was only hard evidence to support a smattering of crew-less satellites reaching that distant solar system.

Either way, it made for a compelling story that had been adapted by countless writers over the years. A tale that Silas likewise enjoyed as a young man, and even now as he remembered it. How he wished he could be there now, he thought as he looked out at the expanse of space for what might be the last time.

He didn't know how the events of the day would go, but he hadn't stayed alive this long by being ignorant of the world around him. He prayed to God for a positive outcome, but the pragmatic side of him knew it was unlikely the Vox would change his position. There were too many forces working against Catherine now, against him. If, or more likely when, she was found guilty, they would come for him too.

He knew intellectually that their lives were quickly spiraling to an end, but perhaps the intense stress or simple dissociation left him unable to process those feelings. The weight of it only left him so incredibly tired.

With a heavy sigh, he got up from his seat by the window and went to his closet. Mr. Beach had already prepared his clothes the night before, so like a robot he dressed in his finest uniform. His insignia of rank and peerage shined to a brilliant luster alongside his medals and campaign ribbons. When he looked at himself in the mirror, he saw the strong, loyal, and confident military commander he knew others expected him to be, but on the inside, he felt like a coward.

He struggled with the guilt those medals and ribbons brought to the surface. In the past, he could ignore those demons but now he was being forced to face them head on. He laughed to himself, a pitiless laugh. *You can't avoid the consequences forever*, he thought.

When he finally emerged from his bedroom, he was surprised to see the meeting table had been arranged with breakfast. Mr. Beach stood quietly nearby as Marcus sipped at a cup of coffee and picked lazily at a plate of eggs. He was up nearly two hours earlier than usual, so it was surprising to see them there already.

"I guess I'm not the only one who couldn't sleep," he said, taking a seat near Marcus.

"It's been a busy night."

Silas raised an eyebrow. "Do I want to know?"

"No, but I have to tell you anyway," he said, setting down his fork and looking seriously at Silas. "The footage from the old governor's office? Well, it's already been sent to the Frumentarii."

Silas set down the coffee mug he was bringing to his lips.

"Why?"

"One of the sarding tech officers. He had been sending reports to Zhou, but with him gone he sent those reports off to the Frumentarii."

"Was the tech officer one of ours?" Silas asked, wondering if the new betrayals had begun.

"No, praise be. It was one of the new people Zhou had saddled us with, but that's the least of our problems now. I know you wanted to wait to decide, but..." Marcus trailed off, leaving the rest unspoken.

"God's bones," Silas knew this was bad, very bad. It wouldn't be long before Ajax knew what really happened. His fate sealed alongside Catherine's. He sank heavily into the chair. He was so tired.

"Where is he now, the tech officer?" he asked.

"Taylor has him locked up in the brig, but no telling how long before someone goes looking for their little birdy. So, what should I tell Taylor and the rest of them?"

"Tell them to prepare for the worst, Tenebris Protocol."

Marcus looked stunned, staring blankly back at Silas.

"Is there a problem?" he asked with a raised eyebrow. "Isn't this what you all wanted from me?"

"Well, I didn't expect you to agree, honestly. I would have stayed with you to the end of course, but I didn't expect...," his voice trailed off. "I always said I would rather go out with a gun in my hand and my best friend by my side." He leaned across the table clasping his hand to Silas's forearm in a show of fidelity. "Malum contineri debet."

"Evil must be contained," Silas repeated, grasping his friend's arm in response.

Marcus pulled back, promptly retrieving his fork and pushing eggs and sausage into his mouth. "One other thing, Corporal Zambrano has gone missing."

"Who?" he asked.

"Namtar Zambrano, the Mercurian from the raid on 132 Aethera, the one you asked me to keep tabs on."

"Yes, right," he said in sudden recognition. He had been so thoroughly distracted he had forgotten about the man completely. Last he heard he was still unconscious from his injuries. He took a sip of his coffee. "Has he died then?"

"No, at least we don't think so. When I say he's missing, I mean he is nowhere to be found. The physicians don't know what happened to him. It's as if he walked off the ship."

"Was he well enough to return to his quarters or something? Wouldn't be the first time a soldier went missing prematurely from the medical bay. What of the people tasked with watching him? Surely, they saw something."

"That's the thing," Marcus said, waving his fork for emphasis. "The medics said he hadn't been conscious since he came back from that mission, and the sentries told me they hadn't seen him leave that medical bed even once in the last six months. The physicians said he has been healing physically, surprisingly well even, but he was still totally unresponsive. Now he's gone."

Silas shook his head. "I can't do anything with that information now. We have more important issues than a missing man-at-arms."

"I agree, but we should make sure he wasn't another one of Zhou's spies. One more thing," Marcus said, and Silas motioned for him to continue.

"The plasma blade I found on him. I had it locked away in my personal safe. The one no one knows about, but now it's missing."

"How can that be?"

"I'm not sure, but I don't think this is all a coincidence."

Silas stroked his chin considering the information. "Inform the security teams to search for him discreetly. He couldn't have gone far. We are in orbit after all."

"I will pass along the order."

"Good, was there anything else?" He hoped there wasn't because he was quickly running out of capacity to handle any more problems, and he was tiring of coincidences.

"No," Marcus said and stood from the table. "I will go find Taylor and the others to personally deliver the orders."

Silas nodded and went back to picking at his meal once Marcus was gone. He was lucky to have someone so close that he could trust with these types of matters.

"Milord, there has been other news, but it hasn't come through the official channels yet," Mr. Beach said from the corner of the room. He had been so quiet that Silas forgot the man was even there.

"What is it, Mr. Beach?"

"Your father, Milord. He is dead. Long live our noble Duke," he said, bowing his head.

Silas returned the bow instinctively with a nod before he realized that Mr. Beach was talking about him.

"Was it..."

"It was as natural as it could be under the circumstances. The honor guard you left behind saw to that."

Silas nodded. The damage had already been done by the poison, but he was glad his father didn't have to endure anymore suffering. He had been near death for so long that the news of his passing registered quickly, but knowing the cause only fueled his simmering anger. His father had been a tough and distant man but not completely unkind. He hoped he would find peace in the Celestial City.

Then he thought of the poison and Simon's likely involvement. With everything that had transpired, he was never able to confront him or do anything useful with the information. Perhaps now it could be used for some advantage, but he didn't immediately see how. Although it did become clear to him why his brother pushed so hard to see Catherine convicted, and it sickened him.

"Thank you for telling me, Mr. Beach. Has this information spread far yet?"

"Your father's staff is delaying the news as long as possible, but it is only a matter of time."

Silas nodded. "See that Marcus knows and tell him to prepare the shuttle. We will descend at once."

Mr. Beach left to fulfill his duty, and Silas was alone. Lost in thought, he stared into his coffee mug, considering the very real possibility that everything he knew was about to end, and soon he would be making his own pilgrimage to the Celestial City.

Luckily, Diana entered the room then. She didn't speak when she saw his face and instead embraced him quietly. He pulled her in tightly and took comfort in one of the last vestiges of good he had left to hold on to. Locked in that embrace, they allowed themselves a release of the built-up emotion they both held onto on the eve of such a terrible day. They knew it would only get harder from here.

Silas, Diana, and their small attaché arrived in New Olympia without fanfare. Their convoy landed in the spaceport adjacent to Trinity Square along with dozens of other craft. The Capital appeared to be busier than he had ever seen it in his lifetime and the spaceport had certainly not seen this many crafts at one time for at least a century or more. It was a pity it took something so terrible to bring so many people together. Well, at least the upper echelons of the Republic anyway.

When they descended through the atmosphere, it was easy to see the multitude of fires burning throughout the greater New Olympia area. Primarily slums and low districts, but fires could be seen spreading in the mid and even some of the high districts. Marcus was right. This was a different time, and the people were hungry for change. Hungry in a way that they had never been before.

Under special rules set forth by the Manus, no armed soldiers were allowed within the entire Capital District except for the Frumentarii and Republican Guard. Normally there was a prohibition on armed troops within the palace, but to extend that to the entire capital was unprecedented. Those few who carried plasma blades were not prohibited from wearing them, as they were not deemed a significant enough threat.

All of this made the execution of the Tenebris Protocol more challenging but not impossible. It was an extremely dangerous game they were about to play, but the Republic left him with no choice.

Either the world would be born anew from the darkness, or it would descend into a long night. He wasn't sure he would survive the day to be around for either, but he felt that was okay too. God would judge him now or in the Celestial City. If anything, he was anxious for that sentence to come to pass. He only hoped his daughter wouldn't be joining him on that pilgrimage.

He held Diana's hand tightly as much to reassure himself as her. Whatever came next, they were all in this together.

Marcus must have been sensing his worry because he leaned close as they walked and whispered into his ear, "We will get her out of here."

Silas grabbed his shoulder and stopped his friend as they walked toward the gallery where they would observe the final moments of the trial. His guards, handpicked from among his most loyal soldiers, fanned out protectively to offer what privacy and security they could.

"Thank you, Marcus, you have been a better friend to me than I have ever deserved. Go now and see to your own affairs,"

"Sard off if you think I'm leaving you both now. You are all the family I have left. What other affairs are there to manage? Feeding my cat? The mangey thing doesn't even like me. Anyway, I told you I will be with you till the end," he said defiantly.

Silas and Diana had to stifle laughs.

"The cat mirrors your own behavior, you know," Diana quipped to her brother, and he shot her a steely look.

"Not the time, Diana!" he retorted, raising his voice.

He didn't expect his friend to budge, but he knew he had to try. "Then please go and find the others. Support us from afar." What he left unsaid was that it would leave Marcus with the best chance to escape if or more likely when things went awry.

Marcus grimaced, but Silus remained quiet. It was important to him that Marcus make his own decision. Much to his chagrin, instead of arguing he nodded in acquiescence. Silas locked forearms once again, neither able to speak further for fear of breaking them both. Then Marcus hugged his sister and departed in silence. Silas and Diana shared a glance, their worries left unsaid. *Only God knows what will happen now*, he thought as he made the sign of the star and cross over his chest.

With his best friend gone, he continued toward Trinity Square, his wife, and his loyal coterie of knights by his side. Gwen was among them and moved to stand by his side, and he was thankful for it. Her presence was comforting in its own gruff way.

"This is a sarding circus," Gwen said as they made their way through the carefully cordoned off areas of the square. Soon these areas would be filled with spectators, but for now they were mostly empty, save for the Republican Guardsmen clad in their blue burnished uniforms. However, some were noticeably wearing battle armor, and the sight made his heartbeat quicken.

"If I still had the ear of the Vox or Manus, I would have advised against this. There is no way to keep so many people contained," he said.

"You don't need to contain them if you are willing to kill them all," she said coldly.

"How much collateral damage would that cause? A large portion of the nobility and even the high districts will be here. The Republic might want them dead, but they also can't rule this planet without them. Least of all the rest of the system."

"Maybe, but I still don't trust this," Gwen said.

"Me neither, but this is our only choice for now," he said, knowing that they had to go along with things. Even the Tenebris Protocol was a long shot, and they all knew it. The Republic had them at a severe disadvantage.

When they reached the designated area, the crowd parted to allow them access to the front. Many of those already assembled stumbled over themselves to avoid any contact with the party.

It was here that Silas was forced to part ways with his escort, despite Gwen's protests. He offered her a reassuring nod and gripped her arm. They would remain in this rear section while Silas was directed to a raised platform further along in the center of the square. This area was reserved for the lords, ladies, and other high-ranking Republic officials in attendance.

Although others were already there, they avoided making eye contact with him or Diana as they approached the front railing. Diana leaned closer to him. They didn't speak, but they didn't need to. Proximity to each other was enough to ease the tension for them both.

From his vantage point, he could see the platform where the Vox and Manus would sit to pass their final judgment on the accused, who would stand at a small dais in front of the golden thrones, behind the dais and at the center of the formation of stages and viewing galleries was the pyre. It would loom ominously over the accused, casting its macabre shadow. The theatrics of it made his stomach churn.

The streaming banners, bearing the nine-pointed star and cross flapping in the light breeze. The day was warm and dry as it usually was this high up on the flanks of Olympus Mons. It would have been a beautiful day if not for the dark proceedings, but it wouldn't be long now, and so he would wait in silence for the coming trial with Diana by his side.

It wasn't long until his brother's voice manifested like an unbidden rooster. Silas didn't turn to look at him. Instead, he remained standing at attention, his hands crossed behind his back and Diana standing stoically by his side, as if this were another military parade.

"I assume by now you have heard the news, brother, or should I say, Duke Beckett. I was a bit disappointed to only hear of our dear father's passing now, but I was always the last to know anything. Duchess Beckett, I congratulate you on your ascension as well, however brief it might be," his brother said like the snake that he was. Did he know no ounce of shame? Silas knew the answer, but he didn't take the bait despite the rage that bubbled under the surface of his stoic facade.

"It's a pity that you only found this level of self-control now," Simon said when Silas didn't budge. "Ah, yes. Here is my son now. Doing well despite your reckless actions," his brother said, motioning his arm to the side. Silas cocked his head slightly to see Praefectus Ajax approach, along with Simon's son Henry, who still bore visible signs of his recent injuries.

He walked with a limp, and bandages could be seen on his head and neck. Silas hadn't been allowed to visit the boy but was glad to see him well. Yet he remained silent. With a man like Simon, it was best to not give him anything to work with.

"Cat still has your tongue, I see. No matter," Simon said, waving his hand dismissively. "Luckily there are still others in this Republic who believe in loyalty, service, and the rule of law."

Simon leaned in to whisper in Silas's ear, "We know what you did. Enjoy your crown for now, because soon it will fall from your severed head, and your tainted branch will be pruned from the Beckett tree once and for all."

It was at that moment Silas knew it was over. To the depth of his bones, he knew there would be no reconciliation, no miracle of leniency, no chance at a normal life. Because of him, Catherine would burn, and with her Diana.

Yet he remained free of chains and could only assume it was to ensure he saw it all before he joined them on the pyre. They wished to punish him in the worst way they could imagine.

"I know you poisoned our father," Silas said, turning to look at Simon. "You are nothing more than a coward and a snake. You chose a pact with the devil, succumbing to his whispers through your own weakness. You could have chosen to rise through your own merits, but instead you schemed and cheated. You ride the coattails of others and shout from the mountain top that you yourself are the victor." Silas laughed bitterly. "You are nothing more than a parasite. So spare me your diatribe about loyalty. You have none, save to your own sick delusions."

The corners of Simon's mouth turned upward into a crazed smile. There was no shred of remorse and no attempt to shy away from the accusations. Whatever shred of familial love Silas might have shared for him was gone forever in that instant.

"I am glad you know it was me," Simon said, returning his stare. Silas wasn't surprised by his admission. He had believed it from the moment Kaya had told him in that alley, but it still hurt to have his suspicions confirmed so roughly.

Simon continued, "Finally, I can come out from under the shadow you and father cast over me. You call me a snake, and I welcome it. Without you blocking the sun, I can finally warm my scales, but first I will warm myself by the flames of the pyre," he said chuckling as if madness had finally consumed him. The sneer never left Simon's face as he walked away toward where his son and Ajax stood watching him.

Silas locked eyes with Henry and saw nothing but sorrow and pain. He couldn't imagine what it would be like to grow up under the guidance of such a monster. He felt for the boy, but his own pain was too great now to do anything about anyone else.

Silas instinctively pulled Diana closer and turned their backs to the demons before they could sap his resolve. He thought his brother might have lost whatever shred of humanity he had left, but now he wasn't sure he ever possessed any at all.

He wished for nothing more than to cut them down where they stood. The only thing stopping him was Diana's warm body pressed against his. He wanted to hold her close and be free of the tormenting clouds that had followed him now for so long. She had held strong for so long, but now she began to weep, and he ran his hand through her hair.

It was something he had always done in stressful times, but it felt like such a paltry exercise in the face of what was coming. She ran her fingers along his arm in her own comforting gesture. Despite her own stress and fears, she still tried to care for him.

The Hospitaller in her would never allow for anything else, and he loved her for it. In that moment especially, he welcomed her touch and appreciated it even more. He knew she had her own misgivings about his behavior and certainly about his family, but she put that aside now. She was a far better woman than he ever deserved.

Maybe he could earn her love again now that they stood hand in hand, their somber faces looking toward the pyre as they mentally prepared to meet the coming storm.

Kaya

June, 4103 U.E.T.—Amaranthine Palace, Mars

"This is taking too long," Kaya muttered as their small team pushed their way through the crowd. Reina was at the front on point. Aron was close to her side. Several other Prometheus agents shadowed closely behind.

"I told you already that we can't afford to make a scene so far away. We need to get into position," Reina whispered back.

"It will all be over at this rate by the time we get to the main dais."

"Be quiet and follow. You know it's important to-"

"Yes, follow the plan, I get it. I know where we are going and who is here," Kaya said cutting Reina off.

"And I know these buildings better than anyone," Aron added.

"Both of you shouldn't talk so much," Reina whispered, annoyed. She had already given them both a long talk about what she called "operational security," which neither of them took very seriously. They both knew plenty about staying undetected and didn't need a lecture.

"Relax, everyone is out for the blood of the traitor. They aren't listening to anybody like us," Kaya said as she adjusted her cowl after bumping past a well-dressed man in a business suit. Kaya, Aron, and the others were all dressed like average mid district residents. Mainly technical professionals who worked long hours in engineering or skilled labor jobs.

Their job was simple on the surface, to blend in with the crowd and wait for a signal. They had been provided with a list of high-value targets that they would try to rescue or capture once the chaos started. Then they would rendezvous back at the spaceport for extraction back to the deep canyons south and east of New Olympia where Jimmy had begun moving non-essential personnel weeks earlier. There they would hide out until tensions cooled and they could formulate their next move.

The problem was that Catherine wasn't on their list. Jimmy had said others were assigned to extricate her if possible because it would be too dangerous for them to be that close to the dais.

Aelius might have told her Catherine wouldn't be martyred, but she didn't trust him. So her only goal was making sure Catherine didn't burn for her mother's dream, even if she hadn't voiced this to the others. She felt like it was her responsibility. Except now she worried they wouldn't be able to get to Catherine in time.

She shoved past another group of mechanics by the looks of them and cursed them for stopping in the middle of the massive flow of humanity into Trinity Square.

She didn't notice right away that their eyes were glued to a scene erupting off to their side.

"Shit, we have to go. Come on–" Reina began to say but was cut off as a loud crash of glass and whoosh of air accompanied a ball of fire that erupted out of the crowd to their left.

The crowd immediately near them began to panic as everyone tried to get away from the flames or more likely the indiscriminate retribution of the guardsman that would come next. Aron grabbed her by the arm to steady her in the push of the crowd as Reina tried to make it back to them. The press of humanity made it impossible, and they were quickly becoming separated.

"Sarding hell!" Kaya shouted and tried to fight her way toward Reina, but even with Aron's bodyweight added to hers they were no match for the press of dozens of frightened people trying to simultaneously run toward and away from the main square.

"Go, I will meet you!" the older woman shouted back as she elbowed a charging man in his throat to clear her own path.

"Shit, shit, shit," Kaya repeated as she scrambled to look over the crowd for a path. Her time with the Coalition made her language more colorful than it had been before.

"Come on! I know a way," Aron said, pulling her through the crowd, physically pushing past confused and frightened citizens.

They ducked under a series of pipes and wires into what looked like a utility corridor. They caught their breath, panting from the effort as people continued to scream and shout nearby. Then they heard the quick blasts of gunfire and an unnatural silence.

"Is there a way out of here?" she asked him.

"Yeah, come on. This will connect to another entrance on the other side of these buildings."

Kaya looked back to make sure no one was following and motioned for him to lead the way.

They arrived at another similar entry point, but this one remained orderly, despite the chaos they had wadded through. Given the noise levels, it was not surprising these people didn't hear the commotion happening not far away.

Over the hum of voices she could hear a cheer go up from the square beyond. The proceedings were starting and their group was so very late. Sarding hell, this was bad, very bad. She looked furiously for some other path to where they needed to be.

"Come on, let's try this way," she said, pulling Aron toward a cordoned off area that led into a series of covered hallways along the edge of the square.

They walked past the first set of plain-dressed attendants without incident. They were serving more as guides for the crowds than guards to keep anyone out of restricted areas and they hadn't tried to stop them.

"Do you know where you are going?" Aron asked as they shuffled quickly through the series of corridors. For the moment at least they blended in with the staff going about their assigned tasks for the event.

"Yes, sort of anyway. I used to walk this way with Henry sometimes. It should lead us back around to the main dais."

"We don't have credentials for any of this," he whispered harshly, trying to get her to stop moving. "This isn't part of the plan. We need to stick to the main entrances. If they catch us and lock down the square—"

"Forget the sarding plan. We need to get to her now. There isn't much time," she said, not bothering to look back. He would know she meant Hex. Kaya was going to get her out of here, one way or another. Aelius should never have convinced her to do this in the first place.

"That absolutely isn't part of the plan!" He grabbed her arm and tried to physically stop her. Moving his face closer to hers so they wouldn't be overheard, he said, "We aren't soldiers, Kaya. This isn't what we are here for."

"I'm so tired of being told what I can and can't do. She's not the one who's supposed to be there, and I'm not going to let her die."

"Then leave it to the others. Let them do what they are trained to do. They will get her," he pleaded.

"What if Jimmy lied, or Aelius? It wouldn't be the first time."

Aron looked at her, the worry on his face plain to see, but he didn't release his grip on her arm. "There is no chance you can do what you are saying, Kaya. Don't be ridiculous," he tried to plead again, but she already wasn't listening.

"Then go find Reina without me," she said, giving her arm a strong yank to pry it free. She heard him curse as she turned and began to run in the direction of the dais. If he didn't believe in her now, then she knew everything she needed to know. There was no time for convincing or planning. She had to act and quickly.

She would find a quiet place where she could wait for the signal and be in position to get to Catherine herself. If she broke Catherine free, she thought they would have a chance to fight their way out until others could join them. If not, she would die in her mother's footsteps, and that felt okay too.

There was no more sign of Aron once she reached the corridor she was looking for. In the distance through the archway, she could see the back of what had to be the main dais or viewing area. Between her and the opening was a cadre of heavily armored Frumentarii and Republican Guardsmen. She would have to find another way through.

She noticed an older woman in bishop's robes walk down a side corridor and decided to follow her. At the end of the hallway, she disappeared through an archway guarded by a single armored republican guardsman holding a lightning pike at the ready. Her heart began to quicken as she approached behind, confidently as if she was perfectly meant to be there.

The guard looked at her, and she instinctively held up the badge that hung from her neck. The guard glanced at it and then looked her up and down. With a nod, he waved her through, likely assuming if she had gotten this far she was supposed to be there, and what harm could one seemingly unarmed girl do anyway? She was nearly overcome with elation until a familiar voice called out behind her.

"You, stop right there. This section is reserved for Sanctum use only," Victoria said in her posh Venusian accent.

Kaya stopped, and the guard tensed. She took a step back, turning to see Victoria standing at the end of the corridor. She noticed Victoria's acolyte robes had been replaced by those of a cleric.

Victoria stared for a moment until she spoke. "Kaya," she said simply when recognition came to her. Then her confusion turned to anger. "I don't know why you came back here, but I told you I would never help you again," Victoria said coldly, her eyes condemning her even more than her words. "Headmistress! Come quickly!" Victoria shouted into the hallway.

Kaya struggled to formulate a response, but it wasn't long before Headmistress Blaiset, trailed closely by Professor Moreau came around the corner behind Victoria.

Professor Moreau and Headmistress Blaiset looked annoyed to be summoned in such a way until they saw Kaya and recognition came to them as well. Professor Moreau seemed disappointed to see her and shook her head slightly.

Meanwhile, Headmistress Blaiset's demeanor changed, and she looked like a cat that had finally caught a mouse it had been chasing. "Well, if that isn't Miss Kaya Vardan herself. What a pleasant surprise," the old crow said with venom dripping from every word.

The guard, noticing something was off, took up a defensive stance, waiting for some kind of instruction.

This was all going south very quickly, and Kaya looked furiously for an escape, but she was cornered. If only she was actually a mouse, she might have had some means of escape through some crevice, but now she had four people in her way, and who knew how many were beyond the sight of the corridor?

She thought maybe she could run to them for aid and lean on the fact she had been kidnap as an alibi, but that idea felt useless in the face of Victoria and the disguise she had no explanation for. No, they knew something was off. Their body language said as much. Whether Victoria sold her out after her visit, she couldn't say, but it hardly mattered now.

"There is no escaping now, girl," Headmistress Blaiset cooed as if confirming Kaya's thoughts. "The lost hens always come home eventually," she said to no one in particular. "Guardsman, seize the girl and take her to the holding cells."

Kaya had only a split second to decide what to do, but she knew there was only one option, and that was to fight with everything she had. She drew her plasma blade with a practiced motion and swiped out instinctively at the guard, burning a deep gouge through his forearm, which forced him to drop his pike. He let out a scream, but it was drowned out by the ear-piercing sound that came from Victoria's mouth.

Kaya held the blade at his unarmored throat as he clutched at his arm. The ceremonial armor seemed to lack a lot of the protection of battle armor, she thought absently.

The headmistress snarled, but if she seemed scared of the blade she didn't show it. Instead, she stomped forward effortlessly, taking up the pike from the ground. "This is a shame, girl. I had hoped you could be repurposed, but it has become clear that isn't an option. Remember what I told you when you first arrived here?" she said, motioning to Kaya's blade. "I told you I would kill you if you ever wielded that blade in my presence again."

She charged at Kaya with the outstretched pike, intent on stabbing her through the middle. Kaya instinctively jumped back, and the guardsman took the opportunity to try to wrestle the blade from her hand.

She swiped out at the guard, catching the man in the throat and stopping him in his tracks. Unable to scream, he writhed on the floor, clutching at his singed neck, but Kaya had no time to focus on his wounds as she batted away at the pike. She was too slow as the electrified metal sliced into her non-sword arm, leaving a bloody gash and dropping her to her knees. She fought against the electricity coursing through her body to remain upright, but it was no use. Her body lost its strength, and she dropped her mother's blade.

She fought with every ounce of strength to keep the woman from skewering her, but she was failing. She didn't know where the old crow had learned to use the weapon so skillfully, but it didn't matter. Her mother's dream would die with her. She stumbled, struggling against the electrical charge, and crashed into the wall as the headmistress moved inside her guard with the spear, for what would surely be the final thrust to her chest.

Kaya closed her eyes, waiting for the searing pain, but it never came. Instead, seconds went by, and she opened her eyes to see the headmistress fall to her knees, a blood-soaked knife held in Professor Moreau's hand.

Victoria screamed in the background, her typical panicked scream, and turned to run back the way they had come.

"Go! I will try to stop her," Moreau said, and Kaya stared at her blankly for a long moment. "Kaya, now!" She put a hand on Kaya's shoulder. None of this made sense, but Kaya had no time to figure out what was happening. She took her blade from the ground and nodded to the professor and turned to go under the archway and into the main square where the crowd cheered before the dais.

The small tunnel led to a series of stairways where she could reach the higher-placed viewing galleries, but she knew if she went onto any of them she would be found instantly. Instead of doing that, she darted under the nearest stage, hoping the decorative cloth covering their bottoms would hide her presence.

Ducking under the support beams, she reached the front of the stage and pulled aside the cloth enough to get a clear view but still hide her body. She realized that despite her haste, despite the blood on her hands, she was too late, but where was the signal? Did she miss it? Catherine was tied to a post, surrounded by bundles of sticks and grass. *Oh no*, she thought.

The crowd had gone eerily quiet as the Manus Gremory approached Catherine, a ceremonial candle held in her left hand and a scepter in the right that was said to have belonged to the last Solar Emperor. The slender woman wore ceremonial red and white robes of office, and she looked every bit the messenger of God, but her message was one of death.

The Vox sat behind her on his golden throne, quiet and observing like a conqueror, but what had he conquered? He inherited a dying world and did nothing to fix it. Instead, he passed judgment on those who tried and called it progress.

"Catherine Beckett, the voice of God has spoken, and your life has been forfeit for crimes against man and God," intoned Gremory in her monotone voice.

Kaya stood too stunned to look away. Where was the sarding signal? Why wasn't anyone doing anything? How would she stop this now? She thought frantically for an answer.

She looked back at the sounds behind her. They must have found the guard, and now soon they would find her. It was over. She had lost.

However, Catherine seemed unfazed by the approaching angel of death. She didn't cry out like Victoria or hide in the shadows like Kaya was doing now. She stood proud and strong, a far cry from the crumpled form Kaya had so recently seen. It was as if she was energized by the very spirit of the cosmos, and it held her tall and steady through the maelstrom.

Then she did something odd. She turned toward Kaya and smiled. Not a cruel or mocking smile but a peaceful one. Not at Kaya, no, at someone above her. It was as if she were saying, "I'm okay" and "Remember me proudly."

Oh God, she thought. Her father was above her now watching this all unfold. Even now she wanted him to know she wasn't afraid. It was the bravest thing she had ever seen.

Unfazed by her smile, the Manus continued her deadly ritual. "Your body is a vessel for sin and must be cleansed by the light and flame. Only in the purity of the heat can your soul be spared and with it the rest of humanity. Be cleansed, my child, and may God's light find you in the darkness," she intoned before placing the candle amongst the bundles of sticks and grass.

As the flames erupted, so did the atmosphere of the square. Above her, the stomping of feet was the loudest as a man's voice cried out, and others seemed to try and restrain him. Kaya drew the hilt of her blade and considered her next move. She couldn't bear to watch Catherine's sacrifice.

She wanted to act, but she knew that would be suicide, and she was afraid, but she was running out of time. As the flames grew ever larger, obscuring Kaya's view, she was forced to look away as even the heat from her vantage point became palpable.

It felt like an eternity, but it was likely only moments until the screams started. Kaya felt sick, but she kindled her blade, right before the gunshots rang out, followed by quick successive blasts of explosions. The signal came too late.

Kaya braced herself as the scaffolding around her lurched with the ground and all hell broke loose.

Silas

June, 4103 U.E.T.—Trinity Square, Mars

Silas's world lurched along with his body as he was thrown violently to the ground from a sudden blast to the east. The sound of Falcons burning fast overhead drowned out the noise of the panicked people as they attempted to flee in every possible direction.

The cacophony of sounds didn't drown out the screams of his daughter that rang out in his head. He didn't know if they were real or imagined, but he cried out for her. Getting to his feet, he attempted to rush to the nearby flames but was cut off by Ajax, who drew his ceramic blade and leveled it at Silas.

"No, I will watch your child burn, and worse yet you will watch. It is only the first of many punishments for what you did to my boy."

Silas screamed and tried to charge through the man, not even bothering to draw his own weapon. Ajax easily blocked the clumsy movement and threw him to the ground. Silas was bleeding, he realized now as he reached up to his forehead. It didn't matter, he thought as he tried to stand back up on shaky legs.

He looked frantically for Diana and realized she stood off to his side, a chair in her hand. She was holding it defensively toward Henry, who held his plasma blade kindled and ready.

"Henry, stand down. That's an order," Silas tried to say, and Ajax laughed.

"The boy won't be listening to you after what you did while he nearly bled to death." Henry for his part looked confused and tried to back away from Diana as he clutched his side. He didn't look like he wanted to fight her.

Silas looked for his brother but noticed him already off in the distance with the Vox and Manus, who were quickly evacuating the square. Still a coward, he thought.

"Out of my way, Ajax," he screamed again as he drew his blade and this time swiped out in a series of quick blows, hoping to take him by surprise and break free of the gallery. He needed to get to Catherine.

Ajax again blocked his blows and countered with a series of his own strikes. Ajax landed a deep gash to his side and Silas stumbled. Ajax was quick and practiced in a way he wasn't expecting, and he struggled to maintain his focus through the blood in his eyes.

"Diana, run!" he shouted and struck back at Ajax, ignoring the pain of his side. Silas swiped low at his legs before twisting upward to slash deeply into the man's bicep. It was then Ajax's turn to be on the defensive.

Diana turned to run, but her path was blocked as an armored Frumentarii knight climbed onto the stage, his ceramic blade at the ready. Diana swung furiously at the knight with her makeshift weapon, only briefly keeping the man at bay.

She wasn't making much progress as the frumentario slashed easily through the piece of furniture leaving it crumbling to pieces in her hand. Diana might be a knight by association, but she was no soldier, and on top of that she was unarmed.

Ajax swung again, but Silas was able to parry the strike, moving into the man's guard and hitting him with his fist as he tried to bring his blade down for a killing blow. However, Ajax was again able to roll away and disengage.

Then a new person joined the stage as gunfire erupted around them. A young girl in mechanic's clothes wielding a plasma blade swung out at Ajax, and he was forced to defend against her strikes while keeping an eye on Silas. Using the opportunity, he sprung to his feet and lashed out as Ajax knocked the girl down toward Henry.

His charge was cut short as heavy railgun rounds slammed into the stage between them forcing Ajax to retreat backward. Ajax seemed to assess it was time to go and shouted for Henry to retreat, but when Silas looked over Henry was checking on the girl who writhed on the ground in obvious pain.

Another round of railgun fire rained down on the stage, and Diana was forced to retreat at the same time the frumentario charged her earning a barrage of railgun rounds for his trouble. He fell limply to the stage but Diana tripped over a chair in her retreat and fell back toward Henry.

Silas tried to reach for her, to stop her fall, but it all happened too quickly. Before she could arrest her fall, Henry turned out of what could only be instinct and stabbed out with his blade defensively at the form approaching him, skewering Diana perfectly through the chest.

They all stood there stunned as Henry snuffed his blade, a faraway expression on his face. Ajax ran back to Henry, to pull him away as Silas struggled back to his feet. As they left, Silas looked from the crumbled form of his wife to the girl and then back to where the pyre now sat fully charred. The slumped form of his daughter was clearly visible. The fire had been hot and smokey enough to kill her but not so hot as to burn away the body. It was likely some sick part of their plan.

He began to break down as he crawled to where Diana was lying, hoping that somehow the strike had missed her vital organs, but he knew that was hopeless. He had seen enough sword wounds in his life.

The gunfire didn't stop and only grew closer along with the explosions. The energy domes over the capital glowed brightly as ordnance rained down on it from above, energy spidering out from the point of impact in brilliant blooms of light.

He didn't care. He clutched at his wife's body, as if he could bring her back to life with only his prayers. He had destroyed his family. What more was there for him now?

"Lord Beckett, please, come with me," a voice called through the haze of his grief. His vision was blurry from tears and the blood that dripped from his forehead. It took him a moment to realize he was being shaken by the shoulders.

"Good, yes, stay with me. We need to get you out of here."

He squinted at the blurry face until realization hit him, "Kaya? Why...what is going on?"

"I can't explain any of that right now, but we need to get you out of here, now," she said more forcefully, pulling him to his feet.

He followed like a puppet pulled on strings, unable to form any coherent thought. He looked back down at his wife and then over to where his daughter... Her body wasn't there any longer. Had she? No, he watched her burn.

Then he noticed a man off to the side holding her charred form, and next to him was Marcus and Gwen. "Take me to my daughter!" he shouted and wiped the blood and tears from his eyes.

Kaya guided him toward the small group, which was quickly growing as they created a defensive circle. Kaya handed him back the hilt of his blade and deposited him into the arms of Marcus.

"Wow, easy. I got you," his friend said as he tried to steady him upright. "Here, let me, help." Marcus poured water from a bottle onto his face before hastily wrapping a cloth around the bleeding gash on his head.

"Catherine, where is she," he called out in a panic.

"I have her, Milord," came a familiar Mercurian voice. Was that Namtar?

"We have her. Don't worry. Where is Diana?" Marcus asked, looking around, and Silas was unable to respond. It was Kaya who responded with a shake of her head and a motion up to the stage.

Marcus cursed as he rushed up to the stage motioning for two of the soldiers to follow him. He came back holding the limp form of his sister, his eyes streaked with tears.

There was fighting breaking out in almost every direction, and Republican Guardsmen and Frumentarii were engaging with unarmored and armored resistance alike. It was clear for Silas to see it was quickly becoming a bloodbath.

"What's going on?" Silas asked through the confusion.

"City has gone crazy. The Coalition has been hitting them hard. We had our team ready for extraction, but it's all gone to hell," Gwen said.

"We initiated the Tenebris Protocol, but they beat us to it. Those Falcons aren't ours, but they took out the anti-air and orbital guns before the Guard knew what hit them. Then fighting broke out in orbit. Lancaster went dark after that," Marcus added, regaining some of his focus as he choked back tears.

"What's the status of our transports?" Silas asked, his trained mind compartmentalizing as he focused on the task at hand.

"Under heavy fire. It will be a fight to get there now. We didn't plan to fight from street to street to get out of here."

"Come on. We don't have time for this. We need to start moving," Kaya said.

"We need a plan first, kid, so unless you have some magic Coalition voodoo like last time we saw you, keep your trap shut," Marcus snapped back, and Kaya glared at him.

"I have a plan," Kaya said. "We need to get to the spaceport."

Before the others could say anything, Namtar spoke, "Listen to the girl. She is right. We need to go there now."

Silas looked to Marcus and then Gwen. Neither of them voiced any complaints, so he motioned for her to lead the way. In their shock, they all seemed amenable to someone who had a plan they didn't need to invent on the spot.

Their party encountered several small pods of resistance through the square, but they were able to neutralize them quickly. Even carrying a body, Namtar fought with a ferocity and grace Silas had never seen before. This looked like the man he had fought with on that asteroid months ago, but it was certainly not him. This was a demon of war unleashed.

His help was vital as they moved swiftly from position to position, trying to avoid the crossfire of the conflicts around them. Especially with Marcus unable to fight and his own injuries slowing him down. Luckily no one seemed focused on them, at least until they got within eyesight of the spaceport entrance.

As their small group approached at a quick jog, gunfire rang out at their feet, forcing them to retreat to a covered position.

"Sarding hell, I knew this was a stupid idea," Marcus said, instinctively shielding Diana's body from the incoming fire.

Meanwhile Kaya threw her hands up in a series of complex hand signals, and the fire stopped.

"You were saying?" she asked with a smug expression that reminded him of Catherine when she was a teenager, but the memory quickly became painful.

"Come on," Kaya repeated as she continued leading them toward the entrance of the spaceport near Trinity Square. They passed through a makeshift barricade armed by Coalition members with their vermillion-colored arm bands.

When they passed, Silas also recognized grizzled soldiers in Mercurian uniforms fighting alongside the Coalition members. The soldiers looked at them warily as they continued firing on the Republic troops advancing behind them.

Once through the armored line, he was surprised to see a familiar face at the entrance.

"Reina, we need medics," Kaya said, motioning to the bodies Marcus and Namtar carried.

"I'm glad to see you guys," she said, her voice becoming more solemn as she looked at the bodies, "but not like this. I'm sorry."

Silas could only nod. His grief was not quite real yet, but his legs finally began to give out from under him as he rushed to the side of his wife and daughter. Marcus joined him in his grief, and they both wept freely.

"Where can we take them for medical?" Gwen said, taking charge of the situation.

"Take them to the Rubah," came the voice of Theodore, who approached from behind a group of soldiers. His clothes were dirty and tattered, but he seemed mostly unharmed. Silas was glad to see he was still alive.

Theodore waved at several soldiers with stretchers to take the bodies of Diana and Catherine to the large frigate that sat in the near distance, its engines humming.

Silas and Marcus fought them at first but relented when Gwen pulled them back. "Not yet, we need to get out of here first and can use your strength. They are in better hands aboard the ship than out here," their friend whispered, and Silas knew she was right.

Marcus grudgingly let go of Diana, and Silas helped him to his feet. They would have to be strong for each other now more than ever.

"Is that our ticket out of here?" Marcus asked once Diana and Catherine were out of sight.

Theodore nodded. "The fleet of Mercury has joined this war and will aid in our escape," he said confidently.

"What of my fleet? Do they remain?" Silas asked no one in particular. He felt so behind what was going on and didn't know who could even answer his question.

Theodore was the one who answered first, "I have gotten word it fights alongside us. Several ships have defected, but the Specter remains yours, High Commander."

A small blessing in a day of curses.

"Come, we should board at once. The Rubah will see us off the planet. We can't hold them here for long. They are disorganized now, but they will soon come down on us with far greater might," Theodore said. Almost on cue, the gun batteries from high above in the palace began raining down fire on their energy dome.

"That pleasure yacht can get through all this?" Marcus said skeptically.

"I assure you she's a more capable ship than you think."

Silas scanned the area, and whether they liked it or not this was by far the largest ship in the area. It was likely their best chance now. Besides, it was where they had taken Diana and Catherine. That was enough reason to follow.

"It's what we have. Come on, load up. I don't think this shield will hold for long," Silas said before anyone else could issue a complaint.

"We have control of the spaceport for now, but it's slipping. We need to evacuate and will only have a brief window to escape when we drop the shields," Theodore said, leading them toward the waiting vessel.

"Where is Aron?" Kaya asked, looking around, panic on her face. Reina pointed to a young man typing furiously into a command terminal nearby. Kaya ran over to him and began speaking with obviously animated language.

Silas turned to Reina for clarity as they walked quickly toward the ship.

Reina shrugged. "I don't know. Those two have an interesting relationship, but whatever magic that kid is doing is holding this energy shield up right now."

Silas's jaw tightened. They were all experienced enough to know what that meant. Someone would have to stay behind to ensure they made it off this rock. If they didn't have remote control of the shields, only someone directly connected to the system could manage it.

"Sarding hell," Marcus said, having obviously come to the same conclusion. "We still have boots on the ground and transports stowed away," he said, trying to offer another option.

Reina looked coldly at him. "We all know what we signed up for here. He will do what it takes. We all will. There's no changing the plan now."

"Come on everyone, load up," Silas said, looking at Marcus, Gwen, and the few others who had gone with them to this point. He let the familiar role of leadership distract him. Meanwhile the barricade they had passed was beginning to take on heavier fire.

Gwen took a deep breath, seemingly coming to her own decision. "Go, sir, we will hold this position. I will see the boy gets out of here."

He began to protest, but she cut him off, "I said get out of here, sir!" He wanted to argue, but there was no time. Gwen most of all knew what she was doing. "Make sure the girl gets on the ship." She saluted him, before turning to hurry over toward Kaya, her gun at the ready. The few soldiers with her hurried to keep up.

"Another ghost," Silas said to no one and turned to board the vessel, guilt weighing heavily on his shoulders as he said a quiet prayer for those who would remain.

Kaya

June, 4103 U.E.T.—Trinity Square, Mars

"You need to leave! This isn't a choice!" Kaya yelled at Aron as he furiously typed into the control panel.

"You're right," he said, strain evident on his face. She could tell it was becoming difficult for him to keep his focus. "If I don't do this, everyone dies. There's no other choice."

"You can die here or have a chance to escape with all of us."

"I can't leave my sister all alone again. I won't do that to her. I need to finish here and get back to where she's hiding with Jimmy and the others," Aron said as sweat dripped down his brow. The explosions were close now. Too close.

"Please," she pleaded with him as a soldier, the older woman, Gwen, came to grab her.

"Lady Vardan, it's time to go," the woman said, taking her by the arm.

"I'm not leaving him!" she said, fighting with the woman.

"You are," she said forcefully. "But I'll make sure he gets on the next transport," she said, looking her in the eye but not releasing her grip. Aron didn't look up from where he was concentrating intently on the console. "Let him do his work," Gwen whispered, and Kaya gritted her teeth.

She pulled away from Gwen long enough to embrace her friend. "I will see you soon," she whispered into his ear, knowing it was probably a lie even as the words left her mouth.

He nodded, but Gwen pulled her away before Aron could say anything else, hurrying her toward the Rubah as sounds of explosions continued to come closer.

The energy dome above them sparkled brilliantly as ordnance rained down. It would have been beautiful if it wasn't for the deadly message it heralded. She had been so distracted by Aron she hadn't even noticed. The violence was unlike anything she had ever seen. This was the first time she had ever seen an energy shield used to block actual weapons. It all made her sick to her stomach.

"Go, get inside," Gwen said, depositing her at the ramp leading into the ship. Soldiers hurried around her, loading what they could in the moments they had left. Reina arrived then and looked relieved as she took her by the arm.

"Good, we don't have much time. Get inside," Reina said and then looked to Gwen, who was already walking away, rifle at the ready. "Aren't you coming?" Reina shouted to the woman over the sound of the ship's engines.

Gwen paused and turned briefly. "We all have things we need to do," she said cryptically before running back toward where Aron still toiled away at the console.

"What does that mean?" Kaya asked Reina as she was practically dragged aboard the vessel.

"Some other time," Reina replied.

Inside the ship, it was a scene of barely organized chaos. Gone was the pleasant leisure vessel she remembered from her trip to Mars what felt like a lifetime ago.

Now the Rubah was a vehicle of war. Soldiers hurried in armored exo-suits while other sailors moved purposefully, carrying out various orders or seeing to their stations. The whirlwind of action and emotions left her lightheaded, and she briefly stumbled before Reina caught her. Her wounded arm dripping blood onto the floor.

"Come on. Stay with me, princess," she said as she carried her toward the bridge. Kaya didn't have the strength to fight it anymore. What was going on? What had she done? She had led them to the spaceport, but was that enough? She was beginning to spiral. She had killed a man! She began shaking.

"I think she's going into shock," she heard Reina say as she was placed down in a chair on the bridge.

"The wound on her arm... Get a bandage. Medics!" came another voice, Theodore?

Then a familiar face came into view. Aelius moved toward her, but what was he doing here? "All will be well," he said in his monotone voice, and she felt a sudden jab into her leg, followed by a sharp burning sensation. She screamed and fought, but then...calm washed over her. The burning went away, and her mind began to clear.

"There, that will help for now," he said.

"What is going on?" she asked, still panting. The room was alight with warning signals, sounds and crew members relaying orders.

"Hang on. It's going to get bumpy. That means everyone," Captain Masoumi shouted as she passed to get into her own command seat at the center of the bridge.

"All personnel, prepare for emergency launch. I repeat, prepare for emergency launch," she said as her voice echoed throughout the ship's main intercom system.

Kaya frantically found the buckles in her seat as the ship shook violently. This was much different than the last time. The others on the bridge did likewise.

"Captain Masoumi, orbital guns are offline, but not for long. Window for launch through vector 3, 9, alpha. You have cover fire. Enemy Falcons are grounded" came a new voice through the bridge's speakers. It was Tiberius! She would recognize that voice anywhere. Her brother had come, like Theodore had said he would.

"Confirmed, Lord Vardan. Initiating launch, standby."

"Copy," he replied, "and, Captain, what of the cactus?"

Masoumi looked back at Kaya. "Onboard."

"Splendid," came her brother's cheerful response. *Did he call me a cactus?*

Then the blood drained from her face as they launched. Untethered objects became flying projectiles through the bridge as Kaya's head slammed back into the seat, the weight and pressure immense as they lurched into the sky.

They were accelerating faster than she had ever experienced, and it took all her power to keep from blacking out. The immense pressure was followed quickly by explosions that rattled the ship's shields, shaking them all even more violently.

"All auxiliary power to shields. We need to get past the short-range guns," the captain calmly relayed to her crew. Kaya could barely move her head, yet the captain seemed nearly unfazed by the maneuver.

While some seemed as calm as she did, there were others who held bleeding heads from where they had been hit by flying coffee cups or clipboards. There were others who struggled to move like Kaya, and there was even a couple that had blacked out completely. Still, most seemed to be doing their jobs to the best of their ability, which Kaya found admirable.

"Shield integrity seventy-four percent," came the cool reply from one of the hardier members of her crew.

"Maintain course, adjust bearing on entry to upper atmosphere, providing coordinates," the captain continued.

"Shield integrity fifty-six percent." The ship continued to shake violently.

Kaya was convinced it would fall to pieces at any moment, and so she closed her eyes, in that moment begging forgiveness for everything she had done that led them all to this horrible moment. Was this how people found God?

Then suddenly, almost as quickly as it started, it was over. The shaking stopped, replaced with the loud hum of the ship's engines and the occasional thump on the shields.

"Shield integrity sixty-three percent. We cleared the range of their guns."

"Good, but we still have the fleet in space to contend with," Captain Masoumi said, getting up from her chair and beginning to swipe through images and external video feeds of what was around them. The bridge was buried deep within the ship and didn't have windows to view the outside directly.

The medics came and bandaged her wounded arm, but she hardly noticed them or the stinging pain.

In the footage, she could see several massive war ships engaged in battle and firing large barrages of ammunition while the bright flashes of nuclear explosions rocked everything around them. It was as terrifying as it was mesmerizing.

"We can't help them with this. We need to continue," Masoumi said solemnly. "Lord Vardan, we must exit the field. I will forward our bearing."

"Copy that, Captain. We will provide an escort. The battle is nearly ours. We will exit this theater and retreat to interplanetary space before they can rally their forces. Inform the high commander that his fleet remains largely intact and will continue with us. I will convene with you all soon."

Then as quickly as it began, it seemed to all be over.

Theodore came over to Kaya and placed a hand on her shoulder. She flinched at the touch. "Go and get some rest. It will be a long journey from here, and you will need it. We can handle this for now."

She nodded at him but didn't speak. The room still spun slightly. Reina moved in to steady her. "I can take her," she offered, her expression strangely warm, but Kaya waved her away.

"No, I will be alright. I know the way," she said and left the bridge, leaving Reina to fend for herself with the others.

The corridors of the ship were still a buzz of activity with sailors moving from station to station. She ignored them as they passed, but occasionally one would reach out to steady her or ask if she needed help. She shooed each of them away in turn. She wanted to sleep.

She eventually reached the old room she and Victoria had used so long ago. She didn't even know if it would be occupied, but she was surprised to find when she opened it that it appeared untouched and unoccupied. There was even a clean bundle of clothes waiting for her. It was odd, but she was too tired to think and instead threw herself onto the bed and promptly fell asleep.

Kaya wasn't sure how long she had been asleep, but when she awoke the ship was noticeably quieter. Rubbing her face, she went to the bathroom. When she admired the wound on her arm, she was glad to see it was relatively shallow, but she would need a fresh bandage. The electricity had been far worse than the blade.

After taking a shower and changing her clothes, she felt the need to walk. Her body was stiff and achy from the exertion of the capital.

The hallways were much calmer now with only the occasional sailor passing by, who would offer polite nods or even slight bows. It felt strangely normal. The warm glow of the ship's lighting told her it was sometime after dawn.

When she reached the observatory, she was surprised to find it full of people, although she shouldn't have been given the events of the previous day. Had it been a day ago already? The ship was probably fuller than it had been in generations.

Except instead of lounging guests, on the ground and tables were injured soldiers in all kinds of conditions. Some looked up at her weakly as she entered. Others were too drugged or injured to notice her arrival. She fought back tears as she investigated their pained and tired but inexplicably happy eyes. She didn't know how they could be happy in a time like this.

She continued walking through the row of makeshift cots and medical beds coming to the large windows. There on the crescent-shaped table where Victoria, her, and Theodore had watched Earth was a charred body, only a single arm exposed from under the white sheet. On the next closest table was another body with its arms crossed over its chest under a white sheet.

Sitting, holding the charred hand delicately was Silas. Marcus meanwhile sat with the other body. Both looked like they hadn't slept in days.

She continued to approach them quietly, not saying a word. Instead, she looked out the large windows at the expansive scene. She assumed they were well clear of Mars and its moons by now, but she wasn't positive. The smoking hulls of warships were coming into view alongside them, but their canons and railguns were quiet now. Friendly ships then, she assumed.

She wondered how many more died. She wondered what happened to Aron, Henry, and even Victoria. At that moment on the stage, Henry had tried to help her, but then he did this, she thought, looking at the covered body that could have only belonged to Silas's wife. Well, she had taken that guard's life. Was that really any different? Maybe not, but she wanted to think it was.

"That bald prophet of yours was looking for you," Marcus said, leaning back to stretch his back audibly, taking his eyes off the covered body for the first time since she arrived.

She nodded. "He can keep looking."

Marcus chuckled and rubbed his eyes. "What a world of shit," he added with a snort.

"I'm sorry," she said softly. It felt like a pathetic attempt to cover up her guilt. She should have, could have done more. If she had gone to Henry in the square that day or gotten to the pyre in time, Catherine and Diana could both be alive.

"For what?" Marcus asked, raising an eyebrow. "Kid, this war has been coming since before you were born. Eventually the republic would have rotted until it began to collapse, and we would be right here where we are, or you or your children. Anyway, there was never any stopping it."

"We are at war then?" she asked, still staring out at the smoking warships wondering where her brother was now.

"Triton is in open rebellion. The Pandora Fleet has defected, and now your brother has almost single-handedly led the destruction of a chunk of the Martian fleet. I would say so, yeah."

She stayed quiet for a long moment. Tiberius did all that?

"What about Aron, Gwen, the others who stayed behind?" she asked.

Marcus shrugged, but Reina spoke. Kaya hadn't noticed her sitting on the floor near the base of one of the windows.

"We lost contact after we got clear of the atmosphere. They were taking heavy fire, but there was an escape plan. A few shuttles made it into orbit, but many more got shot down, and others never took off. We can't say for sure."

Kaya's heart sank, her worst fears being realized.

"Maybe they made it," she offered.

Reina shook her head. "I'm sorry, Princess. It isn't likely. I already checked. They aren't among those who made it to the ships."

"What about Jimmy and the rest of the Coalition forces on the ground? They must still be fighting." She didn't want to abandon any shred of hope she could cling to.

"Probably deep underground by now, in the old mining tunnels and the like. They wouldn't have been able to maintain the attack once the Republic got their act together. We were lucky they were caught so off guard, but now their counterattack will be brutal and swift."

Kaya's sadness turned to anger. "Then why didn't we stay to fight with them? Surely all these ships would have made a difference. You said it yourself. My brother destroyed a large portion of their fleet!"

Reina and Marcus remained quiet under the onslaught of her words.

"We all want to fight," Silas said, breaking the silence, but he never looked up from his daughter's hand. "But we also need to know when we *should* fight. I waited and waited, thinking there was another way, but war is a horrible eventuality. I wished to spare others from it, my family especially, and every citizen that it would inevitably touch, but my indecision brought us here. All over again."

"You couldn't have stopped this," Marcus said.

"Yes, he could," Reina added, and Marcus looked ready to strike her, but Silas spoke up before things escalated.

"She's right. I could have," he said, and Kaya agreed completely.

Silas turned around to look at everyone, releasing his daughter's hand gently. She couldn't imagine how long he had been there. Even in his grief, Kaya wanted to yell at him. To confront him about her mother, but she stayed quiet. He could say what he wanted to say and then she would have the last word.

"Like I could have saved those people in Tiyas during the midnight raids, but I waited, hoping that leadership would choose the better path. The godly path." He sounded angrier as he shook his head. "Orzone offered me a solution. It was clear as day. The man had a brilliant vision for the future, a return to the garden, he called it. He even convinced me of it, but I was young, naive, and my zeal knew few bounds. I argued the Vox would offer amnesty if he gave up the fight and returned things to normal. I genuinely believed the clergy would do it too. What else would shepherds of God do? Oh, how wrong I was."

"What happened?" Kaya asked. She had never heard this story before. All she knew of Orzone was that he was one of the primary Coalition leaders years ago. A terrorist by all official accounts who bankrupted the better part of Mars for his own gain.

"While I kept Orzone busy under the guise of parley, the Frumentarii cleansed their allied districts with fire and radiation. By the time we knew what was going on, it was already too late, but there was no shortage of people who thought it was my plan all along. It wasn't, but they were right to blame me. God's justice is unavoidable, and I have felt its weight."

"The Republic hasn't felt the weight of justice. That's why we needed to stay and fight," Kaya said.

Silas shook his head. "I have nothing left to lose, but all these people around you do. That's why we couldn't stay and fight. We would have lost before we started. Marcus and Reina have it right. We got lucky and caught them off guard, but the Republic's armies are vast and loyal. When mobilized, they are a serious force and not to be underestimated."

"So, you aren't going to do anything at all? Even now?" Kaya asked, her own grief coming out. Her mother had sacrificed everything. Now his daughter and wife had done the same but instead he would rather run and hide. He stared at her with a faraway expression. "You are a coward," she said.

Marcus rose to confront her, and Reina rose to meet him in her defense. Silas waved them both down. Her words seemed to have snapped him from his daze.

"No," he replied with fire in his eyes. He stood up, grunting as he did, holding a bandaged wound on his side. He shouted for everyone nearby to hear, "We will wage a war we can win, a smart war. I'm not waiting any longer. I should have joined this conflict many years ago, but now I am here where God has guided me. I see it so clearly. I will assemble my host and bring it down on them with strength they cannot fathom. The Vox will be silenced, and the Manus dismembered, and from *their* ashes a new world will rise."

A cheer erupted from those around him. The wounded echoing his fervor despite their obvious pain. Marcus likewise joined his friend, shouting a guttural war cry that sent a shiver through Kaya. Even Reina seemed moved by the moment.

She had to know, but she couldn't ask here, not now. Did he even know he had killed her mother. Was what Theodore told her even true? Would he talk so personally to her now if he knew she was the daughter of his arch enemy.

Did it even matter if millions could be saved, the people needed to be who mattered now. This wasn't about petty emotions like revenge, Theodore told her that. She thought he was right or at least she thought her mother would have agreed.

"My mother gave her life for this cause, and so will I," she said after a long pause. She couldn't swear her life to him, but she could pick up her mother's mantle. She would find the truth, but for now they needed his help, and making her mother's dream a reality was more important than anything else.

"I am with you, princess," Reina said with a nod, and Kaya smiled. The older woman's support meant a lot, especially now.

"All is as it should be then," Aelius said in his monotone voice having arrived among them. The others quieted when he spoke. Some looked apprehensive while others seemed excited at the prospect of what he would say.

"The children of Sol have risen to take their rightful place amongst the heavens. This is only the beginning for most of you, the end for some, and a second chance for others. There are many who will try to stop us, more than you can even imagine, but have faith in the spirit of each other, and we can yet see the new dawn."

His words only left her confused, and a glance around the room only confirmed the others must have felt the same.

"Ah, yeah, thanks for that inspirational speech, but..." Marcus began to say, dismissing Aelius, until he was cut off by a sound that emanated from behind him. Then it came again, a muffled cough that shook the soot-stained white sheet.

"By God's bones," Marcus said as Silas rushed to retake his daughter's hand.

Kaya watched as he pulled the sheet from her face, and even through the charred and disfigured appearance Kaya could make out the slightest quiver of her lip. She was breathing, but only barely.

Unable to look any longer, she averted her eyes and noticed she wasn't the only one. Meanwhile the Hospitaler physicians who had been tending to others with less serious wounds ran over to whisk Catherine off. Kaya only assumed they were taking her to the more well-equipped medical bay. Silas and Marcus followed quickly behind them.

She stood staring at their departing backs when Aelius came up beside her.

"I told you she wouldn't be martyred."

"How is it possible? I watched her burn with my own eyes," she said, turning to face him.

His face remained stoic, but he leaned in. Speaking in a whisper, he said, "Some will call it a miracle, but I think you know how it's possible."

Then her mind went back to their visit with Catherine in her cell and the mysterious concoction he had given her. She knew it had to be that, but her mind couldn't piece it together with the things she already knew. Then she started feeling feint. She wanted to speak but couldn't find her words.

"Now isn't the time to talk about this further," he said and drifted off to wherever it was apparitions went when they were done with their hauntings.

"Are you alright, princess? You look pale," Reina said, putting a supporting arm around her.

"I think I need to sit down," she said leaning on the woman for stability.

"Wow, okay. Let's get you back to your room," Reina said and half carried her back to her quarters.

Once inside and Reina had left, she fished through her bag looking for the Solar Empire Insignia she had carried all this time. Sitting on the bed, she held it in her palm and stared at the symbol with its conjoined triangles, thinking back to the note her mother had left her with the same symbol emblazoned on the stationary.

If Catherine had been saved by this concoction, when surely she should have died, did it mean agelessness was real, like Aelius claimed?

If it was, and this was their symbol, the same symbol she found on her mother's note, did it mean her mother might still be alive somewhere? It was a thought that would keep her awake for a long, long time.

EPILOGUE

Tɪʙᴇʀɪᴜs
Jᴜɴᴇ, 4103 U.E.T.—Pᴀʀᴀɢᴏɴ

Tʜᴇ ᴛʀᴀɴsᴍɪssɪᴏɴ ᴄʟɪᴄᴋᴇᴅ off, and Tiberius leaned back in his chair aboard the bridge of his flagship the Paragon. A satisfied look washed over his face as junior officers came to him with reports and updates as the fighting wound down and they prepared their withdrawal. He hadn't realized how much he missed the excitement of battle.

His fleet had sustained damage and taken some losses, but that was to be expected after so many years of stagnation. They would shake off the rust before any of the Republic's admirals grew enough of a spine to fight back.

It looked like he wasn't the only one who seemed excited either. Looking at the faces of his old friends, he saw only exhilaration and triumph.

They were the ones who waited to be plucked all these years from their quiet tombs in the Great Desert. His greatest allies who waited patiently for nearly five hundred years.

Five hundred years to finally be reborn and recover what was stolen from them. Stolen by the Republic worms and their cowardly kin who left them here to fend off the ravenous hoard.

There would be time to settle old scores. For now, he was glad his granddaughter was safe, and that he didn't need to destroy the high commander and his Pandora Fleet. He would need allies for the coming war, even if they were beneath him. The Beckett branch of the dynasty had grown weak over time, but they were still family, he chided himself, however distant.

If he could wait patiently this long, why rush now? The world wasn't ready yet for the truth, and so for now he would continue to wait. There were still a great many amongst his crew that would be shocked to learn the truth, if they even believed it at all. All in due time, he reminded him-self. All in due time.

He left the bridge, his steps lighter than they had been in centuries. His subordinates could see them safely through the final stages of the fighting, so he left for the privacy of his quarters to make one last communication home before the Republic blocked the relays.

He retrieved a cigar, along with a bottle of fine Gaian whisky from his private collection and took a seat. Nothing too fine of course but fine enough to celebrate new beginnings. He would save the best for when the war was finally won, and he claimed his rightful place as Emperor.

He powered on his comm device and entered the desired address. Leaning back and lighting his cigar with a small plasma dagger he waited.

When the comms finally connected, he said, "Mithridates, my son, I bring good news. Your little cactus has been rescued. Now I will need you to fulfill your duty as you swore an oath to do. It is time."

9 7989 89 7 4 9 2 1 8